ERNEST BRAMAH

BEST
MAX CARRADOS
DETECTIVE STORIES

Selected with an Introduction by
E. F. BLEILER

DOVER PUBLICATIONS, INC. NEW YORK

Best Max Carrados Detective Stories, first published by Dover Publications, Inc., in 1972, is a
new selection of stories by Ernest Bramah.
The original source for each story in this collection is indicated in the Note on Sources.

International Standard Book Number: 0-486-20064-7
Library of Congress Catalog Card Number: 70-186096

Manufactured in the United States of America
Dover Publications, Inc.
180 Varick Street
New York, N.Y. 10014

Introduction

Among the outstanding detectives of the first quarter of this century stands Max Carrados, the blind detective with the remarkable compensatory abilities. Along with the Old Man in the Corner, Dr. Thorndyke, Eugene Valmont and Uncle Abner, he offers many adventures that can still be pleasant or exciting to the reader of the 1970's.

Max Carrados, to quote from one of Ernest Bramah's introductions, is "blind, quite blind, but so far from crippling his interests in life or his energies, his blindness has merely impelled him to develop those senses which in most of us lie half dormant and practically unused. Thus you will understand that while he may be at a disadvantage when you are at an advantage, he is at an advantage when you are at a disadvantage." Carrados, it will be seen, can read newspaper headlines and large type by means of his sensitive touch, can sense subtle temperature changes and locate electric light bulbs by their radiation, can identify scents to a degree rivalling a hound, and, of course, can analyze the world of sound vibration with a finesse impossible to any animal.

Max Carrados's blindness is, obviously, a tour de force, since it involves a man who is described as blind, but in actual practice is little less keen in visual perceptions than most men. Carrados, in short, is a blind man who can see perfectly well. Yet the tour de force is strikingly successful; it develops a facet of interest that shows many planes: unexpected ways of obtaining data, plot situations where a blind man can have advantages over a seeing man (as in total darkness), character subtleties, and much else.

The author of the Carrados stories was Ernest Bramah Smith, known in most of his work as Ernest Bramah. Born in Manchester, England, 1868, he was annoyingly successful in evading personal publicity, and most of what can be gathered about him is vague and speculative. He farmed unsuccessfully for a couple of years, then entered journalism, working on the staff of *Today* magazine. In later years he edited a trade magazine for clergymen. Some of the popular articles about him and his work have hinted that he lived in the Orient for a time, where he obtained background for his stories, but there is no real reason to accept this. A small, slender man with facial features reminiscent of his compatriot, Fitzsimmons, the prize fighter, he became nearly a recluse in his later years, although he is said to have been kindly and amiable when sought out. He died in Somerset in 1942. Much of his personality emerges in his fiction: subtle, highly intelligent, cynical, whimsical, charming, sophisticated, yet with a secret liking for coarse melodrama (enlivened with irony), remarkably painstaking in some areas of thought, yet careless in others. He obviously felt an impish delight at pulling his reader's leg, yet sometimes ended by pulling his own as well. In his writing, the verbal level remains his finest achievement, with many elegant, pointed, deft phrases.

Despite the present value of Max Carrados, Ernest Bramah was better known to readers of a generation or so ago as the creator of Kai Lung. Kai Lung, whose adventures extended over several books beginning with *The Wallet of Kai Lung*, was an itinerant professional story-teller in pre-modern China, whose skill at arousing the interest of his audience saved him from many disasters, including the loss of his head. The China these stories portray is partly fanciful, partly sound, something like Hearn, something like the dream world of blue willow chinaware. They abound in felicitous phrases and very effectively prolonged irony, and they have had many admirers, although others find them too precious.

Among Bramah's other works are an account of his own adventure with agriculture, *English Farming and Why I Turned It Up,* and a science-fiction novel, *The Secret of the League,* which has been published as by Smith. A future war story, it is more literate than most members of its genre, although there is no real reason to seek it out and read it. Bramah also wrote a book on British coins: *A Guide to the Varieties and Rarity of English Royal Copper Coins, Charles II— Victoria.* His other fiction includes a rather pointless novel, *A Little Flutter,* and, according to bibliographic sources, scripts which were performed over the British radio. These might be interesting to examine.

The Max Carrados short stories are contained in three collections: *Max Carrados* [1914], which tells how the blind detective became associated with Carlyle, the "inquiry agent," and offers eight cases of Carrados. *The Eyes of Max Carrados* [1924] followed, with nine more stories, and *Max Carrados Mysteries* [1927] with eight more.

An isolated story, "The Bunch of Violets," appears in *The Specimen Case* [1924], along with a couple of other crime stories not up to the Carrados level. This story is familiar from anthologies. The only novel about Max Carrados, *The Bravo of London* [1934], is an occasionally brilliant performance, with fine characterizations, devastating irony, and a great deal of amusing self-parody. It has never been published in America, and is not generally known as a Carrados story, because of errors in the standard reference literature. Other Carrados stories may exist, forgotten, in British periodicals, since most of Bramah's fiction first appeared in such form. A search, however, has not revealed any.

The appeal of Max Carrados in the 1970's is very largely Max Carrados himself—the suave, kindly, resourceful investigator, whom nothing can dismay. His striking personality dominates the series of stories, just as Sherlock Holmes and Dr. Thorndyke dominate their fictional casings. Carrados's abilities and limitations, credible and occasionally incredible, go far toward creating a personality that has survived the death of its author some thirty years.

Carrados's adventures, too, have a freshness to us that is probably greater than it was to his contemporaries. At the time the individual stories were written, many of their situations were stock, but have since dropped out of the writer's toolbox: the spurious haunted house, the inbred mad baronet, Druid circles, death by simulated lightning and so on. Ernest Bramah, however, was always able to impart little and large touches to these situations that elevated them far above their parallel uses by other men. Excellent background, exceptional characterizations, and a personal style created a note of individuality that still survives.

Not all of Carrados's adventures stand up as well as others. Some stories repeat themes done better elsewhere; others violate the essence of the detective story by invoking supernatural *dei ex occulto*; others collapse in form. All these stories have been omitted. What I have selected are my own favorites among the marvelous adventures of that uniquely charming detective, Max Carrados.

E. F. BLEILER

P.E.I.
1971

Contents

The Coin of Dionysius

It was eight o'clock at night and raining, scarcely a time when a business so limited in its clientele as that of a coin dealer could hope to attract any customer, but a light was still showing in the small shop that bore over its window the name of Baxter, and in the even smaller office at the back the proprietor himself sat reading the latest *Pall Mall*. His enterprise seemed to be justified, for presently the door bell gave its announcement, and throwing down his paper Mr. Baxter went forward.

As a matter of fact the dealer had been expecting someone and his manner as he passed into the shop was unmistakably suggestive of a caller of importance. But at the first glance towards his visitor the excess of deference melted out of his bearing, leaving the urbane, self-possessed shopman in the presence of the casual customer.

"Mr. Baxter, I think?" said the latter. He had laid aside his dripping umbrella and was unbuttoning overcoat and coat to reach an inner pocket. "You hardly remember me, I suppose? Mr. Carlyle—two years ago I took up a case for you——"

"To be sure. Mr. Carlyle, the private detective——"

"Inquiry agent," corrected Mr. Carlyle precisely.

"Well," smiled Mr. Baxter, "for that matter I am a coin dealer and not an antiquarian or a numismatist. Is there anything in that way that I can do for you?"

"Yes," replied his visitor; "it is my turn to consult you." He had taken a small wash-leather bag from the inner pocket and now turned something carefully out upon the counter. "What can you tell me about that?"

The dealer gave the coin a moment's scrutiny.

"There is no question about this," he replied. "It is a Sicilian tetradrachm of Dionysius."

"Yes, I know that—I have it on the label out of the cabinet. I can tell you further that it's supposed to be one that Lord Seastoke gave two hundred and fifty pounds for at the Brice sale in '94."

"It seems to me that you can tell me more about it than I can tell you," remarked Mr. Baxter. "What is it that you really want to know?"

"I want to know," replied Mr. Carlyle, "whether it is genuine or not."

"Has any doubt been cast upon it?"

"Certain circumstances raised a suspicion—that is all."

The dealer took another look at the tetradrachm through his magnifying glass, holding it by the edge with the careful touch of an expert. Then he shook his head slowly in a confession of ignorance.

"Of course I could make a guess——"

"No, don't," interrupted Mr. Carlyle hastily. "An arrest hangs on it and nothing short of certainty is any good to me."

"Is that so, Mr. Carlyle?" said Mr. Baxter, with increased interest. "Well, to be quite candid, the thing is out of my line. Now if it was a rare Saxon penny or a doubtful noble I'd stake my reputation on my opinion, but I do very little in the classical series."

Mr. Carlyle did not attempt to conceal his disappointment as he returned the coin to the bag and replaced the bag in the inner pocket.

"I had been relying on you," he grumbled reproachfully. "Where on earth am I to go now?"

"There is always the British Museum."

"Ah, to be sure, thanks. But will anyone who can tell me be there now?"

"Now? No fear!" replied Mr. Baxter. "Go round in the morning——"

"But I must know to-night," explained the visitor, reduced to despair again. "To-morrow will be too late for the purpose."

Mr. Baxter did not hold out much encouragement in the circumstances.

"You can scarcely expect to find anyone at business now," he remarked. "I should have been gone these two hours myself only I happened to have an appointment with an American millionaire who fixed his own time." Something indistinguishable from a wink slid off Mr. Baxter's right eye. "Offmunson he's called, and a bright young pedigree-hunter has traced his descent from Offa, King of Mercia. So he—quite naturally—wants a set of Offas as a sort of collateral proof."

"Very interesting," murmured Mr. Carlyle, fidgeting with his watch. "I should love an hour's chat with you about your millionaire customers—some other time. Just now—look here, Baxter, can't you give me a line of introduction to some dealer in this sort of thing who happens to live in town? You must know dozens of experts."

"Why, bless my soul, Mr. Carlyle, I don't know a man of them away from his business," said Mr. Baxter, staring. "They may live in Park Lane or they may live in Petticoat Lane for all I know. Besides, there aren't so many experts as you seem to imagine. And the two best will very likely quarrel over it. You've had to do with 'expert witnesses,' I suppose?"

"I don't want a witness; there will be no need to give evidence. All I want is an absolutely authoritative pronouncement that I can act on. Is there no one who can really say whether the thing is genuine or not?"

Mr. Baxter's meaning silence became cynical in its implication as he continued to look at his visitor across the counter. Then he relaxed.

"Stay a bit; there is a man—an amateur—I remember hearing wonderful things about some time ago. They say he really does know."

"There you are," explained Mr. Carlyle, much relieved. "There always is someone. Who is he?"

"Funny name," replied Baxter. "Something Wynn or Wynn something." He craned his neck to catch sight of an important motor-car that was drawing to the kerb before his window. "Wynn Carrados! You'll excuse me now, Mr. Carlyle, won't you? This looks like Mr. Offmunson."

Mr. Carlyle hastily scribbled the name down on his cuff. "Wynn Carrados, right. Where does he live?"

"Haven't the remotest idea," replied Baxter, referring the arrangement of his tie to the judgment of the wall mirror. "I have never seen the man myself. Now, Mr. Carlyle, I'm sorry I can't do any more for you. You won't mind, will you?"

Mr. Carlyle could not pretend to misunderstand. He enjoyed the distinction of holding open the door for the transatlantic representative of the line of Offa as he went out, and then made his way through the muddy streets back to his office. There was only one way of tracing a private individual at such short notice—through the pages of the directories, and the gentleman did not flatter himself by a very high estimate of his chances.

Fortune favoured him, however. He very soon discovered a Wynn Carrados living at Richmond, and, better still, further search failed to unearth another. There was, apparently, only one householder at all events of that name in the neighbourhood of London. He jotted down the address and set out for Richmond.

The house was some distance from the station, Mr. Carlyle learned. He took a taxicab and drove, dismissing the vehicle at the gate.
He prided himself on his power of observation and the accuracy of
the deductions which resulted from it—a detail of his business. "It's
nothing more than using one's eyes and putting two and two together," he would modestly declare, when he wished to be depreca-
tory rather than impressive, and by the time he had reached the front
door of "The Turrets" he had formed some opinion of the position
and tastes of the man who lived there.

A man-servant admitted Mr. Carlyle and took in his card—his
private card with the bare request for an interview that would not
detain Mr. Carrados for ten minutes. Luck still favoured him; Mr.
Carrados was at home and would see him at once. The servant,
the hall through which they passed, and the room into which he was
shown, all contributed something to the deductions which the quietly
observant gentleman was half unconsciously recording.

"Mr. Carlyle," announced the servant.

The room was a library or study. The only occupant, a man of
about Carlyle's own age, had been using a typewriter up to the
moment of his visitor's entrance. He now turned and stood up with
an expression of formal courtesy.

"It's very good of you to see me at this hour," apologised the
caller.

The conventional expression of Mr. Carrados's face changed a
little.

"Surely my man has got your name wrong?" he explained. "Isn't
it Louis Calling?"

The visitor stopped short and his agreeable smile gave place to a
sudden flash of anger or annoyance.

"No sir," he replied stiffly. "My name is on the card which you
have before you."

"I beg your pardon," said Mr. Carrados, with perfect good-
humour. "I hadn't seen it. But I used to know a Calling some years
ago—at St. Michael's."

"St. Michael's!" Mr. Carlyle's features underwent another change,
no less instant and sweeping than before. "St. Michael's! Wynn
Carrados? Good heavens! it isn't Max Wynn—old 'Winning' Wynn?"

"A little older and a little fatter—yes," replied Carrados. "*I have*
changed my name you see."

"Extraordinary thing meeting like this," said his visitor, dropping into a chair and staring hard at Mr. Carrados. "I have changed more than my name. How did you recognize me?"

"The voice," replied Carrados. "It took me back to that little smoke-dried attic den of yours where we——"

"My God!" exclaimed Carlyle bitterly, "don't remind me of what we were going to do in those days." He looked round the well-furnished, handsome room and recalled the other signs of wealth that he had noticed. "At all events, you seem fairly comfortable, Wynn."

"I am alternately envied and pitied," replied Carrados, with a placid tolerance of circumstance that seemed characteristic of him. "Still, as you say, I am fairly comfortable."

"Envied, I can understand. But why are you pitied?"

"Because I am blind," was the tranquil reply.

"Blind!" exclaimed Mr. Carlyle, using his own eyes superlatively. "Do you mean—literally blind?"

"Literally. . . . I was riding along a bridle-path through a wood about a dozen years ago with a friend. He was in front. At one point a twig sprang back—you know how easily a thing like that happens. It just flicked my eye—nothing to think twice about."

"And that blinded you?"

"Yes, ultimately. It's called amaurosis."

"I can scarcely believe it. You seem so sure and self-reliant. Your eyes are full of expression—only a little quieter than they used to be. I believe you were typing when I came. . . . Aren't you having me?"

"You miss the dog and the stick?" smiled Carrados. "No; it's a fact."

"What an awful affliction for you, Max. You were always such an impulsive, reckless sort of fellow—never quiet. You must miss such a fearful lot."

"Has anyone else recognized you?" asked Carrados quietly.

"Ah, that was the voice, you said," replied Carlyle.

"Yes; but other people heard the voice as well. Only I had no blundering, self-confident eyes to be hoodwinked."

"That's a rum way of putting it," said Carlyle. "Are your ears never hoodwinked, may I ask?"

"Not now. Nor my fingers. Nor any of my other senses that have to look out for themselves."

"Well, well," murmured Mr. Carlyle, cut short in his sympathetic emotions. "I'm glad you take it so well. Of course, if you find it an advantage to be blind, old man——" He stopped and reddened. "I beg your pardon," he concluded stiffly.

"Not an advantage perhaps," replied the other thoughtfully. "Still it has compensations that one might not think of. A new world to explore, new experiences, new powers awakening; strange new perceptions; life in the fourth dimension. But why do you beg my pardon, Louis?"

"I am an ex-solicitor, struck off in connexion with the falsifying of a trust account, Mr. Carrados," replied Carlyle, rising.

"Sit down, Louis," said Carrados suavely. His face, even his incredibly living eyes, beamed placid good-nature. "The chair on which you will sit, the roof above you, all the comfortable surroundings to which you have so amiably alluded, are the direct result of falsifying a trust account. But do I call you 'Mr. Carlyle' in consequence? Certainly not, Louis."

"I did not falsify the account," cried Carlyle hotly. He sat down however, and added more quietly: "But why do I tell you all this? I have never spoken of it before."

"Blindness invites confidence," replied Carrados. "We are out of the running—human rivalry ceases to exist. Besides, why shouldn't you? In my case the account *was* falsified."

"Of course that's all bunkum, Max" commented Carlyle. "Still, I appreciate your motive."

"Practically everything I possess was left to me by an American cousin, on the condition that I took the name of Carrados. He made his fortune by an ingenious conspiracy of doctoring the crop reports and unloading favourably in consequence. And I need hardly remind you that the receiver is equally guilty with the thief."

"But twice as safe. I know something of that, Max. . . . Have you any idea what my business is?"

"You shall tell me," replied Carrados.

"I run a private inquiry agency. When I lost my profession I had to do something for a living. This occurred. I dropped my name, changed my appearance and opened an office. I knew the legal side down to the ground and I got a retired Scotland Yard man to organize the outside work."

"Excellent!" cried Carrados. "Do you unearth many murders?"

"No," admitted Mr. Carlyle; "our business lies mostly on the conventional lines among divorce and defalcation."

"That's a pity," remarked Carrados. "Do you know, Louis, I

always had a secret ambition to be a detective myself. I have even thought lately that I might still be able to do something at it if the chance came my way. That makes you smile?"

"Well, certainly, the idea——"

"Yes, the idea of a blind detective—the blind tracking the alert—"

"Of course, as you say, certain facilities are no doubt quickened," Mr. Carlyle hastened to add considerately, "but, seriously, with the exception of an artist, I don't suppose there is any man who is more utterly dependent on his eyes."

Whatever opinion Carrados might have held privately, his genial exterior did not betray a shadow of dissent. For a full minute he continued to smoke as though he derived an actual visual enjoyment from the blue sprays that travelled and dispersed across the room. He had already placed before his visitor a box containing cigars of a brand which that gentleman keenly appreciated but generally regarded as unattainable, and the matter-of-fact ease and certainty with which the blind man had brought the box and put it before him had sent a questioning flicker through Carlyle's mind.

"You used to be rather fond of art yourself, Louis," he remarked presently. "Give me your opinion of my latest purchase—the bronze lion on the cabinet there." Then, as Carlyle's gaze went about the room, he added quickly: "No, not that cabinet—the one on your left."

Carlyle shot a sharp glance at his host as he got up, but Carrados's expression was merely benignly complacent. Then he strolled across to the figure.

"Very nice," he admitted. "Late Flemish, isn't it?"

"No, It is a copy of Vidal's 'Roaring Lion.' "

"Vidal?"

"A French artist." The voice became indescribably flat. "He, also, had the misfortune to be blind, by the way."

"You old humbug, Max!" shrieked Carlyle, "you've been thinking that out for the last five minutes." Then the unfortunate man bit his lip and turned his back towards his host.

"Do you remember how we used to pile it up on that obtuse ass Sanders, and then roast him?" asked Carrados, ignoring the half-smothered exclamation with which the other man had recalled himself.

"Yes," replied Carlyle quietly. "This is very good," he continued, addressing himself to the bronze again. "How ever did he do it?"

"With his hands."

"Naturally. But, I mean, how did he study his model?"

"Also with his hands. He called it 'seeing near.' "

"Even with a lion—handled it?"

"In such cases he required the services of a keeper, who brought the animal to bay while Vidal exercised his own particular gifts. . . . You don't feel inclined to put me on the track of a mystery, Louis?"

Unable to regard this request as anything but one of old Max's unquenchable pleasantries, Mr. Carlyle was on the point of making a suitable reply when a sudden thought caused him to smile knowingly. Up to that point, he had, indeed, completely forgotten the object of his visit. Now that he remembered the doubtful Dionysius and Baxter's recommendation he immediately assumed that some mistake had been made. Either Max was not the Wynn Carrados he had been seeking or else the dealer had been misinformed; for although his host was wonderfully expert in the face of his misfortune, it was inconceivable that he could decide the genuineness of a coin without seeing it. The opportunity seemed a good one of getting even with Carrados by taking him at his word.

"Yes," he accordingly replied, with crisp deliberation, as he re-crossed the room; "yes, I will, Max. Here is the clue to what seems to be a rather remarkable fraud." He put the tetradrachm into his host's hand. "What do you make of it?"

For a few seconds Carrados handled the piece with the delicate manipulation of his finger-tips while Carlyle looked on with a self-appreciative grin. Then with equal gravity the blind man weighed the coin in the balance of his hand. Finally he touched it with his tongue.

"Well?" demanded the other.

"Of course I have not much to go on, and if I was more fully in your confidence I might come to another conclusion——"

"Yes, yes," interposed Carlyle, with amused encouragement.

"Then I should advise you to arrest the parlourmaid, Nina Brun, communicate with the police authorities of Padua for particulars of the career of Helene Brunesi, and suggest to Lord Seastoke that he should return to London to see what further depredations have been made in his cabinet."

Mr. Carlyle's groping hand sought and found a chair, on to which he dropped blankly. His eyes were unable to detach themselves for a single moment from the very ordinary spectacle of Mr. Carrados's mildly benevolent face, while the sterilized ghost of his now forgotten amusement still lingered about his features.

"Good heavens!" he managed to articulate, "how do you know?"

"Isn't that what you wanted of me?" asked Carrados suavely.

"Don't humbug, Max," said Carlyle severely. "This is no joke." An undefined mistrust of his own powers suddenly possessed him in the presence of this mystery. "How do you come to know of Nina Brun and Lord Seastoke?"

"You are a detective, Louis," replied Carrados. "How does one know these things? By using one's eyes and putting two and two together."

Carlyle groaned and flung out an arm petulantly.

"Is it all bunkum, Max? Do you really see all the time—though that doesn't go very far towards explaining it."

"Like Vidal, I see very well—at close quarters," replied Carrados, lightly running a forefinger along the inscription on the tetradrachm. "For longer range I keep another pair of eyes. Would you like to test them?"

Mr. Carlyle's assent was not very gracious; it was, in fact, faintly sulky. He was suffering the annoyance of feeling distinctly unimpressive in his own department; but he was also curious.

"The bell is just behind you, if you don't mind," said his host. "Parkinson will appear. You might take note of him while he is in."

The man who had admitted Mr. Carlyle proved to be Parkinson.

"This gentleman is Mr. Carlyle, Parkinson," explained Carrados the moment the man entered. "You will remember him for the future?"

Parkinson's apologetic eye swept the visitor from head to foot, but so lightly and swiftly that it conveyed to that gentleman the comparison of being very deftly dusted.

"I will endeavour to do so, sir," replied Parkinson, turning again to his master.

"I shall be at home to Mr. Carlyle whenever he calls. That is all."

"Very well, sir."

"Now, Louis," remarked Mr. Carrados briskly, when the door had closed again, "you have had a good opportunity of studying Parkinson. What is he like?"

"In what way?"

"I mean as a matter of description. I am a blind man—I haven't seen my servant for twelve years—what idea can you give me of him? I asked you to notice."

"I know you did, but your Parkinson is the sort of man who has very little about him to describe. He is the embodiment of the ordinary. His height is about average——"

"Five feet nine," murmured Carrados. "Slightly above the mean."

"Scarcely noticeably so. Clean-shaven. Medium brown hair. No particularly marked features. Dark eyes. Good teeth."

"False," interposed Carrados. "The teeth—not the statement."

"Possibly," admitted Mr. Carlyle. "I am not a dental expert and I had no opportunity of examining Mr. Parkinson's mouth in detail. But what is the drift of all this?"

"His clothes?"

"Oh, just the ordinary evening dress of a valet. There is not much room for variety in that."

"You noticed, in fact, nothing special by which Parkinson could be identified?"

"Well, he wore an unusually broad gold ring on the little finger of the left hand."

"But that is removable. And yet Parkinson has an ineradicable mole—a small one, I admit—on his chin. And you a human sleuth-hound. Oh, Louis!"

"At all events," retorted Carlyle, writhing a little under this good-humoured satire, although it was easy enough to see in it Carrados's affectionate intention—"at all events, I dare say I can give as good a description of Parkinson as he can give of me."

"That is what we are going to test. Ring the bell again."

"Seriously?"

"Quite. I am trying my eyes against yours. If I can't give you fifty out of a hundred I'll renounce my private detectorial ambition for ever."

"It isn't quite the same," objected Carlyle, but he rang the bell.

"Come in and close the door, Parkinson," said Carrados when the man appeared. "Don't look at Mr. Carlyle again—in fact, you had better stand with your back towards him, he won't mind. Now describe to me his appearance as you observed it."

Parkinson tendered his respectful apologies to Mr. Carlyle for the liberty he was compelled to take, by the deferential quality of his voice.

"Mr. Carlyle, sir, wears patent leather boots of about size seven and very little used. There are five buttons, but on the left boot one button—the third up—is missing, leaving loose threads and not the more usual metal fastener. Mr. Carlyle's trousers, sir, are of a dark material, a dark grey line of about a quarter of an inch width on a darker ground. The bottoms are turned permanently up and are, just now, a little muddy, if I may say so."

"Very muddy," interposed Mr. Carlyle generously. "It is a wet night, Parkinson."

"Yes, sir; very unpleasant weather. If you will allow me, sir, I will brush you in the hall. The mud is dry now, I notice. Then, sir," continued Parkinson, reverting to the business in hand, "there are dark green cashmere hose. A curb-pattern key-chain passes into the left-hand trouser pocket."

From the visitor's nether garments the photographic-eyed Parkinson proceeded to higher ground, and with increasing wonder Mr. Carlyle listened to the faithful catalogue of his possessions. His fetter-and-link albert of gold and platinum was minutely described. His spotted blue ascot, with its gentlemanly pearl scarfpin, was set forth, and the fact that the buttonhole in the left lapel of his morning coat showed signs of use was duly noted. What Parkinson saw he recorded, but he made no deductions. A handkerchief carried in the cuff of the right sleeve was simply that to him and not an indication that Mr. Carlyle was, indeed, left-handed.

But a more delicate part of Parkinson's undertaking remained. He approached it with a double cough.

"As regards Mr. Carlyle's personal appearance, sir——"

"No, enough!" cried the gentleman concerned hastily. "I am more than satisfied. You are a keen observer, Parkinson."

"I have trained myself to suit my master's requirements, sir," replied the man. He looked towards Mr. Carrados, received a nod and withdrew.

Mr. Carlyle was the first to speak.

"That man of yours would be worth five pounds a week to me, Max," he remarked thoughtfully. "But, of course——"

"I don't think that he would take it," replied Carrados, in a voice of equally detached speculation. "He suits me very well. But you have the chance of using his services—indirectly."

"You still mean that—seriously?"

"I notice in you a chronic disinclination to take me seriously, Louis. It is really—to an Englishman—almost painful. Is there something inherently comic about me or the atmosphere of The Turrets?"

"No, my friend," replied Mr. Carlyle, "but there is something essentially prosperous. That is what points to the improbable. Now what is it?"

"It might be merely a whim, but it is more than that," replied Carrados. "It is, well, partly vanity, partly *ennui*, partly"—certainly there was something more nearly tragic in his voice than comic now —"partly hope."

Mr. Carlyle was too tactful to pursue the subject.

"Those are three tolerable motives," he acquiesced. "I'll do anything you want, Max, on one condition."

"Agreed. And it is?"

"That you tell me how you knew so much of this affair." He tapped the silver coin which lay on the table near them. "I am not easily flabbergasted," he added.

"You won't believe that there is nothing to explain—that it was purely second-sight?"

"No," replied Carlyle tersely: "I won't."

"You are quite right. And yet the thing is very simple."

"They always are—when you know," soliloquised the other. "That's what makes them so confoundedly difficult when you don't."

"Here is this one then. In Padua, which seems to be regaining its old reputation as the birthplace of spurious antiques, by the way, there lives an ingenious craftsman named Pietro Stelli. This simple soul, who possesses a talent not inferior to that of Cavino at his best, has for many years turned his hand to the not unprofitable occupation of forging rare Greek and Roman coins. As a collector and student of certain Greek colonials and a specialist in forgeries I have been familiar with Stelli's workmanship for years. Latterly he seems to have come under the influence of an international crook called— at the moment—Dompierre, who soon saw a way of utilizing Stelli's genius on a royal scale. Helene Brunesi, who in private life is—and really is, I believe—Madame Dompierre, readily lent her services to the enterprise."

"Quite so," nodded Mr. Carlyle, as his host paused.

"You see the whole sequence, of course?"

"Not exactly—not in detail," confessed Mr. Carlyle.

"Dompierre's idea was to gain access to some of the most celebrated cabinets of Europe and substitute Stelli's fabrications for the genuine coins. The princely collection of rarities that he would thus amass might be difficult to dispose of safely, but I have no doubt that he had matured his plans. Helene, in the person of Nina Brun, an Anglicised French parlourmaid—a part which she fills to perfection—was to obtain wax impressions of the most valuable pieces and to make the exchange when the counterfeits reached her. In this way it was obviously hoped that the fraud would not come to light until long after the real coins had been sold, and I gather that she has already done her work successfully in general houses. Then, impressed by her excellent references and capable manner, my housekeeper engaged her, and for a few weeks she went about her duties here. It was fatal to this detail of the scheme, however, that I have the misfortune to be blind. I am told that Helene has so innocently angelic a face as to disarm suspicion, but I was incapable of being impressed and that good material was thrown away. But one morning my material fingers—which, of course, knew nothing of Helene's angelic face—discovered an unfamiliar touch about the surface of my favourite Euclideas, and, although there was doubtless nothing to be seen, my critical sense of smell reported that wax had been recently pressed against it. I began to make discreet inquiries and in the meantime my cabinets went to the local bank for safety. Helene countered by receiving a telegram from Angiers, calling her to the death-bed of her aged mother. The aged mother succumbed; duty compelled Helene to remain at the side of her stricken patriarchal father, and doubtless The Turrets was written off the syndicate's operations as a bad debt."

"Very interesting," admitted Mr. Carlyle; "but at the risk of seeming obtuse"—his manner had become delicately chastened—"I must say that I fail to trace the inevitable connexion between Nina Brun and this particular forgery—assuming that it is a forgery."

"Set your mind at rest about that, Louis," replied Carrados. "It is a forgery, and it is a forgery that none but Pietro Stelli could have achieved. That is the essential connexion. Of course, there are accessories. A private detective coming urgently to see me with a notable tetradrachm in his pocket, which he announces to be the clue to a remarkable fraud—well, really, Louis, one scarcely needs to be blind to see through that."

"And Lord Seastoke? I suppose you happened to discover that Nina Brun had gone there?"

"No, I cannot claim to have discovered that, or I should certainly have warned him at once when I found out—only recently—about the gang. As a matter of fact, the last information I had of Lord Seastoke was a line in yesterday's *Morning Post* to the effect that he was still at Cairo. But many of these pieces——" He brushed his finger almost lovingly across the vivid chariot race that embellished the reverse of the coin, and broke off to remark: "You really ought to take up the subject, Louis. You have no idea how useful it might prove to you some day."

"I really think I must," replied Carlyle grimly. "Two hundred and fifty pounds the original of this cost, I believe."

"Cheap, too; it would make five hundred pounds in New York to-day. As I was saying, many are literally unique. This gem by Kimon is—here is his signature, you see; Peter is particularly good at lettering—and as I handled the genuine tetradrachm about two years ago, when Lord Seastoke exhibited it at a meeting of our society in Albemarle Street, there is nothing at all wonderful in my being able to fix the locale of your mystery. Indeed, I feel that I ought to apologize for it all being so simple."

"I think," remarked Mr. Carlyle, critically examining the loose threads on his left boot, "that the apology on that head would be more appropriate from me."

The Knight's Cross Signal Problem

"Louis," exclaimed Mr. Carrados, with the air of genial gaiety that Carlyle had found so incongruous to his conception of a blind man, "you have a mystery somewhere about you! I know it by your step."

Nearly a month had passed since the incident of the false Dionysius had led to the two men meeting. It was now December. Whatever Mr. Carlyle's step might indicate to the inner eye it betokened to the casual observer the manner of a crisp, alert, self-possessed man of business. Carlyle, in truth, betrayed nothing of the pessimism and despondency that had marked him on the earlier occasion.

"You have only yourself to thank that it is a very poor one," he retorted. "If you hadn't held me to a hasty promise——"

"To give me an option on the next case that baffled you, no matter what it was——"

"Just so. The consequence is that you get a very unsatisfactory affair that has no special interest to an amateur and is only baffling because it is—well——"

"Well, baffling?"

"Exactly, Max. Your would-be jest has discovered the proverbial truth. I need hardly tell you that it is only the insoluble that is finally baffling and this is very probably insoluble. You remember the awful smash on the Central and Suburban at Knight's Cross Station a few weeks ago?"

"Yes," replied Carrados, with interest. "I read the whole ghastly details at the time."

"You read?" exclaimed his friend suspiciously.

"I still use the familiar phrases," explained Carrados, with a smile. "As a matter of fact, my secretary reads to me. I mark what I want to hear and when he comes at ten o'clock we clear off the morning papers in no time."

"And how do you know what to mark?" demanded Mr. Carlyle cunningly.

Carrados's right hand, lying idly on the table, moved to a newspaper near. He ran his finger along a column heading, his eyes still turned towards his visitor.

" 'The Money Market. Continued from page 2. British Railways,' " he announced.

"Extraordinary," murmured Carlyle.

"Not very," said Carrados. "If someone dipped a stick in treacle and wrote 'Rats' across a marble slab you would probably be able to distinguish what was there, blindfold."

"Probably," admitted Mr. Carlyle. "At all events we will not test the experiment."

"The difference to you of treacle on a marble background is scarcely greater than that of printers' ink on newspaper to me. But anything smaller than pica I do not read with comfort, and below long primer I cannot read at all. Hence the secretary. Now the accident, Louis."

"The accident: well, you remember all about that. An ordinary Central and Suburban passenger train, non-stop at Knight's Cross, ran past the signal and crashed into a crowded electric train that was just beginning to move out. It was like sending a garden roller down a row of handlights. Two carriages of the electric train were flattened out of existence; the next two were broken up. For the first time on an English railway there was a good stand-up smash between a heavy steam-engine and a train of light cars, and it was 'bad for the coo.' "

"Twenty-seven killed, forty something injured, eight died since," commented Carrados.

"That was bad for the Co.," said Carlyle. "Well, the main fact was plain enough. The heavy train was in the wrong. But was the engine-driver responsible? He claimed, and he claimed vehemently from the first, and he never varied one iota, that he had a 'clear' signal —that is to say, the green light, it being dark. The signalman concerned was equally dogged that he never pulled off the signal—that it was at 'danger' when the accident happened and that it had been for five minutes before. Obviously, they could not both be right."

"Why, Louis?" asked Mr. Carrados smoothly.

"The signal must either have been up or down—red or green."

"Did you ever notice the signals on the Great Northern Railway, Louis?"

"Not particularly, Why?"

"One winterly day, about the year when you and I were concerned in being born, the engine-driver of a Scotch express received the 'clear' from a signal near a little Huntingdon station called Abbots Ripton. He went on and crashed into a goods train and into the thick of the smash a down express mowed its way. Thirteen killed and the usual tale of injured. He was positive that the signal gave him a 'clear'; the signalman was equally confident that he had never pulled it off the 'danger.' Both were right, and yet the signal was in working order. As I said, it was a winterly day; it had been snowing hard and the snow froze and accumulated on the upper edge of the signal arm until its weight bore it down. That is a fact that no fiction writer dare have invented, but to this day every signal on the Great Northern pivots from the centre of the arm instead of from the end, in memory of that snowstorm."

"That came out at the inquest, I presume?" said Mr. Carlyle.

"We have had the Board of Trade inquiry and the inquest here and no explanation is forthcoming. Everything was in perfect order. It rests between the word of the signalman and the word of the engine-driver—not a jot of direct evidence either way. Which is right?"

"That is what you are going to find out, Louis?" suggested Carrados.

"It is what I am being paid for finding out," admitted Mr. Carlyle frankly. "But so far we are just where the inquest left it, and, between ourselves, I candidly can't see an inch in front of my face in the matter."

"Nor can I," said the blind man, with a rather wry smile. "Never mind. The engine-driver is your client, of course?"

"Yes," admitted Carlyle. "But how the deuce did you know?"

"Let us say that your sympathies are enlisted on his behalf. The jury were inclined to exonerate the signalman, weren't they? What has the company done with your man?"

"Both are suspended. Hutchins, the driver, hears that he may probably be given charge of a lavatory at one of the stations. He is a decent, bluff, short-spoken old chap, with his heart in his work. Just now you'll find him at his worst—bitter and suspicious. The thought of swabbing down a lavatory and taking pennies all day is poisoning him."

"Naturally. Well, there we have honest Hutchins: taciturn, a little touchy perhaps, grown grey in the service of the company, and manifesting quite a bulldog-like devotion to his favourite 538."

"Why, that actually was the number of his engine—how do you know it?" demanded Carlyle sharply.

"It was mentioned two or three times at the inquest, Louis," replied Carrados mildly.

"And you remembered—with no reason to?"

"You can generally trust a blind man's memory, especially if he has taken the trouble to develop it."

"Then you will remember that Hutchins did not make a very good impression at the time. He was surly and irritable under the ordeal. I want you to see the case from all sides."

"He called the signalman—Mead—a 'lying young dog,' across the room, I believe. Now, Mead, what is he like? You have seen him, of course?"

"Yes. He does not impress me favourably. He is glib, ingratiating, and distinctly 'greasy.' He has a ready answer for everything almost before the question is out of your mouth. He has thought of everything."

"And now you are going to tell me something, Louis," said Carrados encouragingly.

Mr. Carlyle laughed a little to cover an involuntary movement of surprise.

"There is a suggestive line that was not touched at the inquiries," he admitted. "Hutchins has been a saving man all his life, and he has received good wages. Among his class he is regarded as wealthy. I daresay that he has five hundred pounds in the bank. He is a widower with one daughter, a very nice-mannered girl of about twenty. Mead is a young man, and he and the girl are sweethearts—have been informally engaged for some time. But old Hutchins would not hear of it; he seems to have taken a dislike to the signalman from the first, and latterly he had forbidden him to come to his house or his daughter to speak to him."

"Excellent, Louis," cried Carrados in great delight. "We shall clear your man in a blaze of red and green lights yet and hang the glib, 'greasy' signalman from his own signal-post."

"It is a significant fact, seriously?"

"It is absolutely convincing."

"It may have been a slip, a mental lapse on Mead's part which he discovered the moment it was too late, and then, being too cowardly to admit his fault, and having so much at stake, he took care to make detection impossible. It may have been that, but my idea is rather that probably it was neither quite pure accident nor pure design. I can imagine Mead meanly pluming himself over the fact that the life of this man who stands in his way, and whom he must cordially dislike, lies in his power. I can imagine the idea becoming an obsession as he dwells on it. A dozen times with his hand on the lever he lets his mind explore the possibilities of a moment's defection. Then one day he pulls the signal off in sheer bravado—and hastily puts it at danger again. He may have done it once or he may have done it oftener before he was caught in a fatal moment of irresolution. The chances are about even that the engine-driver would be killed. In any case he would be disgraced, for it is easier on the face of it to believe that a man might run past a danger signal in absentminded-ness, without noticing it, than that a man should pull off a signal and replace it without being conscious of his actions."

"The fireman was killed. Does your theory involve the certainty of the fireman being killed, Louis?"

"No," said Carlyle. "The fireman is a difficulty, but looking at it from Mead's point of view—whether he has been guilty of an error or a crime—it resolves itself into this: First, the fireman may be killed. Second, he may not notice the signal at all. Third, in any case he will loyally corroborate his driver and the good old jury will dis-count that."

Carrados smoked thoughtfully, his open, sightless eyes merely appearing to be set in a tranquil gaze across the room.

"It would not be an improbable explanation," he said presently. "Ninety-nine men out of a hundred would say: 'People do not do these things.' But you and I, who have in our different ways studied criminology, know that they sometimes do, or else there would be no curious crimes. What have you done on that line?"

To anyone who could see, Mr. Carlyle's expression conveyed an answer.

"You are behind the scenes, Max. What was there for me to do? Still I must do something for my money. Well, I have had a very close inquiry made confidentially among the men. There might be a whisper of one of them knowing more than had come out—a man restrained by friendship, or enmity, or even grade jealousy. Nothing came of that. Then there was the remote chance that some private person had noticed the signal without attaching any importance to it then, one who would be able to identify it still by something associated with the time. I went over the line myself. Opposite the signal the line on one side is shut in by a high blank wall; on the other side are houses, but coming below the butt-end of a scullery the signal does not happen to be visible from any road or from any window."

"My poor Louis!" said Carrados, in friendly ridicule. "You were at the end of your tether?"

"I was," admitted Carlyle. "And now that you know the sort of job it is I don't suppose that you are keen on wasting your time over it."

"That would hardly be fair, would it?" said Carrados reasonably. "No, Louis, I will take over your honest old driver and your greasy young signalman and your fatal signal that cannot be seen from anywhere."

"But it is an important point for you to remember, Max, that although the signal cannot be seen from the box, if the mechanism had gone wrong, or anyone tampered with the arm, the automatic indicator would at once have told Mead that the green light was showing. Oh, I have gone very thoroughly into the technical points, I assure you."

"I must do so too," commented Mr. Carrados gravely.

"For that matter, if there is anything you want to know, I dare say that I can tell you," suggested his visitor. "It might save your time."

"True," acquiesced Carrados. "I should like to know whether anyone belonging to the houses that bound the line there came of age or got married on the twenty-sixth of November."

Mr. Carlyle looked across curiously at his host.

"I really do not know, Max," he replied, in his crisp, precise way. "What on earth has that got to do with it, may I inquire?"

"The only explanation of the Pont St. Lin swing-bridge disaster of '75 was the reflection of a green bengal light on a cottage window."

Mr. Carlyle smiled his indulgence privately.

"My dear chap, you mustn't let your retentive memory of obscure happenings run away with you," he remarked wisely. "In nine cases out of ten the obvious explanation is the true one. The difficulty, as here, lies in proving it. Now, you would like to see these men?"

"I expect so; in any case, I will see Hutchins first."

"Both live in Holloway. Shall I ask Hutchins to come here to see you—say to-morrow? He is doing nothing."

"No," replied Carrados. "To-morrow I must call on my brokers and my time may be filled up."

"Quite right; you mustn't neglect your own affairs for this—experiment," assented Carlyle.

"Besides, I should prefer to drop in on Hutchins at his own home. Now, Louis, enough of the honest old man for one night. I have a lovely thing by Eumenes that I want to show you. To-day is— Tuesday. Come to dinner on Sunday and pour the vials of your ridicule on my want of success."

"That's an amiable way of putting it," replied Carlyle. "All right, I will."

Two hours later Carrados was again in his study, apparently, for a wonder, sitting idle. Sometimes he smiled to himself, and once or twice he laughed a little, but for the most part his pleasant, impassive face reflected no emotion and he sat with his useless eyes tranquilly fixed on an unseen distance. It was a fantastic caprice of the man to mock his sightlessness by a parade of light, and under the soft brilliance of a dozen electric brackets the room was as bright as day. At length he stood up and rang the bell.

" I suppose Mr. Greatorex isn't still here by any chance, Parkinson?" he asked, referring to his secretary.

"I think not, sir, but I will ascertain," replied the man.

"Never mind. Go to his room and bring me the last two files of *The Times*. Now"—when he returned—"turn to the earliest you have there. The date?"

"November the second."

"That will do. Find the Money Market; it will be in the Supplement. Now look down the columns until you come to British Railways."

"I have it, sir."

"Central and Suburban. Read the closing price and the change."

"Central and Suburban Ordinary, $66\frac{1}{2}$–$67\frac{1}{2}$, fall $\frac{1}{8}$. Preferred Ordinary, 81–$81\frac{1}{2}$, no change. Deferred Ordinary, $27\frac{1}{2}$–$27\frac{3}{4}$, fall $\frac{1}{4}$. That is all, sir."

"Now take a paper about a week on. Read the Deferred only."

"27–$27\frac{1}{4}$, no change."

"Another week."

"$29\frac{1}{2}$–30, rise $\frac{5}{8}$."

"Another."

"$31\frac{1}{2}$–$32\frac{1}{2}$, rise 1."

"Very good. Now on Tuesday the twenty-seventh November."

"$31\frac{7}{8}$–$32\frac{3}{4}$, rise $\frac{1}{2}$."

"Yes. The next day."

"$24\frac{1}{2}$–$23\frac{1}{2}$, fall 9."

"Quite so, Parkinson. There had been an accident, you see."

"Yes, sir. Very unpleasant accident. Jane knows a person whose sister's young man has a cousin who had his arm torn off in it— torn off at the socket, she says, sir. It seems to bring it home to one, sir."

"That is all. Stay—in the paper you have, look down the first money column and see if there is any reference to the Central and Suburban."

"Yes, sir. 'City and Suburbans, which after their late depression on the projected extension of the motor bus service, had been steadily creeping up on the abandonment of the scheme, and as a result of their own excellent traffic returns, suffered a heavy slump through the lamentable accident of Thursday night. The Deferred in particular at one time fell eleven points as it was felt that the possible dividend, with which rumour has of late been busy, was now out of the question.' "

"Yes; that is all. Now you can take the papers back. And let it be a warning to you, Parkinson, not to invest your savings in speculative railway deferreds."

"Yes, sir. Thank you, sir, I will endeavour to remember." He lingered for a moment as he shook the file of papers level. "I may say, sir, that I have my eye on a small block of cottage property at Acton. But even cottage property scarcely seems safe from legislative depredation now, sir."

The next day Mr. Carrados called on his brokers in the city. It is to be presumed that he got through his private business quicker than he expected, for after leaving Austin Friars he continued his journey to Holloway, where he found Hutchins at home and sitting morosely before his kitchen fire. Rightly assuming that his luxuriant car would involve him in a certain amount of public attention in Klondyke Street, the blind man dismissed it some distance from the house, and walked the rest of the way, guided by the almost imperceptible touch of Parkinson's arm.

"Here is a gentleman to see you, father," explained Miss Hutchins, who had come to the door. She divined the relative positions of the two visitors at a glance.

"Then why don't you take him into the parlour?" grumbled the ex-driver. His face was a testimonial of hard work and general sobriety but at the moment one might hazard from his voice and manner that he had been drinking earlier in the day.

"I don't think that the gentleman would be impressed by the difference between our parlour and our kitchen," replied the girl quaintly, "and it is warmer here."

"What's the matter with the parlour now?" demanded her father sourly. "It was good enough for your mother and me. It used to be good enough for you."

"There is nothing the matter with it, nor with the kitchen either." She turned impassively to the two who had followed her along the narrow passage. "Will you go in, sir?"

"I don't want to see no gentleman," cried Hutchins noisily. "Unless"—his manner suddenly changed to one of pitiable anxiety— "unless you're from the Company sir, to—to——"

"No; I have come on Mr. Carlyle's behalf," replied Carrados, walking to a chair as though he moved by a kind of instinct.

Hutchins laughed his wry contempt.

"Mr. Carlyle!" he reiterated; "Mr. Carlyle! Fat lot of good he's been. Why don't he *do* something for his money?"

"He has," replied Carrados, with imperturbable good-humour; "he has sent me. Now, I want to ask you a few questions."

"A few questions!" roared the irate man. "Why, blast it, I have done nothing else but answer questions for a month. I didn't pay Mr. Carlyle to ask me questions; I can get enough of that for nixes. Why don't you go and ask Mr. Herbert Ananias Mead your few questions—then you might find out something."

There was a slight movement by the door and Carrados knew that the girl had quietly left the room.

"You saw that, sir?" demanded the father, diverted to a new line of bitterness. "You saw that girl—my own daughter, that I've worked for all her life?"

"No," replied Carrados.

"The girl that's just gone out—she's my daughter," explained Hutchins.

"I know, but I did not see her. I see nothing. I am blind."

"Blind!" exclaimed the old fellow, sitting up in startled wonderment. "You mean it, sir? You walk all right and you look at me as if you saw me. You're kidding surely."

"No," smiled Carrados. "It's quite right."

"Then it's a funny business, sir—you what are blind expecting to find something that those with their eyes couldn't," ruminated Hutchins sagely.

"There are things that you can't see with your eyes, Hutchins."

"Perhaps you are right, sir. Well, what is it you want to know?"

"Light a cigar first," said the blind man, holding out his case and waiting until the various sounds told him that his host was smoking contentedly. "The train you were driving at the time of the accident was the six-twenty-seven from Notcliff. It stopped everywhere until it reached Lambeth Bridge, the chief London station on your line. There it became something of an express, and leaving Lambeth Bridge at seven-eleven, should not stop again until it fetched Swanstead on Thames, eleven miles out, at seven-thirty-four. Then it stopped on and off from Swanstead to Ingerfield, the terminus of that branch, which it reached at eight-five."

Hutchins nodded, and then, remembering, said: "That's right, sir."

"That was your business all day—running between Notcliff and Ingerfield?"

"Yes, sir. Three journeys up and three down mostly."

"With the same stops on all the down journeys?"

"No. The seven-eleven is the only one that does a run from the Bridge to Swanstead. You see, it is just on the close of the evening rush, as they call it. A good many late business gentlemen living at Swanstead use the seven-eleven regular. The other journeys we stop at every station to Lambeth Bridge, and then here and there beyond."

"There are, of course, other trains doing exactly the same journey —a service, in fact?"

"Yes, sir. About six."

"And do any of those—say, during the rush—do any of those run non-stop from Lambeth to Swanstead?"

Hutchins reflected a moment. All the choler and restlessness had melted out of the man's face. He was again the excellent artisan, slow but capable and self-reliant.

"That I couldn't definitely say, sir. Very few short-distance trains pass the junction, but some of those may. A guide would show us in a minute but I haven't got one."

"Never mind. You said at the inquest that it was no uncommon thing for you to be pulled up at the 'stop' signal east of Knight's Cross Station. How often would that happen—only with the seven-eleven, mind."

"Perhaps three times a week; perhaps twice."

"The accident was on a Thursday. Have you noticed that you were pulled up oftener on a Thursday than on any other day?"

A smile crossed the driver's face at the question.

"You don't happen to live at Swanstead yourself, sir?" he asked in reply.

"No," admitted Carrados. "Why?"

"Well, sir, we were *always* pulled up on Thursday; practically always, you may say. It got to be quite a saying among those who used the train regular; they used to look out for it."

Carrados's sightless eyes had the one quality of concealing emotion supremely. "Oh," he commented softly, "always; and it was quite a saying, was it? And *why* was it always so on Thursday?"

"It had to do with the early closing, I'm told. The suburban traffic was a bit different. By rights we ought to have been set back two minutes for that day, but I suppose it wasn't thought worth while to alter us in the time-table so we most always had to wait outside Three Deep tunnel for a west-bound electric to make good."

"You were prepared for it then?"

"Yes, sir, I was," said Hutchins, reddening at some recollection, "and very down about it was one of the jury over that. But, mayhap once in three months, I did get through even on a Thursday, and it's not for me to question whether things are right or wrong just because they are not what I may expect. The signals are my orders, sir—stop! go on! and it's for me to obey, as you would a general on the field of battle. What would happen otherwise! It was nonsense what they said about going cautious; and the man who stated it was a barber who didn't know the difference between a 'distance' and a 'stop' signal down to the minute they gave their verdict. My orders, sir, given me by that signal, was 'Go right ahead and keep to your running time!' "

Carrados nodded a soothing assent. "That is all, I think," he remarked.

"All!" exclaimed Hutchins in surprise. "Why, sir, you can't have got much idea of it yet."

"Quite enough. And I know it isn't pleasant for you to be taken along the same ground over and over again."

The man moved awkwardly in his chair and pulled nervously at his grizzled beard.

"You mustn't take any notice of what I said just now, sir," he apologized. "You somehow make me feel that something may come of it; but I've been badgered about and accused and cross-examined from one to another of them these weeks till it's fairly made me bitter against everything. And now they talk of putting me in a lavatory—me that has been with the company for five and forty years and on the foot-plate thirty-two—a man suspected of running past a danger signal."

"You have had a rough time, Hutchins; you will have to exercise your patience a little longer yet," said Carrados sympathetically.

"You think something may come of it, sir? You think you will be able to clear me? Believe me, sir, if you could give me something to look forward to it might save me from——" He pulled himself up and shook his head sorrowfully. "I've been near it," he added simply.

Carrados reflected and took his resolution.

"To-day is Wednesday. I think you may hope to hear something from your general manager towards the middle of next week."

"Good God, sir! You really mean that?"

"In the interval show your good sense by behaving reasonably. Keep civilly to yourself and don't talk. Above all"—he nodded towards a quart jug that stood on the table between them, an incident that filled the simple-minded engineer with boundless wonder when he recalled it afterwards—"above all, leave that alone."

Hutchins snatched up the vessel and brought it crashing down on the hearthstone, his face shining with a set resolution.

"I've done with it, sir. It was the bitterness and despair that drove me to that. Now I can do without it."

The door was hastily opened and Miss Hutchins looked anxiously from her father to the visitors and back again.

"Oh, whatever is the matter?" she exclaimed. "I heard a great crash."

"This gentleman is going to clear me, Meg, my dear," blurted out the old man irrepressibly. "And I've done with the drink for ever."

"Hutchins! Hutchins!" said Carrados warningly.

"My daughter, sir; you wouldn't have her not know?" pleaded Hutchins, rather crest-fallen. "It won't go any further."

Carrados laughed quietly to himself as he felt Margaret Hutchins's startled and questioning eyes attempting to read his mind. He shook hands with the engine-driver without further comment, however, and walked out into the commonplace little street under Parkinson's unobtrusive guidance.

"Very nice of Miss Hutchins to go into half-mourning, Parkinson," he remarked as they went along. "Thoughtful, and yet not ostentatious."

"Yes, sir," agreed Parkinson, who had long ceased to wonder at his master's perceptions.

"The Romans, Parkinson, had a saying to the effect that gold carries no smell. That is a pity sometimes. What jewellery did Miss Hutchins wear?"

"Very little, sir. A plain gold brooch representing a merry-thought —the merry-thought of a sparrow, I should say, sir. The only other article was a smooth-backed gun-metal watch, suspended from a gun-metal bow."

"Nothing showy or expensive, eh?"

"Oh dear no, sir. Quite appropriate for a young person of her position."

"Just what I should have expected." He slackened his pace. "We are passing a hoarding, are we not?"

"Yes, sir."

"We will stand here a moment. Read me the letterpress of the poster before us."

"This 'Oxo' one, sir?"

"Yes."

" 'Oxo,' sir."

Carrados was convulsed with silent laughter. Parkinson had infinitely more dignity and conceded merely a tolerant recognition of the ludicrous.

"That was a bad shot, Parkinson," remarked his master when he could speak. "We will try another."

For three minutes, with scrupulous conscientiousness on the part of the reader and every appearance of keen interest on the part of the hearer, there were set forth the particulars of a sale by auction of superfluous timber and builders' material.

"That will do," said Carrados, when the last detail had been reached. "We can be seen from the door of No. 107 still?"

"Yes, sir."

"No indication of anyone coming to us from there?"

"No, sir."

Carrados walked thoughtfully on again. In the Holloway Road they rejoined the waiting motor-car.

"Lambeth Bridge Station" was the order the driver received.

From the station the car was sent on home and Parkinson was instructed to take two first-class singles for Richmond, which could be reached by changing at Stafford Road. The "evening rush" had not yet commenced and they had no difficulty in finding an empty carriage when the train came in.

Parkinson was kept busy that journey describing what he saw at various points between Lambeth Bridge and Knight's Cross. For a quarter of a mile Carrados's demands on the eyes and the memory of his remarkable servant were wide and incessant. Then his questions ceased. They had passed the "stop" signal, east of Knight's Cross Station.

The following afternoon they made the return journey as far as Knight's Cross. This time, however, the surroundings failed to interest Carrados. "We are going to look at some rooms," was the information he offered on the subject, and an imperturbable "Yes, sir" had been the extent of Parkinson's comment on the unusual proceeding. After leaving the station they turned sharply along a road that ran parallel with the line, a dull thoroughfare of substantial, elderly houses that were beginning to sink into decrepitude. Here and there a corner residence displayed the brass plate of a professional occupant, but for the most part they were given up to the various branches of second-rate apartment letting.

"The third house after the one with the flagstaff," said Carrados.

Parkinson rang the bell, which was answered by a young servant, who took an early opportunity of assuring them that she was not tidy as it was rather early in the afternoon. She informed Carrados, in reply to his inquiry, that Miss Chubb was at home, and showed them into a melancholy little sitting-room to await her appearance.

"I shall be 'almost' blind here, Parkinson," remarked Carrados, walking about the room. "It saves explanation."

"Very good, sir," replied Parkinson.

Five minutes later, an interval suggesting that Miss Chubb also found it rather early in the afternoon, Carrados was arranging to take rooms for his attendant and himself for the short time that he would be in London, seeing an oculist.

"One bedroom, mine, must face north," he stipulated. "It has to do with the light."

Miss Chubb replied that she quite understood. Some gentlemen, she added, had their requirements, others their fancies. She endeavoured to suit all. The bedroom she had in view from the first *did* face north. She would not have known, only the last gentleman, curiously enough, had made the same request.

"A sufferer like myself?" inquired Carrados affably.

Miss Chubb did not think so. In his case she regarded it merely as a fancy. He had said that he could not sleep on any other side. She had had to turn out of her own room to accommodate him, but if one kept an apartment-house one had to be adaptable; and Mr. Ghoosh was certainly very liberal in his ideas.

"Ghoosh? An Indian gentleman, I presume?" hazarded Carrados.

It appeared that Mr. Ghoosh was an Indian. Miss Chubb confided that at first she had been rather perturbed at the idea of taking in "a black man," as she confessed to regarding him. She reiterated, however, that Mr. Ghoosh proved to be "quite the gentleman." Five minutes of affability put Carrados in full possession of Mr. Ghoosh's manner of life and movements—the dates of his arrival and departure, his solitariness and his daily habits.

"This would be the best bedroom," said Miss Chubb.

It was a fair-sized room on the first floor. The window looked out on to the roof of an outbuilding; beyond, the deep cutting of the railway line. Opposite stood the dead wall that Mr. Carlyle had spoken of.

Carrados "looked" round the room with the discriminating glance that sometimes proved so embarrassing to those who knew him.

"I have to take a little daily exercise," he remarked, walking to the window and running his hand up the woodwork. "You will not mind my fixing a 'developer' here, Miss Chubb—a few small screws?"

Miss Chubb thought not. Then she was sure not. Finally she ridiculed the idea of minding with scorn.

"If there is width enough," mused Carrados, spanning the upright critically. "Do you happen to have a wooden foot-rule convenient?"

"Well, to be sure!" exclaimed Miss Chubb, opening a rapid succession of drawers until she produced the required article. "When we did out this room after Mr. Ghoosh, there was this very ruler among the things that he hadn't thought worth taking. This is what you require, sir?"

"Yes," replied Carrados, accepting it, "I think this is exactly what I require." It was a common new white-wood rule, such as one might buy at any small stationer's for a penny. He carelessly took off the width of the upright, reading the figures with a touch; and then continued to run a finger-tip delicately up and down the edges of the instrument.

"Four and seven-eighths," was his unspoken conclusion.

"I hope it will do sir."

"Admirably," replied Carrados. "But I haven't reached the end of my requirements yet, Miss Chubb."

"No, sir?" said the landlady, feeling that it would be a pleasure to oblige so agreeable a gentleman, "what else might there be?"

"Although I can see very little I like to have a light, but not any kind of light. Gas I cannot do with. Do you think that you would be able to find me an oil lamp?"

"Certainly, sir. I got out a very nice brass lamp that I have specially for Mr. Ghoosh. He read a good deal of an evening and he preferred a lamp."

"That is very convenient. I suppose it is large enough to burn for a whole evening?"

"Yes, indeed. And very particular he was always to have it filled every day."

"A lamp without oil is not very useful," smiled Carrados, following her towards another room, and absent-mindedly slipping the foot-rule into his pocket.

Whatever Parkinson thought of the arrangement of going into second-rate apartments in an obscure street it is to be inferred that his devotion to his master was sufficient to overcome his private emotions as a self-respecting "man." At all events, as they were approaching the station he asked, and without a trace of feeling, whether there were any orders for him with reference to the proposed migration.

"None, Parkinson," replied his master. "We must be satisfied with our present quarters."

"I beg your pardon, sir," said Parkinson, with some constraint. "I understand that you had taken the rooms for a week certain."

"I am afraid that Miss Chubb will be under the same impression. Unforeseen circumstances will prevent our going, however. Mr. Greatorex must write to-morrow, enclosing a cheque, with my regrets, and adding a penny for this ruler which I seem to have brought away with me. It, at least, is something for the money."

Parkinson may be excused for not attempting to understand the course of events.

"Here is your train coming in, sir," he merely said.

"We will let it go and wait for another. Is there a signal at either end of the platform?"

"Yes, sir; at the further end."

"Let us walk towards it. Are there any of the porters or officials about here?"

"No, sir; none."

"Take this ruler. I want you to go up the steps—there are steps up the signal, by the way?"

"Yes, sir."

"I want you to measure the glass of the lamp. Do not go up any higher than is necessary, but if you have to stretch be careful not to mark off the measurement with your nail, although the impulse is a natural one. That has been done already."

Parkinson looked apprehensively round and about. Fortunately the part was a dark and unfrequented spot and everyone else was moving towards the exit at the other end of the platform. Fortunately, also, the signal was not a high one.

"As near as I can judge on the rounded surface, the glass is four and seven-eighths across," reported Parkinson.

"Thank you," replied Carrados, returning the measure to his pocket, "four and seven-eighths is quite near enough. Now we will take the next train back."

Sunday evening came, and with it Mr. Carlyle to The Turrets at the appointed hour. He brought to the situation a mind poised for any eventuality and a trenchant eye. As the time went on and the impenetrable Carrados made no illusion to the case, Carlyle's manner inclined to a waggish commiseration of his host's position. Actually, he said little, but the crisp precision of his voice when the path lay open to a remark of any significance left little to be said.

It was not until they had finished dinner and returned to the library that Carrados gave the slightest hint of anything unusual being in the air. His first indication of coming events was to remove the key from the outside to the inside of the door.

"What are you doing, Max?" demanded Mr. Carlyle, his curiosity overcoming the indirect attitude.

"You have been very entertaining, Louis," replied his friend, "but Parkinson should be back very soon now and it is as well to be prepared. Do you happen to carry a revolver?"

"Not when I come to dine with you, Max," replied Carlyle, with all the aplomb he could muster. "Is it usual?"

Carrados smiled affectionately at his guest's agile recovery and touched the secret spring of a drawer in an antique bureau by his side. The little hidden receptacle shot smoothly out, disclosing a pair of dull-blued pistols.

"To-night, at all events, it might be prudent," he replied, handing one to Carlyle and putting the other into his own pocket. "Our man may be here at any minute, and we do not know in what temper he will come."

"Our man!" exclaimed Carlyle, craning forward in excitement. "Max! you don't mean to say that you have got Mead to admit it?"

"No one has admitted it," said Carrados. "And it is not Mead."

"Not Mead. ... Do you mean that Hutchins——?"

"Neither Mead nor Hutchins. The man who tampered with the signal—for Hutchins was right and a green light *was* exhibited—is a young Indian from Bengal. His name is Drishna and he lives at Swanstead."

Mr. Carlyle stared at his friend between sheer surprise and blank incredulity.

"You really mean this, Carrados?" he said.

"My fatal reputation for humour!" smiled Carrados. "If I am wrong, Louis, the next hour will expose it."

"But why—why—why? The colossal villainy, the unparalleled audacity!" Mr. Carlyle lost himself among incredulous superlatives and could only stare.

"Chiefly to get himself out of a disastrous speculation," replied Carrados, answering the question. "If there was another motive—or at least an incentive—which I suspect, doubtless we shall hear of it."

"All the same, Max, I don't think that you have treated me quite fairly," protested Carlyle, getting over his first surprise and passing to a sense of injury. "Here we are and I know nothing, absolutely nothing, of the whole affair."

"We both have our ideas of pleasantry, Louis," replied Carrados genially. "But I dare say you are right and perhaps there is still time to atone." In the fewest possible words he outlined the course of his investigations. "And now you know all that is to be known until Drishna arrives."

"But will he come?" questioned Carlyle doubtfully. "He may be suspicious."

"Yes, he will be suspicious."

"Then he will not come."

"On the contrary, Louis, he will come because my letter will make him suspicious. He *is* coming; otherwise Parkinson would have telephoned me at once and we should have had to take other measures."

"What did you say, Max?" asked Carlyle curiously.

"I wrote that I was anxious to discuss an Indo-Scythian inscription with him, and sent my car in the hope that he would be able to oblige me."

"But is he interested in Indo-Scythian inscriptions?"

"I haven't the faintest idea," admitted Carrados, and Mr. Carlyle was throwing up his hands in despair when the sound of a motor-car wheels softly kissing the gravel surface of the drive outside brought him to his feet.

"By Gad, you are right, Max!" he exclaimed, peeping through the curtains. "There is a man inside."

"Mr. Drishna," announced Parkinson a minute later.

The visitor came into the room with leisurely self-possession that might have been real or a desperate assumption. He was a slightly built young man of about twenty-five, with black hair and eyes, a small, carefully trained moustache, and a dark olive skin. His physiognomy was not displeasing, but his expression had a harsh and supercilious tinge. In attire he erred towards the immaculately spruce.

"Mr. Carrados?" he said inquiringly.

Carrados, who had risen, bowed slightly without offering his hand.

"This gentleman," he said, indicating his friend, "is Mr. Carlyle, the celebrated private detective."

The Indian shot a very sharp glance at the object of this description. Then he sat down.

"You wrote me a letter, Mr. Carrados," he remarked, in English that scarcely betrayed any foreign origin, "a rather curious letter, I may say. You asked me about an ancient inscription. I know nothing of antiquities; but I thought, as you had sent, that it would be more courteous if I came and explained this to you."

"That was the object of my letter," replied Carrados.

"You wished to see me?" said Drishna, unable to stand the ordeal of the silence that Carrados imposed after his remark.

"When you left Miss Chubb's house you left a ruler behind." One lay on the desk by Carrados and he took it up as he spoke.

"I don't understand what you are talking about," said Drishna guardedly. "You are making some mistake."

"The ruler was marked at four and seven-eighths inches—the measure of the glass of the signal lamp outside."

The unfortunate young man was unable to repress a start. His face lost its healthy tone. Then, with a sudden impulse, he made a step forward and snatched the object from Carrados's hand.

"If it is mine I have a right to it," he exclaimed, snapping the ruler in two and throwing it on to the back of the blazing fire. "It is nothing."

"Pardon me, I did not say that the one you have so impetuously disposed of was yours. As a matter of fact, it was mine. Yours is—elsewhere."

"Wherever it is you have no right to it if it is mine," panted Drishna, with rising excitement. "You are a thief, Mr. Carrados. I will not stay any longer here."

He jumped up and turned towards the door. Carlyle made a step forward, but the precaution was unnecessary.

"One moment, Mr. Drishna," interposed Carrados, in his smoothest tones. "It is a pity, after you have come so far, to leave without hearing of my investigations in the neighbourhood of Shaftesbury Avenue."

Drishna sat down again.

"As you like," he muttered. "It does not interest me."

"I wanted to obtain a lamp of a certain pattern," continued Carrados. "It seemed to me that the simplest explanation would be to say that I wanted it for a motor-car. Naturally I went to Long Acre. At the first shop I said: 'Wasn't it here that a friend of mine, an Indian gentleman, recently had a lamp made with a green glass that was nearly five inches across?' No, it was not there but they could make me one. At the next shop the same; at the third, and fourth, and so on. Finally my persistence was rewarded. I found the place where the lamp had been made, and at the cost of ordering another I obtained all the details I wanted. It was news to them, the shopman informed me, that in some parts of India green was the danger colour and therefore tail lamps had to show a green light. The incident made some impression on him and he would be able to identify their customer—who paid in advance and gave no address —among a thousand of his countrymen. Do I succeed in interesting you, Mr. Drishna?"

"Do you?" replied Drishna, with a languid yawn. "Do I look interested?"

"You must make allowance for my unfortunate blindness," apologized Carrados, with grim irony.

"Blindness!" exclaimed Drishna, dropping his affectation of unconcern as though electrified by the word, "do you mean—really blind—that you do not see me?"

"Alas, no," admitted Carrados.

The Indian withdrew his right hand from his coat pocket and with a tragic gesture flung a heavy revolver down on the table between them.

"I have had you covered all the time, Mr. Carrados, and if I had wished to go and you or your friend had raised a hand to stop me, it would have been at the peril of your lives," he said, in a voice of melancholy triumph. "But what is the use of defying fate, and who successfully evades his destiny? A month ago I went to see one of our people who reads the future and sought to know the course of certain events. 'You need fear no human eye,' was the message given to me. Then she added: 'But when the sightless sees the unseen, make your peace with Yama.' And I thought she spoke of the Great Hereafter!"

"This amounts to an admission of your guilt," exclaimed Mr. Carlyle practically.

"I bow to the decree of fate," replied Drishna. "And it is fitting to the universal irony of existence that a blind man should be the instrument. I don't imagine, Mr. Carlyle," he added maliciously, "that you, with your eyes, would ever have brought that result about."

"You are a very cold-blooded young scoundrel, sir!" retorted Mr. Carlyle. "Good heavens! do you realize that you are responsible for the death of scores of innocent men and women?"

"Do *you* realize, Mr. Carlyle, that you and your Government and your soldiers are responsible for the death of thousands of innocent men and women in my country every day? If England was occupied by the Germans who quartered an army and an administration with their wives and their families and all their expensive paraphernalia on the unfortunate country until the whole nation was reduced to the verge of famine, and the appointment of every new official meant the callous death sentence on a thousand men and women to pay his salary, then if you went to Berlin and wrecked a train you would be hailed a patriot. What Boadicea did and—and Samson, so have I. If they were heroes, so am I."

"Well, upon my word!" cried the highly scandalized Carlyle,

"what next! Boadicea was a—er—semi-legendary person, whom we may possibly admire at a distance. Personally, I do not profess to express an opinion. But Samson, I would remind you, is a Biblical character. Samson was mocked as an enemy. You, I do not doubt, have been entertained as a friend."

"And haven't I been mocked and despised and sneered at every day of my life here by your supercilious, superior, empty-headed men?" flashed back Drishna, his eyes leaping into malignity and his voice trembling with sudden passion. "Oh! how I hated them as I passed them in the street and recognized by a thousand petty insults their lordly English contempt for me as an inferior being—a nigger. How I longed with Caligula that a nation had a single neck that I might destroy it at one blow. I loathe you in your complacent hypocrisy, Mr. Carlyle, despise and utterly abominate you from an eminence of superiority that you can never even understand."

"I think we are getting rather away from the point, Mr. Drishna," interposed Carrados, with the impartiality of a judge. "Unless I am misinformed, you are not so ungallant as to include everyone you have met here in your execration?"

"Ah, no," admitted Drishna, descending into a quite ingenuous frankness. "Much as I hate your men I love your women. How is it possible that a nation should be so divided—its men so dull-witted and offensive, its women so quick, sympathetic and capable of appreciating?"

"But a little expensive, too, at times?" suggested Carrados.

Drishna sighed heavily.

"Yes; it is incredible. It is the generosity of their large nature. My allowance, though what most of you would call noble, has proved quite inadequate. I was compelled to borrow money and the interest became overwhelming. Bankruptcy was impracticable because I should have then been recalled by my people, and much as I detest England a certain reason made the thought of leaving it unbearable."

"Connected with the Arcady Theatre?"

"You know? Well, do not let us introduce the lady's name. In order to restore myself I speculated on the Stock Exchange. My credit was good through my father's position and the standing of the firm to which I am attached. I heard on reliable authority, and very early, that the Central and Suburban, and the Deferred especially, was safe to fall heavily, through a motor bus amalgamation that was then a secret. I opened a bear account and sold largely. The shares fell, but only fractionally, and I waited. Then, unfortunately, they began to go up. Adverse forces were at work and rumours were put about. I could not stand the settlement, and in order to carry over an account I was literally compelled to deal temporarily with some securities that were not technically my own property."

"Embezzlement, sir," commented Mr. Carlyle icily. "But what is embezzlement on the top of wholesale murder!"

"That is what it is called. In my case, however, it was only to be temporary. Unfortunately, the rise continued. Then, at the height of my despair, I chanced to be returning to Swanstead rather earlier than usual one evening, and the train was stopped at a certain signal to let another pass. There was conversation in the carriage and I learned certain details. One said that there would be an accident some day, and so forth. In a flash—as by an inspiration—I saw how the circumstance might be turned to account. A bad accident and the shares would certainly fall and my position would be retrieved. I think Mr. Carrados has somehow learned the rest."

"Max," said Mr. Carlyle, with emotion, "is there any reason why you should not send your man for a police officer and have this monster arrested on his own confession without further delay?"

"Pray do so, Mr. Carrados," acquiesced Drishna. "I shall certainly be hanged, but the speech I shall prepare will ring from one end of India to the other; my memory will be venerated as that of a martyr; and the emancipation of my motherland will be hastened by my sacrifice."

"In other words," commented Carrados, "there will be disturbances at half-a-dozen disaffected places, a few unfortunate police will be clubbed to death, and possibly worse things may happen. That does not suit us, Mr. Drishna."

"And how do you propose to prevent it?" asked Drishna, with cool assurance.

"It is very unpleasant being hanged on a dark winter morning; very cold, very friendless, very inhuman. The long trial, the solitude and the confinement, the thoughts of the long sleepless night before, the hangman and the pinioning and the noosing of the rope, are apt to prey on the imagination. Only a very stupid man can take hanging easily."

"What do you want me to do instead, Mr. Carrados?" asked Drishna shrewdly.

Carrados's hand closed on the weapon that still lay on the table between them. Without a word he pushed it across.

"I see," commented Drishna, with a short laugh and a gleaming eye. "Shoot myself and hush it up to suit your purpose. Withhold my message to save the exposures of a trial, and keep the flame from the torch of insurrectionary freedom."

"Also," interposed Carrados mildly, "to save your worthy people a good deal of shame, and to save the lady who is nameless the unpleasant necessity of relinquishing the house and the income which you have just settled on her. She certainly would not then venerate your memory."

"What is that?"

"The transaction which you carried through was based on a felony and could not be upheld. The firm you dealt with will go to the courts, and the money, being directly traceable, will be held forfeit as no good consideration passed."

"Max!" cried Mr. Carlyle hotly, "you are not going to let this scoundrel cheat the gallows after all?"

"The best use you can make of the gallows is to cheat it, Louis," replied Carrados. "Have you ever reflected what human beings will think of us a hundred years hence?"

"Oh, of course I'm not really in favour of hanging," admitted Mr. Carlyle.

"Nobody really is. But we go on hanging. Mr. Drishna is a dangerous animal who for the sake of pacific animals must cease to exist. Let his barbarous exploit pass into oblivion with him. The disadvantages of spreading it broadcast immeasurably outweigh the benefits."

"I have considered," announced Drishna. "I will do as you wish."

"Very well," said Carrados. "Here is some plain notepaper. You had better write a letter to someone saying that the financial difficulties in which you are involved make life unbearable."

"But there are no financial difficulties—now."

"That does not matter in the least. It will be put down to an hallucination and taken as showing the state of your mind."

"But what guarantee have we that he will not escape?" whispered Mr. Carlyle.

"He cannot escape," replied Carrados tranquilly. "His identity is too clear."

"I have no intention of trying to escape," put in Drishna, as he wrote. "You hardly imagine that I have not considered this eventuality, do you?"

"All the same," murmured the ex-lawyer, "I should like to have a jury behind me. It is one thing to execute a man morally; it is another to do it almost literally."

"Is that all right?" asked Drishna, passing across the letter he had written.

Carrados smiled at this tribute to his perception.

"Quite excellent," he replied courteously. "There is a train at nine-forty. Will that suit you?"

Drishna nodded and stood up. Mr. Carlyle had a very uneasy feeling that he ought to do something but could not suggest to himself what.

The next moment he heard his friend heartily thanking the visitor for the assistance he had been in the matter of the Indo-Scythian inscription, as they walked across the hall together. Then a door closed.

"I believe that there is something positively uncanny about Max at times," murmured the perturbed gentleman to himself.

The Mystery of the Vanished Petition Crown

Max Carrados always seemed inclined to laugh quietly if anyone happened to mention the curious disappearance of the Willington Petition Crown. Why he should have been amused rarely came out at such times, perhaps because it is not expedient for one private collector openly to accuse another private collector of barefaced theft (whatever misgivings the majority may secretly admit of one another's morals), but the extent of his knowledge in the affair will emerge from the following pages.

As a specialist in Greek tetradrachms Carrados would naturally only have a condescending interest in any of the non-classical branches of numismatics, but it was an interest that drew him to every word of coin news that appeared. As his delicate fingertips skimmed the morning paper headings at breakfast one day they "read" for him a line that promised some entertainment, and the item was duly blue-pencilled for consideration later. It was no effort for the blind man to pick out all the essentials of the newspaper's contents in this way; he could even, though not with the same facility, read the ordinary smaller type, but where there was no special reason for this it was his custom to mark off such paragraphs for his secretary's subsequent attention. This was in the nature of their ordinary daily routine, and an hour later Greatorex noticed and read aloud the following extract from the *Daily Record:*

"RARE COIN DISAPPEARS

"Auction Room Sensation

"Collectors and dealers who forgathered at Messrs. Lang & Leng's well-known sale-rooms yesterday in the hope of bidding for an exceptionally fine specimen of the celebrated Petition Crown of Charles II were doomed to disappointment. When the lot in question was reached and the coin was displayed at the tables it was discovered that something was wrong. The Petition Crown, which had previously been on view for several days and up to the hour of the sale, had disappeared and a comparatively valueless coin of a somewhat similar type occupied its numbered receptacle.

"Immediate search among the other lots, both sold and unsold, failed to reveal any trace of the missing rarity and the whole affair is so far shrouded in mystery.

"Piquancy is added to the incident by the fact that the last person to see and handle the coin was a well-known lady journalist, who, however, disclaims any numismatic cravings. After inspecting the coin merely as a rare and valuable curiosity the lady in question returned the tray containing it to the attendant in charge, who at once replaced it in the cabinet. As already stated, when it was next required the crown had vanished.

"The Petition Crown holds the auction record among English coins, an example having realised £500 some years ago. It is generally stated that only fifteen specimens of this excessively rare coin were ever struck, and all but two or three are now in public collections and therefore out of the reach of enthusiasts. The crown owes its name to the interesting circumstances of its origin. The English engraver, Thomas Simon, having been supplanted in Charles the Second's favour by his Dutch rival, Roettier, the former put all his skill and genius into the creating of a super-coin, which took the form of a crown piece, with the following quaint inscription neatly engraved around the edge:

" 'Thomas Simon most humbly prays your Majesty to compare this his tryall piece with the Dutch, and if more truly drawn and embossd, more gracefully orderd, and more accurately engraven, to releive him.'

"Sad to relate, although Simon's work is admittedly superior to that of 'the Dutch,' his petition was in vain. Still worse, the royal patron of the arts allowed his 'most humble's' salary and working expenses for several years to remain unpaid, so that after the engraver's death his widow had also to 'petition'—for £2,164 long overdue."

"That's rather like another plant where a string of pearls was changed some years ago," volunteered Greatorex, laying aside the paper in favour of his own reminiscences. He was a cheerful, mercurial youth who conceived that the more important part of his duty was to regale Mr. Carrados with his personal views on life and affairs, nor, strange to say, did his employer very often undeceive him. "Do you remember the one I mean, sir?"

"Yes; they mulled that by not copying the sale label closely enough, and the attendant noticed it when the necklace was laid down again. There was a woman in that business also. But the two cases have nothing in common really."

"How do you mean? Both were at auction sales; both——"

"True," interrupted Carrados, "but those things are only superficial. The essential motives fall into two quite different classes. Good pearls are always readily saleable, and it is simply a matter of rearranging them and making them up in a different form. But what is a man going to do with a Petition Crown? Wear it on his watch-chain? As a marketable piece of loot he might as well carry off a Turner from the National Gallery, or, indeed, one of the lions from Trafalgar Square. Its trade value is about one and ninepence for the melting-pot."

"Oh, come, sir," protested Greatorex. "This account speaks of a few other specimens knocking about. Surely in a year or two's time this one couldn't be positively identified as stolen?"

Max Carrados turned to pull open a drawer of his desk and took out the top pamphlet of a number it contained.

"Here is Lang's catalogue of this sale," he said, passing it across. "I haven't gone into it, but very likely that crown will be illustrated among the plates at the end. Just see."

"Quite right, sir. It is Lot 64, and it is reproduced in one of those photographic process types here on Plate 2."

"Take a glass and look into it. It is described as exceptionally fine, but you will almost certainly find a number of small cuts and dents here and there on the surface."

"Yes; I see what you mean. They don't show ordinarily."

"All the same they label the specimen as definitely as if it was a numbered bank-note. The simplest way out of that would be to carry it loose in your pocket for a few years. That would reduce its cabinet value to one-half, but it would effectually wipe out its identity. The trouble would be that whenever you started to dispose of it you would be pointedly asked for the pedigree. What collection had it come from last? All these little details are on record and easily available. No, it's amateur work, whoever it may be, Greatorex."

"I was rather hoping that perhaps someone would bring it round here to offer sooner or later," remarked the adventurous Greatorex, still examining the plate. "I'll bet I could spot it by that scratch over his majesty's eye."

"Then you will certainly be disappointed," was the unpromising reply. "If the coin really has been stolen—and that's a palpable 'if' so far—ten to one its immediate destination is the private drawer of some collector who will be content to handle and gloat over it in secret for the remaining days of his life."

"And then I suppose it all comes out when he goes off?"

"It may. But I have heard a curious story of an old fellow who had a few pieces in his collection that he never showed. When he thought that he only had a short time left he took a coal hammer and in five minutes the rarities were effectually put beyond any fear of identification."

"My Sunday hat!" exclaimed Mr. Greatorex, compelled to a generous admiration. "Some collectors are hot stuff!"

With that decorous epitaph the subject was laid to rest, with no indication that it would ever be raised again. But—just as one may meet three piebald horses in the course of one short walk—the Petition Crown was fated to persist, and before lunch-time a telephone call from Mr. Carlyle had resurrected it. The period of interment had been just short of three hours.

"Busy, Max?" chirruped the familiar voice of his friend the inquiry agent—incurably brisk and debonair even after its ten miles' journey along the wire. "Not to me? Dear old chap! Well, I dare say you've read all about the disappearance of Lord Willington's—er—Petition Crown in the paper this morning? I thought you might be interested as it's something in your line."

"Greatorex is, at all events," replied Mr. Carrados. "He was half expecting that someone might bring it here in the course of the day. Do you—strictly between ourselves, of course—do you happen to have it for disposal, Louis?"

"Do I happen to have it for disposal?" repeated Mr. Carlyle in a slightly mystified tone. "I thought you would have read that the coin has been stolen. However, Max, in my office at this moment there is a young lady who is very much concerned at being implicated in the affair. Frankly, as the auctioneers are naturally doing all that can be done to solve the riddle, I did not see how I could be of any real service to her, and I told her so. But she seemed so disappointed that as a—er—well——"

"As a sort of forlorn hope?" suggested the listener maliciously.

"Not at all; most certainly not!" protested Mr. Carlyle indignant-ly. "I explained that as you were both a keen coin collector yourself and an enthusiast in certain branches of criminal research, if—*if,* mind you, Max—you cared to hear what she had to say, you would be in an exceptional position to give her a word of advice. And that is really the long and the short of the whole matter, my mordacious friend."

"Very likely, my ingenious sleuth, but I imagine that there is a small piece missing somewhere. You were not wont to turn young and beautiful suppliants from your office door. What is the real reason of this professional reluctance on your part?"

"Max," came along Mr. Carlyle's cautiously-restrained voice—the listener could divine how near the moving lips were to the mouth-piece—"I will speak to you as one gentleman to another when there is no danger of being overheard. Miss Frensham is young, but she is *not* beautiful, and to put it in that way is to pay her a noticeable compliment. She is also, I gather, regrettably hard up. Now, as I never conceal from my clients, my business is conducted on a purely financial basis, whereas you amuse yourself for—the other thing. Doubtless I could earn a few honest but ill-spared guineas at this young lady's expense, but I cannot satisfy myself that she would be any the wiser for the outlay. And so——"

"All right, you old humbug," said Carrados amiably; "send her along. So far as the portents go I am with you in not seeing that there is much to be done for her, but if she finds any satisfaction in talking about it you can tell her that I shall be here for the next few hours."

Miss Frensham evidently did foresee some satisfaction in talking about it, for she came at once. In view of her circumstances, Carrados could not but deem her rather extravagant, for nothing but a taxi from door to door could explain the promptness of her arrival. Mr. Carlyle had not maligned her looks: plain she undoubtedly was, not in any sense describably ugly but with a sort of pug-dog grotes-query. Her dress made no attempt to counteract physical deficiencies, but when she spoke Carrados's unemotional face instantly lit up with pleasure, for, unexpected in such a setting, her voice had the rare quality of gracious music.

"How good of you to let me come in this way, Mr. Carrados!" she exclaimed as they shook hands. "I don't know which I have to thank the more—you or Mr. Carlyle."

"I think I shall claim the major share," said the blind man lightly. "Not for any particular merit, but because I am so very pleased to hear you."

"To hear—— Oh, yes; of course he told me or I really should not have guessed. You know what it's all about?"

"I infer that you are the lady of the paragraph," and the lifted hand indicated the open sheet of the *Record* lying nearby.

"Yes, in a sense I am." Miss Frensham seemed troubled for a moment. "But I am not really a 'well-known lady journalist,' Mr. Carrados. I am only a very obscure one—hardly a real journalist at all. That was just swank, and also because I felt sure that under that description no one who knew would ever think of *me*."

"Oh," said Mr. Carrados with an amused and deepening interest, "so in addition to being the heroine of the adventure you wrote it up?"

"Yes, ultimately I did. At first I was too upset to think about that. But I had gone to the place yesterday to see if there wasn't a 'news-story' in this Petition Crown—nothing but 'news-stories' are worth while, you know—and it seemed rather a pity to miss it when it turned out to be a very much better 'news-story' than I had ever expected. And then I knew that if I got my 'copy' taken I could keep my own name out. I had particular reasons for wishing that."

Carrados nodded without showing any curiosity about the reasons. "What is it exactly that you want to do now?" he asked.

"Well, I feel that I am really under suspicion of having taken the coin—I don't see how they can think anything else in the circumstances—and the only way of clearing myself is to find out who did take it. Knowing that I didn't, I naturally think that it must be the attendant there, because he seems to have been the only other person who could have done."

"Reverse the argument, and the attendant, knowing that he didn't, naturally thinks that it must be you, because you seem to be the only other person who could have done. And so both sides get into difficulties along that obvious line. Suppose we ignore the two palpable suspects—yourself and the attendant. Now who else might it have been?"

"That is the difficulty, Mr. Carrados; it could have been no one else. I returned the coin to the attendant; he put it back in the case and remained on duty there until he displayed it on the tray to show round. Then it was discovered to have been taken."

"I suppose," said Carrados tentatively, "you really were the last to inspect the coin? Sitting there you would probably have noticed if anyone else had asked for it?"

"I only know what they said, but no one seemed to have any doubt about it. I went out to—to get some lunch and when I got back the sale was going on."

"Ah," said the blind man thoughtfully. "Of course you would have to. Suppose you tell me the—the 'news-story' all through."

"I hoped that you would let me," replied the girl. "But I was afraid of taking up too much of your time. Well, I have been living by journalism for some time now. Rather suddenly I had to support myself by some kind of work, and there was nothing else that I seemed able to do. I have always been fond of writing, and I had quite a lot of stories and articles and poems that I had been told by friends were quite good enough to print. I brought them to London with me, but somehow they didn't seem so much thought of here. I got to know one or two other girls who wrote, and they told me that my sort of stuff would be all right when I got into the peerage or became a leading lady, but if I wanted to live meanwhile it was absolutely necessary to cultivate a 'news-nose.' I soon saw what they meant: it wasn't absolutely necessary that it should be news you wrote, but it had to give the impression that it was."

"Miss Frensham, I have been a practical journalist myself," remarked Carrados. "You had grasped the sacred torch."

"At all events, I could just keep the domestic pot boiling after that. It was rather a near thing sometimes, but there was someone—he is a sub-editor on the *Daily Record* actually—who helped me more than I can ever say. He told me of this sale. 'There's a coin to be sold that's expected to break the record,' he said; and he explained to me which it was. 'There ought to be a "news-story" in it if it does— say two hundred words in the ordinary way, four hundred if you can make it kick. I'll try and put it through.' I thought that I had made it kick, so I went to four hundred."

"Yes," agreed her auditor, "I certainly think you can claim that amount of movement."

"I didn't know anything about a coin auction, of course, but I looked up Simon in the biographical dictionary at the B.M. reading-room and then went on to the place. That was yesterday—the morning of the sale. There were two or three others—men—looking at the coins—nothing to what I had expected—and one attendant who gave out the drawers in which they were arranged as they were asked for.

"I expected some sort of formality before they let me see the crown—so valuable—but there was really nothing at all. I just said, 'Can I see No. 64, please?' and he simply pulled one of the shallow drawers out of its case and put it down before me on the table. There were about a dozen other lots in the drawer, each in its separate little box. Then he turned his back on me to attend to something else. I believe that I could have picked up the coin and walked out of the place with it."

"We are a trustful people both in war and peace," conceded Mr. Carrados. "But I think you would have found that you couldn't quite do that."

"Well, I didn't try—though it certainly did occur to me that there might be a stunt of some sort in it: you look out for them when one means a week's good keep. I made a few notes that I thought I could work in and then found that it was just one o'clock—the sale was to begin at a quarter past. As the attendant took the coins away I asked him how fast they sold them.

" 'If you only want to see that lot sold, miss, a quarter to two will be in plenty of time. If you reckon a hundred lots to the hour you'll be well on the safe side.'

"I thanked him and went out. That was really all I had to do with the coin. I never saw it again. When I got back to the sale-room the auction was going on. Even then there were only about twelve or fifteen people there. They sat at the tables—I suppose you know how they are arranged, as a sort of hollow oblong, with the auctioneer at one end and the attendant showing the coins up and down the middle?—and a few sitting here and there about the room. I didn't sit down; I stood between the table and the door waiting for the price of Lot 64, which was the only thing I wanted.

"When he got to it there was a slight stir of interest, though a more lethargic set of enthusiasts I never saw. I always imagined that collectors were a most excitable race who lost their heads at bidding and went on and on madly. These might have been buying arrowroot for all the emotion they showed."

"Half of them would be dealers who had long ago got over all human enthusiasms; the remainder would be collectors, too afraid lest the others should think that they were keen on something. And then?"

"The attendant was carrying the coin round on a little tray when one man picked it up and looked at it. 'Hullo!' he said and passed it to the next. 'This is the wrong lot,' said that one, and then the auctioneer leaned over and called to the attendant, 'Come, come, my lad—No. 64,' and the attendant said, 'This *is* No. 64,' in an aggrieved way and showed him the numbered box. Then the attendant and those near that end began to look among the unsold lots, and after that they all turned out the sold lots—they had mostly been put into little envelopes—and when they came to the end of these every one looked at every one else and said nothing. Then I think they began it all over again—the hunting, I mean—when the auctioneer hit on his desk.

" 'This is an important lot. Very sorry, but we can't go on with the selling until we know more where we are. I suppose someone did see the Petition Crown this morning?'

"Two or three men said that they had, and the attendant, looking round, recognised me.

" 'That lady was the last to see the lot before the sale, sir,' I heard him say. 'Better ask her.'

" 'Did you——' began the auctioneer, and then, I suppose, recognising that I mightn't like to carry on a shouting conversation across the room, he added, 'Do you mind coming round here?'

"I went round the tables to where he was sitting, and he continued:

" 'Did you see this lot before the sale? Our man thinks that you were the last to have it out.'

" 'Yes,' I admitted. 'I saw it, and it was there when I returned the drawer. Of course I don't know that I was the last, but it was about one o'clock.'

" 'No one had it out later, Muir?'

" 'No, sir. I've been on this spot ever since, and that tray hasn't been asked for.'

"The auctioneer seemed to consider, and every one else looked first at one and then the other of us. I began to feel very uncomfortable.

" 'I suppose it really was the Petition Crown you saw at one o'clock?' he asked after a bit.

" 'I suppose it must have been,' I replied. 'I copied the "Petition" from the edge into this notebook.'

" 'Well, that fixes it all right. You see how awkward it is for us, Miss—Miss——'

"I gave him my name.

" 'Miss Frensham. We have to do the best we can in the circumstances. I can't say at the moment on whom the loss will fall—if the coin really proves to have disappeared—but the figure is considerable. Now every one else in the room is known to us by sight; we have the names and addresses of them all.'

" 'You have my name,' I said, 'and I am living at the Allied Arts Hostel in Lower Gower Street.'

" 'Thank you,' he replied, writing it down. 'But of course that means very little to us. Is there anyone convenient who knows you personally to whom we can refer? You must understand that this does not imply any sort of suspicion of your *bona fides*; it is only putting you on equal terms with the rest of the company.'

"I thought for a moment. I saw a great many unpleasant possibilities. Most of all I knew that I wanted to keep this from my people.

" 'The editor of the *Daily Record* knows me slightly,' I replied; 'but I don't see that he can say anything beyond that. And as to suspicion, I am afraid that you already have some. If you have any ladies on your staff I am quite willing to turn out everything I have before them'—I thought that perhaps this would settle the matter off-hand, and I couldn't help adding rather viciously: 'and after that I dare say the rest of the company will do the same before you.'

" 'Yes,' he considered, 'but you've been out for half-an-hour, so that that would really prove nothing. At lunch I suppose?'

"I began to see that things were fitting in rather unpleasantly for me.

" 'Yes,' I said.

" 'Perhaps I had better note where you went. We don't know where this may land us, and in the end it may be to your interest to have a waitress or someone who can identify you over that time.'

" 'I'm afraid I can't do that,' I had to say. 'There was no one who noticed me.'

" 'Surely—— Well, anyhow, the place?'

"I shook my head. He looked at me for a moment and then wrote something down. . . . You think that was very suspicious, Mr. Carrados?"

"Your advocate never thinks that anything you do is suspicious," replied the suave listener. "Probably they would."

"They seemed to. Well, Mr. Carrados, I don't mind telling you, but somehow I couldn't say it before that—I felt—unfriendly battery of eyes. . . . My lunch consisted of three very unladylike thick slices of bread-and-butter, and I ate them as I walked slowly up and down the stairs at a tube station. So, you see, there could be no corroboration."

"Perhaps we shall do better—not even require it," he replied quietly. "What happened next?"

"I don't think that there was much more. They gave up looking for the coin. The auctioneer said that he had telephoned to someone—his solicitor or Scotland Yard, I imagined, but I didn't hear which—to know what ought to be done, and he hoped that everyone would remain until they knew. Then the sale began again. I went across and sat down on a chair away from the table. I had no interest in the sale—in fact I hated it—and after a time I took out my pad and tried to write the paragraph. Very soon the sale came to an end and the men began to go—I suppose they had been told to. I waited, for I wasn't going to seem in a hurry, until I was the only person left. After a bit the man who had been selling came in and seemed rather surprised to see me still there. He said he hoped I didn't think that I was being detained, and I said, 'Oh, no, I was just finishing something.' He said that that was all right, only they were going to lock up the room then and have it thoroughly looked over to-day—it was just possible that something might turn up, though he was rather afraid that it would remain a mystery to the end. He was quite nice about it, and told me several curious things that had happened in connection with sales in the past. Then I left and he locked the door after us and, I believe, took the key."

Carrados laughed appreciatively.

"Yes, it was rather like the proverb about the stolen horse, wasn't it?" said the girl. "But I suppose they felt that even the unlikeliest chance must be taken. Anyway, they have certainly sent inquiries both to my Hostel and to the *Record* office. That's chiefly why I want to have my poor character restored. Every one says, 'Of course, Miss Frensham, nobody would think for a moment——' But what else are they to think privately? The thing has gone and I am branded as the last to handle it."

"Yes, yes," said Carrados, beginning to walk about the room and to touch one familiar object after another in his curiously unhesitating way. "That unfortunate 'last' has obsessed you and all the others until it has shut out every real consideration. Your account of the whole business—quite clear so far as it goes—is entirely based on the fact that you were the last, and the attendant knew you were the last, and the auctioneer was told you were the last, and all the others grasped it, and you all proceeded to revolve round that centre.

There stands the man we want, as plain as a pikestaff for us, only you and your lastness get between so persistently that we cannot see him."

"I'm very sorry," faltered Miss Frensham, rather taken aback.

"That's all right, my dear young lady," said an entirely benevolent Carrados. "We are getting on very nicely on the whole, and soon you will begin to tell me the things I really want to know."

"Indeed I will tell you anything," she protested.

"Of course you will—as soon as I have the gumption to ask. In the meantime what do you really think of the celebrated Petition Crown now that you've seen it?"

This light conversational opening struck Miss Frensham as rather an unpropitious way of grappling with the problem of the theft, but she had just professed her general willingness.

"Well," she replied with conscientious effort, "it chiefly struck me as rather absurd that people should be willing to pay so much for this one when other coins, apparently almost like it, could be had for a few shillings."

"Yes; very true." The blind man appeared to consider this naïve expression deeply. "As a collector myself of course that goes home. You are not a collector, in any sense, Miss Frensham?"

"No, indeed."

"I was wondering," speculated Carrados in the same idle vein, "how you happened to know that."

"Oh, very simply. There were about a dozen other lots in the drawer the man put before me. One of them consisted of quite a number of crown pieces, and they struck me as being so like the Petition Crown at a glance that out of curiosity I compared them. When it came to the sale they made only a few pounds for the lot."

"You compared them—side by side?"

"Yes. I—I——" As she spoke Miss Frensham suddenly went very white, half rose from her chair, and sat down again. The charming voice trailed off into a gasp.

"You remember something now? You—possibly—changed them somehow?"

"*I did!* I see it all. I remember exactly how it went. What a dreadful thing!"

"Tell me what happened."

"I was waiting for the attendant to turn so that I could tell him I had finished. It was then that I took up these two coins—the

Petition Crown and one from another box—to compare. There was a man near me who had seemed to be watching—at least I thought so—and just then I looked up and caught his eyes on me. I suppose it made me nervous; anyway I dropped one of the crowns back into the drawer. It made a great clatter as it fell among the others and I felt that it would be almost a crime there to knock a coin like that. I just slipped the other into its place and pushed the drawer away as the attendant turned. And now I see clearly as can be that I returned them wrong."

"That is our real starting-point," said Carrados happily. "Now we can proceed."

"But it must have been found out. All the sold lots were looked over again."

"Oh, yes; it must have been found out. But exactly when? The man who was observing you—did you hear his name?"

"No."

"Where did he sit during the sale?"

"He sat—yes, that's rather curious. You remember that after talking to the auctioneer I went and sat down away from the table? Well, when the selling was going on again this man kept hovering round. Presently he bent down to me and said, 'Excuse me, but you have taken my seat.' 'What on earth do you mean?' I retorted, for it was just at the time that I was feeling exasperated. 'There was nothing on the chair, and there are a dozen others there,' and I pointed to the whole empty row. Then he said, 'Oh, I beg your pardon' and went and sat down on another."

"Isn't it splendid!" exclaimed Carrados in one of his rare bursts of enthusiasm. "No sooner have we got rid of you and the attendant as the only possible culprits than we find the real man absolutely fighting to make himself known—doing everything he can to attract our attention—struggling like a chicken emerging from its shell. Soon you will tell me that you found his hand on the back of your chair."

"Oh!" cried Miss Frensham in sharp surprise. "How can you possibly know that?"

"I did not; but it was worth while suggesting to you."

"It's absolutely true. I certainly shouldn't have thought it worth while mentioning, but just at the end of the sale, when every one got up, he passed behind me, and stopping, he put his hand—rather gratuitously it seemed—on my chair and asked me if I had heard what the last lot made. I said that I wasn't taking the least notice, and he went away. What does it mean?"

"At the moment it means that we must telephone to Lang's to keep the stable door locked—don't put your trust in proverbs, Miss Frensham. And there are a few questions I want them to have settled before I call there."

"I dare say I'm an idiot," said the lady frankly, "but I'm beginning to get rather excited. Isn't there anything that I can do to help?"

"Why, yes," he smiled with friendly understanding. "Make out the list for me. We need the catalogue—it's over there. Now which was the lot of crowns you compared with?"

"This one—No. 56," she replied, after studying the pages. " 'Charles II, Crowns, various dates, in fine condition generally, 7.' "

"That's sufficient. You have your pad? Now write:

"Confidential. Please ascertain
"(1) Who bought Lot 56?
"(2) What man, if any, left the sale-room about one o'clock and returned before Lot 56 was sold?
"(3) What man, if any, returned after the sale for something he had left in the room?

"Of course," he seemed to apologise, "that gives away the whole show to you."

"Ye—es," replied Miss Frensham dutifully.

Mr. Carrados insisted on his visitor remaining for lunch. He even arranged that no one else should be present on the occasion, and the guest, justly annoyed at this characteristic masculine act of delicacy, repaid him by discovering the appetite of the proverbial fairy. The ghosts of three slabs of bread-and-butter stood between her and that generous table; and, reflecting on that, the whimsical maiden sought her own means to dispel the spectre.

"It is really my fault that the coin has gone," she found occasion to remark. "Almost as much as though I had taken it. If it never turns up again I can't be satisfied until I have made it good."

Carrados was naturally horrified. Was she mad? Had she forgotten its record?

"My dear young lady, don't be romantic. The coin is insured, or ought to be. Why, it would cripple you for years—for ever."

"Oh, no," she retorted airily. "We all expect to make our fortunes. And I really have some money that I don't use."

"Yes?" he smiled, and in the character of her intimate adviser the words slipped out: "How much?"

"Well," she considered with deliberate effect, "I think it varies. . . . But"—with devastating clearness—"it is somewhere about three thousand pounds a year."

"I beg your pardon?" stammered Carrados. "No, no; don't say it again. I heard perfectly. I see. I understand. You ran away from it?"

"I ran away—if you call it running away—from several things. If you could see me, Mr. Carrados, you would understand that I am endowed with an almost supernatural plainness. It is too obvious even for the glass to conceal from me. At school, where politeness is not one of the compulsory subjects, I was 'Pup,' 'Puggy,' 'Ki-ki,' 'Balcombe Beauty,' 'Snarleywow,' and other shafts of endearment. I was not petted. Even my mother found it a little trying. . . . And yet as I grew up I learned that I could be astonishingly popular with most men. The things I said were witty, the things I did were clever, my taste was exquisite, and they were all prepared to marry me. . . . But when I happened to wander into the society of strange men who had missed hearing of my pecuniary worth, my word! No one noticed that I hadn't a seat, no one thought of asking me to dance, to sing, to skate. They didn't see me. And if I opened my mouth they very rarely even heard me. And then if a really pretty girl happened to come into the circle! What an instant preening up of the fishy-eyed old men and a strutting round of the bored-to-death young ones! They didn't even take the trouble to hide anything from me: I might have been a man too. I could watch them licking their lips and arranging their attractions. Oh—h! do you wonder that I went sick among it all? There was a man my father wanted me to marry; well, at all events a decent sort of male, it seemed. I was beginning to think that I might as well when *that* came out. No, it doesn't really matter what. My father thought it needn't make any difference! Mother assured me that it was nicer not to notice these things! When I said that it made all the difference and that I had already noticed a great many things and that I was going away out into the world to see if it was the same everywhere and meant to begin by earning my own living of course I raised a tremendous storm. Then—if I must go—they wanted to arrange things for me, so that everything should be quite nice. But they'd been arranging for me all my life and that was just what I wanted to disarrange. In the end I got my way—you see, I was in rather a strong position—subject to certain conditions. Father stipulated that I didn't get into any 'damned mess,' or back I should have to go. Mother hoped that her girlie would remain unspotted from the world. So here I am. And that's the whole story, Mr. Carrados, and the reason why I'm so anxious to keep out of what I am sure my father would call a—ahem—mess."

"Poor Louis!" thought his friend. Then aloud, "And is human nature entirely transformed by the five-mile radius, Miss Frensham?"

"No," she admitted seriously. "But at least I know exactly where I am. There is no competition to carry my parcel or to run my errands—I hope I haven't given the impression that I want it?—but if anything I do does happen to get praised I can believe it honest; if I make a friend I can really feel that it is for myself. . . . I am no longer, as I heard of one 'admirer' dubbing me, 'The Girl with the Golden Mug.' "

Both laughed. Then he grew almost pensive.

"After laughing at that let me say something," he ventured at length. "When you needn't fear having to meet a man's eyes ever he may be privileged to an unusual frankness. . . . Think as little of looks as you do of lucre, Miss Frensham. I can know nothing of the features you so dispraise: to me you would always be the girl with the golden voice. I am sure that someone else will see you—as you think you are—as little as I do, and to him you will always be the girl with the golden heart."

"You kind man!" she responded. "Well . . . perhaps there is!"

*   *   *   *   *

When Carrados got down to Lang & Leng's a few hours later he found that the seller on the previous day had been Mr. Travis, a gentleman to whom he was by no means a stranger.

"Very glad to have your suggestions, of course, Carrados," remarked Mr. Travis graciously. "Are you looking into it on Lord Willington's behalf? Miss Frensham's! You don't say so!"

"I have a weakness for being on the winning side," remarked the blind man.

"Well, as to that, I don't know that it's exactly a case of a winning side or a losing side. Unless you call us the losing side, egad! This is the room. You want to look—to go round it?"

"I should like to. One never knows."

"Oh, we've been thoroughly over it this morning. Heaven knows what we could expect, but it seemed the natural thing to do. Yes, it's still being kept locked, since you asked."

"Anyone wanting to go in for anything!"

"No—only Mr. Marrabel, who called for his gloves after the sale; they'd been taken to the office though."

"Marrabel!" thought the patient worker in the dark. "Yes, of course—Marrabel the dilettante."

"And, by the way, that reminds me," continued Mr. Travis. "Oh yes, sit anywhere you like. That list you sent through. You're not going to suspect Marrabel of any connection? Because, strangely enough, his name is the answer to each of your inquiries."

"I should scarcely describe it as a case for suspicion," replied Carrados. "Still, one thinks of every one."

"We can eliminate Mr. Marrabel at all events, I think. He did not look at any of the lots yesterday. He only bought No. 56, and both Muir and I noticed that he did not touch the coins when he got them—just put them on an empty chair by his side until the hue and cry was raised, and then he passed the box over to the table for someone to verify—all there and the correct number."

"Very convincing," assented Carrados.

"I mean it rather shows that there isn't much to be gained by looking for so-called 'clues' at this end, don't you think? Marrabel as a case in point. Of course we shall be delighted to put any information or facilities that we may have at your disposal, Carrados, both out of consideration for yourself and as due to your client. But what *we* chiefly want is to get the coin back. And the people we have put on to it seem to be extending themselves in that direction. By to-morrow every curio-dealer, pawnbroker, and leading collector will be on the look out. America will be notified, for they think that the coin may be quite likely offered there. A reward is being offered to make it worth anybody's while. In the next number of the *Bric-a-brac Collector* there will be an ingenuous advertisement from a wealthy colonial anxious to buy rare milled silver coins; don't be deceived by it."

"I won't," promised Mr. Carrados. "But all this must come rather expensive."

"Doubtless it is. But the fact is, since the thing has gone, Willington's people are persuading themselves that it might have made a fantastic price. That is why we are only anxious to get it back again."

"Oh!" Polite unconcern was Carrados's note. He seldom denied himself these rare moments when, perhaps, a week's patient labour ran down to a needle-point. "Of course I'm more interested in my client. But as the coin is all you want—why, here it is!"

"What—what's—that?" articulated Mr. Travis.

"The Petition Crown," replied the arch-humbug, continuing to hold out his hand. "Delighted to be the means of restoring it to you, Travis."

"It *is* the Petition Crown," murmured Travis. "Good God! You brought it?"

"On the contrary, I found it here."

"Found it? Where?"

"Beneath the seat of this chair."

"You knew that it was there? Do you mean that Miss Frensham told you?"

"I knew that it should be here, and Miss Frensham certainly told me."

"She hid it there?"

"Not at all. She did not know that it was here. She told me where it was, but she did not know that she was telling me."

"Then I'm hanged if I understand," complained Mr. Travis. "Can't you be human once in a way, Carrados? Damn it all, man, we went to school together!"

"Sit down," said Carrados, "and I'll be as human as you like. . . . Did you ever commit a crime, Travis?"

"Not really," confessed the auctioneer with admirable sang-froid. "I robbed an orchard when I was ten, but that——"

"Robbing orchards at ten scarcely counts, does it? Well, I have the advantage because there is no form of villainy that I haven't gone through in all its phases. Theoretically, of course, but so far as working out the details is concerned and preparing for emergencies, efficiently and with craftsmanlike pride. Whenever I fail to get to sleep at night—rather frequently, I'm sorry to say—I commit a murder, forgery, a robbery or what not, with all its ramifications. It's much more soothing than counting sheep and it never fails to get me off. The point is, that the criminal mind is rarely original, and I find that in nine cases out of ten that sort of crime is committed exactly as I have already done it. Being a collector myself, of course, I've robbed coin auctions frequently. I know precisely how it should be done and what is to be avoided. Marrabel did the correct things, but he overlooked the contingency of someone else also thinking of them."

"But Marrabel, my dear fellow! He must be almost in Debrett. Think!"

"Oh, yes. But he makes a speciality of getting choice things for nothing, provided there is no risk."

"And there is no risk here?"

"None at all; practically none if he's content to take his loss. But is he? We shall see. However, this is what has happened so far:

"Miss Frensham started the business by mixing Lots 56 and 64 without knowing it at the time. She had come to get a newspaper par out of the sale if she could, and was taking an intelligent interest in the subject when she happened to catch Marrabel overlooking her. Well, being nervy and rather touchy she dropped the Petition Crown on to the other crowns in Lot 56 and put the one from that lot into box No. 64.

"Marrabel evidently grasped that. It might prove a golden opportunity. Doubtless he took five minutes to consider the position. Then he hied him off to his Mayfair flat and returned with an appropriate coin in his pocket, well in time to purchase Lot 56. What did it cost him?"

"Three-fifteen," said Mr. Travis.

"You know well enough, Travis, that although a single-coin lot is generally taken up by someone as it goes round the table, half a dozen coins, like Lot 56, are seldom touched. At the most they are glanced at. When Muir turned them out on to his tray, what had been at the top naturally got hidden. When he returned them to the box, to hand over to the buyer, the Petition Crown perhaps came to the top again. Marrabel, seated in an unusually retiring position, doubtless received his booty with an appropriate gesture of uncon-cern and laid it carelessly on the next chair. Good. No risk so far.

"He had at least four minutes in which to act. You and Muir thought he paid no attention to the purchase because he didn't hold the box and examine the contents. Quite natural; but of course you weren't actually watching him and he was out to mask his move-ments. All in good time the exchange was made. But now the element of risk came in: he had the thing in his possession.

"Your amateur is always self-conscious. Marrabel could have walked off then, but that would certainly have put him in an equivocal position. Yet supposing it came to being searched? And Miss Frensham, you may remember, did throw out the suggestion. Whether he had reconnoitred in advance we need not speculate; but here beneath his chair, without moving, Marrabel found an ideal crevice for his loot: tight, hidden, accessible.

"He could now move away from the dangerous spot, and he did when the chase began, putting his purchase on the table with a fine indifference for someone else to verify. He stayed away from this chair so long that a curious thing occurred. Miss Frensham took it.

"In one way Marrabel was now on velvet. The leading suspect had drawn a red herring across his tracks, for if by any chance the crown should come to light here Miss Frensham was hopelessly involved. Then presently the situation eased; the sale was coming to an end and there was no suggestion now of search or of anyone being detained. His only desire was to recover the coin and to get away. But the lady seemed set here, and Marrabel, ignorant of her intentions, made his first bad move. He claimed the chair, fully expecting to be given it at once.

"As it happened Miss Frensham didn't budge. She is far from being an ordinary meek young person, and the immediate events hadn't gone to soothe her. She was sitting there quietly writing, and, taken on the surface, it was sheerly an impertinence on the man's part. She had had occasion to notice Marrabel already. In strictly feminine terms she told him to go to the devil, and Marrabel, now beginning to feel jerky, veered off.

"The sale comes to an end. Every one begins to go. Is Marrabel to hang about aimlessly until this chair is vacant and then deliberately come and sit here for no obvious reason? The man's tightened nerves won't hear of it. Act naturally and there is no risk at all. Return later—to-morrow, next week, it doesn't matter, the coin is snugly waiting. And then, good heavens! the thing flashes on him. The chairs are all alike! Next week, to-morrow, even after the sale they may be rearranged, moved, taken to another room, and he will have to go sitting on one after another, an object for all to marvel at. What's to be done? Why plainly to mark the chair before it is too late, and here, Travis, under my fingers, is the cross that our man broke his pencil on."

"Very ingenious," admitted Mr. Travis, "and in the face of this evidence"—delicately balancing the recovered crown upon a finger-tip—"it would be mean to argue. But, you know, Carrados, Miss Frensham *did* sit here last."

"Inflexible man!" replied Carrados. "Well, when is your next sale?"

"Friday—enamels. On view for one day only."

"So much the better. You can have it in here? Keep it close till then and I will be here early. And just make sure that Marrabel is sent his catalogue, won't you?"

*   *   *   *   *

There was nothing at all unusual to be noticed about the sale-rooms on Thursday morning, and Mr. Marrabel strolled round in perfect composure. With praiseworthy restraint he had not hastened there, and the group of conspirators in the private office had to amuse themselves as best they could for at least two hours.

Marrabel was interested in enamels, as he was in all precious things, and he wandered from point to point consulting his catalogue, examining a piece and marking a price as he had done a score of times before—as every one else was doing then. Finally he sat down to review his list: nothing could be more natural. Satisfied, he rose to go.

Outside the room an attendant came across to speak to him: the signal had been passed.

"Do you mind stepping into Mr. Travis's office, sir? I think he wants to see you about something."

The message was polite and not wholly unusual, but Marrabel's throat went dry.

"Not now," he said, quickening his step. "I have an important—— Back in half an hour, tell him."

It was too late for that easy manoeuvre to carry. Across the hall there was another form between him and the outer door. Nor did the first one obligingly retire.

"Beg pardon, sir, but I understand it's rather particular, sir."

Then Marrabel must have known that something had miscarried.

"Oh, curse it, all right," he snapped and, watched at every step, he went.

"It's about the Petition Crown that disappeared at the last coin sale." The urbane Travis never had a less relished job. "We have received certain information and we may have to take proceedings. Do you wish to make any statement?"

Marrabel had dimly foreseen this possibility, and he had given some thought to a satisfactory explanation, but in the end he had left it to be decided by the circumstances of the moment, because there was no perfectly satisfactory explanation to be thought of.

"Well," he said, affecting a light laugh, "that's an unnecessarily brutal way of putting it, because, as a matter of fact, I was bringing the crown to return to you, and I have it in my pocket at the moment. It was only this morning I discovered it when I came to look into that lot I bought. How it got there and how it came to be missed by the dolts who looked I can't say. Personally I didn't examine one of the coins until to-day."

"I see," remarked Mr. Travis. "But I understand that you were leaving the place just now?"

"You understand quite right. I intended handing you the crown, but when I got here and realised how cursed unpleasant it might be I funked it. I decided to send the damned thing back by post without a word."

"At all events you have it for us now?"

"Yes, here it is," and Marrabel took a coin from his pocket with alacrity, and laying it on the desk turned hopefully to go.

"Thanks, but—one moment—what is this?"

The unhappy man looked at the coin he had just produced and turned paler than before.

"I must have picked up the wrong one," he muttered, beginning to recognise the hopeless morass he was floundering into.

"Look again," said a quiet voice as Mr. Carrados appeared on the scene. "Look closer at the coin you brought from your room this morning!"

"You blind devil!" Lightly scratched on the surface of the silver he found the signature "Max Carrados" and the date of that very day. "This is your doing all through!"

"If it is, it is only to show up a scoundrel. You didn't stick at getting two innocent people suspected by your scheme. Let them see you now."

As if worked by machinery an inner door fell open and Miss Frensham and Muir walked in and stood silently regarding him.

"At the sale," continued Carrados pitilessly, "you were both publicly put in a position of some suspicion by the disappearance of a coin. It is right that you should now know that it was deliberately stolen by Mr. Marrabel here. He is the thief and your perfect innocence is established."

"Well, curse it all, it wasn't entirely my fault," snarled Marrabel. "I only accepted what was given me."

"That will be for a judge and jury to assess. You'll give him in charge now, Travis?"

At this prospect Marrabel's last vestige of pretence broke down. All the poltroonery in the man came to the surface with a rush.

"For God's sake don't do that, Travis," he cried, clutching him by the sleeve. "I'll do anything you wish—confess anything you like—only don't have me sent to prison. I'll put all sorts of things your way, and I know crowds of people. Heavens! man, consider what it would mean to me—one of your own class."

"What shall we do, Carrados? We never like to prosecute."

"I know you don't," replied the blind man. "I've already drawn up his confession. Read this and then sign it, Mr. Marrabel, and we will all be witnesses of the spontaneous act of reparation on your part."

"What are you going to do with it?" asked the unfortunate wretch.

"Keep it as a guarantee of future good behaviour, and to vindicate these others if the necessity occurs. And you needn't think of having me knifed to get it back again, because I shan't carry it in my pocketbook."

Marrabel slowly signed and then stabbed the polished desk with the pen he held in a gust of passion that left his fingers pierced and bleeding.

"I'd go willingly to hell if I could first see you skinned alive, Carrados," he said as he turned to leave.

"I am sure you would," retorted Max Carrados pleasantly. "But I don't think that anything to do with me need affect your destination. Now go."

This did not happen last year nor yet the year before. Miss Frensham married her sub-editor, and their children—now old enough to go to school—frequently take prizes at quite important beauty competitions. Mr. Marrabel almost immediately left these inhospitable shores, and after a seemly interval appeared in flourishing conditions in New York. Not that American connoisseurs know less than English ones do, but they know less of Mr. Marrabel.

The Holloway Flat Tragedy

A good many years ago, when chance brought Max Carrados and Louis Carlyle together again and they renewed the friendship of their youth, the blind man's first inquiry had been a jesting, "Do you unearth many murders, Louis?" and the private detective's reply a wholly serious, "No; our business lies mostly on the conventional lines among defalcation and divorce." Since that day Carlyle's business had increased beyond the fondest dreams of its creator, but "defalcation and divorce" still constituted the bulwarks of his prosperity. Yet from time to time a more sensational happening or a more romantic course raised a case above the commonplace, but none, it is safe to say, ever rivalled in public interest the remarkable crime which was destined to become labelled in the current Press as "The Holloway Flat Tragedy."

It was Mr. Carlyle's rule to see all callers who sought his aid, for the very nature of their business precluded clients from willingly unbosoming themselves to members of his office staff. Afterwards, they might accept the discreet attention of tactful subordinates, but for the first impression Carlyle well knew the value of his sympathetic handshake, his crisply reassuring voice, his—if need be—humanly condoning eye, and his impeccably prosperous person and surroundings. Men and women, guilty and innocent alike, pouring out their stories felt that at last they were really "understood," and, to give Louis Carlyle his due, the deduction was generally fully justified.

To the quiet Bampton Street establishment one September afternoon there came a new client who gave the name of Poleash and wished to see Mr. Carlyle in person. There was, as usual, no difficulty about that, and, looking up from his desk, Louis registered the impression of an inconspicuous man, somewhere in the thirties. He used spectacles, wore a moustache, and his clothes were a lounge suit of dark material, cut on the simple lines affected by the prudent man who reflects that he may be wearing that selfsame garment two or three seasons hence. There was a slight air of untidiness—or rather, perhaps, an absence of spruceness in any detail—about his general appearance, and the experienced observer put him down as a middle-class worker in any of the clerical, lower professional, or non-manual walks of life.

"Now, Mr. Poleash, sit down and tell me what I can do for you," said Carlyle when they had shaken hands—a rite to which the astute gentleman attached no slight importance and invariably offered. "Some trouble or little difficulty, I suppose, umph? But first let me get your name right and have your address for reference. You can rely on this, Mr. Poleash"—the inclination of Mr. Carlyle's head and the arrest of his lifted pen were undeniably impressive—"every word you utter is strictly confidential."

"Oh, that'll be all right, I'm sure," said the visitor carelessly. "It is rather out-of-the-way all the same, and at first——"

"The name?" insinuated Mr. Carlyle persuasively.

"Albert Henry Poleash: P-o-l-e-a-s-h—twelve Meridon House, Sturgrove Road, Holloway."

"Thank you. Now, if you will."

"Of course I could tell you in a dozen words, but I expect you'd need to know the circumstances, so perhpas I may as well begin where I think you'll understand it best from."

"By all means," assented Mr. Carlyle heartily; "by all means. In your own words and exactly as it occurs to you. I'm entirely at your service, so don't feel hurried. Do you care——" The production of a plain gold case completed the inquiry.

"To begin with," said Mr. Poleash, after contributing a match to their common purpose, "I may say that I'm a married man, living with my wife at that address—a smallish flat which suits us very well as we have no children. Neither of us has any near relations either and we keep ourselves pretty much to ourselves. Our only servant is a daily woman, who seems able to do everything that we require."

"One moment, if you please," interposed Mr. Carlyle briskly. "I don't want you to do anything but tell your story in your own way, Mr. Poleash, but if you would indicate by a single word the nature of the event that concerns us it would enable me to judge which points are likely to be most vital to our purpose. Theft—divorce—blackmail——"

"No—murder," replied Mr. Poleash with literal directness.

"Murder!" exclaimed the startled professional. "Do you mean that a murder has been committed?"

"No, not yet. I am coming to that. For ordinary purposes I generally describe myself as a rent-collector, but that is because official Jacks-in-office seem to have a morbid suspicion of anyone who is obviously not a millionaire calling himself independent. As a matter of fact, I have quite enough private income to serve my purpose. Most of it comes from small house property scattered about London. I see to the management of this myself and personally collect the rents. It takes a few days a week, gives me an interest, keeps me in exercise, and pays as well as anything else I could be doing in the time."

"Quite so," encouraged the listener.

"That's always there," went on Mr. Poleash, continuing his leisurely narrative with no indication of needing any encouragement, "but now and then I take up other work if it suits me—certain kinds of special canvassing; sometimes research. I don't want to slave making more money than we have the need of, and I don't want ever to find that we haven't enough money for anything we may require."

"Ideal," contributed Mr. Carlyle. "You are a true philosopher."

"My wife also has no need to be dependent on anyone either," continued Mr. Poleash, without paying the least attention to the suave compliment. "As a costume designer and fashion artist she is fully qualified to earn her living, and in fact up to a couple of years ago she did work of that kind regularly. Then she had a long illness that made a great change in her. This brings me to one of the considerations that affect whatever I may wish to do: the illness left her a nervous wreck—jumpy, excitable, not altogether reasonable."

"Neurasthenia," was Mr. Carlyle's seasonable comment. "The symptom of the age."

"Very likely. It doesn't affect me—at least it doesn't affect me directly. Living in the same house with Mrs. Poleash, it's bound to affect me, because I have to consider how every blessed thing I do will affect her. And just lately something very lively indeed has come along.

"There is a girl in a shop that I got friendly with—no, I don't want you to put her name down yet. It began a year or eighteen months—— But I don't suppose that matters. The only thing I really think that I'm to blame about is that I never told her I was married. As first there was no reason why I should; afterwards—well, there was a certain amount of reason why I shouldn't. Anyhow, I suppose that it was bound to come out sooner or later, and it did, a few weeks ago. She said, quite nicely, that she thought we ought to get married as things were, and then, of course, I had to explain that we couldn't.

"I really hadn't the ghost of an idea that she'd take it so terribly to heart as she did. There's nothing of the Don Juan about me, as you can see at a glance. The thing had simply come about—one step leading to another. But she fainted clean away, and when she came to again she was like a solid block of ice to everything I said. And then to cap matters who should appear at that moment but a fellow she'd been half engaged to before I came along. She'd frequently spoken about this man—his jealousy and temper and so on —and begged me never to let him pick a quarrel with me. 'Peter' was the only name I ever heard him called by, but he was a foreign-looking fellow—an Italian, I think."

" 'Pietro,' perhaps?" suggested Mr. Carlyle.

"No; 'Peter' she called him. 'Please take me back home, Peter,' was all she said, and off they went together without a word from either to me. Whenever I've seen her since it's been the same. 'Will I please leave her as there is nothing to be said?' and I've been trying to think of all manner of arrangements to put things right."

"The only arrangement that would seem likely to do that is the one that's out of your power to make," said Mr. Carlyle.

"I suppose so. However, this Peter evidently had a different idea. This is what happened two nights ago. I woke up in the dark—it was about three o'clock I found afterwards—with one of those feelings you get that you've forgotten to do something. It was a letter that I should have posted: it was important that it got delivered some time the next day—the same day by then—and there it was in my breast pocket. I knew if I left it that I should never be up in time for the first morning dispatch, so I determined to slip out then and make sure of it.

"It would only be a matter of twenty minutes or so. There is a pillar-box nearer, but that isn't cleared early. I pulled on a few things and prepared to tiptoe out when a fresh thought struck me.

"Mrs. Poleash is a very uncertain sleeper nowadays, and if she is disturbed it's ten to one if she gets off again, and for that reason we use different rooms. I knew better than wake her up to tell her I was going out, but at the same time there was just the possibility that she might wake and, hearing some noise, look in at my door to see if I was all right. If she found me gone she would nearly have a fit. On the spur of the moment I pushed the bolster down the bed and rucked up my dressing gown—it was lying about—above it. In the poor light it served very well for a sleeping man, and I knew that she would not disturb me.

"In less time than I'd given myself I had done my business and was back again at the building. I was entering—my hand was on the knob of the outer door in fact—when the door was pulled sharply open from the other side and another man and I came face to face on the step. We both fell back a bit, I think, but the next moment he had pushed past me and was hurrying down the street. There was just enough light from the lamp across the way for me to be certain of him; it was Peter, and I'm pretty sure that he was equally sharp in recognising me.

"Of course I went up the stairs in double quick time after that. The door of the flat was as I had left it—simply on the handle as I had put up the latch catch, never dreaming of anyone coming along in that time—and all was quiet and undisturbed inside. But one thing was different in my room, although it took me a few minutes to discover it. There was a clean cut through my dressing gown, through the sheet, through the bolster. Someone, Mr. Carlyle, had driven a knife well home before he discovered his mistake."

"But that was plain evidence of an attempt to murder," declared Mr. Carlyle feelingly—he disliked crimes of violence from every point of view. "Your business is obviously to inform the police."

"No," replied the visitor slowly; "no. Of course I thought of that, but I soon had to let it slide. What would it mean? Visits, inquiries, cross-examinations, explanations. Everything must come out. After a sufficient exhibition of nerve-storm Mrs. Poleash would set about getting a divorce and I should have to go through that. Then I suppose I should have to marry the other one, and, when all's said and done, that's the last thing I really want. In any case, my home would be broken up and my whole life spoiled. No, if it comes to that I might just as well be dead."

"Then what do you propose doing, may I ask? Calmly waiting to be assassinated?"

"That's exactly what I came to see you about. You know my position, my difficulty. I understand that you are a man of wide experience. Putting aside the police and certain publicity, what should you advise?"

"Well, well," admitted the expert, "it's rather a formidable handicap, but we will do the best for you that is to be done. Can you indicate exactly what you want?"

"I can easily indicate exactly what I don't want. I don't want to be murdered or molested and I don't want Mrs. Poleash to get wind of what's been going on."

"Why not go away for a time? Meanwhile we could find out who your man is and keep him under observation."

"I might do that—unless Kitty took it into her head that she didn't want to go, and then, of course, I couldn't leave her alone in the flat just now. After Tuesday night's business—this is what concerns me most—should you think it likely that the fellow would come again or not?"

Mr. Carlyle pondered wisely. The longer he took over an opinion, he had discovered—providing he kept up the right expression—the greater weight attached to his pronouncement.

"No," he replied with due authority. "I should say not—not in anything like the same way. Of course he will naturally assume that you will now take due precautions—probably imagine that the police are after him. What sort of fastenings have you to your doors and windows?"

"Nothing out of the way. They are old flats and not in very good repair. The outer door is never kept locked, night or day. The front door of our flat has a handle, a latch lock, and a mortice lock. During the day it is simply kept on the latch; at night we fasten the other lock, but do not secure the latch, so that the woman can let herself in when she comes—she has one set of keys, I another, and Mrs. Poleash the third."

"But when you were out on Tuesday night there was no lock fastened, I understand?"

"That is so. Simply the handle to turn. I purposely fastened the latch lock out of action as I found at the door that I hadn't the keys with me and I didn't want to go back to the room again."

"And the inner doors?"

"They have locks, but few now work—either the key is lost or the lock broken. We never trouble about them—except Kitty's room. She has scrupulously locked that at night, since she has had burglars among other nerve fancies."

Mr. Carlyle shook his head.

"You ought at the very least to have the locks put right at once. Practically all windows are fitted with catches that a child can push back with a table-knife."

"That's all very well, but, you see, if I get a locksmith in I shall have to make up some cock-and-bull story about house-breaking to Mrs. Poleash, and that will set her off. And, anyway, we are on the third story up."

"If you are going to consider your wife's nerves at every turn, my dear sir," remarked Mr. Carlyle with some contempt, from the security of his single state, "you will begin to find yourself in rather a tight fix, I am afraid. How are you going to account for the cut linen, for instance?"

"Oh, I've arranged all that," replied Mr. Poleash, nodding saga-ciously. "My dressing gown she will never notice. The sheet and bolster case—it was a hot night so there was only a single sheet fortunately—I have hidden away in a drawer for the present and put others in their place. I shall buy another of each and burn or lose these soon—Kitty doesn't keep a very close check on things. The bolster itself I can sew up well enough before it's noticed."

"You may be able to keep it up," was Mr. Carlyle's dubious admission. "At all events," he continued, "as I understand it, you want me to advise you on the lines of taking no direct action against the man you call Peter and at the same time adopting no precautions that would strike Mrs. Poleash as being unusual?"

"Nothing that would suggest burglars or murder to her just now," assented Poleash. "Yes; that's about what it comes to. You may be able to give me a useful tip or two. If not—well, I know it's a tough proposition and I don't grudge the outlay."

"At least let us see," replied the professional man, never failing on the side of lack of self-confidence. "Now as regards——"

It redounds to Louis Carlyle's credit as an inquiry agent that in an exacting world no serious voice ever accused him of taking unearned money; for so long as there was anything to be learned he plied his novel client with questions, explored surmises and bestowed advice. Even when they had come to the end of useful conversation and the prolific notebook had been closed Carlyle lingered on the topic.

"It's an abnormal situation, Mr. Poleash, and full of professional interest. I shall keep it in mind, you may be sure, and if anything further occurs to me, why, I will let you know."

"Please don't write on any account," begged Mr. Poleash with sudden earnestness. "In fact, I'd ask you to put a line to that effect across my address. You see, I'm liable to be out at any post time, and if my wife should happen to get curious about a strange letter, why, that, in the language of the kerb, would blow the gaff."

"I see," assented Mr. Carlyle. "Very well; it shall be just as you like."

"And if I can settle with you now," continued Poleash; "for of course I don't want to have an account sent. Then some day—say next week—I might look in to report and to hear if you have anything further to suggest."

"You might, in the meanwhile, consider the most practical course —that of having your man kept under observation."

"I will," promised the other. "But so far I'm all in favour of letting sleeping dogs lie."

Not unnaturally Mr. Carlyle had heard that line before and had countered it.

"True, but it is as well to know when they wake up again," he replied. With just the necessary touch of dignity and graciousness he named and received the single guinea at which he assessed the interview and began to conduct Mr. Poleash towards the door— not the one by which he had entered from the waiting-room but another leading directly down into the street. "Have you lost something?"

"Only my hat and things—I left them in your ante-room." He held up his gloved left hand as though it required a word of explanation. "I keep this on because I am short of a finger, and I've noticed that some people don't like to see it."

"We'll go out that way instead then—it's all the same," remarked Carlyle, as he crossed to the other door.

Two later callers were sitting in the waiting-room, and at the sight of them Mr. Carlyle's somewhat cherubic face at once assumed an expression of the heartiest welcome. But beyond an unusually melli-fluent "Good afternoon!" he said nothing until his departing client was out of hearing. Names were not paraded in those precincts. With a muttered apology Mr. Poleash recovered his belongings from among the illustrated papers and hurried away.

"And why in the world have you been waiting here, Max, instead of sending in to me?" demanded the hospitable Carlyle with a show of indignation.

"Business," replied Mr. Carrados tersely. "*Your* business, understand. Your chief minion was eager to blow a message through to you but 'No,' I said, 'we'll take our proper turn.' Why should I interrupt the Bogus Company Promoter's confession or cut short the Guilty Husband's plea?"

"Joking apart, that fellow who just went brought a very remarkable story," said Mr. Carlyle. "I should be glad to know what you would have had to say to him when we have time to go into it." (Do not be too ready to condemn the gentleman as an arrant humbug and this a gross breach of confidence: Max Carrados had been appointed Honorary Consultant to the firm, so that what would have otherwise been grave indiscretions were strictly business discussions.)

"In the meantime the suggestion is that you haven't taken a half-day off lately and that Monday morning is a convenient time."

"Generous man! What is happening on Monday morning then?"

"Something rather surprising in wireless at the Imperial Salon—ten to twelve-thirty. I know it's the sort of thing you'll be interested in, and I have two tickets and want someone fairly intelligent to go with."

"An ideal chain of circumstances," rippled Mr. Carlyle. "I shall endeavour to earn the price of my seat."

"I am sure you will succeed," retorted Carrados. "By the way, it's free."

To a strain of this intellectual horseplay the arrangements for their meeting were made, and that having been the only reason for the call, Mr. Carrados departed under Parkinson's watchful escort. In due course the wireless demonstration took place, but (although an invention then for the first time shown bore no small part in one of the blind man's subsequent cases) it is unnecessary to accompany them inside the hall, for with the enigma centring in Mr. Poleash that event had no connection. It is only touched upon as bringing Carrados and his friend together at that hour, for as they walked along Pall Mall after lunching Mr. Carlyle suddenly gave a whistle of misgiving and surprise and stopped a hurrying newsboy.

"Holloway Flat Tragedy," he read from the bill as he investigated sundry pockets for the exact coin. "By gad, if that should happen to be——"

"Poleash! My God, it is!" he exclaimed as soon as his eye had found the paragraph concerned—a mere inch in the "Stop Press" news. "Poor beggar! Tshk! Tshk!"—his clicking tongue expressed disapproval and regret. "He ought to have known better after what had happened. It was madness. I wonder what he actually did——"

"Your remarkable caller of last Thursday, Louis?"

"Yes; but how do you come to know?"

"A trifling indiscretion on his part. With a carelessness that must be rare among your clients I should say, Mr. Poleash dropped one of his cards under the table in your waiting-room, where the conscientious Parkinson discovered it."

"Well, the unfortunate chap doesn't need cards now. Listen, Max.

"NORTH LONDON TRAGEDY

"Early this morning a charwoman going to a flat in Meridon House, Holloway, made a gruesome discovery. Becoming suspicious at the untouched milk and newspapers, she looked into a bedroom and there found the occupier, a Mr. Poleash, dead in bed. He had received shocking injuries, and everything points to deliberate murder. Mrs. Poleash is understood to be away on a holiday in Devonshire."

"Of course Scotland Yard takes it up now, but I must put my information at their service. They're devilish lucky, too. I can practically hand over the miscreant to them and they will scoop the credit."

"I was to hear about that," Carrados reminded him. "Suppose we walk across to Scotland Yard, and you can tell me on the way."

At the corner of Derby Street they encountered two men who had just turned out of the Yard. The elder had the appearance of being a shrewd farmer, showing his likely son the sights of London and keeping a wideawake eye for its notorious pitfalls. To pursue appearances a step farther they might even have been calling to recover the impressive umbrella that the senior carried.

"Beedel," dropped Mr. Carlyle beneath his breath, but his friend was already smiling recognition.

"The very man," said Carrados genially. "I'll wager you can tell us something about the Poleash arrangements, inspector."

The two plain-clothes men exchanged amused glances.

"I can tell you this much, Mr. Carrados," replied Inspector Beedel, in unusually good spirits, "my nephew George here is going to do the work and I'm going to look after the bouquets at the finish. We're on our way there now."

"Couldn't be better," said the blind man. "Perhaps you wouldn't mind us going up there with you?"

"Very pleased," replied Beedel. "We were making for the station."

"You may as well help to fill our taxi," suggested Carrados. "Mr. Carlyle may have something to tell you on the way."

On the whole Mr. Carlyle would have preferred to make his disclosure to head-quarters, but the convenience of the arrangement was not to be denied, and with a keen appreciation of the astonishing piece of luck Beedel and George heard the story of the inquiry agent's client.

"It looks like being simply a matter of finding this girl, if the conditions up there bear out this tale," remarked George, between satisfaction at so veritable a clue and a doubt whether he would not have preferred a more complicated case. "Did you happen to get her name and address, sir?"

"No," admitted Mr. Carlyle with a slight aloofness, "it did not arise. Poleash was naturally reluctant to bring in the lady more than he need and I did not press him."

"Makes no odds," conceded George generously. "Shop-girl—kept company with a foreigner—known as Peter. Even without anything else there ought to be no difficulty in finding her."

Sturgrove Road was not deserted, and there was a rapid concentration about the door of Meridon House "to see the 'tecs arrive." On the whole, public opinion was disappointed in their appearance, but the action of George in looking up at the frontage of the building and then glancing sharply right and left along the road was favourably commented on. The policeman stationed at the outer door admitted them at once.

A sergeant and a constable of the local division were in possession of No. 12, and the scared daily woman, temporarily sustained by their impression of absolute immobility, was waiting in the kitchen to indicate whatever was required. Greetings on a slightly technical plane passed between the four members of the force.

"Mrs. Poleash has been sent for, I suppose?" asked Mr. Carlyle.

"We telephoned from our office to Torquay some hours ago," replied the sergeant. "They'll send an officer to the place she's staying at and break it to her as well as possible. That's the course we usually follow." He took out a weighty presentation watch and considered it. "Torquay. I don't suppose she could be here yet."

"Not even if she was in first go," amplified his subordinate.

"Well," suggested George, "suppose we look round?"

The bedroom was the first spot visited. There was nothing unusual to be seen, apart from the outline of the bed, its secret now hidden beneath a decorous covering—nothing beyond the rather untidy details of the occupant's daily round. All these would in due course receive a careful scrutiny, but at the moment one point drew every eye.

"Hold one another's hands," advised the sergeant, as he prepared to turn down the sheet. The hovering charwoman gave a scream and fled.

"That's a wild beast been at work," said Inspector Beedel, coolly drawing nearer to appreciate the details.

"My word, yes!" agreed George, following a little reluctantly.

"Shocking! Shocking!" Mr. Carlyle made no pretence about turning away.

"Killed at the first blow," continued the sergeant, indicating, "though it's not the only one. Then his face slashed about like a fancy loaf till his own mother wouldn't know him. Something dreadful, isn't it? Finger gone? Oh, that's an old affair. What're you to make of it all?"

"Revenge—revenge and rage and sheer bloodthirstiness," summed up Mr. Carlyle. "Was anything taken?"

"Nothing disturbed so far as we can see, and the old party there" —a comprehensive. nod in the direction of the absent charlady— "says that all the things she knows of seem to be right."

"What time do they put it at?" asked Beedel.

"Dr. Meadows has been here. Midnight Saturday to early Sunday morning, he said. That agrees with the people at the flat opposite hearing the door locked at about ten on Saturday night and the Sunday morning milk and paper not being touched."

"Milk-can on the doorstep all day, I suppose?" suggested someone.

"Yes; people opposite noticed it, but thought nothing of it. They knew Mrs. Poleash was going away on Saturday and thought that he might have gone with her. Mrs. Jones, she doesn't come on Sundays, so nothing was found out till this morning."

"May as well hear what she has to say now," said Beedel. "No need to keep her about that I know of."

"Just one minute, please, if you don't mind," put in Mr. Carlyle, not so much asking anyone's permission as directing the affair. The sight of a wardrobe had reminded him of the dead man's story, and he was now handling the clothes that hung there with keen anticipation. "There is something that I really came especially to see. This is his dressing gown, and, yes, by Jupiter, it's here!"

He pointed to a clean cut through the material as they gathered round him.

"What's that?" inquired the sergeant, looking from one face to another.

"Previous attempt," replied Beedel shortly.

"There ought to be a sheet and bolster-case somewhere about," continued the eager gentleman, now thoroughly intrigued, and under the impulse of his zeal drawers and cupboards were opened and their contents gingerly displaced.

"Something of the sort here among the shirts," announced George.

"Have them out then. Not likely to be any others put away there." The hidden things were unfolded and displayed and here also the tragic evidence lay clear before them.

"By gad, you know, I half thought he might have dreamt it until this came," confessed Mr. Carlyle to the room at large. "Tshk! Tshk! How on earth the fellow could have gone——" He remembered the quiet figure lying within earshot and finished with a tolerant shrug.

"Let's get on," said Beedel. These details could very well have waited had been his thought all along.

"I'll fold the things," volunteered Mr. Carrados. All the others had satisfied their curiosity by glance or scrutiny and he was free to take his time. He took up the loose bundle in his arms and with the strange impulse towards light that so often moved him he turned away from them and sought the window.

"Now, missis, come along and tell us all about it," called out the young constable.

"No," interposed the inspector kindly, "the poor creature's upset enough already without bringing her in here again. Stay where you are, Mrs. Jones, we're coming there," he announced from the door, and they filed along the skimpy passage into the dingy kitchen. "Now can you just tell us quietly what you know about this bad business?"

Mrs. Jones's testimony, given on the frequently expressed understanding that she was quite prepared to be struck dead at any point of it if she deviated from the strictest line of truth, did not disclose any new feature, while its frequent references to the lives and opinions of friends not concerned in the progress of the drama threatened now and then to stifle the narrative with a surfeit of pronouns. But she was listened to with patience and complimented on her nerve. Mrs. Jones sadly shook her antique black bonnet and disclaimed the quality.

"I could do nothing but stand and scream," she confessed wistfully, referring to the first dreadful moment at the bedroom door.

"I stood and screamed three times before I could get myself away. The poor gentleman! What harm was he, for to be done in like that!"

There was a string of questions from one or another of the company before she was finally dismissed—generally from Beedel or George with Mr. Carlyle's courteously assertive voice intervening once or twice: the Poleashes had few visitors that she had ever seen —she was only there from eight to six—and she had never known of anyone staying with them; no one had knocked at the door for anything on Saturday; she had not noticed anyone whom she could call to mind as "a foreigner" loitering about or at the door recently (a foreign family lived at No. 5, but they were well spoken of); neither Mr. or Mrs. Poleash had talked to her of anything uncommon of late—the gentleman was mostly out and "she" wasn't one of the friendly sort; the couple seemed to get on together "as well as most," and she had never heard a "real" quarrel; Mrs. Poleash had gone off for a week (she understood) about noon on Saturday, and Mr. Poleash had accompanied her to Paddington (as he had mentioned on his return for tea); she had last seen him at about five o'clock on Saturday, when she left, a little earlier than usual; she knew nothing of the ashes in the kitchen grate, not having had a fire there for weeks past; the picture post card (passed round) from Mrs. Poleash, announcing her arrival at Torquay, she had found on the hall floor together with the Sunday paper; she was to go on just the same while Mrs. Poleash was away, coming daily to "do up," and so on; it was a regular arrangement "week in and week out."

"That seems to be about all?" summed up Inspector Beedel, looking round. "We have your address, Mrs. Jones, and you're sure to hear from us about something pretty soon."

"Before you go," said a matter-of-fact voice from the door, "do you happen to remember what you were doing last Thursday afternoon?" It was the first question that Mr. Carrados had put, and they had scarcely noticed whether he had re-joined them yet or not.

"Last Thursday afternoon?" repeated Mrs. Jones helplessly. "Oh, Lor', sir, my head's in that whirl——"

"Yes, but it isn't so difficult if you think—early closing day, you know."

This stimulus proved effective and the charwoman remembered. She had something special to remember by. On Thursday morning Mrs. Poleash had passed on to her a single ticket for that afternoon's performance at the Parkhurst Theatre, and told her that she could go after she had washed up the dinner things.

"So that you were not here at all on Thursday afternoon? Just one more thing, Mrs. Jones. Sooner or later a photograph of your master will be wanted. Is there one anywhere about?"

"The only one I know of stands on the sideboard in the little room. There may be others put away, but not being what you might call curious, sir——"

"I'm sure you're not," agreed Carrados. "Now, as you go you shall point it out to us so that there can be no mistake."

"You couldn't make no mistake because there's only that and one of her stands there," explained Mrs. Jones, but she proceeded to comply. "There it——"

"Yes?" said the blind man, close upon her.

"I'm sorry, sir, indeed. I must have made a mistake——"

"I don't think you made any mistake," he urged. "I don't think you really think so either."

"I'm that mithered I don't rightly know what to think," she declared. "That isn't him."

"Is it the frame? No, don't touch it—that might be unlucky, you know—but you can remember that."

"It's the frame, right enough. I ought to know, the times I've dusted it."

"Then the photograph has been changed: there's nothing unlikely in that. When was the last time that you noticed the other one there?"

Quite recently, it would seem, but taking refuge behind her whirling head Mrs. Jones held out against precision. It might have been Friday or it might have been Saturday. Carrados forbore to press her more exactly, and she departed, sustained by the advice of Authority that she should have nothing to say to nobody, under the excuse, if need be, that she had answered enough questions already for one day.

"While we are here," said the sergeant—they were still in the "little room," the only one that looked out on the front—"you might as well see where he got in." He went to the window and indicated certain marks on the wood- and stone-work. "We found the lower sash still a few inches up when we came."

"Went the same way as he came, I suppose," suggested George.

"Must have done. All the keys are accounted for, and Mrs. Jones found the front door locked as usual. And why not; why shouldn't he? There's the balcony, and you hardly have to lean out to see the stairway window not a yard away. Why, it's as easy as ring-a-roses. Might have been made for it."

"Tshk! Tshk!" fumed Mr. Carlyle unhappily. "After what I said. And not one of the locks has been seen to."

"Locks?" echoed the young policeman, appearing that moment at the door. "Why, here is a chap with tools, says he's come to repair and fit the locks!"

"Well, if this isn't the fair *nefus ultra*!" articulated the sergeant. "However, show him in, lad."

The locksmith, looking scarcely less alarmed than if he had fallen into a den of thieves, had a very short and simple tale to tell. His shop was in the Seven Sisters Road, and on Friday afternoon a gentleman had called there and arranged with him to come on Monday and repair some locks. He had given the name of Poleash and that address. The man knew nothing of what had taken place and had come as fixed.

"It's a pity you didn't happen to make it Saturday, Mr. Hipwaite," said Inspector Beedel, as he took a note of this new evidence. "It might—I don't say it would, but it might—have prevented murder being done."

"But that's the very thing I was not to do," declared Hipwaite, with some warmth. " 'Don't come on Saturday because the wife is very nervous, and if she thinks burglars are about she'll have a fit,' he said—those very words. 'She'll be away on Monday, and then by the time she comes back she mayn't notice.' Was I likely to come on Saturday?"

Plainly he was not. "That's all right," it was conceded, "but there's nothing in your line doing to-day." So Mr. Hipwaite departed, more than half persuaded that he had been hardly used and not in the least mollified by being concerned in so notable a tragedy.

"Before I go," resumed the sergeant, leading the way back to the kitchen, "there's one other thing I must hand over. You heard what Mrs. Jones said about the fire—that there hadn't been one for weeks as they always used the stove?"

"That's what I asked her," George reminded him. "Someone has had a fire here."

"Correct," continued the officer imperturbably. "It's also what I asked her a couple of hours before you came. Someone's had a fire here. Who and what for? Well, I've had the cinders out to see and now I'll make over to you what there was."

"Glove fasteners," commented the inspector. "All the metal there was about them. Millions of the pattern, I suppose."

"Burned his gloves after the job—they must have been in a fair mess," said George. " 'Audubon Frères' they're stamped—foreign make."

"That reminds me—there's one thing more." It was produced from the sergeant's pocket-book, a folded fragment of paper, charred along its edge. "It's from the hearth; evidently a bit that fell out when the fire was made. Foreign newspaper, you will see; Italian it looks to me."

Mr. Carlyle, Inspector Beedel, and George exchanged appreciative glances. Upon this atmosphere of quiet satisfaction there fell something almost like a chuckle.

"Did anyone happen to notice if he had written '*Si parla Italiano*' in red on the wall over the bed?" inquired the guileless voice.

The young constable, chancing to be the nearest person to the door, rose to this mendacious suggestion by offering to go and see. The others stared at the blind man in various stages of uncertainty.

"No, no," called out Mr. Carlyle feelingly. "There is no need to look, thank you. When you know Mr. Carrados as well as I do you will understand that although there is always something in what he says it is not always the something you think it is. Now, Max, pray enlighten the company. Why should the murderer write 'Italian spoken' over the bed?"

"Obviously to make sure that you shouldn't miss it," replied Mr. Carrados.

"Well," remarked the sergeant, demonstrating one or two simple exercises in physical drill as a suitable preparation, "I may as well be going. I don't understand Italian myself. Nor Dutch either," he added cryptically.

Mr. Carlyle also had nothing more to stay for. "If you have done here, Max——" he began, and turned only to find that Carrados was no longer there.

"Your friend has just gone to the front room, sir," said the constable, catching the words as he passed. "Funny to see a blind man getting about so——" But a sudden crash of glass from the direction referred to cut short the impending compliment.

It was, as Carrados explained, entirely his own preposterous fault.

Nothing but curiosity about the size of the room had impelled him to touch the walls, and the picture, having a weak cord or an insecure nail . . . had it not brought something else down in its fall?

"Only the two frames from the sideboard, so far as I can see," replied Carlyle. "All the glass is shattered. But I don't suppose that Mrs. Poleash will be in a condition to worry about trifles. Jolly good thing you aren't hurt, that's all."

"Of course I should like to replace the damage," said the delinquent.

Inspector Beedel said nothing, but as he looked on he recalled one or two other mischances in the past, and being of an introspective nature he continued to massage his chin thoughtfully.

*   *   *   *   *

Three days later the inquest on the body of Albert Henry Poleash was opened. It was of the merest formal description, proof of identity and a bare statement of the cause of death being the only evidence put forward. An adjournment for a week was then declared.

At the resumed inquiry the story of Poleash's death was taken forward, and the newspaper reader for the first time was encouraged to see in it the promise of a first-class popular sensation. Louis Carlyle related the episode of his unexpected client. Corroboration of that wildly romantic story was forthcoming from many sides. Mr. Hipwaite carried the drama two days later by describing the dead man's visit to his shop, the order to repair the locks, and his own futile journey to the flat. Mrs. Jones, skilfully piloted among dates and details, was in evidence as the discoverer of the body. Two doctors—a private practitioner called hurriedly in at the first alarm and the divisional surgeon—agreed on all essential points, and the police efficiently bridged the narration at one stage and another and contrived to present a faithful survey of the tragedy.

But the most arresting figure of the day, though her evidence was of very slight account and mainly negative, was the unhappy widow. As she moved into the witness-box, a wan, graceful creature in her unaccustomed, but, it may be said, not unattractive crêpe, a rustle of compassion stirred the court and Mr. Carlyle, who had come prejudiced against her, as an automatic reflex of his client's fate, chirruped sympathy.

Mrs. Poleash gave her testimony in a low voice, not particularly attractive in its tone, and she looked straight before her with eyes neither downcast nor wandering. Her name, she said, was Katherine Poleash, her age twenty-nine. She knew nothing of the tragedy, having been in Torquay at the time. She had gone there on the Saturday afternoon, her husband seeing her off from Paddington. Their relationship was perfectly friendly, but not demonstrative. Her husband was a considerate but rather reserved man with no especial interests. Up to two years ago she had been accustomed to earn her own living, but a nervous breakdown had interfered with her capacity for work. It was on account of that illness that she had generally occupied a separate bedroom; it had left her nervous in many ways, but she was surprised to hear that she should have been described as exacting or ill-tempered.

" 'Not wholly reasonable and excitable,' were the precise terms used, I think," put in Mr. Carlyle gallantly.

"It's much the same," she replied apathetically.

Continuing, she had no knowledge at all of any intrigue between her husband and a shop-girl, such as had been referred to, nor had she ever heard of the man Peter, either by name or as an Italian. She could not suggest in what quarter of London the shop in question was likely to be as the deceased was accustomed to go about a good deal. The police already had a list of the various properties he owned. At the conclusion of her evidence Mrs. Poleash seemed to be on the point of fainting and had to be assisted out.

There was nothing to be gained by a further adjournment. The cause of death—the real issue before that court—was reasonably clear. The jury brought in a verdict of "Wilful Murder against Some Person or Persons Unknown." Before the reporters left the police asked that the Press should circulate a request for anyone having knowledge of a shop-assistant who had been friendly with a foreigner known as Peter or Pietro, or with a man answering to Mr. Poleash's description, to communicate with them either at New Scotland Yard or to any local station. The Press promised to comply and offered to publish photographs of Mr. Poleash as a means toward that end, only to learn that no photograph possessing identification value could be found. So began the memorable paperchase for an extremely nebulous shop-assistant and a foreigner whose description began and ended with the sobriquet "Peter the Italian."

* * * * *

"I was wondering if you or Inspector Beedel would come round one day to see me," said Mr. Carrados as George was shown into the study at The Turrets. Two full weeks had elapsed since the conclusion of the inquest and the newspaper value of the Holloway Flat Tragedy had sunk from a column opposite leader page to a six-line fill-up beneath "Home and General." "Your uncle used often to drop in to entertain me with the progress of his cases."

"That wasn't his way of looking at it, Mr. Carrados. He used to say that when it came to seeing through a brick wall you were— well, hell!"

"Curious," remarked Mr. Carrados. "I don't remember ever hearing Inspector Beedel make use of that precise expression."

George went a trifle red and laughed to demonstrate his self-possession.

"Well, perhaps I dropped a word of my own in by accident," he said. "But that was what he meant—in a complimentary sense, of course. As a matter of fact, it was on his advice that I ventured to trouble you now."

"Not 'trouble,'" protested the blind man, ever responsive to the least touch of diffidence. "That's another word the inspector wouldn't use about me, I'm sure."

"You're very kind," said George, accepting a cigarette, "and as I had to come this way to see another—oh, my Lord, another!—shop-girl, why, I thought——"

"Ah; how is the case going?"

"It's no go, Mr. Carrados. We've seen thousands of shop-girls and hundreds of Italian Peters. I'm beginning to think," said the visitor, watching Mr. Carrados's face as he propounded the astonishing heresy, "that there is no such person."

"Yes?" replied Carrados unmoved. "It is always as well to look beyond the obvious, isn't it? What does the inspector say?"

"He says, 'I should like to know what Mr. Carrados really meant by "Italian spoken," and what he really did when he smashed that picture.'"

Carrados laughed his appreciation as he seemed actually to watch the blue smoke curling upwards.

"How easy it is to give a straightforward answer when a plain question is asked," he replied. "By 'Si parla Italiano' I ventured to insinuate my own private opinion that there was no Italian Peter;

when I broke the picture I tried to obtain some definite evidence of someone there was."

George waited in the hope of this theme developing, but his host seemed to consider that he had said all that was necessary, and it is difficult to lead on a man into disclosures when you cannot fix him with your eye.

"Poleash may have been mistaken himself," he continued tentatively; "or he may have purposely misled Mr. Carlyle on details, with the idea of getting his advice but not entirely trusting him to the full extent."

"He may," admitted the placid smoker.

"One thing I can't understand is how ever the man set about keeping company with a girl without spending more on her than he seems to have done. We found a small pocket diary that he entered his current expenses in, and there isn't a single item for chocolates, flowers, theatres, or anything of that sort."

"A diary?"

"Oh, he didn't keep a diary; only entered cash, and rents received, and so on. Here it is, if you care to—examine it."

"Thank you, I should. I wonder what our friend Carlyle charged for the consultation?"

"I don't remember seeing that," admitted George, referring to the pages. "Thursday, the 3rd, wasn't it? No, curiously enough, that doesn't appear. . . . I wonder if he never put down any of these what you might call questionable items for fear of Mrs. Poleash seeing?"

"Not unnaturally," agreed Carrados. "You found nothing else of interest then—no addresses or new names?"

"Nothing at all. Oh, that page you've got is only his memorandum of sizes and numbers and so on."

"Yes; quite a useful habit, isn't it?" The long, vibrant fingers touched off line after line without a pause or stumble. "When he made this handy list Albert Henry Poleash little thought——Boots, size 9; hat, size $7\frac{1}{8}$; collars, size 16; gloves, size $8\frac{3}{4}$; watch, No. 31903; weight, 11st 8lbs. There we have the man: *Ex pede Herculem*, as the motto has it—only in this case of course the hat and gloves are more useful."

"Very true, sir," said George, whose instinct was to keep a knowing front on all occasions.

When Parkinson was summoned to the room some time later he

found his master there alone. Every light was blazing on, and, sitting at his desk, Mr. Carrados confronted a single sheet of paper. With his trained acuteness for the minutiæ of every new condition Parkinson immediately took mental photographs of the sheet of paper with its slim written column, of the position and appearance of the chair George had used, of the number and placing of cigarette ends and matches, of all the details connected with the tray and contents, and of a few other matters. It was his routine.

"Close the door and come in," said Carrados. "I want you to carry your mind back about four weeks to the last occasion when we called at Mr. Carlyle's office together. As we sat in the waiting-room I asked you if the things left there belonged to anyone we knew."

"I remember the circumstance perfectly, sir."

"I want the articles described. The gloves?"

"There was only one glove—that for the right hand. It was a dark grey *suède*, moderately used, and not of the best cut. The fastening was a press button stamped 'Audubon Frères.' The only marking inside the glove was the size, $7\frac{1}{2}$."

Carrados made a note on the sheet before him. "The hat?" he said. "What size was that?"

"The size of the hat, printed on an octagonal white ticket, was $6\frac{3}{4}$, sir."

"Excellent, so far, When the caller passed through you saw him for a moment. Apart from clothes, which do not matter just now, was there any physical peculiarity that would identify him?"

"He had a small dark mole beneath the left eye. The lobe of his right ear was appreciably less than the other. The nail of the middle finger of the right hand was corrugated from an injury at some time."

Carrados made a final note on the paper before him.

"Very good indeed, Parkinson," he remarked. "That is all I wanted."

*   *   *   *   *

A month passed and nothing happened. Occasionally a newspaper, pressed for a subject, commented on the disquieting frequency with which undetected murder could be done, and among other instances mentioned the Holloway Flat Tragedy and deplored the ease with which Peter the Italian had remained at large. The name by that time struck the reader as distantly familiar.

Then one evening early in November Beedel rang Mr. Carrados up. The blind man happened to take the call himself, and at the first words he knew that the dull, patient shadowing of weeks was about to fructify.

"Yes, Inspector Beedel himself, sir," said the voice at the other end. "I'm speaking from Beak Street. The two you know of have just gone to the Restaurant X in Warsaw Street. The lady has booked two seats at the Alhambra for to-night, so we expect them to be there for the best part of an hour."

"I'll come at once," replied Carrados. "What about Carlyle?"

"He's been notified. Back entrance in Boulton Court," said the inspector. "I'm off there now myself."

It was the first time that the two the blind man "knew of" had met since the watch was set, and their correspondence had been singularly innocuous. Yet not a breath of suspicion had been raised and the same elaborate care that had prompted Mr. Carrados to bring down a picture to cover the abstraction of a small square of glass had been maintained throughout.

"Nice private little room upstairs, saire," insinuated the proprietor as "the two" looked round. He guessed that they shunned publicity, and he was right, although not entirely so. With a curt nod the man led the way up the narrow stairway to the equivocal little den on the first floor. The general room below had not been crowded, but this one was wholly empty.

"Quite like old times," said the woman with an unmusical laugh as she threw off her cloak—there was little indication of the sorrowing widow now, "I thought we had better fight shy of the 'Toledo' for the future."

" 'M yes," replied her companion slowly, looking dubiously about him—he no longer wore glasses or moustache, nor was his left hand, the glove now removed, deficient of a finger. "The only thing is whether it isn't too soon for us to be about together at all."

"Pha!" she snapped expressively. "They've gone to sleep again. There isn't a thing—no not a single detail—gone wrong. The most that could happen would be a raid here to look for Peter the Italian!"

"For God's sake don't keep on that," he urged in a low voice. "Your husband was a brute to you by what you say, and I'm not sorry now it's done, but I want to forget it all. You had your way: I've done everything you planned. Now you are free and decently well off and as soon as it's safe we can really marry—if you still will."

"If I still will," she repeated, looking at him meaningly. "Do you know, Dick, I think it may become desirable sooner even than I thought."

"Sssh!" he warned; "here comes someone. You order, Kitty—you always have done! Anything will suit me." He turned to arrange his overcoat across an empty chair and reassured his hand among the contents of the nearest pocket.

Downstairs, in his nondescript living-room, the proprietor of the Restaurant X was being very quickly and efficiently made to understand just so much of the situation as turned on his immediate and complete acceptance of it. In the presence of authority so vigorously expressed the stout gentleman bowed profusely, lowered his voice, and from time to time placed a knowing finger on his lips in agreement.

"Hallo," said the man called "Dick" as a different attendant brought a dish. "Where has our other waiter got to?"

"Party of regular customers as always has him just come in," explained the new one. " 'Ope you don't mind, sir."

"Not a brass button."

"It's all right, inspector," reported the "waiter." "He has the three marks you said—mole, ear, nail."

"Certain of the woman?"

"Mrs. Poleash, sure as snow."

"Any reference to it?"

"Don't think so while I'm about. Drama just now. Has his little gun handy."

"Take this in now. Leave the door open and see if you can make him talk up. . . . If you two gentlemen will step just across there I think you'll be able to hear."

Carrados smiled as he proceeded to comply.

"I have already heard," he said. "It is the voice of the man who called on Mr. Carlyle on September the third."

"I think it is the voice," admitted Mr. Carlyle when he had tiptoed back again. "I really think so, but after two months I should not be prepared to swear."

"He is the man," repeated Carrados deliberately.

Inspector Beedel, clinking something quietly in his pocket, nodded to his waiter.

"Morgan follows you in with the coffee," he said. "Put it down on the table, Morgan, and stand beside the woman. Call me as soon as you have him."

It was the sweet that the first waiter was to take, and with it there was a sauce. It was not exactly overturned, but there was an awkward movement and a few drops were splashed. With a clumsy apology the waiter, napkin in hand, leaned across the customer to remove a spot that marked his coat-sleeve.

"Here!" exclaimed the startled man. "What the devil are you up to?"

It was too late. Speech was the only thing left to him then. His wrists were already held in a trained, relentless grasp; he was pressed helplessly back into his chair at the first movement of resistance. Kitty Poleash rose from her seat with a dreadful coldness round her heart, felt a hand upon her shoulder, cast one fearful glance around, and sank down upon her chair again. Before another word was spoken Inspector Beedel had appeared, and the grip of bone and muscle on the straining wrists was changed to one of steel. Less than thirty seconds bridged the whole astonishing transformation.

"Richard Crispinge, you are charged with the murder of this woman's husband. Katherine Poleash, you are held as an accessory." The usual caution followed. "Get a taxi to the back entrance, Morgan."

Half a dozen emotions met on Crispinge's face as he shot a glance at his companion and then faced the accuser again.

"You're crazy," he panted, still labouring from the effort. "I've never even seen the man."

"I shouldn't say anything now, if I were you," advised Beedel, on a quite human note. "You may find out later that we know more than you might think."

What followed could not have been charged against human foresight, for at a later stage it was shown that a certain cable failed and in a trice one side of Warsaw Street was involved in darkness. What happened in that darkness—where they had severally stood and after—who moved or spoke—whose hand was raised—were all matters of dispute, but suddenly the black was stabbed by a streak of red, a little crack—scarcely more than the sharp bursting of a paper bag—nearly caught up to it, and almost slowly to the waiting ears came the sound of strain and the long crash of falling glass and china.

"A lamp from down there!" snapped Beedel's sorely-tried voice, as the ray of an electric torch whirled like a pygmy searchlight and then centred on a tumbled thing lying beyond the table. "Look alive!"

"They say there is gas somewhere," announced Mr. Carlyle, striking a match as he ran in. "Ah, here it it."

No need to ask then what had happened, though how it had happened could never be set quite finally at rest; for if Kitty Poleash was standing now, whereas before she had sat, the weapon lay beyond her reach close to the shackled hands. A curious apathy seemed to fall upon the room as though the tang of the drifting wisp of smoke dulled their alertness, and when the woman moved slowly towards her lover Beedel merely picked the pistol up and waited. With a terrible calmness she knelt by the huddled form and raised the inert head.

"Good-bye, my dear," she said quietly, kissing the dead lips for the last time; "it's over." And with a strange tragic fitness she added, in the words of another fatal schemer, "We fail!"

She seemed to be the only one who had any business there; Beedel was abstracted; Carlyle and Carrados felt like spectators walking on a stage when the play is over. In the street below the summoned taxi throbbed unheeded; they were waiting for another equipage now. When that had moved off with its burden Kitty Poleash would follow her captors submissively, like a dog without a home.

"It isn't a feather in our caps to have a man slip away like that," remarked the inspector moodily as the two joined him for a word before they left; "but, of course, as far as they are both concerned, it's the very best that could have happened."

"In what way do you mean the best?" demanded Mr. Carlyle with a professional keenness for the explicit.

"Why, look at what will happen now. He's saved all the trouble and thought of being hanged, which it was bound to be in the end, and has got it over without a moment's worry. She will get the full benefit of it as well, because her counsel will now be able to pile it all up against the fellow and claim that he exercised an irresistible influence over her. Personally, I should say that it's twelve of one and thirteen of the other, and I don't know that she isn't the thirteen, but she is about as likely to be hanged as I am to be made superintendent tomorrow."

*   *   *   *   *

"Max," said Mr. Carlyle, as they sat smoking together the same night, "when you think of the elaboration of that plot it was appalling."

"Curious," replied Carrados thoughtfully. "To me it seems absolutely simple and inevitable. Perhaps that is because I should have done it—fundamentally, that is—just the same way myself."

"And got caught the same way?"

"There were mistakes made. If you decide to kill a man you must do it either secretly or openly. If you do it secretly and it comes to light you are done for. If you do it openly there is the chance of putting another appearance on the crime.

"These two—Crispinge and Mrs. Poleash—knew that in the ordinary way the killing of the husband would immediately attract suspicion to the wife. Under the fierce scrutiny it could not long be hidden that the woman had a lover, and the disclosure would be fatal. Indeed, if Poleash had lived, that fact must shortly have come to light, and it was the sordid determinaion to secure his income for themselves before he discovered the intrigue and divorced his wife that sealed his fate and forced an early issue.

"If you intend to commit a murder, Louis, and know that suspicion will automatically fall on you, what is the first thing that you would wish to effect? Obviously that it should fall on someone else more strongly. But as the arrest of that someone else would upset the plan, you would naturally make his identity such that he would have the best chance of remaining at large. The most difficult person to find is one who does not exist.

"There you have the whole strategy of the sorry business. Everything hinged on that, and when you once possess that clue you not only see why everything happened as it did but you can confidently forecast exactly what will happen. To go on believing that you had talked with the real Poleash it was necessary that you should never actually see the man as he was. Hence the disfigurement. What assailant would act in that way? Only one maddened by a jealous fury. The Southern people are popularly the most jealous and revengeful, so we must have a native of Italy or Spain, and the Italian is the more credible of the two. Similarly, Mr. Hipwaite is brought in to add another touch of corroboration to your tale. But why Mr. Hipwaite from a mile away? There is a locksmith quite near at hand; I made it my business to call on him, and I learned that, as I expected, he knew Poleash by sight. Plainly he would never have served the purpose."

"Perhaps I ought to have been more sceptical of the fellow's tale," conceded Mr. Carlyle; "but, you know, Max, I have a dozen fresh people call on me every month with queer stories, and it's not once in a million times that this would happen. I, at any rate, saw nothing to rouse suspicion. You say he made mistakes?"

"Crispinge, among divers other things he's failed in, has been an actor, and with Mrs. Poleash's coaching on facts there is no doubt that he carried the part all right. Being wise after the event, we may say that he overstressed the need of secrecy. The idea of the previous attack, designed, of course, to throw irrefutable evidence into the scales, was too pronounced. Something slighter would have served better. Personally, I think it was excess of caution to send Mrs. Jones out on the Thursday afternoon. She could have been relied upon to be too 'mithered' for her recollections to carry any weight. It was necessary to destroy the only reliable photograph of Poleash, but the risk ought to have been taken of burning it before she went off to establish her unassailable alibi, and not leaving it for her accomplice to do. In the event, by handling the frame after he had burned his gloves, Crispinge furnished us with the solitary finger-print that linked up his identity."

"He had been convicted then?"

"Blackmail, six years ago, and other things before. A mixture of weakness and violence, he has always gravitated towards women for support. But the great mistake—the vital oversight—the alarm signal to my perceptions——"

"Yes?"

"Well, I should really hardly like to mention it to anyone but you. The sheet and the bolster-case that so convincingly turned up to clinch your client's tale once and for all demolished it. They had never been on Poleash's bed, believe me, Louis. What a natural thing for the woman to take them from her own, and yet how fatal! I sensed that damning fact as soon as I had them in my hands, and in a trice the whole fabric of deception, so ingeniously contrived, came down in ruins. Nothing —nothing—could ever retrieve that simple, deadly blunder."

The Disappearance of Marie Severe

"I wonder if you might happen to be interested in this case of Marie Severe, Mr. Carrados?"

If Carrados's eyes had been in the habit of expressing emotion they would doubtless have twinkled as Inspector Beedel thus casually introduced the subject of the Swanstead on Thames schoolgirl whose inexplicable disappearance two weeks earlier had filled column upon column of every newspaper with excited speculation until the sheer impossibility of keeping the sensation going without a shred of actual fact had relegated Marie Severe to the obscurity of an occasional paragraph.

"If you are concerned with it, I am sure that I shall be interested, Inspector," said the blind man encouragingly. "It is still being followed, then?"

"Why, yes, sir, I have it in hand, but as for following it—well, 'following' is perhaps scarcely the word now."

"Ah," commented Carrados. "There was very little to follow, I remember."

"I don't think that I've ever known a case of the kind with less, sir. For all the trace she left, the girl might have melted out of existence, and from that day to this, with the exception of that printed communication received by her mother—you remember that, Mr. Carrados?—there hasn't been a clue worth wasting so much as shoe leather on."

"You have had plenty of hints all the same, I suppose?"

Inspector Beedel threw out a gesture of mild despair. It conveyed the patient exasperation of the conscientious and long-suffering man.

"I should say that the case 'took on' remarkably, Mr. Carrados. I doubt if there has been a more popular sensation of its kind for years. Mind you, I'm all in favour of publicity in the circumstances; the photographs and description *may* bring important facts to light, but sometimes it's a bit trying for those who have to do the work at our end. 'Seen in Northampton,' 'seen in Ealing,' 'heard of in West

Croydon,' 'girl answering to the description observed in the waiting-room at Charing Cross,' 'suspicious-looking man with likely girl noticed about the Victoria Dock, Hull,' 'seen and spoken to near Chorley, Lancs,' 'caught sight of apparently struggling in a luxurious motor car on the Portsmouth Road,' 'believed to have visited a Watford picture palace'—they've all been gone into as carefully as though we believed that each one was the real thing at last."

"And you haven't, eh?"

The Inspector looked round. He knew well enough that they were alone in the study at The Turrets, but the action had become something of a mannerism with him.

"I don't mind admitting to *you*, sir, that I've never had any other opinion than that the father of the little girl went down that day and got her away. Where she is now, and whether dead or alive, I can't pretend to say, but that he's at the bottom of it I'm firmly convinced. And what's more," he added with slow significance, "I *hope* so."

"Why in particular?" inquired the other.

Beedel felt in his breast-pocket, took out a formidable wallet, and from among its multitudinous contents selected a cabinet photograph sheathed in its protecting envelope of glazed transparent paper.

"If you could make out anything of what this portrait shows, you'd understand better what I mean, Mr. Carrados," he replied delicately.

Carrados shook his head but nevertheless held out his hand for the photograph.

"No good, I'm afraid," he confessed before he took it. "A print of this sort is one of the few things that afford no graduation to the sense of touch. No, no"—as he passed his finger-tips over the paper —"a gelatino-chloride surface of mathematical uniformity, Inspector, and nothing more. Now had it been the negative——"

"I am sure that that could be procured if you wished to have it, Mr. Carrados. Anyway, I dare say that you've seen in some of the papers what this young girl is like. She is ten years old and big— at least tall—for her age. This picture is the last taken—some time this year—and I am told that it is just like her."

"How should you describe it, Inspector?"

"I am not much good at that sort of thing," said the large man with a shy awkwardness, "but it makes as sweet a picture as ever I've seen. She is very straight-set, and yet with a sort of gracefulness such as a young wild animal might have. It's a full-faced position, and she is looking straight out at you with an expression that is partly serious and partly amused, and as noble and gracious with it all as a young princess might be. I have children of my own, Mr. Carrados, and of course I think they're very nice and pretty, but this—this is quite a different thing. Her hair is curly without being in separate curls, and the description calls it black. Eyes dark brown with straight eyebrows, complexion a sort of glowing brown, small regular teeth. Of course we have a full description of what she was wearing and so forth."

"Yes, yes," assented Carrados idly. "The Van Brown Studio, Photographers, eh? These people are quite well off, then?"

"Oh yes; very nice house and good position—Mrs. Severe, that is to say. You will remember that she obtained a divorce from her husband four or five years ago. I've turned up the particulars and it wasn't what you'd call a bad case as things go, but the lady seemed determined, and in the end Severe didn't defend. She had five or six hundred a year of her own, but he had nothing beyond his salary, and he threw his position up then, and ever since he has been going steadily down. He's almost on the last rung now and picks up his living casual."

"What's the case against him?"

"Well, it scarcely amounts to a case as yet because there is no evidence of his being seen with the child, nor is there anything to connect him with her after the disappearance. Still, it is a working hypothesis. If it was the act of a tramp or a maniac, experience goes to show that we should have found her, dead or alive, by now. Mrs. Severe is all for it being her husband. Of course the decree gave her the custody of Marie. Severe asked to be allowed to see her occasionally, and at first a servant took the child to have tea with him once a month. That was at his rooms. Then he asked to be met in one of the parks or at a gallery. He hadn't got so much as a room then, you see, sir. At last the servant reported that he had grown so shabby as to shame her that the child should be seen with him, though she did say that he was always sober and very kind to Marie, bringing her a little toy or something even when he didn't seem to have sixpence for himself. After that the visits were stopped altogether. Then about a month ago these two, husband and wife, met accidentally in the street. Severe said that he hoped to be doing a bit better soon, and asked for the visits to be continued. How it would have gone I cannot say, but Mrs. Severe happened to have a friend with her, an American lady called Miss Julp, who seems to be living with her now, and the middle-aged female—she's a hard sister, that Cornelia Julp, I should say—pushed her way into the conversation and gave her views on his conduct until Severe must have had some trouble with his hands. Finally Mrs. Severe had an unfortunate impulse to end the discussion by giving her husband a bank-note. She says she got the most awful look she ever saw on any face. Then Severe very deliberately tore up the note, dropped the pieces down a gutter grid that they were standing near, dusted his fingers on his handkerchief, raised his hat and walked away without another word. That was the last she saw of him, but she professes to have been afraid of something happening ever since."

"Then something happens, and so, of course, it must be Severe?" suggested Carrados.

"It does look a bit like that so far, I must admit, sir," assented the Inspector. "Still, Mrs. Severe's opinions aren't quite all. Severe's account of his movements on the afternoon in question—say between twelve-thirty and four in particular—are not satisfactory. Latterly he has been occupying a miserable room off Red Lion Street. He went out at twelve and returned about five—that he doesn't deny. Says he spent the time walking about the streets and in the Holborn news-room, but can mention no one who saw him during those five hours. On the other hand, a porter at Swanstead station identifies him as a passenger who alighted there from the 1.17 that afternoon."

"From a newspaper likeness?"

"In the first instance, Mr. Carrados. Afterwards in person."

"Did they speak, or is it merely visual?"

"Only from what he saw of him."

"Struck, I suppose, by the remarkable fact that the passenger wore a hat and a tie—as shown in the picture, or inspired to notice him closely by something indescribably suggestive in the passenger's way of giving up his ticket? It may be all right, Beedel, I admit, but I heartily distrust the weight of importance that these casual identifications are being given on vital points nowadays. Are you satisfied with this yourself?"

"Only as corroborative, sir. Until we find the girl or some trace of her we're bound to make casts in the hope of picking up a line. Well, then there's the letter Mrs. Severe received."

"Have you that with you?"

The Inspector took up the wallet that he had not yet returned to his pocket and selected another enclosure.

"It's a very unusual form," he commented as he handed the envelope to Mr. Carrados and waited for his opinion.

The blind man passed his finger-tips across the paper and at once understood the point of singularity. The lines were printed, but not in consecutive form, every letter being on a little separate square of paper. It was evident that they had been cut out from some other sheet and then pasted on the envelope to form the address.

"London, E.C., 5.30 p.m., 15th May," read Carrados from the postmark.

"The day of the kidnapping. There is a train from Swanstead arriving at Lambeth Bridge at 4.47," remarked Beedel.

"What was your porter doing when that left?"

"He was off duty, sir."

Carrados took out the enclosure and read it off as he had already done the envelope, but with a more deliberative touch, for the print was smaller. The type and the paper were suggestive of a newspaper origin. In most cases whole words had been found available.

"Do not be alarmed," ran the patchwork message. "The girl is in good hands. Only risk lies in pressing search. Wait and she will return uninjured."

"You have identified the newspaper?"

"Yes; it is all cut from *The Times* of May the 13th. The printing on the back of the words fixes it absolutely. Premeditated, Mr. Carrados."

"The whole incident points to that. The date of the newspaper means little, but the deliberate selection of words, the careful way they have been cut out and aligned, taken in conjunction with the time the child disappeared and the time that this was posted—yes, I think you may assume premeditation, Inspector."

"Stationery of the commonest description; immediate return to London, and the method of a man who used this print because he feared that under any disguise his handwriting might be recognised."

Carrados nodded.

"Severe cannot hope to retain the child, of course," he remarked casually. "What motive do you infer?"

"Mrs. Severe is convinced that it is to distress her, out of revenge."

"And this letter is to reassure her?"

The Inspector bit his lip as he smiled at the quiet thrust.

"It might also be to influence her towards suspending search," he suggested.

"At all events I dare say that it has reassured her?"

"In a certain way, yes, it has. It has enabled us to establish that the act is not one of casual lust or vagabondage. There is an alternative that we naturally did not suggest to her."

"And that is?"

"Another Thelby Wood case, Mr. Carrados. The maniacal infatuation of someone who would be the last to be suspected. Some man of good position, a friend and neighbour possibly, who sees this beautiful young creature—the school friend of his own daughters or sitting before him in church it may be—and becomes the slave of his diseased imagination until he is prepared to risk everything for that one overpowering object. A primitive man for the time, one may say, or, even worse, a satyr or a gorilla."

"I wonder," observed Carrados thoughtfully, "if you also have ever felt that you would like to drop it and become a monk, Inspector. Or a stylite on a pole."

Beedel laughed softly and then rubbed his chin in the same contemplative spirit.

"I think I know what you mean, sir," he admitted. "It's a black page. But," he added with wholesome philosophy, "after all, it *is* only a page in a longish book. And if I was in a monastery there'd be one or two more things done that I've helped to keep undone."

"Including the cracking of my head, Inspector? Very true. We must take the world as we find it and ourselves as we are. And I wish that I could agree with you about Severe. It would be a more endurable outlook: spite and revenge are at least decent human motives. Unfortunately, the only hint I can offer is a negative one." He indicated the printed cuttings on the sheet that Beedel had submitted to him. "This photo-mountant costs about sixpence a pot, but you can buy a bottle of gum for a penny."

"Well, sir," said Beedel, "I did think of having that examined, but I waited for you to see the letter as it stood. After all, it didn't strike me as a point one could put much reliance on."

"Quite right," assented Mr. Carrados, "there is nothing personal or definite in it. It may suggest a photographer, amateur or professional, but it would be preposterous to assume so much from this alone. Severe, even, may have—— There are hundreds of chances. I should disregard it for the moment."

"There is nothing more to be got from the letter?"

"There may be, but it is rather elusive at present. What has been done with it?"

"I received it from Mrs. Severe and it has been in my possession ever since."

"You haven't submitted it to a chemist for any purpose?"

"No, sir. I gave a copy of the wording to some newspaper gentlemen, but no one but myself has handled it."

"Very good. Now if you care to leave it with me for a few days——"

Inspector Beedel expressed his immediate willingness and would have added his tribute of obligation for Mr. Carrados's service, but the blind man cut him short.

"Don't rely on anything, Inspector," he warned him. "I am afraid that this resolves itself into a game of chance. Just one touch of luck may give us a winning point, or it may go the other way. In any case there is no reason why I should not motor round by Swanstead one of these days when I am out. If anything fresh turns up before you hear from me you had better telephone me. Now exactly where did this happen?"

The actual facts surrounding the disappearance of Marie Severe constituted the real mystery of the case. Arling Avenue, Swanstead, was one of those leisurely suburban roads where it is impossible to imagine anything happening hurriedly from the delivery of an occasional telegram to the activity of the local builder. Houses, detached houses each surrounded by its rood or more of garden, had been built here and there along its length at one time or another, but even the most modern one had now become matured, and the vacant plots between them had reverted from the condition of "eligible sites" into very passable fields of buttercups and daisies again, so that Arling Avenue remained a pleasant and exclusive thoroughfare. One side of the road was entirely unbuilt on and afforded the prospect of a level meadow where hay was made and real animals grazed in due season. The inhabitants of Arling Avenue never failed to point out to visitors this evidence of undeniable rurality. It even figured in the prospectus of Homewood, the Arling Avenue day school for girls and little boys which the Misses Chibwell had carried on with equal success and inconspicuousness until the Severe affair suddenly brought them into the glare of a terrifying publicity.

Mrs. Severe's house, The Hollies, was the first in the road, as the road was generally regarded—that is to say, from the direction of the station. Beedel picked up a loose sheet of paper and scored it heavily with a plan of the neighbourhood as he explained the position with some minuteness. Next to The Hollies came Arling Lodge. After Arling Lodge there was one of the vacant plots of ground before the next house was reached, but between the Lodge and the vacant plot was a broad grassy opening, unfenced towards the road, and here the Inspector's pencil underlined the deepest significance, culminating in an ominous X about the centre of the space. Originally the opening had doubtless marked the projection of another road, but the scheme had come to nothing. Occasionally a little band of exploring children with the fictitious optimism of youth pecked among its rank and tangled growth in the affectation of hoping to find blackberries there; once in a while a passing chair-mender or travelling tinker regarded it favourably for the scene of his midday siesta, but its only legitimate use seemed to be that of affording access to the side door of Arling Lodge garden. The Inspector pencilled in the garden door as an afterthought, with the parenthesis that it was seldom used and always kept locked. Then he followed out the Avenue as far as the school, indicating all the houses and other features. The whole distance traversed did not exceed two hundred yards.

A few minutes before two o'clock on the afternoon of her disappearance Marie Severe set out as usual for Miss Chibwell's school. Since the incident of the unfortunate encounter with her former husband Mrs. Severe had considered it necessary to exercise a peculiar vigilance over her only child. Thenceforward Marie never went out alone; never, with the exception of the short walk to school and back, that is to say, for in that quiet straight road, in the full light of day, it was ridiculous to imagine that anything could happen. It was ridiculous, but all the same the vaguely uneasy woman generally walked to the garden gate with the little girl and watched her until the diminished figure passed, with a last gay wave of hand or satchel, out of her sight into the school yard.

"That's how it would have been on this occasion," narrated Beedel, "only just as they got to the garden gate a tradesman whom Mrs. Severe wanted to speak with drove up and passed in by the back way. The lady looked along the avenue, and as it happened at that moment Miss Chibwell was standing in the road by her gate. No one else was in sight, so it isn't to be wondered at that Mrs.

Severe went back to the house immediately without another thought.

"That was the last that has been seen of Marie. As a matter of fact, Miss Chibwell turned back into her garden almost as soon as Mrs. Severe did. When the child did not appear for the afternoon school the mistress thought nothing of it. She is a little short-sighted and although she had seen the two at their gate she concluded that they were going out together somewhere. Consequently it was not until four o'clock, when Marie did not return home, that the alarm was raised."

Continuous narration was not congenial to Inspector Beedel's mental attitude. He made frequent pauses as though to invite cross-examination. Sometimes Carrados ignored the opening, at others he found it more convenient to comply.

"The inference is that someone was waiting in this space just beyond Arling Lodge?" he now contributed.

"I think it is reasonable to assume that, sir. Premeditated, we both admit. Doubtless a favourable opportunity was being looked for and there it was. At all events there"—he tapped the **X** as the paper lay beneath Carrados's hand—"there is the very last trace that we can rely on."

"The scent, you mean?"

"Yes, Mr. Carrados. We got one of our dogs down the next morning and put him on the trail. We gave him the scent of a boot and from the gate he brought us without a pause to where I have marked this **X**. There the line ended. There can be no doubt that from that point the girl had been picked up and carried. That is a very remarkable thing. It could scarcely have been done openly past the houses. The fences on all sides are of such a nature that it is incredible for any man to have got an unwilling or insensible burden of that sort over without at least laying it down in the process. If our dog is to be trusted, it wasn't laid down. Some sort of a vehicle remains. We find no recent wheel-marks and no one seems to have seen anything that would answer about at that time."

"You are determined to mystify me, Inspector," smiled Carrados.

"I'm that way myself, sir," said the detective.

"And I know you too well to ask if you have done this and that—"

"I've done everything," admitted Beedel modestly.

"Is this **X** spot commanded by any of the houses? Here is Arling Lodge——"

"There is one window overlooking, but now the trees are too

much out for anything to be seen. Besides, it's only a passage window. Dr. Ellerslie took me up there himself to settle the point."

"Ellerslie—Dr. Ellerslie?"

"The gentleman who lives there. At least he doesn't live altogether there, as I understand that he has it for a week-end place. Boating, I believe, sir. His regular practice is in town."

"Harley Street? Prescott Ellerslie, do you know?"

"That is the same, Mr. Carrados."

"Oh, a very well-known man. He has a great reputation as an operator for peritonitis. Nothing less than fifty guineas a time, Inspector." Perhaps the fee did not greatly impress Mr. Carrados, but doubtless he judged that it would interest Inspector Beedel. "And this house on the other side—Lyncote?"

"A retired Indian army colonel lives there—Colonel Doige."

"I mean as regards overlooking the spot."

"No; it is quite cut off from there. It cannot be seen."

Carrados's interpreting finger stopped lightly over a detail of the plan that it was again exploring. The Inspector's pencil had now added a line of dots leading from The Hollies gate to the X.

"The line the dog took," Beedel explained, following the other's movement. "You notice that the girl turned sharply out of the avenue into this opening at right angles."

"I was just considering that."

"Something took her attention suddenly or someone called her there—I wonder what, Mr. Carrados."

"I wonder," echoed the blind man, raising the anonymous letter to his face again.

Mr. Carrados frequently professed to find inspiration in the surroundings of light and brilliance to which his physical sense was dead, but when he wished to go about his work with everyone else at a notable disadvantage he not unnaturally chose the dark. It was therefore night when, in accordance with his promise to Beedel, he motored round by Swanstead, or, more exactly, it was morning, for the clock in the square ivied tower of the parish church struck two as the car switchbacked over the humped bridge from Middlesex into Surrey.

"This will do, Harris; wait here," he said a little later. He knew that there were trees above and wide open spaces on both sides. The station lay just beyond, and from the station to Arling Avenue was a negligible step. Even at that hour Arling Avenue might have been awake to the intrusion of an alien car of rather noticeable proportions.

The adaptable Harris picked out Mr. Carrados's most substantial rug and went to sleep, to dream of a wayside cycle shop and tea-rooms where he could devote himself to pedigree Wyandottes. With Parkinson at his elbow Carrados walked slowly on to Arling Avenue. What was lacking on Beedel's plan Parkinson's eyes supplied; on a subtler plane, in the moist, warm night, full of quiet sounds and earthy odours, other details were filled in like the work of a lightning cartoonist before the blind man's understanding.

They walked the length of the avenue once and then returned to the grassy opening where the last trace of Marie Severe had evaporated.

"I will stay here. You walk on back to the highroad and wait for me. I may be some time. If I want you, you will hear the whistle."

"Very good, sir." Parkinson knew of old that there were times when his master would have no human eye upon him as he went about his work, and with a magnificent stolidity the man had not a particle of curiosity. It did not even occur to him to wonder. But for nearly half-an-hour the more inquiring creatures of the night looked down—or up, according to their natures—to observe the strange attitudes and quiet persistence of the disturber of the solitude as he crossed and recrossed their little domain, studied its boundaries, and explored every corner of its miniature thickets. A single petal picked up near the locked door to the garden of Arling Lodge seemed a small return for such perseverance, but it is to be presumed that the patient search had not been in vain, for it was immediately after the discovery that Carrados left the opening, and with the cool effrontery that marked his methods he opened the front gate of Dr. Ellerslie's garden and made his way with slow but unerring insight along the boundary wall.

"A blind man," he had once replied to Mr. Carlyle's nervous remonstrance—"a blind man carries on his face a sufficient excuse for every indiscretion."

It was nearly three o'clock when, by the light of the street lamp at the corner of the avenue and the highroad, Parkinson saw his master approaching. But to the patient and excellent servitor's disappointment Carrados at that moment turned back and retraced his steps in the same leisurely manner. As a matter of fact, a new consideration had occurred to the blind man and he continued to pace up and down the footpath as he considered it.

"Oh, sir!"

He stopped at once, but betraying no surprise, without the start which few can restrain when addressed suddenly in the dark. It was always dark to him, but was it ever sudden? Was he indeed ignorant of the obscure figure that had appeared at the gate during his perambulation?

"I have seen you walking up and down at this hour and I wondered —I wondered whether you had any news."

"Who are you?" he asked.

"I am Mrs. Severe. My little girl Marie disappeared from here two weeks ago. You must surely know about it; everybody does."

"Yes, I know," he admitted. "Inspector Beedel told me."

"Oh, Inspector Beedel!" There was obvious disappointment in her voice. "He is very kind and promises—but nothing comes of it, and the days go on, the days go on," she repeated tragically.

"Ida! Ida!" Someone was calling from one of the upper windows, but Carrados was speaking also and Mrs. Severe merely waved her hand back towards the house without responding.

"Your little girl was very fond of flowers?"

"Oh yes, indeed." The pleasant recollection dwarfed the poor lady's present sense of calamity and for a moment she was quite bright. "She loved them. She would bury her face in a bunch of flowers and drink their scent. She almost lived in the garden. They were more to her than toys or dolls, I am sure. But how do you know?"

"I only guessed."

"Ida! Ida!" The rather insistent, nasally querulous voice was raised again and this time Mrs. Severe replied.

"Yes, dear, immediately," she called back, still lingering, however, to discover whether she had anything to hope from this outlandish visitant.

"Had Marie been ill recently?" Carrados detained her with the question.

"Ill! Oh no." The reply was instant and emphatic. It was almost —if one could credit a mother's pride in her child's health being carried to such a length—it was almost resentful.

"Nothing that required the services of a doctor?"

"Marie never requires the services of a doctor." The tone, distant and constrained, made it clear that Mrs. Severe had given up any expectations in this quarter. "My child, I am glad to say, does not know what illness means," she added deliberately.

"Ida! Oh, here you are." The very unromantically accoutred form of a keen-visaged, middle-aged female, padding heavily in bedroom slippers along the garden walk, gave its quietus to the situation. "What a scare you gave me, dearie. Why, whoever——"

"Good-night," said Mrs. Severe, turning from the gate.

Carrados raised his hat and resumed his interrupted stroll. He had not sought the interview and he made no effort to prolong it, for there was little to be got from that source.

"A strange flare of maternal pride," he remarked in his usual detached fashion as he rejoined Parkinson.

About five o'clock on the same day—five o'clock in the afternoon, let it be understood—Inspector Beedel was called to the telephone.

"Oh, nothing fresh so far, Mr. Carrados," he reported when he identified his caller. "I shan't forget to let you know whenever there is."

"But I think that possibly there is," replied Mr. Carrados. "Or at least there might be if you went down to Arling Lodge and insisted on seeing the child who slept there last night."

"Arling Lodge? Dr. Ellerslie's? You don't mean to say, sir——"

"That is for you to satisfy yourself. Dr. Ellerslie is a widower with no children. Marie Severe was drugged by phronolal on some flowers which she was given. Phronolal is a new anaesthetic which is practically unknown outside medical circles. She was carried into the garden of Arling Lodge and into the house. The bunch of flowers was thrown down temporarily inside the wall, probably while the door was relocked. The girl's hair caught on a raspberry cane six yards from the back door along the path leading there. Ellerslie had previously sent away the two people who look after the place— a housekeeper and her husband who sees to the garden. That letter, by the way, was associable with phronolal. Now you have all that I know, Inspector, and I hope to goodness that I am clear of it."

"But, good heavens, Mr. Carrados, this is really terrible!" protested Beedel, moved to emotion in spite of his rich experience of questionable humanity. "A man in his position! Is he a maniac?"

"I don't know. To tell you frankly, Inspector, I haven't gone an inch further than I was compelled to go in order to be sure. Make use of the information as you like, but I don't want to have anything more to do with the case. It isn't a pleasant thing to have pulled down a man like Ellerslie—a callous, exacting machine in the operating-room, one hears, but a man who was doing fine work—saving useful lives every day. I'm sick of it, Beedel, that's all."

"I understand, sir. Still, there's the other side, isn't there, after all? Of course I'll keep your name out of it as you wish, but I shall be given a good deal of credit that I oughtn't to accept. If you don't do anything for a few weeks the papers are always more complimentary when you do do it."

"I'm afraid that you will have to put up with that," replied Carrados drily.

There was an acquiescent laugh from the other end and a reference to the speaker's indebtedness. Then: "Well, I'll get the necessary authority and go down at once, sir."

"Yes. Good-bye," said Carrados. He hung up the receiver with the only satisfaction that he had experienced since he had fixed on Ellerslie—satisfaction to have done with it. The thing was unpalatable enough in itself, and to add another element of distaste, through one or two circumstances that had come his way in the past, he had an actual regard for the surgeon whom some called brutal, but who was universally admitted to be splendidly efficient. It would have been a much more congenial business to the blind man to clear him than to implicate. He betook himself to a tray of Sicilian coins of the autonomous period to get the taste out of his mouth and swore that he would not read a word of any stage of the proceedings.

"A Mr. Severe wishes to see you, sir."

So it happened that about an hour after he had definitely shelved his interest in the case Max Carrados was again drawn into its complications. Had Severe been merely a well-to-do suppliant, perhaps . . . but the blind man had enough of the vagabond spirit to ensure his sympathy towards one whom he knew, on the contrary, to be extremely ill-to-do. In a flash of imagination he saw the outcast walking from Red Lion Street to Richmond, and, denied admission, from Richmond back to Red Lion Street again, because he hadn't sixpence to squander, the man who always bought a little toy . . .

"It is nearly seven, isn't it, Parkinson? Mr. Severe will stay and dine with me," were almost the first words the visitor heard.

"Very well, sir."

"I? Dine?" interposed Severe quickly. "No, no. I really——"

"If you will be so good as to keep me company," said Carrados with suave determination. Parkinson retired, knowing that the thing was settled. "I am quite alone, Mr. Severe, and my selfishness takes that form. If a man calls on me about breakfast-time he must stay to breakfast, at lunch-time to lunch, and so on."

"Your friends, doubtless," suggested Severe with latent bitterness.

"Well, I am inclined to describe anyone who will lighten my darkness for an hour as a friend. You would yourself in the circumstances, you know." And then, quite unconsciously, under this treatment the years of degradation slipped from Severe and he found himself accepting the invitation in the conventional phrases and talking to his host just as though they were two men of the same world in the old times. Guessing what had brought him, and knowing that it mattered little or nothing then, Carrados kept his guest clear of the subject of the disappearance until they were alone again after dinner. Then, to be denied no longer, Severe tackled it with a blunt inquiry:

"Scotland Yard has been consulting you about Marie, Mr. Carrados?"

"Surely that is not in the papers?"

"I don't know," replied Severe, "but they aren't my authority. Among the people I have mostly to do with many shrewd bits of information circulate that never get into the Press. Sometimes they are mere beadwork, of course, but quite often they have ground. Just at present I am something of a celebrity in my usual haunts— I am 'Jones' in town, by the way, but my identity has come out— and everything to do with the notorious Severe affair comes round to me. I hear that Inspector Beedel, who has the case in hand, has just been to see you. Your co-operation is inferred."

"And if so?" queried Carrados.

"If so," continued his visitor, "I have a word to say. Beedel got it into his thick, unimaginative skull that I must be the kidnapper because, on the orthodox 'motive' lines, he couldn't fix on anyone else. As a matter of fact, Mr. Carrados, I have rather too much affection for my little daughter to have taken her out of a comfortable home. My unfortunate wife may have her faults—I don't mind admitting that she has—serious faults and a great many of them, but she would at least give Marie decent surroundings. When I heard of the child's disappearance—it was in the early evening papers the next morning—I was distracted. I dreaded every edition to see a placard announcing that the body had been found and to read the usual horrible details of insane or bestial outrage. I searched my pockets and found a shilling and a few coppers. Without any clear idea of what I expected to do, I tore off to the station and spent my money on a third single to Swanstead."

"Oh," interposed Carrados, "the 1.17 arrival?"

Severe laughed contemptuously.

"The station porter, you mean?" he said. "Yes; that bright youth merely predated his experience by twenty-four hours when he saw that there was bunce in it a few days later. Oh, I dare say he really thought it then. As for me, before I had got to Swanstead I had realised my mistake. What could I do in any case? Nothing that the least efficient local bobby could not do much better. Least of all did I wish to meet Ida—Mrs. Severe. No; I walked out of the station, turned to the right instead of the left and padded back to town."

"And you have come now, a fortnight or more later, to tell me this, Mr. Severe?"

"Well, I have come to have small hopes of Beedel. At first I didn't care two straws what they thought, expecting every hour to hear the worst. But that may not have happened. Two weeks have passed without anything being found, so that the child may be alive somewhere. If you are taking it up there is a chance—provided only that you don't let them obsess you with the idea that I have had anything to do with it."

"I don't imagine that you have had anything to do with it, Mr. Severe, and I believe that Marie is still alive."

"Thank God for that," said Severe with sudden intensity. "I am very, very glad to hear you express that opinion, Mr. Carrados. I don't suppose that I shall see much of the girl as time goes on or that she will be taught to regard the Fifth Commandment very seriously. All the same, the relief of hearing that makes me your debtor for ever. . . . Anxious as I am, I will be content with that. I won't worry you for your clues or your ideas . . . but I will tell you one thing. It may amuse you. *My* notion, a few days ago, of what might have happened——"

"Yes?" encouraged his host.

"It shows you the wild ideas one gets in such circumstances. My former wife is, if I may be permitted to say so, the most amiable and devoted creature in the world. Subject to that, I will readily concede that a more self-opinionated, credulous, dogmatically wrong-headed and crank-ridden woman does not exist. There isn't

a silly fad that she hasn't taken up—and what's more tragic, absolutely believed in for the time—from ozonised milk to rhythmic yawning.
Some time ago she was swept into Christian Science. An atrocious
harpy called Julp—a professional 'healer'—fastened on her and has
dominated her ever since. Well, fantastic as it seems now, I was
actually prepared to believe that Marie had been ill and under their
really sincere but grotesque 'healing' had died. Then to hide the
failure of their creed or because they got panic-stricken——"

Then Carrados interrupted, an incivility he rarely committed.

"Yes, yes, I see," he said quickly. "But your daughter never is ill?"

"Never ill? Marie? Oh, isn't she! In the past six months I've——"

"But Mrs. Severe deliberately said—her words—that Marie 'does
not know what illness means.'"

"That's their jargon. They hold that illness does not exist and so
it has no meaning. But I should describe Marie as a delicate child
on the whole—bilious attacks and so on."

"Christian Scientists . . . gastric trouble . . . Prescott Ellerslie?
Good heavens! This comes of half doing a thing," muttered Carrados.

"Nothing wrong, I hope?" ventured the visitor.

"Wait." Severe wondered what the deuce turn the business was
taking, but there being no incentive to do anything else, he waited.
Coffee, rather more fragrant that that purveyed at the nocturnal
stall, and fat Egyptian cigarettes of a subtle aroma somehow failed
nevertheless to make the time pass quickly. Yet five minutes would
have covered Carrados's absence.

"Nothing wrong, but an unfortunate oversight," he remarked
when he returned. "I was too late to catch Beedel, so we must try to
mend matters at the other end if we can. I shall have to ask you to
go with me. I have ordered the car and I can tell you how we stand
on the way."

"I shall be glad if you can make any use of me," said Severe.

"I hope that I may. And as for anything being wrong," added
Carrados with deliberation, "so far as Marie is concerned I think
we may find that the one thing necessary for her future welfare has
been achieved."

"That's all I ask," said Severe.

"But it isn't all that I ask," retorted the blind man almost sharply.

This time there was nothing clandestine about the visit to Arling
Avenue. On the contrary, the pace they kept up made it necessary
that the horn should give pretty continuous notice of their presence.

If it was a race, however, they had the satisfaction of being successful: the manner—more suggestive of the trained nurse than the domestic servant—of the maid who came to the door of Arling Lodge made it clear to Carrados, apart from any other indication, that the catastrophe of Beedel's arrival had not yet been launched. When the young person at the door began conscientiously, but with obvious inexperience, to prevaricate with the truth, the caller merely accepted her statements and wrote a few words on his card.

"When Dr. Ellerslie does return, will you please give him this at once?" he said. "I will wait."

It is to be inferred that the great specialist's return had been providentially timed, for Carrados was scarcely seated when Prescott Ellerslie hurried into the room with the visiting-card in his hand.

"Mr. Carrados?" he postulated. "Will you please explain this rather unusually worded request for an interview?"

"Certainly I will," replied Carrados. "The wording is prompted by the necessity of compelling your immediate attention. The interview is the outcome of my desire to be of use to you."

"Thank you," said Ellerslie with non-committal courtesy. "And the occasion?"

"The occasion is the impending visit of Inspector Beedel from Scotland Yard, not, this time, to look out of your landing window, but to demand the surrender of the missing Marie Severe and, if you deny any knowledge of her, armed with authority to search your house."

"Oh," replied the doctor with astonishing composure. "And if the situation develops on the lines which you have so pointedly indicated, how do you propose to help me?"

"That depends a little on your explanation of the circumstances."

"Surely between Mr. Carrados and Scotland Yard there is nothing that remains to be explained!"

"Mr. Carrados can only speak for himself," replied the blind man with unmoved good humour. "And in his case there are several things to be explained. There is probably not a great deal of time before the Inspector's arrival, but there may be enough if you are disposed——"

"Very well," acquiesced Ellerslie. "You are quite right in assuming Marie Severe to be in this house. I had her brought here . . . out of revenge, to redress an old and very grievous injury. Perhaps you had guessed that?"

"Not in those terms," said Carrados mildly.

"Yet so it was. Ten years ago a very sweet and precious little child, my only daughter, was wantonly done to death by an ignorant and credulous woman who had charge of her, in the tenets of her faith. It is called Christian Science. The opportunity was put before me and to-day I stand convicted of having outraged every social and legal form by snatching Marie Severe from just that same fate."

Carrados nodded gravely.

"Yes," he assented. "That is the thing I missed."

"I used to see her on her way to school, whenever I was here," went on the doctor wistfully, "and soon I came to watch for her and to know the times at which she ought to pass. She was of all living creatures the gayest and the most vivid, glowing and vibrant with the compelling joy of life, a little being of wonderful grace, delicacy and charm. She has, I found when I came to know her somewhat, that distinction of manner which one is prone to associate unreasonably only with the children of the great and wealthy—a young nobility. In much the reminded me constantly of my own lost child; in other ways she attracted me by her diversity. Such, Mr. Carrados, was the nature of my interest in Marie Severe.

"I don't know the Severes and I have never even spoken to the mother. I believe that she has only lived here about a year, and in any case I have no concern in the social life of Swanstead. But a few months ago my worthy old housekeeper struck up an acquaintance with one of Mrs. Severe's servants, a staid, middle-aged person who had gone into the family as Marie's nurse. The friendship begun down our respective gardens—they adjoin—developed to the stage of these two dames taking tea occasionally with one another. My Mrs. Glass is a garrulous old woman. Hitherto my difficulty had often been to keep her quiet. Now I let her talk and deftly steered the conversation. I learned that my neighbours were Christian Scientists and had a so-called 'healer' living with them. The information struck me with a sudden dread.

" 'I suppose they are never ill, then?' I inquired carelessly.

"Mrs. Severe had not been ill since she had embraced Christian Science, and Miss Julp was described in a phrase obviously of her own importing as being 'all selvage.' The servants were allowed to see a doctor if they wished, although they were strongly pressed to have done with such 'trickery' in dispelling a mere 'illusion.'

" 'And isn't there a child?' I asked.

"Marie, it appeared, had from time to time suffered from the 'illusion' that she had not felt well—had suffered pain. Under Miss Julp's spiritual treatment the 'hallucination' had been dispelled. Mrs. Glass had laughed, looked very knowing and then given her friend away in her appreciation of the joke. The faithful nurse had accepted the situation and as soon as her mistress's back was turned had doctored Marie according to her own simple notions. Under this double influence the child had always picked up again, but the two women had ominously speculated what would happen if she fell 'really ill.' I led her on to details of the sicknesses—their symptoms, frequency and so on. It was a congenial topic between the motherly old creature and the nurse and I could not have had a better medium. I learned a good deal from her chatter. It did not reassure me.

"From that time, without allowing my interest to appear, I sought better opportunities to see the child. I inspired Mrs. Glass to suggest to the nurse that Miss Marie might come and explore the garden here—it is a large and tangled place, such as an adventuring child would love to roam in, and this one, as I found, was passionately fond of flowers and growing things and birds and little animals. I got a pair of tame squirrels and turned them loose here. You can guess her enchantment when she discovered them. I went out with nuts for her to give them and we were friends at once. All the time I was examining her without her knowledge. I don't suppose it ever occurred to her that I might be a doctor. The result practically confirmed the growing suspicion that everything I had heard pointed to. And the tragic irony of the situation was that it had been appendicitis that my child—*my* child—had perished from!"

"Oh, so this was appendicitis, then?"

"Yes. It was appendicitis of that insidious and misleading type to which children are particularly liable. These apparently negligible turns at invervals of weeks were really inflammation of the appendix and the condition was inevitably passing into one of general suppurative peritonitis. Very soon there would come another 'illusion' according to the mother and Miss Julp, another 'bilious turn' according to the nurse, similar to those already experienced, but apparently more obstinate. The Christian Scientists would argue with it, Hannah would surreptitiously dose it. This time, however, it would hang on. Still there would be no really very alarming symptoms to wring the natural affection of the mother, nothing severe enough to drive the nurse into mutiny. The pulse running at about 140 would be the last thing they would notice."

"And then?" Ellerslie was pacing the room in savage indignation, but Carrados had Beedel's impending visit continually before him.

"Then she would be dead. Quite suddenly and unceremoniously this fair young life, which in ten minutes I could render immune from this danger for all the future, would go clean out—extinguished to demonstrate that appendicitis does not exist and that Mind is All in All. If my diagnosis was correct there could be no appeal, no shockful realisation of the true position to give the mother a chance. It would be inevitable, but it would be quite unlooked for.

"What was I to do, should you say, Mr. Carrados, in this emergency? I had dealt with these fanatics before and I knew that if I took so unusual a course as to go to Mrs. Severe I should at the best be met by polite incredulity and a text from Mrs. Mary Baker Eddy's immortal work. And by doing that I should have made any other line of action risky, if not impossible. You, I believe, are a humane man. What was I to do?"

"What you did do," said his visitor, "was about the most dangerous thing that a doctor could be mixed up in."

"Oh, no," replied Ellerslie, "he does a much more dangerous thing whenever he operates on a septiferous subject, whenever he enters a fever-stricken house. To career and reputation, you would say; but believe me, Mr. Carrados, life is quite as important as livelihood, and every doctor does that sort of thing every day. Well, like many very ordinary men whom you may meet, I am something of a maniac and something of a mystic. Incredible as it will doubtless seem to the world to-morrow, I found that, at the risk of my professional career, at the risk, possibly, of a criminal conviction, the greatest thing that I should ever do would be to save this one exquisite young life. Elsewhere other men just as good could take my place, but here it was I and I alone."

"Well, you did it?" prompted Carrados. "I must remind you that the time presses and I want to know the facts."

"Yes I did it. I won't delay with the precautions I had taken in securing the child or with the scheme that I had worked out for returning her. I believed that I had a very good chance of coming through undiscovered and I infer that I have to thank you that I did not. Marie has not the slightest idea where she is and when I go into the room I am sufficiently disguised. She thinks that she has had an accident."

"Of course you must have had assistance?"

"I have had the devoted help of an assistant and two nurses, but the whole responsibility is mine. I managed to send off Mrs. Glass and her husband for a holiday so as to keep them out of it. That was after I had decided upon the operation. To justify what I was about to do there had to be no mistake about the necessity. I contrived a final test.

"Less than three weeks ago I saw Hannah and the little girl come to the house one afternoon. Shortly afterwards Mrs. Glass knocked at my door. Could she ask Hannah to tea and, as Mrs. Severe and her friend were being out until late, might Miss Marie also stay? There was, as she knew, no need for her to ask me, but my housekeeper is primitive in her ideas of duty. Of course I readily assented, but I suggested that Marie should have tea with me; and so it was arranged.

"Before tea she amused herself about the garden. I told her to gather me a bunch of flowers and when she came in with them I noticed that she had scratched her arm with a thorn. I hurried through the meal, for I had then determined what to do. When we had finished, without ringing the bell, I gave her a chair in front of the fire and sat down opposite her. There was a true story about a clever goose that I had promised her.

" 'But you are going to sleep, Marie,' I said, looking at her fixedly. 'It is the heat of the fire.'

" 'I think I must be,' she admitted drowsily. 'Oh, how silly. I can scarcely keep my eyes open.'

" 'You are going to sleep,' I repeated. 'You are very, very tired.' I raised my hand and moved it slowly before her face. 'You can hardly see my hand now. Your eyes are closed. When I stop speaking you will be asleep.' I dropped my hand and she was fast asleep.

"I had made my arrangements and had everything ready. From her arm, where the puncture of the needle was masked by the scratch, I secured a few drops of blood. Then I applied a simple styptic to the place and verified by a more leisurely examination some of the symptoms I had already looked for. When I woke her, a few minutes later, she had no inkling of what had passed.

"Why,' I was saying as she awakened, 'I don't believe that you have heard a word about old Solomon!'

"I applied the various laboratory tests to the blood which I had obtained without delay. The result, taken in conjunction with the other symptoms, was conclusive. I was resolved upon my course from that moment. The operation itself was simple and completely successful. The condition demonstrated the pressing necessity for what I did. Marie Severe will probably outlive her mother now—especially if the lady remains faithful to Christian Science. As for the sequel . . . I am sorry, but I don't regret."

*   *   *   *   *

"A surprise, eh, Inspector?"

Inspector Beedel, accompanied by Mrs. Severe and—if the comparative degree may be used to indicate her relative importance—even more accompanied by Miss Julp, had arrived at Arling Lodge and been given immediate admission. It was Carrados who thus greeted him.

Beedel looked at his friend and then at Dr. Ellerslie. With unconscious habit he even noticed the proportions of the room, the position of the door and window, and the chief articles of furniture. His mind moved rather slowly, but always logically, and in cases where "sound intelligence" sufficed he was rarely unsuccessful. He had brought Mrs. Severe to identify Marie, whom he had never seen, and his men remained outside within whistle-call in case of any emergency. He now saw that he might have to shift his ground and he at once proceeded cautiously.

"Well, sir," he admitted, "I did not expect to see you here."

"Nor did I anticipate coming. Mrs. Severe"—he bowed to her—"I think that we have already met informally. Your friend, Miss Julp, unless I am mistaken? It is a good thing that we are all here."

"That is my name, sir," struck in the recalcitrant Cornelia, "but I am not aware——"

"At the gate early—very early—this morning, Miss Julp. I recognise your step. But accept my assurance, my dear lady"—for Miss Julp had given a start of maidenly confusion at the recollection—"that although I heard, I did *not* see you. Well, Inspector, I have since found that I misled you. The mistake was mine—a fundamental error. You were right. Mrs. Severe was right. Dr. Ellerslie is unassailably right. I speak for him because it was I who fastened an unsupportable motive on his actions. Marie Severe is in this house, but she was received here by Dr. Ellerslie in his professional capacity and strictly in the relation of doctor and patient. . . . Mr. Severe has at length admitted that he alone is to blame. You see, you were right after all."

"Arthur! Oh!" exclaimed Mrs. Severe, deeply moved.

"But why," demanded the other lady hostilely, "why should the man want her here?"

"Mr. Severe was apprehensive on account of his daughter's health," replied Carrados gravely. "His story is that, fearing something serious, he submitted her to this eminent specialist, who found a dangerous—a critical—condition that could only be removed by immediate operation. Dr. Ellerslie has saved your daughter's life, Mrs. Severe."

"Fiddlesticks!" shouted Miss Julp excitedly. "It's an outrage—a criminal outrage. An operation! There was no danger—there couldn't be with *me* at hand. You've done it this time, *Doctor* Ellerslie. My gosh, but this will be a case!"

Mrs. Severe sank into a chair, pale and trembling.

"I can scarcely believe it," she managed to say. "It is a crime. Dr. Ellerslie—no doctor had the right. Mr. Severe has no authority whatever. The court gave me sole control of Marie."

"Excuse me," put in Carrados with the blandness of perfect self-control and cognisance of his point, "excuse me, but have you ever informed Dr. Ellerslie of that ruling?"

"No," admitted Mrs. Severe with faint surprise. "No. Why should I?"

"Quite so. Why should you? But have you any knowledge that Dr. Ellerslie is acquainted with the details of your unhappy domestic differences?"

"I do not know at all. What do these things matter?"

"Only this: Why should Dr. Ellerslie question the authority of a parent who brings his child? It shows at least that he is the one who is concerned about her welfare. For all Dr. Ellerslie knew, you might be the unauthorised one, Mrs. Severe. A doctor can scarcely be expected to withhold a critical operation while he investigates the family affairs of his patients."

"But all this time—this dreadful suspense. He must have known."

Carrados shrugged his shoulders and seemed to glance across the room to where their host had so far stood immovable.

"I did know, Mrs. Severe. I could not help knowing. But I knew something else, and to a doctor the interests of his patient must overrule every ordinary consideration. Should the occasion arise, I shall be prepared at any time to justify my silence."

"Oh, the occasion will arise and pretty sharp, don't you fear," chimed in the irrepressible Miss Julp. "There's a sight more in this business, Ida, than we've got at yet. A mighty cute idea putting up Severe now. I never did believe that he was in it. He's a piece too mean-spirited to have the nerve. And where is Arthur Severe now? Gone, of course; quit the country and at someone else's expense."

"Not at all," said Carrados very obligingly. "Since you ask, Miss Julp"—he raised his voice—"Mr. Severe!"

The door opened and Severe strolled into the room with great sang-froid. He bowed distantly to his wife and nodded familiarly to the police official.

"Well, Inspector," he remarked, "you've cornered me at last, you see."

"I'm not so sure of that," retorted Beedel shortly.

"Oh, come now; you are too modest. My unconvincing alibi that you broke down. The printed letter so conclusively from my hand. And Grigson—your irrefutable, steadfast witness from the station here, Inspector. There's no getting round Grigson now, you know."

Beedel rubbed his chin helpfully but made no answer. Things seemed to have reached a momentary impasse.

"Perhaps we may at least all sit down," suggested Ellerslie, to break the silence. "There are rather a lot of us, but I think the chairs will go round."

"If I wasn't just dead tired I would sooner drop than sit down in the house of a man calling himself a doctor," declared Miss Julp. Then she sat down rather heavily. Sharp on the action came a piercing yell, a deep-wrung "Yag!" of pain and alarm, and the lady was seen bounding to her feet, to turn and look suspiciously at the place she had just vacated.

"It was a needle, Cornelia," said Mrs. Severe, who sat next to her. "See, here it is."

"Dear me, how unfortunate," exclaimed Ellerslie, following the action; "one of my surgical needles. I do hope that it has been properly sterilised since the last operation."

"What's that?" demanded Miss Julp sharply.

"Well," explained the doctor slowly, "I mean that there is such a thing as blood-poisoning. At least," he amended, "for me there is such a thing as blood-poisoning. For you, fortunately, it does not exist. Any more than pain does," he added thoughtfully.

"Do you mean," demanded Miss Julp with slow precision, "that through your carelessness, your criminal carelessness, I run any risk of blood-poisoning?"

"Cornelia!" exclaimed Mrs. Severe in pale incredulity.

"Of course not," retorted the surgeon. "How can you if such a thing does not exist?"

"I don't care whether it exists or not——"

"Cornelia!" repeated her faithful disciple in horror.

"Be quiet, Ida. This is my business. It isn't like an ordinary illness. I've always had a horror of blood-poisoning. I have nightmares about it. My father died of it. He had to have glass tubes put in his veins, and the night he died—— Oh, I tell you I can't stand the thought of it. There's nothing else I believe in, but blood-poisoning——" She shuddered. "I tell you, doctor," she declared with a sudden descent to the practical, "if I get laid up from this you'll have to stand the racket, and pretty considerable damages as well."

"But at the worst this is a very simple matter," protested Ellerslie. "If you will let me dress the place——"

Miss Julp went as red as a swarthy-complexioned lady of forty-five could be expected to go.

"How can I let you dress the place?" she snapped. "It is——"

"Oh, Cornelia, Cornelia!" exclaimed Mrs. Severe reproachfully, through her disillusioned tears, "would you really be so false to the great principles which you have taught me?"

"I have a trained nurse here," suggested the doctor. "She would do it as well as I could."

"Are you really going?" demanded Mrs. Severe, for there was no doubt that Miss Julp was going and going with alacrity.

"I don't abate one iota of my principles, Ida," she remarked. "But one has to discriminate. There are natural illnesses and there are unnatural illnesses. We say with truth that there can be no death, but no one will deny that Christian Scientists do, as a matter of fact, in the ordinary sense, die. Perhaps this is rather beyond you yet, dear, but I hope that some day you will see it in the light of its deeper mystery."

"Do you?" replied Mrs. Severe with cold disdain. "At present I only see that there is one law of indulgence for yourself and another for your dupes."

"After all," interposed Ellerslie, "this embarrassing discussion need never have arisen. I now see that the offending implement is only one of Mrs. Glass's darning needles. How careless of her! You need have no fear, Miss Julp."

"Oh, you coward!" exclaimed Miss Julp breathlessly. "You coward! I won't stay here a moment longer. I will go home."

"I won't detain you," said Mrs. Severe as Cornelia passed her. "Your home is in Chicago, I believe? Ann will help you to pack."

Carrados rose and touched Beedel on the arm.

"You and I are not wanted here, Inspector," he whispered. "The bottom's dropped out of the case," and they slipped away together.

Mrs. Severe looked across the room towards her late husband, hesitated and then slowly walked up to him.

"There is a great deal here that I do not understand," she said, "but is not this so, that you were willing to go to prison to shield this man who has been good to Marie?"

Severe flushed a little. Then he dropped his deliberate reply.

"I am willing to go to hell for this man for his goodness to Marie," he said curtly.

"Oh!" exclaimed Mrs. Severe with a little cry. "I wish—— You never said that you would go to hell for me!"

The outcast stared. Then a curious look, a twisted smile of tenderness and half-mocking humour crossed his features.

"My dear," he responded gravely, "perhaps not. But I often thought it!"

Dr. Ellerslie, who had followed out the last two of his departing guests, looked in at the door.

"Marie is awake, I hear," he said. "Will you go up now, Mrs. Severe?"

With a shy smile the lady held out her hand towards the shabby man.

"You must go with me, Arthur," she stipulated.

The Mystery of the Poisoned Dish of Mushrooms

Some time during November of a recent year, newspaper readers who are in the habit of being attracted by curious items of quite negligible importance might have followed the account of the tragedy of a St. Abbots schoolboy which appeared in the Press under the headings, "Fatal Dish of Mushrooms," "Are Toadstools Distinguishable?" or some similarly alluring title.

The facts relating to the death of Charlie Winpole were simple and straightforward and the jury sworn to the business of investigating the cause had no hesitation in bringing in a verdict in accordance with the medical evidence. The witnesses who had anything really material to contribute were only two in number, Mrs. Dupreen and Robert Wilberforce Slark, M.D. A couple of hours would easily have disposed of every detail of an inquiry that was generally admitted to have been a pure formality, had not the contention of an interested person delayed the inevitable conclusion by forcing the necessity of an adjournment.

Irene Dupreen testified that she was the widow of a physician and lived at Hazlehurst, Chesset Avenue, St. Abbots, with her brother. The deceased was their nephew, an only child and an orphan, and was aged twelve. He was a ward of Chancery and the Court had appointed her as guardian, with an adequate provision for the expenses of his bringing up and education. That allowance would, of course, cease with her nephew's death.

Coming to the particulars of the case, Mrs. Dupreen explained that for a few days the boy had been suffering from a rather severe cold. She had not thought it necessary to call in a doctor, recognising it as a mild form of influenza. She had kept him from school and restricted him to his bedroom. On the previous Wednesday, the day before his death, he was quite convalescent, with a good pulse and a normal temperature, but as the weather was cold she decided still to keep him in bed as a measure of precaution. He had a fair appetite, but did not care for the lunch they had, and so she had asked him, before going out in the afternoon, if there was anything that he would especially fancy for his dinner. He had thereupon expressed a partiality for mushrooms, of which he was always very fond.

"I laughed and pulled his ear," continued the witness, much affected at her recollection, "and asked him if that was his idea of a suitable dish for an invalid. But I didn't think that it really mattered in the least then, so I went to several shops about them. They all said that mushrooms were over, but finally I found a few at Lackington's, the greengrocer in Park Road. I bought only half-a-pound; no one but Charlie among us cared for them and I thought that they were already very dry and rather dear."

The connection between the mushrooms and the unfortunate boy's death seemed inevitable. When Mrs. Dupreen went upstairs after dinner she found Charlie apparently asleep and breathing soundly. She quietly removed the tray and without disturbing him turned out the gas and closed the door. In the middle of the night she was suddenly and startlingly awakened by something. For a moment she remained confused, listening. Then a curious sound coming from the direction of the boy's bedroom drew her there. On opening the door she was horrified to see her nephew lying on the floor in a convulsed attitude. His eyes were open and widely dilated; one hand clutched some bed-clothes which he had dragged down with him, and the other still grasped the empty water-bottle that had been by his side. She called loudly for help and her brother and then the servant appeared. She sent the latter to a medicine cabinet for mustard leaves and told her brother to get in the nearest available doctor. She had already lifted Charlie on to the bed again. Before the doctor arrived, which was in about half-an-hour, the boy was dead.

In answer to a question the witness stated that she had not seen her nephew between the time she removed the tray and when she found him ill. The only other person who had seen him within a few hours of his death had been her brother, Philip Loudham, who had taken up Charlie's dinner. When he came down again he had made the remark: "The youngster seems lively enough now."

Dr. Slark was the next witness. His evidence was to the effect that about three-fifteen on the Thursday morning he was hurriedly called to Hazlehurst by a gentleman whom he now knew to be Mr.

Philip Loudham. He understood that the case was one of convulsions and went provided for that contingency, but on his arrival he found the patient already dead. From his own examination and from what he was told he had no hesitation in diagnosing the case as one of agaric poisoning. He saw no reason to suspect any of the food except the mushrooms, and all the symptoms pointed to bhurine, the deadly principle of *Amanita Bhuroides,* or the Black Cap, as it was popularly called, from its fancied resemblance to the head-dress assumed by a judge in passing death sentence, coupled with its sinister and well-merited reputation. It was always fatal.

Continuing his evidence, Dr. Slark explained that only after maturity did the Black Cap develop its distinctive appearance. Up to that stage it had many of the characteristics of *Agaricus campestris,* or common mushroom. It was true that the gills were paler than one would expect to find, and there were other slight differences of a technical kind, but all might easily be overlooked in the superficial glance of the gatherer. The whole subject of edible and noxious fungi was a difficult one and at present very imperfectly understood. He, personally, very much doubted if true mushrooms were ever responsible for the cases of poisoning which one occasionally saw attributed to them. Under scientific examination he was satisfied that all would resolve themselves into poisoning by one or other of the many noxious fungi that could easily be mistaken for the edible varieties. It was possible to prepare an artificial bed, plant it with proper spawn and be rewarded by a crop of mushroom-like growth of undoubted virulence. On the other hand, the injurious constituents of many poisonous fungi passed off in the process of cooking. There was no handy way of discriminating between the good and the bad except by the absolute identification of species. The salt test and the silver-spoon test were all nonsense and the sooner they were forgotten the better. Apparent mushrooms that were found in woods or growing in the vicinity of trees or hedges should always be regarded with the utmost suspicion.

Dr. Slark's evidence concluded the case so far as the subpœnaed witnesses were concerned, but before addressing the jury the coroner announced that another person had expressed a desire to be heard. There was no reason why they should not accept any evidence that was tendered, and as the applicant's name had been mentioned in the case it was only right that he should have the opportunity of replying publicly.

Mr. Lackington thereupon entered the witness-box and was sworn. He stated that he was a fruiterer and greengrocer, carrying on a business in Park Road, St. Abbots. He remembered Mrs. Dupreen coming to his shop two days before. The basket of mushrooms from which she was supplied consisted of a small lot of about six pounds, brought in by a farmer from a neighbouring village, with whom he had frequent dealings. All had been disposed of and in no other case had illness resulted. It was a serious matter to him as a tradesman to have his name associated with a case of this kind. That was why he had come forward. Not only with regard to mushrooms, but as a general result, people would become shy of dealing with him if it was stated that he sold unwholesome goods.

The coroner, intervening at this point, remarked that he might as well say that he would direct the jury that, in the event of their finding the deceased to have died from the effects of the mushrooms or anything contained among them, there was no evidence other than that the occurrence was one of pure mischance.

Mr. Lackington expressed his thanks for the assurance, but said that a bad impression would still remain. He had been in business in St. Abbots for twenty-seven years and during that time he had handled some tons of mushrooms without a single complaint before. He admitted, in answer to the interrogation, that he had not actually examined every mushroom of the half-pound sold to Mrs. Dupreen, but he weighed them, and he was confident that if a toadstool had been among them he would have detected it. Might it not be a cooking utensil that was the cause?

Dr. Slark shook his head and was understood to say that he could not accept the suggestion.

Continuing, Mr. Lackington then asked whether it was not possible that the deceased, doubtless an inquiring, adventurous boy and as mischievous as most of his kind, feeling quite well again and being confined to the house, had got up in his aunt's absence and taken something that would explain this sad affair? They had heard of a medicine cabinet. What about tablets of trional or veronal or something of that sort that might perhaps look like sweets?—— It was all very well for Dr. Slark to laugh, but this matter was a serious one for the witness.

Dr. Slark apologised for smiling—he had not laughed—and gravely remarked that the matter was a serious one for all concerned in the inquiry. He admitted that the reference to trional and veronal in this connection had, for the moment, caused him to forget the surroundings. He would suggest that in the circumstances perhaps the coroner would think it desirable to order a more detailed examination of the body to be made.

After some further discussion the coroner, while remarking that in most cases an analysis was quite unnecessary, decided that in view of what had transpired it would be more satisfactory to have a complete autopsy carried out. The inquest was accordingly adjourned.

A week later most of those who had taken part in the first inquiry assembled again in the room of the St. Abbots Town Hall which did duty for the Coroner's Court. Only one witness was heard and his evidence was brief and conclusive.

Dr. Herbert Ingpenny, consulting pathologist to St. Martin's Hospital, stated that he had made an examination of the contents of the stomach and viscera of the deceased. He found evidence of the presence of the poison bhurine in sufficient quantity to account for the boy's death, and the symptoms, as described by Dr. Slark and Mrs. Dupreen in the course of the previous hearing, were consistent with bhurine poisoning. Bhurine did not occur naturally except as a constituent of *Amanita Bhuroides*. One-fifth of a grain would be fatal to an adult; in other words, a single fungus in the dish might poison three people. A child, especially if experiencing the effects of a weakening illness, would be even more susceptible. No other harmful substance was present.

Dr. Ingpenny concluded by saying that he endorsed his colleague's general remarks on the subject of mushrooms and other fungi, and the jury, after a plain direction from the coroner, forthwith brought in a verdict in accordance with the medical evidence.

It was a foregone conclusion with anyone who knew the facts or had followed the evidence. Yet five days later Philip Loudham was arrested suddenly and charged with the astounding crime of having murdered his nephew.

It is at this point that Max Carrados makes his first appearance in the Winpole tragedy.

A few days after the arrest, being in a particularly urbane frame of mind himself, and having several hours with no demands on them that could not be fitly transferred to his subordinates, Mr. Carlyle looked round for some social entertainment and with a benevolent condescension very opportunely remembered the existence of his niece living at Groat's Heath.

"Elsie will be delighted," he assented to the suggestion. "She is rather out of the world up there, I imagine. Now if I get there at four, put in a couple of hours . . ."

Mrs. Bellmark was certainly pleased, but she appeared to be still more surprised, and behind that lay an effervescence of excitement that even to Mr. Carlyle's complacent self-esteem seemed out of proportion to the occasion. The reason could not be long withheld.

"Did you meet anyone, Uncle Louis?" was almost her first inquiry.

"Did I meet anyone?" repeated Mr. Carlyle with his usual precision. "Um, no, I cannot say that I met anyone particular. Of course——"

"I've had a visitor and he's coming back again for tea. Guess who it is? But you never will. Mr. Carrados."

"Max Carrados!" exclaimed her uncle in astonishment. "You don't say so. Why, bless my soul, Elsie, I'd almost forgotten that you knew him. It seems years ago—— What on earth is Max doing in Groat's Heath?"

"That is the extraordinary thing about it," replied Mrs. Bellmark. "He said that he had come up here to look for mushrooms."

"Mushrooms?"

"Yes; that was what he said. He asked me if I knew of any woods about here that he could go into and I told him of the one down Stonecut Lane."

"But don't you know, my dear child," exclaimed Mr. Carlyle, "that mushrooms growing in woods or even near trees are always to be regarded with suspicion? They may look like mushrooms, but they are probably poisonous."

"I didn't know," admitted Mrs. Bellmark; "but if they are, I imagine Mr. Carrados will know."

"It scarcely sounds like it—going to a wood, you know. As it happens, I have been looking up the subject lately. But, in any case, you say that he is coming back here?"

"He asked me if he might call on his way home for a cup of tea, and of course I said, 'Of course.'"

"Of course," also said Mr. Carlyle. "Motoring, I suppose."

"Yes, a big grey car. He had Mr. Parkinson with him."

Mr. Caryle was slightly puzzled, as he frequently was by his friend's proceedings, but it was not his custom to dwell on any topic that involved an admission of inadequacy. The subject of Carrados and his eccentric quest was therefore dismissed until the sound of a formidable motor car dominating the atmosphere of the quiet suburban road was almost immediately followed by the entrance of the blind amateur. With a knowing look towards his niece Carlyle had taken up a position at the farther end of the room, where he remained in almost breathless silence.

Carrados acknowledged the hostess's smiling greeting and then nodded familiarly in the direction of the playful guest.

"Well, Louis," he remarked, "we've caught each other."

Mrs. Bellmark was perceptibly startled, but rippled musically at the failure of the conspiracy.

"Extraordinary," admitted Mr. Carlyle, coming forward.

"Not so very," was the dry reply. "Your friendly little maid"— to Mrs. Bellmark—"mentioned your visitor as she brought me in."

"Is it a fact, Max," demanded Mr. Carlyle, "that you have been to—er—Stonecut Wood to get mushrooms?"

"Mrs. Bellmark told you?"

"Yes. And did you succeed?"

"Parkinson found something that he assured me looked just like mushrooms."

Mr. Carlyle bestowed a triumphant glance on his niece.

"I should very much like to see these so-called mushrooms. Do you know, it may be rather a good thing for you that I met you."

"It is always a good thing for me to meet you," replied Carrados. "You shall see them. They are in the car. Perhaps I shall be able to take you back to town?"

"If you are going very soon. No, no, Elsie"—in response to Mrs. Bellmark's protesting "Oh!"—"I don't want to influence Max, but I really must tear myself away the moment after tea. I still have to clear up some work on a rather important case I am just completing. It is quite appropriate to the occasion, too. Do you know all about the Winpole business, Max?"

"No," admitted Carrados, without any appreciable show of interest. "Do you, Louis?"

"Yes," responded Mr. Carlyle with crisp assurance, "yes, I think that I may claim I do. In fact it was I who obtained the evidence that induced the authorities to take up the case against Loudham."

"Oh, do tell us all about it," exclaimed Elsie. "I have only seen something in the *Indicator*.

Mr. Carlyle shook his head, hemmed and looked wise, and then gave in.

"But not a word of this outside, Elsie," he stipulated. "Some of the evidence won't be given until next week and it might be serious."

"Not a syllable," assented the lady. "How exciting! Go on."

"Well, you know, of course, that the coroner's jury—very rightly, according to the evidence before them—brought in a verdict of accidental death. In the circumstances it was a reflection on the business methods or the care or the knowledge or whatever one may decide of the man who sold the mushrooms, a greengrocer called Lackington. I have seen Lackington, and with a rather remarkable pertinacity in the face of the evidence he insists that he could not have made this fatal blunder—that in weighing so small a quantity as half-a-pound, at any rate, he would at once have spotted anything that wasn't quite all right."

"But the doctor said, Uncle Louis——"

"Yes, my dear Elsie, we know what the doctor said, but, rightly or wrongly, Lackington backs his experience and practical knowledge against theoretical generalities. In ordinary circumstances nothing more would have come of it, but it happens that Lackington has for a lodger a young man on the staff of the local paper, and for a neighbour a pharmaceutical chemist. These three men talked things over more than once—Lackington restive under the damage that had been done to his reputation, the journalist stimulating and keen for a newspaper sensation, the chemist contributing his quota of practical knowledge. At the end of a few days a fabric of circumstance had been woven which might be serious or innocent according to the further development of the suggestion and the manner in which it could be met. These were the chief points of the attack:

"Mrs. Dupreen's allowance for the care and maintenance of Charlie Winpole ceased with his death, as she had told the jury. What she did not mention was that the deceased boy would have come into an inheritance of some fifteen thousand pounds at age and that this fortune now fell in equal shares to the lot of his two nearest relatives—Mrs. Dupreen and her brother, Philip.

"Mrs. Dupreen was by no means in easy circumstances. Philip Loudham was equally poor and had no assured income. He had tried several forms of business and now, at about thirty-five, was spending his time chiefly in writing poems and painting water-colours, none of which brought him any money so far as one could learn.

"Philip Loudham, it was admitted, took up the food round which the tragedy centred.

"Philip Loudham was shown to be in debt and urgently in need of money. There was supposed to be a lady in the case—I hope I need say no more, Elsie."

"Who is she?" asked Mrs. Bellmark with poignant interest.

"We do not know yet. A married woman, it is rumoured, I regret to say. It scarcely matters—certainly not to you, Elsie. To continue:

"Mrs. Dupreen got back from her shopping in the afternoon before her nephew's death at about three o'clock. In less than half-an-hour Loudham left the house and going to the station took a return ticket to Euston. He went by the 3.41 and was back in St. Abbots at 5.43. That would give him barely an hour in town for whatever business he transacted. What was that business?

"The chemist next door supplied the information that although bhurine only occurs in nature in this one form, it can be isolated from the other constituents of the fungus and dealt with like any other liquid poison. But it was a very exceptional commodity, having no commercial uses and probably not half-a-dozen retail chemists in London had it on their shelves. He himself had never stocked it and never been asked for it.

"With this suggestive but by no means convincing evidence," continued Mr. Carlyle, "the young journalist went to the editor of *The Morning Indicator*, to which he acted as St. Abbots correspondent, and asked him whether he cared to take up the inquiry as a 'scoop.' The local trio had carried it as far as they were able. The editor of the *Indicator* decided to look into it and asked me to go on with the case. This is how my connection with it arose."

"Oh, that's how newspapers get to know things?" commented Mrs. Bellmark. "I often wondered."

"It is one way," assented her uncle.

"An American development," contributed Carrados. "It is a little overdone there."

"It must be awful," said the hostess. "And the police methods! In the plays that come from the States——" The entrance of the friendly hand-maiden, bringing tea, was responsible for the platitudinous wave. The conversation, in deference to Mr. Carlyle's scruples, marked time until the door closed on her departure.

"My first business," continued the inquiry agent, after making himself useful at the table, "was naturally to discover among the

chemists in London whether a sale of bhurine coincided with Philip
Loudham's hasty visit. If this line failed, the very foundation of the
edifice of hypothetical guilt gave way; if it succeeded . . . Well, it
did succeed. In a street off Caistor Square, Tottenham Court Road
—Trenion Street—we found a man called Lightcraft, who at once
remembered making such a sale. As bhurine is a specified poison,
the transaction would have to be entered, and Lightcraft's book
contained this unassailable piece of evidence. On Wednesday, the
sixth of this month, a man signing his name as 'J. D. Williams,' and
giving '25 Chalcott Place' as the address, purchased four drachms
of bhurine. Lightcraft fixed the time as about half-past four. I went
to 25 Chalcott Place and found it to be a small boarding-house.
No one of the name of Williams was known there."

If Mr. Caryle's tone of finality went for anything, Philip Loudham
was as good as pinioned. Mrs. Bellmark supplied the expected note
of admiration.

"Just fancy!" was the form it took.

"Under the Act the purchaser must be known to the chemist?"
suggested Carrados.

"Yes," agreed Mr. Carlyle; "and there our friend Lightcraft may
have let himself in for a little trouble. But, as he says—and we must
admit that there is something in it—who is to define what 'known
to' actually means? A hundred people are known to him as regular
or occasional customers and he has never heard their names; a
score of names and addresses represent to him regular or occasional
customers whom he has never seen. This 'J. D. Williams' came in
with an easy air and appeared at all events to know Lightcraft. The
face seemed not unfamiliar and Lightcraft was perhaps a little too
facile in assuming that he *did* know him. Well, well, Max, I can
understand the circumstances. Competition is keen—especially
against the private chemist—and one may give offence and lose a
customer. We must all live."

"Except Charlie Winpole," occurred to Max Carrados, but he
left the retort unspoken. "Did you happen to come across any
inquiry for bhurine at other shops?" he asked instead.

"No," replied Carlyle, "no, I did not. It would have been an
indication then, of course, but after finding the actual place the
others would have no significance. Why do you ask?"

"Oh, nothing. Only don't you think that he was rather lucky to
get it first shot if our St. Abbots authority was right?"

"Yes, yes; perhaps he was. But that is of no interest to us now. The great thing is that a peculiarly sinister and deliberate murder is brought home to its perpetrator. When you consider the circumstances, upon my soul, I don't know that I have ever unmasked a more ingenious and cold-blooded ruffian."

"Then he has confessed, uncle?"

"Confessed, my dear Elsie," said Mr. Carlyle, with a tolerant smile, "no, he has not confessed—men of that type never do. On the contrary, he asserted his outraged innocence with a considerable show of indignation. What else was he to do? Then he was asked to account for his movements between 4.15 and 5 o'clock on that afternoon. Egad, the fellow was so cocksure of the safety of his plans that he hadn't even taken the trouble to think that out. First he denied that he had been away from St. Abbots at all. Then he remembered. He had run down to town in the afternoon for a few things.—What things?—Well, chiefly stationery.—Where had he bought it?—At a shop in Oxford Street; he did not know the name.—Would he be able to point it out?—He thought so.—Could he identify the attendant?—No, he could not remember him in the least.—Had he the bill?—No, he never kept small bills.—How much was the amount?—About three or four shillings.—And the return fare to Euston was three-and-eightpence. Was it not rather an extravagant journey?—He could only say that he did so.—Three or four shillings' worth of stationery would be a moderate parcel. Did he have it sent? —No, he took it with him.—Three or four shillings' worth of stationery in his pocket?—No, it was in a parcel.—Too large to go in his pocket?—Yes.—Two independent witnesses would testify that he carried no parcel. They were townsmen of St. Abbots who had travelled down in the same carriage with him. Did he still persist that he had been engaged in buying stationery? Then he declined to say anything further—about the best thing he could do."

"And Lightcraft identifies him?"

"Um, well, not quite so positively as we might wish. You see, a fortnight has elapsed. The man who bought the poison wore a moustache—put on, of course—but Lightcraft will say that there is a resemblance and the type of the two men the same."

"I foresee that Mr. Lightcraft's accommodating memory for faces will come in for rather severe handling in cross-examination," said Carrados, as though he rather enjoyed the prospect.

"It will balance Mr. Philip Loudham's unfortunate forgetfulness for localities, Max," rejoined Mr. Carlyle, delivering the thrust with his own inimitable aplomb.

Carrados rose with smiling acquiescence to the shrewdness of the riposte.

"I will be quite generous, Mrs. Bellmark," he observed. "I will take him away now, with the memory of that lingering in your ears —all my crushing retorts unspoken."

"Five-thirty, egad!" exclaimed Mr. Carlyle, displaying his imposing gold watch. "We must—or, at all events, I must. You can think of them in the car, Max."

"I do hope you won't come to blows," murmured the lady. Then she added: "When will the real trial come on, Uncle Louis?"

"The Sessions? Oh, early in January."

"I must remember to look out for it." Possibly she had some faint idea of Uncle Louis taking a leading part in the proceedings. At any rate Mr. Carlyle looked pleased, but when adieux had been taken and the door was closed Mrs. Bellmark was left wondering what the enigma of Max Carrados's departing smile had been.

Before they had covered many furlongs Mr. Carlyle suddenly remembered the suspected mushrooms and demanded to see them. A very moderate collection was produced for his inspection. He turned them over sceptically.

"The gills are too pale for true mushrooms, Max," he declared sapiently. "Don't take any risk. Let me drop them out of the window?"

"No." Carrados's hand quietly arrested the threatened action. "No; I have a use for them, Louis, but it is not culinary. You are quite right; they are rank poison. I only want to study them for . . . a case I am interested in."

"A case! You don't mean to say that there is another mushroom poisoner going?"

"No; it is the same."

"But—but you said——"

"That I did not know all about it? Quite true. Nor do I yet. But I know rather more than I did then."

"Do you mean that Scotland Yard——"

"No, Louis." Mr. Carrados appeared to find something rather amusing in the situation. "I am for the other side."

"The other side! And you let me babble out the whole case for the prosecution! Well, really, Max!"

"But you are out of it now? The Public Prosecutor has taken it up?"

"True, true. But, for all that, I feel devilishly bad."

"Then I will give you all the whole case for the defence and so we shall be quits. In fact I am relying on you to help me with it."

"With the defence? I—after supplying the evidence that the Public Prosecutor is acting on?"

"Why not? You don't want to hang Philip Loudham—especially if he happens to be innocent—do you?"

"I don't want to hang anyone," protested Mr. Carlyle. "At least —not—as a private individual."

"Quite so. Well, suppose you and I between ourselves find out the actual facts of the case and decide what is to be done. The more usual course is for the prosecution to exaggerate all that tells against the accused and to contradict everything in his favour; for the defence to advance fictitious evidence of innocence and to lie roundly on everything that endangers his client; while on both sides witnesses are piled up to bemuse the jury into accepting the desired version. That does not always make for impartiality or for justice. . . . Now you and I are two reasonable men, Louis——"

"I hope so," admitted Mr. Carlyle. "I hope so."

"You can give away the case for the prosecution and I will expose the weakness of the defence, so, between us, we may arrive at the truth."

"It strikes me as a deuced irregular proceeding. But I am curious to hear the defence all the same."

"You are welcome to all of it that there yet is. An alibi, of course."

"Ah!" commented Mr. Carlyle with expression.

"So recently as yesterday a lady came hurriedly, and with a certain amount of secrecy, to see me. She came on the strength of the introduction afforded by a mutual acquaintanceship with Fromow, the Greek professor. When we were alone she asked me, besought me, in fact, to tell her what to do. A few hours before Mrs. Dupreen had rushed across London to her with the tale of young Loudham's arrest. Then out came the whole story. This woman—well, her name is Guestling, Louis—lives a little way down in Surrey and is married. Her husband, according to her own account—and I have certainly heard a hint about it elsewhere—leads her a studiedly outrageous existence; an admired silken-mannered gentleman in society, a tolerable polecat at home, one infers. About a year ago Mrs. Guestling made the acquaintance of Loudham, who was staying in that neighbourhood painting his pretty unsaleable country lanes and golden sunsets. The inevitable, or, to accept the lady's protestations, half the inevitable, followed. Guestling, who adds an insatiable jealousy to his other domestic virtues, vetoed the new acquaintance and thenceforward the two met hurriedly and furtively in town. Had either of them any money they might have snatched their destinies from the hands of Fate and gone off together, but she has nothing and he has nothing and both, I suppose, are poor weak mortals when it comes to doing anything courageous and outright in this censorious world. So they drifted, drifting but not yet wholly wrecked."

"A formidable incentive for a weak and desperate man to secure a fortune by hook or crook, Max," said Carlyle drily.

"That is the motive that I wish to make you a present of. But, as you will insist on your side, it is also a motive for a weak and foolish couple to steal every brief opportunity of a secret meeting. On Wednesday, the sixth, the lady was returning home from a visit to some friends in the Midlands. She saw in the occasion an opportunity and on the morning of the sixth a message appeared in the personal column of *The Daily Telegraph*—their usual channel of communication—making an assignation. That much can be established by the irrefutable evidence of the newspaper. Philip Loudham kept the appointment and for half-an-hour this miserably happy pair sat holding each other's hands in a dreary deserted waiting-room of Bishop's Road Station. That half-hour was from 4.14 to 4.45. Then Loudham saw Mrs. Guestling into Praed Street Station for Victoria, returned to Euston and just caught the 5.7 St. Abbots."

"Can this be corroborated—especially as regards the precise time they were together?"

"Not a word of it. They chose the waiting-room at Bishop's Road for seclusion and apparently they got it. Not a soul even looked in while they were there."

"Then, by Jupiter, Max," exclaimed Mr. Carlyle with emotion, "you have hanged your client!"

Carrados could not restrain a smile at his friend's tragic note of triumph.

"Well, let us examine the rope," he said with his usual imperturbability.

"Here it is." It was a trivial enough shred of evidence that the inquiry agent took from his pocket-book and put into the expectant hand; in point of fact, the salmon-coloured ticket of a "London General" motor omnibus.

"Royal Oak—the stage nearest Paddington—to Tottenham Court Road—the point nearest Trenion Street," he added significantly.

"Yes," acquiesced Carrados, taking it.

"The man who bought the bhurine dropped that ticket on the floor of the shop. He left the door open and Lightcraft followed him to close it. That is how he came to pick the ticket up, and he remembers that it was not there before. Then he threw it into a waste-paper basket underneath the counter, and that is where we found it when I called on him."

"Mr. Lightcraft's memory fascinates me, Louis," was the blind man's unruffled comment. "Let us drop in and have a chat with him?"

"Do you really think that there is anything more to be got in that quarter?" queried Carlyle dubiously. "I have turned him inside out, you may be sure."

"True; but we approach Mr. Lightcraft from different angles. You were looking for evidence to prove young Loudham guilty. I am looking for evidence to prove him innocent."

"Very well, Max," acquiesced his companion. "Only don't blame me if it turns out as deuced awkward for your man as Mrs. G. has done. Shall I tell you what a counsel may be expected to put to the jury as the explanation of that lady's evidence?"

"No, thanks," said Carrados half sleepily from his corner. "I know. I told her so."

"Oh, very well. I needn't inform you, then," and debarred of that satisfaction Mr. Carlyle withdrew himself into his own corner, where he nursed an indulgent annoyance against the occasional perversity of Max Carrados until the stopping of the car and the variegated attractions displayed in a shop window told him where they were.

Mr. Lightcraft made no pretence of being glad to see his visitors. For some time he declined to open his mouth at all on the subject that had brought them there, repeating with parrot-like obstinacy to every remark on their part, "The matter is *sub judice*. I am unable to say anything further," until Mr. Carlyle longed to box his ears and bring him to his senses. The ears happened to be rather prominent, for they glowed with sensitiveness, and the chemist was otherwise a lank and pallid man, whose transparent ivory skin and well-defined moustache gave him something of the appearance of a waxwork.

"At all events," interposed Carrados, when his friend turned from the maddening reiteration in despair, "you don't mind telling me a few things about bhurine—apart from this particular connection?"

"I am very busy," and Mr. Lightcraft, with his back towards the shop, did something superfluous among the bottles on a shelf.

"I imagine that the time of Mr. Max Carrados, of whom even you may possibly have heard, is as valuable as yours, my good friend," put in Mr. Carlyle with scandalised dignity.

"Mr. Carrados?" Lightcraft turned and regarded the blind man with interest. "I did not know. But you must recognise the unenviable position in which I am put by this gentleman's interference."

"It is his profession, you know," said Carrados mildly, "and, in any case, it would certainly have been someone. Why not help me to get you out of the position?"

"How is that possible?"

"If the case against Philip Loudham breaks down and he is discharged at the next hearing you would not be called upon further."

"That would certainly be a mitigation. But why should it break down?"

"Suppose you let me try the taste of bhurine," suggested Carrados. "You have some left?"

"Max, Max!" cried Mr. Carlyle's warning voice, "aren't you aware that the stuff is a deadly poison? One-fifth of a grain——"

"Mr. Lightcraft will know how to administer it."

Apparently Mr. Lightcraft did. He filled a graduated measure with cold water, dipped a slender glass rod into a bottle that was not kept on the shelves, and with it stirred the water. Then into another vessel of water he dropped a single spot of the dilution.

"One in a hundred and twenty-five thousand, Mr. Carrados," he said, offering him the mixture.

Carrados just touched the liquid with his lips, considered the impression and then wiped his mouth.

"Now for the smell."

The unstoppered bottle was handed to him and he took in its exhalation.

"Stewed mushrooms!" was his comment. "What is it used for, Mr. Lightcraft?"

"Nothing that I know of."

"But your customer must have stated an application."

The pallid chemist flushed a little at the recollection of that incident.·

"Yes," he conceded. "There is a good deal about the whole business that is still a mystery to me. The man came in shortly after I had lit up and nodded familiarly as he said: 'Good-evening, Mr. Lightcraft.' I naturally assumed that he was someone whom I could not quite place. 'I want another half-pound of nitre,' he said, and I served him. Had he bought nitre before, I have since tried to recall and I cannot. It is a common enough article and I sell it every day. I have a poor memory for faces I am willing to admit. It has hampered me in business many a time. We chatted about nothing in particular as I did up the parcel. After he had paid and turned to go he looked back again. 'By the way, do you happen to have any bhurine?' he inquired. Unfortunately I had a few ounces. 'Of course you know its nature?' I cautioned him. 'May I ask what you require it for?' He nodded and held up the parcel of nitre he had in his hand. 'The same thing,' he replied, 'taxidermy.' Then I supplied him with half-an-ounce."

"As a matter of fact, is it used in taxidermy?"

"It does not seem to be. I have made inquiry and no one knows of it. Nitre is largely used, and some of the dangerous poisons—arsenic and mercuric chloride, for instance—but not this. No, it was a subterfuge."

"Now the poison book, if you please."

Mr. Lightcraft produced it without demur and the blind man ran his finger along the indicated line.

"Yes; this is quite satisfactory. Is it a fact, Mr. Lightcraft, that not half-a-dozen chemists in London stock this particular substance? We are told that"

"I can quite believe it. I certainly don't know of another."

"Strangely enough, your customer of the sixth seems to have come straight here. Do you issue a price-list?"

"Only a localised one of certain photographic goods. Bhurine is not included."

"You can suggest no reason why Mr. Phillip Loudham should be inspired to presume that he would be able to procure this unusual drug from you? You have never corresponded with him nor come across his name or address before?"

"No. As far as I can recollect, I know nothing whatever of him."

"Then as yet you must assume that it was pure chance. By the way, Mr. Lightcraft, how does it come that *you* stock this rare poison, which has no commercial use and for which there is no demand?"

The chemist permitted himself to smile at the blunt terms of the inquiry.

"In the ordinary way I don't stock it," he replied. "This is a small quantity which I had over from my own use."

"Your own use? Oh, then it has a use after all?"

"No, scarcely that. Some time ago it leaked out in a corner of the photographic world that a great revolution in colour photography was on the point of realisation by the use of bhurine in one of the processes. I, among others, at once took it up. Unfortunately it was another instance of a discovery that is correct in theory breaking down in practice. Nothing came of it."

"Dear, dear me," said Carrados softly, with sympathetic understanding in his voice; "what a pity. You are interested in photography, Mr. Lightcraft?"

"It is the hobby of my life, sir. Of course most chemists dabble in it as a part of their business, but I devote all my spare time to experimenting. Colour photography in particular."

"Colour photography; yes. It has a great future. This bhurine process—I suppose it would have been of considerable financial value if it had worked?"

Mr. Lightcraft laughed quietly and rubbed his hands together. For the moment he had forgotten Loudham and the annoying case and lived in his enthusiasm.

"I should rather say it would, Mr. Carrados," he replied. "It would have been the most epoch-marking thing since Gaudin produced the first dry plate in '54. Consider it—the elaborate processes of Dyndale, Eiloff and Jupp reduced to the simplicity of a single contact print giving the entire range of chromatic variation. Financially it will scarcely bear thinking about by artificial light."

"Was it widely taken up?" asked Carrados.

"The bhurine idea?"

"Yes. You spoke of the secret leaking out. Were many in the know?"

"Not at all. The group of initiates was only a small one and I should imagine that, on reflection, every man kept it to himself. It certainly never became public. Then when the theory was definitely exploded, of course no one took any further interest in it."

"Were all who were working on the same lines known to you, Mr. Lightcraft?"

"Well, yes; more or less I suppose they would be," said the chemist thoughtfully. "You see, the man who stumbled on the formula was a member of the Iris—a society of those interested in this subject, of which I was the secretary—and I don't think it ever got beyond the committee."

"How long ago was this?"

"A year—eighteen months. It led to unpleasantness and broke up the society."

"Suppose it happened to come to your knowledge that one of the original circle was quietly pursuing his experiments on the same lines with bhurine—what should you infer from it?"

Mr. Lightcraft considered. Then he regarded Carrados with a sharp, almost a startled, glance and then he fell to biting his nails in perplexed uncertainty.

"It would depend on who it was," he replied.

"Was there by any chance one who was unknown to you by sight but whose address you were familiar with?"

"Paulden!" exclaimed Mr. Lightcraft. "Paulden, by heaven! I do believe you're right. He was the ablest of the lot and he never came to the meetings—a corresponding member. Southem, the original man who struck the idea, knew Paulden and told him of it. Southem was an impractical genius who would never be able to make anything work. Paulden—yes, Paulden it was who finally persuaded Southem that there was nothing in it. He sent a report to the same effect to be read at one of the meetings. So Paulden is taking up bhurine again——"

"Where does he live?" inquired Carrados.

"Ivor House, Wilmington Lane, Enstead. As secretary I have written there a score of times."

"It is on the Great Western—Paddington," commented the blind man. "Still, can you get out the addresses of the others in the know, Mr. Lightcraft?"

"Certainly, certainly. I have the book of membership. But I am convinced now that Paulden was the man. I believe that I did actually see him once some years ago, but he has grown a moustache since."

"If you had been convinced of that a few days ago it would have saved us some awkwardness," volunteered Mr. Carlyle with a little dignified asperity.

"When you came before, Mr. Carlyle, you were so convinced yourself of it being Mr. Loudham that you wouldn't hear of me thinking of anyone else," retorted the chemist. "You will bear me out also that I never positively identified him as my customer. Now here is the book. Southem, Potter's Bar. Voynich, Islington. Crawford, Streatham Hill. Brown, Southampton Row. Vickers, Clapham Common. Tidey, Fulham. All those I knew quite well—associated with them week after week. Williams I didn't know so closely. He is dead. Bigwood has gone to Canada. I don't think anyone else was in the bhurine craze—as we called it afterwards."

"But now? What would you call it now?" queried Carrados.

"Now? Well, I hope that you will get me out of having to turn up at court and that sort of thing, Mr. Carrados. If Paulden is going on experimenting with bhurine again on the sly I shall want all my spare time to do the same myself!"

A few hours later the two investigators rang the bell of a substantial detached house in Enstead, the little country town twenty miles out in Berkshire, and asked to see Mr. Paulden.

"It is no good taking Lightcraft to identify the man," Carrados had decided. "If Paulden denied it, our friend's obliging record in that line would put him out of court."

"I maintain an open mind on the subject," Carlyle had replied. "Lightcraft is admittedly a very bending reed, but there is no reason why he should not have been right before and wrong to-day."

They were shown into a ceremonial reception-room to wait. Mr. Carlyle diagnosed snug circumstances and the tastes of an indoors, comfort-loving man in the surroundings.

The door opened, but it was to admit a middle-aged matronly lady with good-humour and domestic capability proclaimed by every detail of her smiling face and easy manner.

"You wished to see my husband?" she asked with friendly courtesy.

"Mr. Paulden? Yes, we should like to," replied Carlyle, with his most responsive urbanity. "It is a matter that need not occupy more than a few minutes."

"He is very busy just now. If it has to do with the election"—a local contest was at its height—"he is not interested in politics and scarcely ever votes." Her manner was not curious, but merely reflected a business-like desire to save trouble all round.

"Very sensible too, ve-ry sensible indeed," almost warbled Mr.

Carlyle with instinctive cajolery. "After all," he continued, mendaciously appropriating as his own an aphorism at which he had laughed heartily a few days before in the theatre, "after all, what does an election do but change the colour of the necktie of the man who picks our pockets? No, no, Mrs. Paulden, it is merely a—um—quite personal matter."

The lady looked from one to the other with smiling amiability.

"Some little mystery," her expression seemed to say. "All right; I don't mind, only perhaps I could help you if I knew."

"Mr. Paulden is in his dark-room now," was what she actually did say. "I am afraid, I am really afraid that I shan't be able to persuade him to come out unless I can take a definite message."

"One understands the difficulty of tempting an enthusiast from his work," suggested Carrados, speaking for the first time. "Would it be permissible to take us to the door of the dark-room, Mrs. Paulden, and let us speak to your husband through it?"

"We can try that way," she acquiesced readily, "if it is really so important."

"I think so," he replied.

The dark-room lay across the hall. Mrs. Paulden conducted them to the door, waited a moment and then knocked quietly.

"Yes?" sang out a voice, rather irritably one might judge, from inside.

"Two gentlemen have called to see you about something, Lance—"

"I cannot see anyone when I am in here," interrupted the voice with rising sharpness. "You know that, Clara——"

"Yes, dear," she said soothingly; "but listen. They are at the door here and if you can spare the time just to come and speak you will know without much trouble if their business is as important as they think."

"Wait a minute," came the reply after a moment's pause, and then they heard someone approach the door from the other side.

It was a little difficult to know exactly how it happened in the obscure light of the corner of the hall. Carrados had stepped nearer to the door to speak. Possibly he trod on Mr. Carlyle's toe, for there was a confused movement; certainly he put out his hand hastily to recover himself. The next moment the door of the dark-room jerked open, the light was let in and the warm odours of a mixed and vitiated atmosphere rolled out. Secure in the well-ordered discipline of his excellent household, Mr. Paulden had neglected the precaution of locking himself in.

"Confound it all," shouted the incensed experimenter in a towering rage, "confound it all, you've spoiled the whole thing now!"

"Dear me," apologised Carrados penitently, "I am so sorry. I think it must have been my fault, do you know. Does it really matter?"

"Matter!" stormed Mr. Paulden, recklessly flinging open the door fully now to come face to face with his disturbers—"matter letting a flood of light into a darkroom in the middle of a delicate experiment!"

"Surely it was very little," persisted Carrados.

"Pshaw," snarled the angry gentleman; "it was enough. You know the difference between light and dark, I suppose?"

Mr. Carlyle suddenly found himself holding his breath, wondering how on earth Max had conjured that opportune challenge to the surface.

"No," was the mild and deprecating reply—the appeal *ad misericordiam* that had never failed him yet—"no, unfortunately I don't, for I am blind. That is why I am so awkward."

Out of the shocked silence Mrs. Paulden gave a little croon of pity. The moment before she had been speechless with indignation on her husband's behalf. Paulden felt as though he had struck a suffering animal. He stammered an apology and turned away to close the unfortunate door. Then he began to walk slowly down the hall.

"You wished to see me about something?" he remarked, with matter-of-fact civility. "Perhaps we had better go in here." He indicated the reception room where they had waited and followed them in. The admirable Mrs. Paulden gave no indication of wishing to join the party.

Carrados came to the point at once.

"Mr. Carlyle," he said, indicating his friend, "has recently been acting for the prosecution in a case of alleged poisoning that the Public Prosecutor has now taken up. I am interested in the defence. Both sides are thus before you, Mr. Paulden."

"How does this concern me?" asked Paulden with obvious surprise.

"You are experimenting with bhurine. The victim of this alleged crime undoubtedly lost his life by bhurine poisoning. Do you mind telling us when and where you acquired your stock of this scarce substance?"

"I have had——"

"No—a moment, Mr. Paulden, before you reply," struck in Carrados with arresting hand. "You must understand that nothing so grotesque as to connect you with a crime is contemplated. But a man is under arrest and the chief point against him is the half-ounce of bhurine that Lightcraft of Trenion Street sold to someone at half-past five last Wednesday fortnight. Before you commit yourself to any statement that it may possibly be difficult to recede from, you should realise that this inquiry will be pushed to the very end."

"How do you know that I am using bhurine?"

"That," parried Carrados, "is a blind man's secret."

"Oh, well. And you say that someone has been arrested through this fact?"

"Yes. Possibly you have read something of the St. Abbots mushroom poisoning case?"

"I have no interest in the sensational ephemera of the Press. Very well; it was I who bought the bhurine from Lightcraft that Wednesday afternoon. I gave a false name and address, I must admit. I had a sufficient private reason for so doing."

"This knocks what is vulgarly termed 'the stuffing' out of the case for the prosecution," observed Carlyle, who had been taking a note. "It may also involve you in some trouble yourself, Mr. Paulden."

"I don't think that you need regard that very seriously in the circumstances," said Carrados reassuringly.

"They must find some scapegoat, you know," persisted Mr. Carlyle. "Loudham will raise Cain over it."

"I don't think so. Loudham, as the prosecution will roundly tell him, has only himself to thank for not giving a satisfactory account of his movements. Loudham will be lectured, Lightcraft will be fined the minimum, and Mr. Paulden will, I imagine, be told not to do it again."

The man before them laughed bitterly.

"There will be no occasion to do it again," he remarked. "Do you know anything of the circumstances?"

"Lightcraft told us something connected with colour photography. You distrust Mr. Lightcraft, I infer?"

Mr. Paulden came down to the heart-easing medium of the street.

"I've had some once, thanks," was what he said with terse expression. "Let me tell you. About eighteen months ago I was on the edge of a great discovery in colour photography. It was my discovery, whatever you may have heard. Bhurine was the medium, and not being then so cautious or suspicious as I have reason to be now, and finding it difficult—really impossible—to procure this substance casually, I sent in an order to Lightcraft to procure me a stock. Unfortunately, in a moment of enthusiasm I had hinted at the anticipated results to a man who was then my friend—a weakling called Southem. Comparing notes with Lightcraft they put two and two together and in a trice most of the secret boiled over.

"If you have ever been within an ace of a monumental discovery you will understand the torment of anxiety and self-reproach that possessed me. For months the result must have trembled in the balance, but even as it evaded me, so it evaded the others. And at last I was able to spread conviction that the bhurine process was a failure. I breathed again.

"You don't want to hear of the various things that conspired to baffle me. I proceeded with extreme caution and therefore slowly. About two weeks ago I had another foretaste of success and immediately on it a veritable disaster. By some diabolical mischance I contrived to upset my stock bottle of bhurine. It rolled down, smashed to atoms on a developing dish filled with another chemical, and the precious lot was irretrievably lost. To arrest the experiments at that stage for a day was to lose a month. In one place and one alone could I hope to replenish the stock temporarily at such short notice and to do it openly after my last experience filled me with dismay. . . . Well, you know what happened, and now, I suppose, it will all come out."

* * * * *

A week after his arrest Philip Loudham and his sister were sitting together in the drawing-room at Hazlehurst, nervous and expectant. Loudham had been discharged scarcely six hours before, with such vindication of his character as the frigid intimation that there was no evidence against him afforded. On his arrival home he had found a letter from Max Carrados—a name with which he was now familiar—awaiting him. There had been other notes and telegrams—messages of sympathy and congratulation, but the man who had brought about his liberation did not include these conventionalities. He merely stated that he proposed calling upon Mr. Loudham at nine o'clock that evening and that he hoped it would be convenient for him and all other members of the household to be at home.

"He can scarcely be coming to be thanked," speculated Loudham, breaking the silence that had fallen on them as the hour approached. "I should have called on him myself to-morrow."

Mrs. Dupreen assented absent-mindedly. Both were dressed in black, and both at that moment had the same thought: that they were dreaming this.

"I suppose you won't go on living here, Irene?" continued the brother, speaking to make the minutes seem tolerable.

This at least had the effect of bringing Mrs. Dupreen back into the present with a rush.

"Of course not," she replied almost sharply and looking at him direct. "Why should I, now?"

"Oh, all right," he agreed. "I didn't suppose you would." Then, as the front-door bell was heard to ring: "Thank heaven!"

"Won't you go to meet him in the hall and bring him in?" suggested Mrs. Dupreen. "He is blind, you know."

Carrados was carrying a small leather case which he allowed Loudham to relieve him of, together with his hat and gloves. The introduction to Mrs. Dupreen was made, the blind man put in touch with a chair, and then Philip Loudham began to rattle off the acknowledgment of gratitude of which he had been framing and rejecting openings for the last half-hour.

"I'm afraid it's no good attempting to thank you for the extraordinary service that you've rendered me, Mr. Carrados," he began, "and, above all, I appreciate the fact that, owing to you, it has been possible to keep Mrs. Guestling's name entirely out of the case. Of course you know all about that, and my sister knows, so it isn't worth while beating about the bush. Well, now that I shall have something like a decent income of my own, I shall urge Kitty—Mrs. Guestling—to apply for the divorce that she is richly entitled to, and when that is all settled we shall marry at once and try to forget the experiences on both sides that have led up to it. I hope," he added tamely, "that you don't consider us really much to blame?"

Carrados shook his head in mild deprecation.

"That is an ethical point that has lain outside the scope of my inquiry," he replied. "You would hardly imagine that I should disturb you at such a time merely to claim your thanks. Has it occurred to you why I should have come?"

Brother and sister exchanged looks and by their silence gave reply.

"We have still to find who poisoned Charlie Winpole."

Loudham stared at their guest in frank bewilderment. Mrs. Dupreen almost closed her eyes. When she spoke it was in a pained whisper.

"Is there anything more to be gained by pursuing that idea, Mr. Carrados?" she asked pleadingly. "We have passed through a week of anguish, coming upon a week of grief and great distress. Surely all has been done that can be done?"

"But you would have justice for your nephew if there has been foul play?"

Mrs. Dupreen made a weary gesture of resignation. It was Loudham who took up the question.

"Do you really mean, Mr. Carrados, that there is any doubt about the cause?"

"Will you give me my case, please? Thank you." He opened it and produced a small paper bag. "Now a newspaper, if you will." He opened the bag and poured out the contents. "You remember stating at the inquest, Mrs. Dupreen, that the mushrooms you bought looked rather dry? They were dry, there is no doubt, for they had then been gathered four days. Here are some more under precisely the same conditions. They looked, in point of fact, like these?"

"Yes," admitted the lady, beginning to regard Carrados with a new and curious interest.

"Dr. Slark further stated that the only fungus containing the poison bhurine—the *Amanita* called the Black Cap, and also by the country folk the Devil's Scent Bottle—did not assume its forbidding appearance until maturity. He was wrong in one sense there, for experiment proved that if the Black Cap is gathered in its young and deceptive stage and kept, it assumes precisely the same appearance as it withers as if it was ripening naturally. You observe." He opened a a second bag and, shaking out the contents, displayed another little heap by the side of the first. "Gathered four days ago," he explained.

"Why, they are as black as ink," commented Loudham. "And the, phew! aroma!"

"One would hardly have got through without you seeing it, Mrs. Dupreen?"

"I certainly hardly think so," she admitted.

"With due allowance for Lackington's biased opinion I also think that his claim might be allowed. Finally, it is incredible that whoever peeled the mushrooms should have passed one of these. Who was the cook on that occasion, Mrs. Dupreen?"

"My maid Hilda. She does all the cooking."

"The one who admitted me?"

"Yes; she is the only servant I have, Mr. Carrados."

"I should like to have her in, if you don't mind."

"Certainly, if you wish it. She is"—Mrs. Dupreen felt that she must put in a favourable word before this inexorable man pronounced judgment—"she is a very good, straightforward girl."

"So much the better."

"I will——" Mrs. Dupreen rose and began to cross the room.

"Ring for her? Thank you," and whatever her intention had been the lady rang the bell.

"Yes, ma'am?"

A neat, modest-mannered girl, simple and nervous, with a face as full, as clear and as honest as an English apple. "A pity," thought Mrs. Dupreen, "that this confident, suspicious man cannot see her now."

"Come in, Hilda. This gentleman wants to ask you something."

"Yes, ma'am." The round, blue eyes went appealingly to Carrados, fell upon the fungi spread out before her, and then circled the room with an instinct of escape.

"You remember the night poor Charlie died, Hilda," said Carrados in his suavest tones, "you cooked some mushrooms for his supper, didn't you?"

"No, sir," came the glib reply.

" 'No,' Hilda!" exclaimed Mrs. Dupreen in wonderment. "You mean 'yes,' surely, child. Of course you cooked them. Don't you remember?"

"Yes, ma'am," dutifully replied Hilda.

"That is all right," said the blind man reassuringly. "Nervous witnesses very often answer at random at first. You have nothing to be afraid of, my good girl, if you will tell the truth. I suppose you know a mushroom when you see it?"

"Yes, sir," was the rather hesitating reply.

"There was nothing like this among them?" He held up one of the poisonous sort.

"No, sir; indeed there wasn't, sir. I should have known then."

"You would have known *then?* You were not called at the inquest, Hilda?"

"No, sir."

"If you had been, what would you have told them about these mushrooms that you cooked?"

"I—I don't know, sir."

"Come, come, Hilda. What could you have told them—something that we do not know? The truth, girl, if you want to save yourself?" Then with a sudden, terrible directness the question cleft her trembling, guilt-stricken little brain: "Where did you get the other mushrooms from that you put with those that your mistress brought?"

The eyes that had been mostly riveted to the floor leapt to Carrados for a single frightened glance, from Carrados to her mistress, to Philip Loudham, and to the floor again. In a moment her face changed and she was in a burst of sobbing.

"Oho, oho, oho!" she wailed. "I didn't know; I didn't know. I meant no harm; indeed I didn't, ma'am."

"Hilda! Hilda!" exclaimed Mrs. Dupreen in bewilderment. "What is it you're saying? What have you done?"

"It was his own fault. Oho, oho, oho!" Every word was punctuated by a gasp. "He always was a little pig and making himself ill with food. You know he was, ma'am, although you were so fond of him. I'm sure I'm not to blame."

"But *what* was it? What *have* you done?" besought her mistress.

"It was after you went out on that afternoon. He put on his things and slipped down into the kitchen without the master knowing. He said what you were getting for his dinner, ma'am, and that you never got enough of them. Then he told me not to tell about his being down, because he'd seen some white things from his bedroom window growing by the hedge at the bottom of the garden and he was going to get them. He brought in four or five and said they were mushrooms and asked me to cook them with the others and not say anything because you'd say too many were not good for him. And I didn't know any difference. Indeed I'm telling you the truth, ma'am."

"Oh, Hilda, Hilda!" was torn reproachfully from Mrs. Dupreen. "You know what we've gone through. Why didn't you tell us this before?"

"I was afraid. I was afraid of what they'd do. And no one ever guessed until I thought I was safe. Indeed I meant no harm to anyone, but I was afraid that they'd punish me instead."

Carrados had risen and was picking up his things.

"Yes," he said, half musing to himself, "I knew it must exist: the one explanation that accounts for everything and cannot be assailed. We have reached the bed-rock of truth at last."

The Ghost at Massingham Mansions

"Do you believe in ghosts, Max?" inquired Mr. Carlyle.

"Only as ghosts," replied Carrados with decision.

"Quite so," assented the private detective with the air of acquiescence with which he was wont to cloak his moments of obfuscation. Then he added cautiously: "And how don't you believe in them, pray?"

"As public nuisances—or private ones for that matter," replied his friend. "So long as they are content to behave as ghosts I am with them. When they begin to meddle with a state of existence that is outside their province—to interfere in business matters and depreciate property—to rattle chains, bang doors, ring bells, predict winners and to edit magazines—and to attract attention instead of shunning it, I cease to believe. My sympathies are entirely with the sensible old fellow who was awakened in the middle of the night to find a shadowy form standing by the side of his bed and silently regarding him. For a few minutes the disturbed man waited patiently, expecting some awful communication, but the same profound silence was maintained. 'Well,' he remarked at length, 'if you have nothing to do, I have,' and turning over went to sleep again."

"I have been asked to take up a ghost," Carlyle began to explain.

"Then I don't believe in it," declared Carrados.

"Why not?"

"Because it is a pushful, notoriety-loving ghost, or it would not have gone so far. Probably it wants to get into *The Daily Mail*. The other people, whoever they are, don't believe in it either, Louis, or they wouldn't have called you in. They would have gone to Sir Oliver Lodge for an explanation, or to the nearest priest for a stoup of holy water."

"I admit that I shall direct my researches towards the forces of this world before I begin to investigate any other," conceded Louis Carlyle. "And I don't doubt," he added, with his usual bland complacence, "that I shall hale up some mischievous or aggrieved

individual before the ghost is many days older. Now that you have
brought me so far, do you care to go on round to the place with
me, Max, to hear what they have to say about it?"

Carrados agreed with his usual good nature. He rarely met his
friend without hearing the details of some new case, for Carlyle's
practice had increased vastly since the night when chance had led
him into the blind man's study. They discussed the cases according
to their interest, and there the matter generally ended so far as Max
Carrados was concerned, until he casually heard the result sub-
sequently from Carlyle's lips or learned the sequel from the newspaper. But these pages are primarily a record of the methods of the
one man whose name they bear and therefore for the occasional
case that Carrados completed for his friend there must be assumed
the unchronicled scores which the inquiry agent dealt capably
with himself. This reminder is perhaps necessary to dissipate the
impression that Louis Carlyle was a pretentious humbug. He was,
as a matter of fact, in spite of his amiable foibles and the self-
assurance that was, after all, merely an asset of his trade, a shrewd
and capable business man of his world, and behind his office manner
nothing concerned him more than to pocket fees for which he felt
that he had failed to render value.

Massingham Mansions proved to be a single block of residential
flats overlooking a recreation ground. It was, as they afterwards
found, an adjunct to a larger estate of similar property situated down
another road. A porter, residing in the basement, looked after the
interests of Massingham Mansions; the business office was placed
among the other flats. On that morning it presented the appearance
of a well-kept, prosperous enough place, a little dull, a little unfinished, a little depressing perhaps; in fact faintly reminiscent of the
superfluous mansions that stand among broad, weedy roads on the
outskirts of overgrown seaside resorts; but it was persistently raining
at the time when Mr. Carlyle had his first view of it.

"It is early to judge," he remarked, after stopping the car in order
to verify the name on the brass plate, "but, upon my word, Max, I
really think that our ghost might have discovered more appropriate
quarters."

At the office, to which the porter had directed them, they found
a managing clerk and two coltish youths in charge. Mr. Carlyle's
name produced an appreciable flutter.

"The governor isn't here just now, but I have this matter in hand," said the clerk with an easy air of responsibility—an effect unfortunately marred by a sudden irrepressible giggle from the least overawed of the colts. "Will you kindly step into our private room?" He turned at the door of the inner office and dropped a freezing eye on the offender. "Get those letters copied before you go out to lunch, Binns," he remarked in a sufficiently loud voice. Then he closed the door quickly, before Binns could find a suitable retort.

So far it had been plain sailing, but now, brought face to face with the necessity of explaining, the clerk began to develop some hesitancy in beginning.

"It's a funny sort of business," he remarked, skirting the difficulty.

"Perhaps," admitted Mr. Carlyle; "but that will not embarrass us. Many of the cases that pass through my hands are what you would call 'funny sorts of business.'"

"I suppose so," responded the young man, "but not through ours. Well, this is at No. 11 Massingham. A few nights ago—I suppose it must be more than a week now—Willett, the estate porter, was taking up some luggage to No. 75 Northanger for the people there when he noticed a light in one of the rooms at 11 Massingham. The backs face, though about twenty or thirty yards away. It struck him as curious, because 11 Massingham is empty and locked up. Naturally he thought at first that the porter at Massingham or one of us from the office had gone up for something. Still it was so unusual—being late at night—that it was his business to look into it. On his way round—you know where Massingham Mansions are?—he had to pass here. It was dark, for we'd all been gone hours, but Willett has duplicate keys and he let himself in. Then he began to think that something must be wrong, for here, hanging up against their number on the board, were the only two keys of 11 Massingham that there are supposed to be. He put the keys in his pocket and went on to Massingham. Green, the resident porter there, told him that he hadn't been into No. 11 for a week. What was more, no one had passed the outer door, in or out, for a good half-hour. He knew that, because the door 'springs' with a noise when it is opened, no matter how carefully. So the two of them went up. The door of No. 11 was locked and inside everything was as it should be. There was no light then, and after looking well round with the lanterns that they carried they were satisfied that no one was concealed there."

"You say lanterns," interrupted Mr. Carlyle. "I suppose they lit the gas, or whatever it is there, as well?"

"It is gas, but they could not light it because it was cut off at the meter. We always cut it off when a flat becomes vacant."

"What sort of a light was it, then, that Willett saw?"

"It was gas, Mr. Carlyle. It is possible to see the bracket in that room from 75 Northanger. He saw it burning."

"Then the meter had been put on again?"

"It is in a locked cupboard in the basement. Only the office and the porters have keys. They tried the gas in the room and it was dead out; they looked at the meter in the basement afterwards and it was dead off."

"Very good," observed Mr. Carlyle, noting the facts in his pocket-book. "What next?"

"The next," continued the clerk, "was something that had really happened before. When they got down again—Green and Willett—Green was rather chipping Willett about seeing the light, you know, when he stopped suddenly. He'd remembered something. The day before the servant at 12 Massingham had asked him who it was that was using the bathroom at No. 11—she of course knowing that it was empty. He told her that no one used the bathroom. 'Well,' she said, 'we hear the water running and splashing almost every night and it's funny with no one there.' He had thought nothing of it at the time, concluding—as he told her—that it must be the water in the bathroom of one of the underneath flats that they heard. Of course he told Willett then and they went up again and examined the bathroom more closely. Water had certainly been run there, for the sides of the bath were still wet. They tried the taps and not a drop came. When a flat is empty we cut off the water like the gas."

"At the same place—the cupboard in the basement?" inquired Carlyle.

"No; at the cistern in the roof. The trap is at the top of the stairs and you need a longish ladder to get there. The next morning Willett reported what he'd seen and the governor told me to look into it. We didn't think much of it so far. That night I happened to be seeing some friends to the station here—I live not so far off—and I thought I might as well take a turn round here on my way home. I knew that if a light was burning I should be able to see the window lit up from the yard at the back, although the gas itself would be out of sight. And, sure enough, there was the light blazing out of one of the windows of No. 11. I won't say that I didn't feel a bit home-sick then, but I'd made up my mind to go up."

"Good man," murmured Mr. Carlyle approvingly.

"Wait a bit," recommended the clerk, with a shame-faced laugh. "So far I had only had to make my mind up. It was then close on midnight and not a soul about. I came here for the keys, and I also had the luck to remember an old revolver that had been lying about in a drawer of the office for years. It wasn't loaded, but it didn't seem quite so lonely with it. I put it in my pocket and went on to Massingham, taking another turn into the yard to see that the light was still on. Then I went up the stairs as quietly as I could and let myself into No. II."

"You didn't take Willett or Green with you?"

The clerk gave Mr. Carlyle a knowing look, as of one smart man who will be appreciated by another.

"Willett's a very trustworthy chap," he replied, "and we have every confidence in him. Green also, although he has not been with us so long. But I thought it just as well to do it on my own, you understand, Mr. Carlyle. You didn't look in at Massingham on your way? Well, if you had you would have seen that there is a pane of glass above every door, frosted glass to the hall doors and plain over each of those inside. It's to light the halls and passages, you know. Each flat has a small square hall and a longish passage leading off it. As soon as I opened the door I could tell that one of the rooms down the passage was lit up, though I could not see the door of it from there. Then I crept very quietly through the hall into the passage. A regular stream of light was shining from above the end door on the left. The room, I knew, was the smallest in the flat—it's generally used for a servant's bedroom or sometimes for a box-room. It was a bit thick, you'll admit—right at the end of a long passage and midnight, and after what the others had said."

"Yes, yes," assented the inquiry agent. "But you went on?"

"I went on, tiptoeing without a sound. I got to the door, took out my pistol, put my hand almost on the handle and then——"

"Well, well," prompted Mr. Carlyle, as the narrator paused provokingly, with the dramatic instinct of an expert raconteur, "what then?"

"Then the light went out. While my hand was within an inch of the handle the light went out, as clean as if I had been watched all along and the thing timed. It went out all at once, without any warning and without the slightest sound from the beastly room beyond. And then it was as black as hell in the passage and something seemed to be going to happen."

"What did you do?"

"I did a slope," acknowledged the clerk frankly. "I broke all the records down that passage, I bet you. You'll laugh, I dare say, and think you would have stood, but you don't know what it was like. I'd been screwing myself up, wondering what I should see in that lighted room when I opened the door, and then the light went out like a knife, and for all I knew the next second the door would open on me in the dark and Christ only knows what come out."

"Probably I should have run also," conceded Mr. Carlyle tactfully. "And you, Max?"

"You see, I always feel at home in the dark," apologised the blind man. "At all events, you got safely away, Mr.——?"

"My name's Elliott," responded the clerk. "Yes, you may bet I did. Whether the door opened and anybody or anything came out or not I can't say. I didn't look. I certainly did get an idea that I heard the bath water running and swishing as I snatched at the hall door, but I didn't stop to consider that either, and if it was, the noise was lost in the slam of the door and my clatter as I took about twelve flights of stairs six steps at a time. Then when I was safely out I did venture to go round to look up again, and there was that damned light full on again."

"Really?" commented Mr. Carlyle. "That was very audacious of him."

"Him? Oh, well, yes, I suppose so. That's what the governor insists, but he hasn't been up there himself in the dark."

"Is that as far as you have got?"

"It's as far as we can get. The bally thing goes on just as it likes. The very next day we tied up the taps of the gas-meter and the water cistern and sealed the string. Bless you, it didn't make a ha'peth of difference. Scarcely a night passes without the light showing, and there's no doubt that the water runs. We've put copying ink on the door handles and the taps and got into it ourselves until there isn't a man about the place that you couldn't implicate."

"Has anyone watched up there?"

"Willett and Green together did one night. They shut themselves up in the room opposite from ten till twelve and nothing happened. I was watching the window with a pair of opera-glasses from an empty flat here—85 Northanger. Then they chucked it, and before

they could have been down the steps the light was there—I could
see the gas as plain as I can see this ink-stand. I ran down and met
them coming to tell me that nothing had happened. The three of us
sprinted up again and the light was out and the flat as deserted as
a churchyard. What do you make of that?"

"It certainly requires looking into," replied Mr. Carlyle diplo-
matically.

"Looking into! Well, you're welcome to look all day and all night
too, Mr. Carlyle. It isn't as though it was an old baronial mansion,
you see, with sliding panels and secret passages. The place has the
date over the front door, 1882—1882 and haunted, by gosh! It was
built for what it is, and there isn't an inch unaccounted for between
the slates and the foundation."

"These two things—the light and the water running—are the only
indications there have been?" asked Mr. Carlyle.

"So far as we ourselves have seen or heard. I ought perhaps to
tell you of something else, however. When this business first started
I made a few casual inquiries here and there among the tenants.
Among others I saw Mr. Belting, who occupies No. 9 Massingham
—the flat directly beneath No. 11. It didn't seem any good making
up a cock-and-bull story, so I put it to him plainly—had he been
annoyed by anything unusual going on at the empty flat above?

" 'If you mean your confounded ghost up there, I have not been
particularly annoyed,' he said at once, 'but Mrs. Belting has, and
I should advise you to keep out of her way, at least until she gets
another servant.' Then he told me that their girl, who slept in the
bedroom underneath the little one at No. 11, had been going on
about noises in the room above—footsteps and tramping and a
bump on the floor—for some time before we heard anything of it.
Then one day she suddenly said that she'd had enough of it and
bolted. That was just before Willett first saw the light."

"It is being talked about, then—among the tenants?"

"You bet!" assented Mr. Elliott pungently. "That's what gets the
governor. He wouldn't give a continental if no one knew, but you
can't tell where it will end. The people at Northanger don't half
like it either. All the children are scared out of their little wits and
none of the slaveys will run errands after dark. It'll give the estate
a bad name for the next three years if it isn't stopped."

"It shall be stopped," declared Mr. Carlyle impressively. "Of
course we have our methods for dealing with this sort of thing, but

in order to make a clean sweep it is desirable to put our hands on the offender *in flagranti delicto*. Tell your—er—principal not to have any further concern in the matter. One of my people will call here for any further details that he may require during the day. Just leave everything as it is in the meanwhile. Good-morning, Mr. Elliott, good-morning. . . . A fairly obvious game, I imagine, Max," he commented as they got into the car, "although the details are original and the motive not disclosed as yet. I wonder how many of them are in it?"

"Let me know when you find out," said Carrados, and Mr. Carlyle promised.

Nearly a week passed and the expected revelation failed to make its appearance. Then, instead, quite a different note arrived:

"*My dear Max,*—I wonder if you formed any conclusion of that Massingham Mansions affair from Mr. Elliott's refined narrative of the circumstances?

"I begin to suspect that Trigget, whom I put on, is somewhat of an ass, though a very remarkable circumstance has come to light which might—if it wasn't a matter of business—offer an explanation of the whole business by stamping it as inexplicable.

"You know how I value your suggestions. If you happen to be in the neighbourhood—not otherwise, Max, I protest—I should be glad if you would drop in for a chat. Yours sincerely,

"*Louis Carlyle.*"

Carrados smiled at the ingenuous transparency of the note. He had thought several times of the case since the interview with Elliott, chiefly because he was struck by certain details of the manifestation that divided it from the ordinary methods of the bogy-raiser, an aspect that had apparently made no particular impression on his friend. He was sufficiently interested not to let the day pass without "happening" to be in the neighbourhood of Bampton Street.

"Max," exclaimed Mr. Carlyle, raising an accusing forefinger, "you have come on purpose."

"If I have," replied the visitor, "you can reward me with a cup of that excellent beverage that you were able to conjure up from somewhere down in the basement on a former occasion. As a matter of fact, I have."

Mr. Carlyle transmitted the order and then demanded his friend's serious attention.

"That ghost at Massingham Mansions——"

"I still don't believe in that particular ghost, Louis," commented Carrados in mild speculation.

"I never did, of course," replied Caryle, "but, upon my word, Max, I shall have to very soon as a precautionary measure. Trigget has been able to do nothing and now he has as good as gone on strike."

"Downed—now what on earth can an inquiry man down to go on strike, Louis? Notebooks? So Trigget has got a chill, like our candid friend Eliott, Eh?"

"He started all right—said that he didn't mind spending a night or a week in a haunted flat, and, to do him justice, I don't believe he did at first. Then he came across a very curious piece of forgotten local history, a very remarkable—er—coincidence in the circumstances, Max."

"I was wondering," said Carrados, "when we should come up against that story, Louis."

"Then you know of it?" exclaimed the inquiry agent in surprise.

"Not at all. Only I guessed it must exist. Here you have the manifestation associated with two things which in themselves are neither usual nor awe-inspiring—the gas and the water. It requires some association to connect them up, to give them point and force. That is the story."

"Yes," assented his friend, "that is the story, and, upon my soul, in the circumstances—well, you shall hear it. It comes partly from the newspapers of many years ago, but only partly, for the circumstances were successfully hushed up in a large measure and it required the stimulated memories of ancient scandal-mongers to fill in the details. Oh yes, it was a scandal, Max, and would have been a great sensation too, I do not doubt, only they had no proper pictorial press in those days, poor beggars. It was very soon after Massingham Mansions had been erected—they were called Enderby House in those days, by the way, for the name was changed on account of this very business. The household at No. 11 consisted of a comfortable, middle-aged married couple and one servant, a quiet and attractive young creature, one is led to understand. As a matter of fact, I think they were the first tenants of that flat."

"The first occupants give the soul to a new house," remarked the blind man gravely. "That is why empty houses have their different characters."

"I don't doubt it for a moment," assented Mr. Carlyle in his incisive way, "but none of our authorities on this case made any reference to the fact. They did say, however, that the man held a good and responsible position—a position for which high personal character and strict morality were essential. He was also well known and regarded in quiet but substantial local circles where serious views prevailed. He was, in short, a man of notorious 'respectability.'

"The first chapter of the tragedy opened with the painful death of the prepossessing handmaiden—suicide, poor creature. She didn't appear one morning and the flat was full of the reek of gas. With great promptitude the master threw all the windows open and called up the porter. They burst open the door of the little bedroom at the end of the passage, and there was the thing as clear as daylight for any coroner's jury to see. The door was locked on the inside and the extinguished gas was turned full on. It was only a tiny room, with no fireplace, and the ventilation of a closed well-fitting door and window was negligible in the circumstances. At all events the girl was proved to have been dead for several hours when they reached her, and the doctor who conducted the autopsy crowned the convincing fabric of circumstances when he mentioned as delicately as possible that the girl had a very pressing reason for dreading an inevitable misfortune that would shortly overtake her. The jury returned the obvious verdict.

"There have been a great many undiscovered crimes in the history of mankind, Max, but it is by no means every ingenious plot that carries. After the inquest, at which our gentleman doubtless cut a very proper and impressive figure, the barbed whisper began to insinuate and to grow in freedom. It is sheerly impossible to judge how these things start, but we know that when once they have been begun they gather material like an avalanche. It was remembered by someone at the flat underneath that late on the fatal night a window in the principal bedroom above had been heard to open, top and bottom, very quietly. Certain other sounds of movement in the night did not tally with the tale of sleep-wrapped innocence. Sceptical busybodies were anxious to demonstrate practically to those who differed from them on this question that it was quite easy to extinguish a gas-jet in one room by blowing down the gas-pipe in another; and in this connection there was evidence that the lady of the flat had spoken to her friends more than once of her sentimental young servant's extravagant habit of reading herself to sleep occasionally with the light full on. Why was nothing heard at the inquest, they demanded, of the curious fact that an open novelette lay on the counterpane when the room was broken into? A hundred trifling circumstances were adduced—arrangements that the girl had been making for the future down to the last evening of her life—interpretable hints that she had dropped to her acquaintances—her views on suicide and the best means to that end: a favourite topic, it would seem, among her class—her possession of certain comparatively expensive trinkets on a salary of a very few shillings a week, and so on. Finally, some rather more definite and important piece of evidence must have been conveyed to the authorities, for we know now that one fine day a warrant was issued. Somehow rumour preceded its execution. The eminently respectable gentleman with whom it was concerned did not wait to argue out the merits of the case. He locked himself in the bathroom, and when the police arrived they found that instead of an arrest they had to arrange the details for another inquest."

"A very convincing episode," conceded Carrados in response to his friend's expectant air. "And now her spirit passes the long winter evenings turning the gas on and off, and the one amusement of his consists in doing the same with the bath-water—or the other way, the other way about, Louis. Truly, one half the world knows not how the other half lives!"

"All your cheap humour won't induce Trigget to spend another night in that flat, Max," retorted Mr. Carlyle. "Nor, I am afraid, will it help me through this business in any other way."

"Then I'll give you a hint that may," said Carrados. "Try your respectable gentleman's way of settling difficulties."

"What is that?" demanded his friend.

"Blow down the pipes, Louis."

"Blow down the pipes?" repeated Carlyle.

"At all events try it. I infer that Mr. Trigget has not experimented in that direction."

"But what will it do, Max?"

"Possibly it will demonstrate where the other end goes to."

"But the other end goes to the meter."

"I suggest not—not without some interference with its progress. I have already met your Mr. Trigget, you know, Louis. An excellent and reliable man within his limits, but he is at his best posted outside the door of a hotel waiting to see the co-respondent go in. He hasn't enough imagination for this case—not enough to carry him away from what would be his own obvious method of doing it to what is someone else's equally obvious but quite different method. Unless I am doing him an injustice, he will have spent most of his time trying to catch someone getting into the flat to turn the gas and water on and off, whereas I conjecture that no one does go into the flat because it is perfectly simple—ingenious but simple—to produce these phenomena without. Then when Mr. Trigget has satisfied himself that it is physically impossible for anyone to be going in and out, and when, on the top of it, he comes across this romantic tragedy— a tale that might psychologically explain the ghost, simply because the ghost is moulded on the tragedy—then, of course, Mr. Trigget's mental process is swept away from its moorings and his feet begin to get cold."

"This is very curious and suggestive," said Mr. Carlyle. "I certainly assumed—— But shall we have Trigget up and question him on the point? I think he ought to be here now—if he isn't detained at the Bull."

Carrados assented, and in a few minutes Mr. Trigget presented himself at the door of the private office. He was a melancholy-looking middle-aged little man, with an ineradicable air of being exactly what he was, and the searcher for deeper or subtler indications of character would only be rewarded by a latent pessimism grounded on the depressing probability that he would never be anything else.

"Come in, Trigget," called out Mr. Carlyle when his employee diffidently appeared. "Come in. Mr. Carrados would like to hear some of the details of the Massingham Mansions case."

"Not the first time I have availed myself of the benefit of your inquiries, Mr. Trigget," nodded the blind man. "Good-afternoon."

"Good-afternoon, sir," replied Trigget with gloomy deference. "It's very handsome of you to put it in that way, Mr. Carrados, sir. But this isn't another Tarporley-Templeton case, if I may say so, sir. That was as plain as a pikestaff after all, sir."

"When we saw the pikestaff, Mr. Trigget; yes, it was," admitted Carrados, with a smile. "But this is insoluble? Ah, well. When I was a boy I used to be extraordinarily fond of ghost stories, I remember, but even while reading them I always had an uneasy suspicion that when it came to the necessary detail of explaining the mystery I should be defrauded with some subterfuge as 'by an ingenious arrangement of hidden wires the artful Muggles had contrived,' etc., or 'an optical illusion effected by means of concealed mirrors revealed the *modus operandi* of the apparition.' I thought that I had been swindled. I think so still. I hope there are no ingenious wires or concealed mirrors here, Mr. Trigget?"

Mr. Trigget looked mildly sagacious but hopelessly puzzled. It was his misfortune that in him the necessities of his business and the proclivities of his nature were at variance, so that he ordinarily presented the curious anomaly of looking equally alert and tired.

"Wires, sir?" he began, with faint amusement.

"Not only wires, but anything that might account for what is going on," interposed Mr. Carlyle. "Mr. Carrados means this, Trigget: you have reported that it is impossible for anyone to be concealed in the flat or to have secret access to it——"

"I have tested every inch of space in all the rooms, Mr. Carrados, sir," protested the hurt Trigget. "I have examined every board and, you may say, every nail in the floor, the skirting-boards, the window frames and in fact wherever a board or a nail exists. There are no secret ways in or out. Then I have taken the most elaborate precautions against the doors and windows being used for surreptitious ingress and egress. They have not been used, sir. For the past week I am the only person who has been in and out of the flat, Mr. Carrados, and yet night after night the gas that is cut off at the meter is lit and turned out again, and the water that is cut off at the cistern splashes about in the bath up to the second I let myself in. Then it's as quiet as the grave and everything is exactly as I left it. It isn't human, Mr. Carrados, sir, and flesh and blood can't stand it—not in the middle of the night, that is to say."

"You see nothing further, Mr. Trigget?"

"I don't indeed, Mr. Carrados. I would suggest doing away with the gas in that room altogether. As a box-room it wouldn't need one."

"And the bathroom?"

"That might be turned into a small bedroom and all the water fittings removed. Then to provide a bathroom——"

"Yes, yes," interrupted Mr. Caryle impatiently, "but we are retained to discover who is causing this annoyance and to detect the means, not to suggest structural alterations in the flat, Trigget. The fact is that after having put in a week on this job you have failed to bring us an inch nearer its solution. Now Mr. Carrados has suggested"—Mr. Carlyle was not usually detained among the finer

shades of humour, but some appreciation of the grotesqueness of
the advice required him to control his voice as he put the matter in
its baldest form—"Mr. Carrados has suggested that instead of spending the time measuring the chimneys and listening to the wall-paper,
if you had simply blown down the gas-pipe——"

Carrados was inclined to laugh, although he thought it rather too
bad of Louis.

"Not quite in those terms, Mr. Trigget," he interposed.

"Blow down the gas-pipe, sir?" repeated the amazed man. "What
for?"

"To ascertain where the other end comes out," replied Carlyle.

"But don't you see, sir, that that is a detail until you ascertain
how it is being done? The pipe may be tapped between the bath and the
cistern. Naturally, I considered that. As a matter of fact, the water-
pipe isn't tapped. It goes straight up from the bath to the cistern in
the attic above, a distance of only a few feet, and I have examined it.
The gas-pipe, it is true, passes through a number of flats, and without
pulling up all the floors it isn't practicable to trace it. But how does
that help us, Mr. Carrados? The gas-tap has to be turned on and
off; you can't do that with these hidden wires. It has to be lit. I've
never heard of lighting gas by optical illusions, sir. Somebody must
get in and out of the flat or else it isn't human. I've spent a week,
a very trying week, sir, in endeavouring to ascertain how it could
be done. I haven't shirked cold and wet and solitude, sir, in the
discharge of my duty. I've freely placed my poor gifts of observation
and intelligence, such as they are, at the service——"

"Not 'freely,' Trigget," interposed his employer with decision.

"I am speaking under a deep sense of injury, Mr. Carlyle,"
retorted Mr. Trigget, who, having had time to think it over, had
now come to the conclusion that he was not appreciated. "I am
alluding to a moral attitude such as we all possess. I am very grieved
by what has been suggested. I didn't expect it of you, Mr. Carlyle,
sir; indeed I did not. For a week I have done everything that it has
been possible to do, everything that a long experience could suggest,
and now, as I understand it, sir, you complain that I didn't blow
down the gas-pipe, sir. It's hard, sir; it's very hard."

"Oh, well, for heaven's sake don't cry about it, Trigget," exclaimed
Mr. Carlyle. "You're always sobbing about the place over something or other. We know you did your best—God help you!" he
added aside.

"I did, Mr. Carlyle; indeed I did, sir. And I thank you for that appreciative tribute to my services. I value it highly, very highly indeed, sir." A tremulous note in the rather impassioned delivery made it increasingly plain that Mr. Trigget's regimen had not been confined entirely to solid food that day. His wrongs were forgotten and he approached Mr. Carrados with an engaging air of secrecy.

"What is this tip about blowing down the gas-pipe, sir?" he whispered confidentially. "The old dog's always willing to learn something new."

"Max," said Mr. Carlyle curtly, "is there anything more that we need detain Trigget for?"

"Just this," replied Carrados after a moment's thought. "The gas-bracket—it has a mantle attachment on?"

"Oh no, Mr. Carrados," confided the old dog with the affectation of imparting rather valuable information, "not a mantle on. Oh, certainly no mantle. Indeed—indeed, not a mantle at all."

Mr. Carlyle looked at his friend curiously. It was half evident that something might have miscarried. Furthermore, it was obvious that the warmth of the room and the stress of emotion were beginning to have a disastrous effect on the level of Mr. Trigget's ideas and speech.

"A globe?" suggested Carrados.

"A globe? No sir, not even a globe, in the strict sense of the word. No globe, that is to say, Mr. Carrados. In fact nothing like a globe."

"What is there, then?" demanded the blind man without any break in his unruffled patience. "There may be another way—but surely—surely there must be some attachment?"

"No," said Mr. Trigget with precision, "no attachment at all; nothing at all; nothing whatsoever. Just the ordinary or common or penny plain gas-jet, and above it the whatyoumaycallit thingamabob."

"The shade—gas consumer—of course!" exclaimed Carrados. "That is it."

"The tin thingamabob," insisted Mr. Trigget with slow dignity. "Call it what you will. Its purpose is self-evident. It acts as a dispirator—a distributor, that is to say——"

"Louis," struck in Carrados joyously, "are you good for settling it to-night?"

"Certainly, my dear fellow, if you can really give the time."

"Good; it's years since I last tackled a ghost. What about——?" His look indicated the other member of the council.

"Would he be of any assistance?"

"Perhaps—then."

"What time?"

"Say eleven-thirty."

"Trigget," rapped out his employer sharply, "meet us at the corner of Middlewood and Enderby Roads at half-past eleven sharp tonight. If you can't manage it I shall not require your services again."

"Certainly, sir; I shall not fail to be punctual," replied Trigget without a tremor. The appearance of an almost incredible sobriety had possessed him in the face of warning, and both in speech and manner he was again exactly the man as he had entered the room. "I regard it as a great honour, Mr. Carrados, to be associated with you in this business, sir."

"In the meanwhile," remarked Carrados, "if you find the time hang heavy on your hands you might look up the subject of 'platinum black.' It may be the new tip you want."

"Certainly, sir. But do you mind giving me a hint as to what 'platinum black' is?"

"It is a chemical that has the remarkable property of igniting hydrogen or coal gas by mere contact," replied Carrados. "Think how useful that may be if you haven't got a match!"

To mark the happy occasion Mr. Carlyle had insisted on taking his friend off to witness a popular musical comedy. Carrados had a few preparations to make, a few accessories to procure for the night's work, but the whole business had come within the compass of an hour and the theatre spanned the interval between dinner at the Palm Tree and the time when they left the car at the appointed meeting-place. Mr. Trigget was already there, in an irreproachable state of normal dejection. Parkinson accompanied the party, bringing with him the baggage of the expedition.

"Anything going on, Trigget?" inquired Mr. Carlyle.

"I've made a turn round the place, sir, and the light was on," was the reply. "I didn't go up for fear of disturbing the conditions before you saw them. That was about ten minutes ago. Are you going into the yard to look again? I have all the keys, of course."

"Do we, Max?" queried Mr. Carlyle.

"Mr. Trigget might. We need not all go. He can catch us up again."

He caught them up again before they had reached the outer door.

"It's still on, sir," he reported.

"Do we use any special caution, Max?" asked Carlyle.

"Oh no. Just as though we were friends of the ghost, calling in the ordinary way."

Trigget, who retained the keys, preceded the party up the stairs till the top was reached. He stood a moment at the door of No. 11 examining, by the light of the electric lamp he carried, his private marks there and pointing out to the others in a whisper that they had not been tampered with. All at once a most dismal wail, lingering, piercing and ending in something like a sob that died away because the life that gave it utterance had died with it, drawled forebodingly through the echoing emptiness of the deserted flat. Trigget had just snapped off his light and in the darkness a startled exclamation sprang from Mr. Carlyle's lips.

"It's all right, sir," said the little man, with a private satisfaction that he had the diplomacy to conceal. "Bit creepy, isn't it? especially when you hear it by yourself up here for the first time. It's only the end of the bath-water running out."

He had opened the door and was conducting them to the room at the end of the passage. A faint aurora had been visible from that direction when they first entered the hall, but it was cut off before they could identify its source.

"That's what happens," muttered Trigget.

He threw open the bedroom door without waiting to examine his marks there and they crowded into the tiny chamber. Under the beams of the lamps they carried it was brilliantly though erratically illuminated. All turned towards the central object of their quest, a tarnished gas-bracket of the plainest description. A few inches above it hung the metal disc that Trigget had alluded to, for the ceiling was low and at that point it was brought even nearer to the gas by corresponding with the slant of the roof outside.

With the prescience so habitual with him that it had ceased to cause remark among his associates Carrados walked straight to the gas-bracket and touched the burner.

"Still warm," he remarked. "And so are we getting now. A thoroughly material ghost, you perceive, Louis."

"But still turned off, don't you see, Mr. Carrados, sir," put in Trigget eagerly. "And yet no one's passed out."

"Still turned off—and still turned on," commented the blind man.

"What do you mean, Max?"

"The small screwdriver, Parkinson," requested Carrados.

"Well, upon my word!" dropped Mr. Carlyle expressively. For in no longer time than it takes to record the fact Max Carrados had removed a screw and then knocked out the tap. He held it up towards them and they all at once saw that so much of the metal had been filed away that the gas passed through no matter how the tap stood. "How on earth did you know of that?"

"Because it wasn't practicable to do the thing in any other way. Now unhook the shade, Parkinson—carefully."

The warning was not altogether unnecessary, for the man had to stand on tiptoes before he could comply. Carrados received the dingy metal cone and lightly touched its inner surface.

"Ah, here, at the apex, to be sure," he remarked. "The gas is bound to get there. And there, Louis, you have an ever-lit and yet a truly 'safety' match—so far as gas is concerned. You can buy the thing for a shilling, I believe."

Mr. Carlyle was examining the tiny apparatus with interest. So small that it might have passed for the mummy of a midget hanging from a cobweb, it appeared to consist of an insignificant black pellet and an inch of the finest wire.

"Um, I've never heard of it. And this will really light the gas?"

"As often as you like. That is the whole bag of tricks."

Mr. Carlyle turned a censorious eye upon his lieutenant, but Trigget was equal to the occasion and met it without embarrassment.

"I hadn't heard of it either, sir," he remarked conversationally. "Gracious, what won't they be getting out next, Mr. Carlyle!"

"Now for the mystery of the water." Carrados was finding his way to the bathroom and they followed him down the passage and across the hall. "In its way I think that this is really more ingenious than the gas, for, as Mr. Trigget has proved for us, the water does not come from the cistern. The taps, you perceive, are absolutely dry."

"It is forced up?" suggested Mr. Carlyle, nodding towards the outlet.

"That is the obvious alternative. We will test it presently." The blind man was down on his hands and knees following the lines of the different pipes. "Two degrees more cold are not conclusive, because in any case the water had gone out that way. Mr. Trigget, you know the ropes, will you be so obliging as to go up to the cistern and turn the water on."

"I shall need a ladder, sir."

"Parkinson."

"We have a folding ladder out here," said Parkinson, touching Mr. Trigget's arm.

"One moment," interposed Carrados, rising from his investigation among the pipes; "this requires some care. I want you to do it without making a sound or showing a light, if that is possible. Parkinson will help you. Wait until you hear us raising a diversion at the other end of the flat. Come, Louis."

The diversion took the form of tapping the wall and skirting-board in the other haunted room. When Trigget presented himself to report that the water was now on Carrados put him to continue the singular exercise with Mr. Carlyle while he himself slipped back to the bathroom.

"The pump, Parkinson," he commanded in a brisk whisper to his man, who was waiting in the hall.

The appliance was not unlike a powerful tyre pump with some modifications. One tube from it was quickly fitted to the outlet pipe of the bath, another trailed a loose end into the bath itself, ready to take up the water. There were a few other details, the work of moments. Then Carrados turned on the tap, silencing the inflow by the attachment of a short length of rubber tube. When the water had risen a few inches he slipped off to the other room, told his rather mystified confederates there that he wanted a little more noise and bustle put into their performance, and was back again in the bathroom.

"Now, Parkinson," he directed, and turned off the tap. There was about a foot of water in the bath.

Parkinson stood on the broad base of the pump and tried to drive down the handle. It scarcely moved.

"Harder," urged Carrados, interpreting every detail of sound with perfect accuracy.

Parkinson set his teeth and lunged again. Again he seemed to come up against a solid wall of resistance.

"Keep trying; something must give," said his master encouragingly. "Here, let me——" He threw his weight into the balance and for a moment they hung like a group poised before action. Then, somewhere, something did give and the sheathing plunger "drew."

"Now like blazes till the bath is empty. Then you can tell the others to stop hammering." Parkinson, looking round to acquiesce, found himself alone, for with silent step and quickened senses

Carrados was already passing down the dark flights of the broad stone stairway.

It was perhaps three minutes later when an excited gentleman in the state of disrobement that is tacitly regarded as falling upon the *punctum coecum* in times of fire, flood and nocturnal emergency shot out of the door of No. 7 and bounding up the intervening flights of steps pounded with the knocker on the door of No. 9. As someone did not appear with the instantaneity of a jack-in-the-box, he proceeded to repeat the summons, interspersing it with an occasional "I say!" shouted through the letter-box.

The light above the door made it unconvincing to affect that no one was at home. The gentleman at the door trumpeted the fact through his channel of communication and demanded instant attention. So immersed was he with his own grievance, in fact, that he failed to notice the approach of someone on the other side, and the sudden opening of the door, when it did take place, surprised him on his knees at his neighbour's doorstep, a large and consequential-looking personage as revealed in the light from the hall, wearing the silk hat that he had instinctively snatched up, but with his braces hanging down.

"Mr. Tupworthy of No. 7, isn't it?" quickly interposed the new man before his visitor could speak. "But why this—homage? Permit me to raise you, sir."

"Confound it all," snorted Mr. Tupworthy indignantly, "you're flooding my flat. The water's coming through my bathroom ceiling in bucketfuls. The plaster'll fall next. Can't you stop it? Has a pipe burst or something?"

"Something, I imagine," replied No. 9 with serene detachment. "At all events it appears to be over now."

"So I should hope," was the irate retort. "It's bad enough as it is. I shall go round to the office and complain. I'll tell you what it is, Mr. Belting: these mansions are becoming a pandemonium, sir, a veritable pandemonium."

"Capital idea; we'll go together and complain: two will be more effective," suggested Mr. Belting. "But not to-night, Mr. Tupworthy. We should not find anyone there. The office will be closed. Say to-morrow——"

"I had no intention of anything so preposterous as going there to-night. I am in no condition to go. If I don't get my feet into hot water at once I shall be laid up with a severe cold. Doubtless you haven't noticed it, but I am wet through to the skin, saturated, sir."

Mr. Belting shook his head sagely.

"Always a mistake to try to stop water coming through the ceiling," he remarked. "It will come, you know. Finds its own level and all that."

"I did not try to stop it—at least not voluntarily. A temporary emergency necessitated a slight rearrangement of our accommodation. I—I tell you this in confidence—I was sleeping in the bathroom."

At the revelation of so notable a catastrophe Mr. Belting actually seemed to stagger. Possibly his eyes filled with tears; certainly he had to turn and wipe away his emotion before he could proceed.

"Not—not right under it?" he whispered.

"I imagine so," replied Mr. Tupworthy. "I do not conceive that I could have been placed more centrally. I received the full cataract in the region of the ear. Well, if I may rely on you that it has stopped, I will terminate our interview for the present."

"Good-night," responded the still tremulous Belting. "Good-night—or good-morning, to be exact." He waited with the door open to light the first flight of stairs for Mr. Tupworthy's descent. Before the door was closed another figure stepped down quietly from the obscurity of the steps leading upwards.

"Mr. Belting, I believe?" said the stranger. "My name is Carrados. I have been looking over the flat above. Can you spare me a few minutes?"

"What, Mr. Max Carrados?"

"The same," smiled the owner of the name.

"Come in, Mr. Carrados," exclaimed Belting, not only without embarrassment, but with positive affection in his voice. "Come in by all means. I've heard of you more than once. Delighted to meet you. This way. I know—I know." He put a hand on his guest's arm and insisted on steering his course until he deposited him in an easy-chair before a fire. "This looks like being a great night. What will you have?"

Carrados put the suggestion aside and raised a corner of the situation.

"I'm afraid that I don't come altogether as a friend," he hinted.

"It's no good," replied his host. "I can't regard you in any other light after this. You heard Tupworthy? But you haven't seen the man, Mr. Carrados. I know—I've heard—but no wealth of the imagination can ever really quite reconstruct Tupworthy, the shoddy magnifico, in his immense porcine complacency, his monumental self-importance. And sleeping right underneath! Gods, but we have lived to-night! Why—why ever did you stop?"

"You associate me with this business?"

"Associate you! My dear Mr. Carrados, I give you the full glorious credit for the one entirely successful piece of low comedy humour in real life that I have ever encountered. Indeed, in a legal and pecuniary sense, I hold you absolutely responsible."

"Oh!" exclaimed Carrados, beginning to laugh quietly. Then he continued: "I think that I shall come through that all right. I shall refer you to Mr. Carlyle, the private inquiry agent, and he will doubtless pass you on to your landlord, for whom he is acting, and I imagine that he in turn will throw all the responsibility on the ingenious gentleman who has put them to so much trouble. Can you guess the result of my investigation in the flat above?"

"Guess, Mr. Carrados? I don't need to guess: I *know*. You don't suppose I thought for a moment that such transparent devices as two intercepted pipes and an automatic gas-lighter would impose on a man of intelligence? They were only contrived to mystify the credulous imagination of clerks and porters."

"You admit it, then?"

"Admit! Good gracious, of course I admit it, Mr. Carrados. What's the use of denying it?"

"Precisely. I am glad you see that. And yet you seem far from being a mere practical joker. Does your confidence extend to the length of letting me into your object?"

"Between ourselves," replied Mr. Belting, "I haven't the least objection. But I wish that you would have—say a cup of coffee. Mrs. Belting is still up, I believe. She would be charmed to have the opportunity——No? Well, just as you like. Now, my object? You must understand, Mr. Carrados, that I am a man of sufficient leisure and adequate means for the small position we maintain. But I am not unoccupied—not idle. On the contrary, I am always busy. I don't approve of any man passing his time aimlessly. I have a number of interests in life—hobbies, if you like. You should appreciate that, as you are a private criminologist. I am—among other things which don't concern us now—a private retributionist. On every side people are becoming far too careless and negligent. An era of irresponsibility has set in. Nobody troubles to keep his word, to carry out literally his undertakings. In my small way I try to set that right by showing them the logical development of their ways. I am, in fact, the sworn enemy of anything approaching sloppiness. You smile at that?"

"It is a point of view," replied Carrados. "I was wondering how the phrase at this moment would convey itself, say, to Mr. Tupworthy's ear."

Mr. Belting doubled up.

"But don't remind me of Tupworthy or I can't get on," he said. "In my method I follow the system of Herbert Spencer towards children. Of course you are familiar with his treatise on 'Education'? If a rough boy persists, after warnings, in tearing or soiling all his clothes, don't scold him for what, after all, is only a natural and healthy instinct overdone. But equally, of course, don't punish yourself by buying him other clothes. When the time comes for the children to be taken to an entertainment little Tommy cannot go with them. It would not be seemly, and he is too ashamed, to go in rags. He begins to see the force of practical logic. Very well. If a tradesman promises—promises explicitly—delivery of his goods by a certain time and he fails, he finds that he is then unable to leave them. I pay on delivery, by the way. If a man undertakes to make me an article like another—I am painstaking, Mr. Carrados: I point out at the time how exactly like I want it—and it is (as it generally is) on completion something quite different, I decline to be easy-going and to be put off with it. I take the simplest and most obvious instances; I could multiply indefinitely. It is, of course, frequently inconvenient to me, but it establishes a standard."

"I see that you are a dangerous man, Mr. Belting," remarked Carrados. "If most men were like you our national character would be undermined. People would have to behave properly."

"If most men were like me we should constitute an intolerable nuisance," replied Belting seriously. "A necessary reaction towards sloppiness would set in and find me at its head. I am always with minorities."

"And the case in point?"

"The present trouble centres round the kitchen sink. It is cracked and leaks. A trivial cause for so elaborate an outcome, you may say, but you will doubtless remember that two men quarrelling once at a spring as to who should use it first involved half Europe in a war, and the whole tragedy of *Lear* sprang from a silly business round a word. I hadn't noticed the sink when we took this flat, but the landlord had solemnly sworn to do everything that was necessary. Is a new sink necessary to replace a cracked one? Obviously. Well, you know what landlords are: possibly you are one yourself. They promise you heaven until you have signed the agreement and then they tell you to go to hell. Suggested that we'd probably broken the sink ourselves and would certainly be looked to to replace it. An excellent servant caught a cold standing in the drip and left. Was I to be driven into paying for a new sink myself? Very well, I thought, if the reasonable complaint of one tenant is nothing to you, see how you like the unreasonable complaints of fifty. The method served a useful purpose too. When Mrs. Belting heard that old tale about the tragedy at No. 11 she was terribly upset; vowed that she couldn't stay alone in here at night on any consideration.

" 'My dear,' I said, 'don't worry yourself about ghosts. I'll make as good a one as ever lived, and then when you see how it takes other people in, just remember next time you hear of another that someone's pulling the string.' And I really don't think that she'll ever be afraid of ghosts again."

"Thank you," said Carrados, rising. "Altogether I have spent a very entertaining evening, Mr. Belting. I hope your retaliatory method won't get you into serious trouble this time."

"Why should it?" demanded Belting quickly.

"Oh, well, tenants are complaining, the property is being depreciated. The landlord may think that he has legal redress against you."

"But surely I am at liberty to light the gas or use the bath in my own flat when and how I like?"

A curious look had come into Mr. Belting's smiling face; a curious note must have sounded in his voice. Carrados was warned and, being warned, guessed.

"You are a wonderful man," he said with upraised hand. "I capitulate. Tell me how it is, won't you?"

"I knew the man at 11. His tenancy isn't really up till March, but he got an appointment in the north and had to go. His two unexpired months weren't worth troubling about, so I got him to sublet the flat to me—all quite regularly—for a nominal consideration, and not to mention it."

"But he gave up the keys?"

"No. He left them in the door and the porter took them away. Very unwarrantable of him; surely I can keep my keys where I like? However, as I had another . . . Really, Mr. Carrados, you hardly imagine that unless I had an absolute right to be there I should penetrate into a flat, tamper with the gas and water, knock the place about, tramp up and down——"

"I go," said Carrados, "to get our people out in haste. Good-night."

"Good-night, Mr. Carrados. It's been a great privilege to meet you. Sorry I can't persuade you . . ."

The Tragedy at Brookbend Cottage

"Max," said Mr. Carlyle, when Parkinson had closed the door behind him, "this is Lieutenant Hollyer, whom you consented to see."

"To hear," corrected Carrados, smiling straight into the healthy and rather embarrassed face of the stranger before him. "Mr. Hollyer knows of my disability?"

"Mr. Carlyle told me," said the young man, "but, as a matter of fact, I had heard of you before, Mr. Carrados, from one of our men. It was in connection with the foundering of the *Ivan Saratov*."

Carrados wagged his head in good-humoured resignation.

"And the owners were sworn to inviolable secrecy!" he exclaimed. "Well, it is inevitable, I suppose. Not another scuttling case, Mr. Hollyer?"

"No, mine is quite a private matter," replied the lieutenant. "My sister, Mrs. Creake—but Mr. Carlyle would tell you better than I can. He knows all about it."

"No, no; Carlyle is a professional. Let me have it in the rough, Mr. Hollyer. My ears are my eyes, you know."

"Very well, sir. I can tell you what there is to tell, right enough, but I feel that when all's said and done it must sound very little to another, although it seems important to me."

"We have occasionally found trifles of significance ourselves," said Carrados encouragingly. "Don't let that deter you."

This was the essence of Lieutenant Hollyer's narrative:

"I have a sister, Millicent, who is married to a man called Creake. She is about twenty-eight now and he is at least fifteen years older. Neither my mother (who has since died) nor I cared very much about Creake. We had nothing particular against him, except, perhaps, the moderate disparity of age, but none of us appeared to have anything in common. He was a dark, taciturn man, and his moody silence froze up conversation. As a result, of course, we didn't see much of each other."

"This, you must understand, was four or five years ago, Max," interposed Mr. Carlyle officiously.

Carrados maintained an uncompromising silence. Mr. Carlyle blew his nose and contrived to impart a hurt significance into the operation. Then Lieutenant Hollyer continued:

"Millicent married Creake after a very short engagement. It was a frightfully subdued wedding—more like a funeral to me. The man professed to have no relations and apparently he had scarcely any friends or business acquaintances. He was an agent for something or other and had an office off Holborn. I suppose he made a living out of it then, although we knew practically nothing of his private affairs, but I gather that it has been going down since, and I suspect that for the past few years they have been getting along almost entirely on Millicent's little income. You would like the particulars of that?"

"Please," assented Carrados.

"When our father died about seven years ago, he left three thousand pounds. It was invested in Canadian stock and brought in a little over a hundred a year. By his will my mother was to have the income of that for life and on her death it was to pass to Millicent, subject to the payment of a lump sum of five hundred pounds to me. But my father privately suggested to me that if I should have no particular use for the money at the time, he would propose my letting Millicent have the income of it until I did want it, as she would not be particularly well off. You see, Mr. Carrados, a great deal more had been spent on my education and advancement than on her; I had my pay, and, of course, I could look out for myself better than a girl could."

"Quite so," agreed Carrados.

"Therefore I did nothing about that," continued the lieutenant. "Three years ago I was over again but I did not see much of them. They were living in lodgings. That was the only time since the marriage that I have seen them until last week. In the meanwhile our mother had died and Millicent had been receiving her income. She wrote me several letters at the time. Otherwise we did not correspond much, but about a year ago she sent me their new address— Brookbend Cottage, Mulling Common—a house that they had taken. When I got two months' leave I invited myself there as a matter of course, fully expecting to stay most of my time with them, but I made an excuse to get away after a week. The place was dismal and unendurable, the whole life and atmosphere indescribably depressing." He looked round with an instinct of caution, leaned forward earnestly, and dropped his voice. "Mr. Carrados, it is my absolute conviction that Creake is only waiting for a favourable opportunity to murder Millicent."

"Go on," said Carrados quietly. "A week of the depressing surroundings of Brookbend Cottage would not alone convince you of that, Mr. Hollyer."

"I am not so sure," declared Hollyer doubtfully. "There was a feeling of suspicion and—before me—polite hatred that would have gone a good way towards it. All the same there *was* something more definite. Millicent told me this the day after I went there. There is no doubt that a few months ago Creake deliberately planned to poison her with some weed-killer. She told me the circumstances in a rather distressed moment, but afterwards she refused to speak of it again—even weakly denied it—and, as a matter of fact, it was with the greatest of difficulty that I could get her at any time to talk about her husband or his affairs. The gist of it was that she had the strongest suspicion that Creake doctored a bottle of stout which he expected she would drink for her supper when she was alone. The weed-killer, properly labelled, but also in a beer bottle, was kept with other miscellaneous liquids in the same cupboard as the beer but on a high shelf. When he found that it had miscarried he poured away the mixture, washed out the bottle and put in the dregs from another. There is no doubt in my mind that if he had come back and found Millicent dead or dying he would have contrived it to appear that she had made a mistake in the dark and drunk some of the poison before she found out."

"Yes," assented Carrados. "The open way; the safe way."

"You must understand that they live in a very small style, Mr. Carrados, and Millicent is almost entirely in the man's power. The only servant they have is a woman who comes in for a few hours every day. The house is lonely and secluded. Creake is sometimes away for days and nights at a time, and Millicent, either through pride or indifference, seems to have dropped off all her old friends and to have made no others. He might poison her, bury the body in the garden, and be a thousand miles away before anyone began even to inquire about her. What am I to do, Mr. Carrados?"

"He is less likely to try poison than some other means now," pondered Carrados. "That having failed, his wife will always be on her guard. He may know, or at least suspect, that others know. No. . . . The common-sense precaution would be for your sister to leave the man, Mr. Hollyer. She will not?"

"No," admitted Hollyer, "she will not. I at once urged that." The young man struggled with some hesitation for a moment and then blurted out: "The fact is, Mr. Carrados, I don't understand Millicent. She is not the girl she was. She hates Creake and treats him with a silent contempt that eats into their lives like acid, and yet she is so jealous of him that she will let nothing short of death part them. It is a horrible life they lead. I stood it for a week and I must say, much as I dislike my brother-in-law, that he has some-thing to put up with. If only he got into a passion like a man and killed her it wouldn't be altogether incomprehensible."

"That does not concern us," said Carrados. "In a game of this kind one has to take sides and we have taken ours. It remains for us to see that our side wins. You mentioned jealousy, Mr. Hollyer. Have you any idea whether Mrs. Creake has real ground for it?"

"I should have told you that," replied Lieutenant Hollyer. "I happened to strike up with a newspaper man whose office is in the same block as Creake's. When I mentioned the name he grinned. 'Creake,' he said, 'oh, he's the man with the romantic typist, isn't he?' 'Well, he's my brother-in-law,' I replied. 'What about the typist?' Then the chap shut up like a knife. 'No, no,' he said, 'I didn't know he was married. I don't want to get mixed up in any-thing of that sort. I only said that he had a typist. Well, what of that? So have we; so has everyone.' There was nothing more to be got out of him, but the remark and the grin meant—well, about as usual, Mr. Carrados."

Carrados turned to his friend.

"I suppose you know all about the typist by now, Louis?"

"We have had her under efficient observation, Max," replied Mr. Carlyle with severe dignity.

"Is she unmarried?"

"Yes; so far as ordinary repute goes, she is."

"That is all that is essential for the moment. Mr. Hollyer opens up three excellent reasons why this man might wish to dispose of his wife. If we accept the suggestion of poisoning—though we have only a jealous woman's suspicion for it—we add to the wish the determination. Well, we will go forward on that. Have you got a photograph of Mr. Creake?"

The lieutenant took out his pocket-book.

"Mr. Carlyle asked me for one. Here is the best I could get."

Carrados rang the bell.

"This, Parkinson," he said, when the man appeared, "is a photograph of a Mr.—— What first name, by the way?"

"Austin," put in Hollyer, who was following everything with a boyish mixture of excitement and subdued importance.

"—of a Mr. Austin Creake. I may require you to recognize him."

Parkinson glanced at the print and returned it to his master's hand.

"May I inquire if it is a recent photograph of the gentleman, sir?" he asked.

"About six years ago," said the lieutenant, taking in this new actor in the drama with frank curiosity. "But he is very little changed."

"Thank you, sir. I will endeavour to remember Mr. Creake, sir."

Lieutenant Hollyer stood up as Parkinson left the room. The interview seemed to be at an end.

"Oh, there's one other matter," he remarked. "I am afraid that I did rather an unfortunate thing while I was at Brookbend. It seemed to me that as all Millicent's money would probably pass into Creake's hands sooner or later I might as well have my five hundred pounds, if only to help her with afterwards. So I broached the subject and said that I should like to have it now as I had an opportunity for investing."

"And you think?"

"It may possibly influence Creake to act sooner than he otherwise might have done. He may have got possession of the principal even and find it very awkward to replace it."

"So much the better. If your sister is going to be murdered it may as well be done next week as next year so far as I am concerned. Excuse my brutality, Mr. Hollyer, but this is simply a case to me and I regard it strategically. Now Mr. Carlyle's organization can look after Mrs. Creake for a few weeks, but it cannot look after her for ever. By increasing the immediate risk we diminish the permanent risk."

"I see," agreed Hollyer. "I'm awfully uneasy but I'm entirely in your hands."

"Then we will give Mr. Creake every inducement and every opportunity to get to work. Where are you staying now?"

"Just now with some friends at St. Albans."

"That is too far." The inscrutable eyes retained their tranquil depth but a new quality of quickening interest in the voice made Mr. Carlyle forget the weight and burden of his ruffled dignity. "Give me a few minutes, please. The cigarettes are behind you, Mr. Hollyer." The blind man walked to the window and seemed to look out over the cypress-shaded lawn. The lieutenant lit a cigarette and Mr. Carlyle picked up *Punch*. Then Carrados turned round again.

"You are prepared to put your own arrangements aside?" he demanded of his visitor.

"Certainly."

"Very well. I want you to go down now—straight from here—to Brookbend Cottage. Tell your sister that your leave is unexpectedly cut short and that you sail to-morrow."

"The *Martian*?"

"No, no; the *Martian* doesn't sail. Look up the movements on your way there and pick out a boat that does. Say you are transferred. Add that you expect to be away only two or three months and that you really want the five hundred pounds by the time of your return. Don't stay in the house long, please."

"I understand, sir."

"St. Albans is too far. Make your excuse and get away from there to-day. Put up somewhere in town, where you will be in reach of the telephone. Let Mr. Carlyle and myself know where you are. Keep out of Creake's way. I don't want actually to tie you down to the house, but we may require your services. We will let you know at the first sign of anything doing and if there is nothing to be done we must release you."

"I don't mind that. Is there nothing more that I can do now?"

"Nothing. In going to Mr. Carlyle you have done the best thing possible; you have put your sister into the care of the shrewdest man in London." Whereat the object of this quite unexpected eulogy found himself becoming covered with modest confusion.

"Well, Max?" remarked Mr. Carlyle tentatively when they were alone.

"Well, Louis?"

"Of course it wasn't worth while rubbing it in before young Hollyer, but, as a matter of fact, every single man carries the life of any other man—only one, mind you—in his hands, do what you will."

"Provided he doesn't bungle," acquiesced Carrados.

"Quite so."

"And also that he is absolutely reckless of the consequences."

"Of course."

"Two rather large provisos. Creake is obviously susceptible to both. Have you seen him?"

"No. As I told you, I put a man on to report his habits in town. Then, two days ago, as the case seemed to promise some interest—for he certainly is deeply involved with the typist, Max, and the thing might take a sensational turn at any time—I went down to Mulling Common myself. Although the house is lonely it is on the electric tram route. You know the sort of market garden rurality that about a dozen miles out of London offers—alternate bricks and cabbages. It was easy enough to get to know about Creake locally. He mixes with no one there, goes into town at irregular times but generally every day, and is reputed to be devilish hard to get money out of. Finally I made the acquaintance of an old fellow who used to do a day's gardening at Brookbend occasionally. He has a cottage and a garden of his own with a greenhouse, and the business cost me the price of a pound of tomatoes."

"Was it—a profitable investment?"

"As tomatoes, yes; as information, no. The old fellow had the fatal disadvantage from our point of view of labouring under a grievance. A few weeks ago Creake told him that he would not require him again as he was going to do his own gardening in future."

"That is something, Louis."

"If only Creake was going to poison his wife with hyoscyamine and bury her, instead of blowing her up with a dynamite cartridge and claiming that it came in among the coal."

"True, true. Still——"

"However, the chatty old soul had a simple explanation for everything that Creake did. Creake was mad. He had even seen him flying a kite in his garden where it was found to get wrecked among the trees. A lad of ten would have known better, he declared. And certainly the kite did get wrecked, for I saw it hanging over the road myself. But that a sane man should spend his time 'playing with a toy' was beyond him."

"A good many men have been flying kites of various kinds lately," said Carrados. "Is he interested in aviation?"

"I dare say. He appears to have some knowledge of scientific subjects. Now what do you want me to do, Max?"

"Will you do it?"

"Implicitly—subject to the usual reservations."

"Keep your man on Creake in town and let me have his reports after you have seen them. Lunch with me here now. 'Phone up to your office that you are detained on unpleasant business and then give the deserving Parkinson an afternoon off by looking after me while we take a motor run round Mulling Common. If we have time we might go on to Brighton, feed at the 'Ship,' and come back in the cool."

"Amiable and thrice lucky mortal," sighed Mr. Carlyle, his glance wandering round the room.

But, as it happened, Brighton did not figure in that day's itinerary. It had been Carrados's intention merely to pass Brookbend Cottage on this occasion, relying on his highly developed faculties, aided by Mr. Carlyle's description, to inform him of the surroundings. A hundred yards before they reached the house he had given an order to his chauffeur to drop into the lowest speed and they were leisurely drawing past when a discovery by Mr. Carlyle modified their plans.

"By Jupiter!" that gentleman suddenly exclaimed, "there's a board up, Max. The place is to be let."

Carrados picked up the tube again. A couple of sentences passed and the car stopped by the roadside, a score of paces past the limit of the garden. Mr. Carlyle took out his notebook and wrote down the address of a firm of house agents.

"You might raise the bonnet and have a look at the engines, Harris," said Carrados. "We want to be occupied here for a few minutes."

"This is sudden; Hollyer knew nothing of their leaving," remarked Mr. Carlyle.

"Probably not for three months yet. All the same, Louis, we will go on to the agents and get a card to view whether we use it to-day or not."

A thick hedge, in its summer dress effectively screening the house beyond from public view, lay between the garden and the road. Above the hedge showed an occasional shrub; at the corner nearest to the car a chestnut flourished. The wooden gate, once white, which they had passed, was grimed and rickety. The road itself was still the unpretentious country lane that the advent of the electric car had found it. When Carrados had taken in these details there seemed little else to notice. He was on the point of giving Harris the order to go on when his ear caught a trivial sound.

"Someone is coming out of the house, Louis," he warned his friend. "It may be Hollyer, but he ought to have gone by this time."

"I don't hear anyone," replied the other, but as he spoke a door banged noisily and Mr. Carlyle slipped into another seat and ensconced himself behind a copy of *The Globe*.

"Creake himself," he whispered across the car, as a man appeared at the gate. "Hollyer was right; he is hardly changed. Waiting for a car, I suppose."

But a car very soon swung past them from the direction in which Mr. Creake was looking and it did not interest him. For a minute or two longer he continued to look expectantly along the road. Then he walked slowly up the drive back to the house.

"We will give him five or ten minutes," decided Carrados. "Harris is behaving very naturally."

Before even the shorter period had run out they were repaid. A telegraph-boy cycled leisurely along the road, and, leaving his machine at the gate, went up to the cottage. Evidently there was no reply, for in less than a minute he was trundling past them back again. Round the bend an approaching tram clanged its bell noisily, and, quickened by the warning sound, Mr. Creake again appeared, this time with a small portmanteau in his hand. With a backward glance he hurried on towards the next stopping-place, and, boarding the car as it slackened down, he was carried out of their knowledge.

"Very convenient of Mr. Creake," remarked Carrados, with quiet satisfaction. "We will now get the order and go over the house in his absence. It might be useful to have a look at the wire as well."

"It might, Max," acquiesced Mr. Carlyle a little dryly. "But if it is, as it probably is, in Creake's pocket, how do you propose to get it?"

"By going to the post office, Louis."

"Quite so. Have you ever tried to see a copy of a telegram addressed to someone else?"

"I don't think I have ever had occasion yet," admitted Carrados. "Have you?"

"In one or two cases I have perhaps been an accessory to the act. It is generally a matter either of extreme delicacy or considerable expenditure."

"Then for Hollyer's sake we will hope for the former here." And Mr. Carlyle smiled darkly and hinted that he was content to wait for a friendly revenge.

A little later, having left the car at the beginning of the straggling High Street, the two men called at the village post office. They had already visited the house agent and obtained an order to view Brookbend Cottage, declining with some difficulty the clerk's persistent offer to accompany them. The reason was soon forthcoming. "As a matter of fact," explained the young man, "the present tenant is under *our* notice to leave."

"Unsatisfactory, eh?" said Carrados encouragingly.

"He's a corker," admitted the clerk, responding to the friendly tone. "Fifteen months and not a doit of rent have we had. That's why I should have liked——"

"We will make every allowance," replied Carrados.

The post office occupied one side of a stationer's shop. It was not without some inward trepidation that Mr. Carlyle found himself committed to the adventure. Carrados, on the other hand, was the personification of bland unconcern.

"You have just sent a telegram to Brookbend Cottage," he said to the young lady behind the brasswork lattice. "We think it may have come inaccurately and should like a repeat." He took out his purse. "What is the fee?"

The request was evidently not a common one. "Oh," said the girl uncertainly, "wait a minute, please." She turned to a pile of telegram duplicates behind the desk and ran a doubtful finger along the upper sheets. "I think this is all right. You want it repeated?"

"Please." Just a tinge of questioning surprise gave point to the courteous tone.

"It will be fourpence. If there is an error the amount will be refunded."

Carrados put down his coin and received his change.

"Will it take long?" he inquired carelessly, as he pulled on his glove.

"You will most likely get it within a quarter of an hour," she replied.

"Now you've done it," commented Mr. Carlyle as they walked back to their car. "How do you propose to get that telegram, Max?"

"Ask for it," was the laconic explanation.

And, stripping the artifice of any elaboration, he simply asked for it and got it. The car, posted at a convenient bend in the road, gave him a warning note as the telegraph-boy approached. Then Carrados took up a convincing attitude with his hand on the gate while Mr. Carlyle lent himself to the semblance of a departing friend. That was the inevitable impression when the boy rode up.

"Creake, Brookbend Cottage?" inquired Carrados, holding out his hand, and without a second thought the boy gave him the envelope and rode away on the assurance that there would be no reply.

"Some day, my friend," remarked Mr. Carlyle, looking nervously toward the unseen house, "your ingenuity will get you into a tight corner."

"Then my ingenuity must get me out again," was the retort. "Let us have our 'view' now. The telegram can wait."

An untidy workwoman took their order and left them standing at the door. Presently a lady whom they both knew to be Mrs. Creake appeared.

"You wish to see over the house?" she said, in a voice that was utterly devoid of any interest. Then, without waiting for a reply, she turned to the nearest door and threw it open.

"This is the drawing-room," she said, standing aside.

They walked into a sparsely furnished, damp-smelling room and made a pretence of looking round, while Mrs. Creake remained silent and aloof.

"The dining-room," she continued, crossing the narrow hall and opening another door.

Mr. Carlyle ventured a genial commonplace in the hope of inducing conversation. The result was not encouraging. Doubtless they would have gone through the house under the same frigid guidance had not Carrados been at fault in a way that Mr. Carlyle had never known him fail before. In crossing the hall he stumbled over a mat and almost fell.

"Pardon my clumsiness," he said to the lady. "I am, unfortunately, quite blind. But," he added, with a smile, to turn off the mishap, "even a blind man must have a house."

The man who had eyes was surprised to see a flood of colour rush into Mrs. Creake's face.

"Blind!" she exclaimed, "oh, I beg your pardon. Why did you not tell me? You might have fallen."

"I generally manage fairly well," he replied. "But, of course, in a strange house——"

She put her hand on his arm very lightly.

"You must let me guide you, just a little," she said.

The house, without being large, was full of passages and inconvenient turnings. Carrados asked an occasional question and found Mrs. Creake quite amiable without effusion. Mr. Carlyle followed them from room to room in the hope, though scarcely the expectation, of learning something that might be useful.

"This is the last one. It is the largest bedroom," said their guide. Only two of the upper rooms were fully furnished and Mr. Carlyle at once saw, as Carrados knew without seeing, that this was the one which the Creakes occupied.

"A very pleasant outlook," declared Mr. Carlyle.

"Oh, I suppose so," admitted the lady vaguely. The room, in fact, looked over the leafy garden and the road beyond. It had a French window opening on to a small balcony, and to this, under the strange influence that always attracted him to light, Carrados walked.

"I expect that there is a certain amount of repair needed?" he said, after standing there a moment.

"I am afraid there would be," she confessed.

"I ask because there is a sheet of metal on the floor here," he continued. "Now that, in an old house, spells dry rot to the wary observer."

"My husband said that the rain, which comes in a little under the window, was rotting the boards there," she replied. "He put that down recently. I had not noticed anything myself."

It was the first time she had mentioned her husband; Mr. Carlyle pricked up his ears.

"Ah, that is a less serious matter," said Carrados. "May I step out on to the balcony?"

"Oh yes, if you like to." Then, as he appeared to be fumbling at the catch, "Let me open it for you."

But the window was already open, and Carrados, facing the various points of the compass, took in the bearings.

"A sunny, sheltered corner," he remarked. "An ideal spot for a deck-chair and a book."

She shrugged her shoulders half contemptuously.

"I dare say," she replied, "but I never use it."

"Sometimes, surely," he persisted mildly. "It would be my favourite retreat. But then——"

"I was going to say that I had never even been out on it, but that would not be quite true. It has two uses for me, both equally romantic; I occasionally shake a duster from it, and when my husband returns late without his latchkey he wakes me up and I come out here and drop him mine."

Further revelation of Mr. Creake's nocturnal habits was cut off, greatly to Mr. Carlyle's annoyance, by a cough of unmistakable significance from the foot of the stairs. They had heard a trade cart drive up to the gate, a knock at the door, and the heavy-footed woman tramp along the hall.

"Excuse me a minute, please," said Mrs. Creake.

"Louis," said Carrados, in a sharp whisper, the moment they were alone, "stand against the door."

With extreme plausibility Mr. Carlyle began to admire a picture so situated that while he was there it was impossible to open the door more than a few inches. From that position he observed his confederate go through the curious procedure of kneeling down on the bedroom floor and for a full minute pressing his ear to the sheet of metal that had already engaged his attention. Then he rose to his feet, nodded, dusted his trousers, and Mr. Carlyle moved to a less equivocal position.

"What a beautiful rose-tree grows up your balcony," remarked Carrados, stepping into the room as Mrs. Creake returned. "I suppose you are very fond of gardening?"

"I detest it," she replied.

"But this *Gloire*, so carefully trained——?"

"Is it?" she replied. "I think my husband was nailing it up recently." By some strange fatality Carrados's most aimless remarks seemed to involve the absent Mr. Creake. "Do you care to see the garden?"

The garden proved to be extensive and neglected. Behind the house was chiefly orchard. In front, some semblance of order had been kept up; here it was lawn and shrubbery, and the drive they had walked along. Two things interested Carrados: the soil at the foot of the balcony, which he declared on examination to be particularly suitable for roses, and the fine chestnut-tree in the corner by the road.

As they walked back to the car Mr. Carlyle lamented that they had learned so little of Creake's movements.

"Perhaps the telegram will tell us something," suggested Carrados. "Read it, Louis."

Mr. Carlyle cut open the envelope, glanced at the enclosure, and in spite of his disappointment could not restrain a chuckle.

"My poor Max," he explained, "you have put yourself to an amount of ingenious trouble for nothing. Creake is evidently taking a few days' holiday and prudently availed himself of the Meteorological Office forecast before going. Listen: '*Immediate prospect for London warm and settled. Further outlook cooler but fine.*' Well, well; I did get a pound of tomatoes for *my* fourpence."

"You certainly scored there, Louis," admitted Carrados, with humorous appreciation. "I wonder," he added speculatively, "whether it is Creake's peculiar taste usually to spend his week-end holiday in London."

"Eh?" exclaimed Mr. Carlyle, looking at the words again, "by gad, that's rum, Max. They go to Weston-super-Mare. Why on earth should he want to know about London?"

"I can make a guess, but before we are satisfied I must come here again. Take another look at that kite, Louis. Are there a few yards of string hanging loose from it?"

"Yes, there are."

"Rather thick string—unusually thick for the purpose?"

"Yes, but how do you know?"

As they drove home again Carrados explained, and Mr. Carlyle sat aghast, saying incredulously: "Good God, Max, is it possible?"

An hour later he was satisfied that it was possible. In reply to his inquiry someone in his office telephoned him the information that "they" had left Paddington by the four-thirty for Weston.

It was more than a week after his introduction to Carrados that Lieutenant Hollyer had a summons to present himself at The Turrets again. He found Mr. Carlyle already there and the two friends were awaiting his arrival.

"I stayed in all day after hearing from you this morning, Mr. Carrados," he said, shaking hands. "When I got your second message I was all ready to walk straight out of the house. That's how I did it in the time. I hope everything is all right?"

"Excellent," replied Carrados. "You'd better have something before we start. We probably have a long and perhaps an exciting night before us."

"And certainly a wet one," assented the lieutenant. "It was thundering over Mulling way as I came along."

"That is why you are here," said his host. "We are waiting for a certain message before we start, and in the meantime you may as well understand what we expect to happen. As you saw, there is a thunderstorm coming on. The Meteorological Office morning forecast predicted it for the whole of London if the conditions remained. That is why I kept you in readiness. Within an hour it is now inevitable that we shall experience a deluge. Here and there damage will be done to trees and buildings; here and there a person will probably be struck and killed."

"Yes."

"It is Mr. Creake's intention that his wife should be among the victims."

"I don't exactly follow," said Hollyer, looking from one man to the other. "I quite admit that Creake would be immensely relieved if such a thing did happen, but the chance is surely an absurdly remote one."

"Yet unless we intervene it is precisely what a coroner's jury will decide has happened. Do you know whether your brother-in-law has any practical knowledge of electricity, Mr. Hollyer?"

"I cannot say. He was so reserved, and we really knew so little of him——"

"Yet in 1896 an Austin Creake contributed an article on 'Alternating Currents' to the American *Scientific World*. That would argue a fairly intimate acquaintanceship."

"But do you mean that he is going to direct a flash of lightning?"

"Only into the minds of the doctor who conducts the postmortem, and the coroner. This storm, the opportunity for which he has been waiting for weeks, is merely the cloak to his act. The weapon which he has planned to use—scarcely less powerful than lightning but much more tractable—is the high voltage current of electricity that flows along the tram wire at his gate."

"Oh!" exclaimed Lieutenant Hollyer, as the sudden revelation struck him.

"Some time between eleven o'clock to-night—about the hour when your sister goes to bed—and one thirty in the morning—the time up to which he can rely on the current—Creake will throw a stone up at the balcony window. Most of his preparation has long been made; it only remains for him to connect up a short length to the window handle and a longer one at the other end to tap the live wire. That done, he will wake his wife in the way I have said. The moment she moves the catch of the window—and he has carefully filed its parts to ensure perfect contact—she will be electrocuted as effectually as if she sat in the executioner's chair in Sing Sing prison."

"But what are we doing here!" exclaimed Hollyer, starting to his feet, pale and horrified. "It is past ten now and anything may happen."

"Quite natural, Mr. Hollyer," said Carrados reassuringly, "but you need have no anxiety. Creake is being watched, the house is being watched, and your sister is as safe as if she slept to-night in Windsor Castle. Be assured that whatever happens he will not be allowed to complete his scheme; but it is desirable to let him implicate himself to the fullest limit. Your brother-in-law, Mr. Hollyer, is a man with a peculiar capacity for taking pains."

"He is a damned cold-blooded scoundrel!" exclaimed the young officer fiercely. "When I think of Millicent five years ago——"

"Well, for that matter, an enlightened nation has decided that electrocution is the most humane way of removing its superfluous citizens," suggested Carrados mildly. "He is certainly an ingenious-minded gentleman. It is his misfortune that in Mr. Carlyle he was fated to be opposed by an even subtler brain——"

"No, no! Really, Max!" protested the embarrassed gentleman.

"Mr. Hollyer will be able to judge for himself when I tell him that it was Mr. Carlyle who first drew attention to the significance of the abandoned kite," insisted Carrados firmly. "Then, of course, its object became plain to me—as indeed to anyone. For ten minutes, perhaps, a wire must be carried from the overhead line to the chestnut-tree. Creake has everything in his favour, but it is just within possibility that the driver of an inopportune train might notice the appendage. What of that? Why, for more than a week he has seen a derelict kite with its yards of trailing string hanging in the tree. A very calculating mind, Mr. Hollyer. It would be interesting to know what line of action Mr. Creake has mapped out for himself afterwards. I expect he has half-a-dozen artistic little touches up his sleeve. Possibly he would merely singe his wife's hair, burn her feet with a red-hot poker, shiver the glass of the French window, and be content with that to let well alone. You see, lightning is so varied in its effects that whatever he did or did not do would be right. He is in the impregnable position of the body showing all the symptoms of death by lightning shock and nothing else but lightning to account for it—a dilated eye, heart contracted in systole, bloodless lungs shrunk to a third the normal weight, and all the rest of it. When he has removed a few outward traces of his work Creake might quite safely 'discover' his dead wife and rush off for the nearest doctor. Or he may have decided to arrange a convincing alibi, and creep away, leaving the discovery to another. We shall never know; he will make no confession."

"I wish it was well over," admitted Hollyer, "I'm not particularly jumpy, but this gives me a touch of the creeps."

"Three more hours at the worst, lieutenant," said Carrados cheerfully. "Ah-ha, something is coming through now."

He went to the telephone and received a message from one quarter; then made another connection and talked for a few minutes with someone else.

"Everything working smoothly," he remarked between times over his shoulder. "Your sister has gone to bed, Mr. Hollyer."

Then he turned to the house telephone and distributed his orders.

"So we," he concluded, "must get up."

By the time they were ready a large closed motor car was waiting. The lieutenant thought he recognised Parkinson in the well-swathed form beside the driver, but there was no temptation to linger for a second on the steps. Already the stinging rain had lashed the drive into the semblance of a frothy estuary; all round the lightning jagged its course through the incessant tremulous glow of more distant lightning, while the thunder only ceased its muttering to turn at close quarters and crackle viciously.

"One of the few things I regret missing," remarked Carrados tranquilly; "but I hear a good deal of colour in it."

The car slushed its way down to the gate, lurched a little heavily across the dip into the road, and, steadying as it came upon the straight, began to hum contentedly along the deserted highway.

"We are not going direct?" suddenly inquired Hollyer, after they had travelled perhaps half-a-dozen miles. The night was bewildering enough but he had the sailor's gift for location.

"No; through Hunscott Green and then by a field-path to the orchard at the back," replied Carrados. "Keep a sharp look out for the man with the lantern about here, Harris," he called through the tube.

"Something flashing just ahead, sir," came the reply, and the car slowed down and stopped.

Carrados dropped the near window as a man in glistening waterproof stepped from the shelter of a lich-gate and approached.

"Inspector Beedel, sir," said the stranger, looking into the car.

"Quite right, Inspector," said Carrados. "Get in."

"I have a man with me, sir."

"We can find room for him as well."

"We are very wet."

"So shall we all be soon."

The lieutenant changed his seat and the two burly forms took places side by side. In less than five minutes the car stopped again, this time in a grassy country lane.

"Now we have to face it," announced Carrados. "The inspector will show us the way."

The car slid round and disappeared into the night, while Beedel led the party to a stile in the hedge. A couple of fields brought them to the Brookbend boundary. There a figure stood out of the black foliage, exchanged a few words with their guide and piloted them along the shadows of the orchard to the back door of the house.

"You will find a broken pane near the catch of the scullery window," said the blind man.

"Right, sir," replied the inspector. "I have it. Now who goes through?"

"Mr. Hollyer will open the door for us. I'm afraid you must take off your boots and all wet things, Lieutenant. We cannot risk a single spot inside."

They waited until the back door opened, then each one divested himself in a similar manner and passed into the kitchen, where the remains of a fire still burned. The man from the orchard gathered together the discarded garments and disappeared again.

Carrados turned to the lieutenant.

"A rather delicate job for you now, Mr. Hollyer. I want you to go up to your sister, wake her, and get her into another room with as little fuss as possible. Tell her as much as you think fit and let her understand that her very life depends on absolute stillness when she is alone. Don't be unduly hurried, but not a glimmer of a light, please."

Ten minutes passed by the measure of the battered old alarum on the dresser shelf before the young man returned.

"I've had rather a time of it," he reported, with a nervous laugh, "but I think it will be all right now. She is in the spare room."

"Then we will take our places. You and Parkinson come with me to the bedroom. Inspector, you have your own arrangements. Mr. Carlyle will be with you."

They dispersed silently about the house. Hollyer glanced apprehensively at the door of the spare room as they passed it, but within was as quiet as the grave. Their room lay at the other end of the passage.

"You may as well take your place in the bed now, Hollyer," directed Carrados when they were inside and the door closed. "Keep well down among the clothes. Creake has to get up on the balcony, you know, and he will probably peep through the window, but he dare come no farther. Then when he begins to throw up stones slip on this dressing-gown of your sister's. I'll tell you what to do after."

The next sixty minutes drew out into the longest hour that the lieutenant had ever known. Occasionally he heard a whisper pass between the two men who stood behind the window curtains, but he could see nothing. Then Carrados threw a guarded remark in his direction.

"He is in the garden now."

Something scraped slightly against the outer wall. But the night was full of wilder sounds, and in the house the furniture and the boards creaked and sprung between the yawling of the wind among the chimneys, the rattle of the thunder and the pelting of the rain. It was a time to quicken the steadiest pulse, and when the crucial moment came, when a pebble suddenly rang against the pane with a sound that the tense waiting magnified into a shivering crash, Hollyer leapt from the bed on the instant.

"Easy, easy," warned Carrados feelingly. "We will wait for another knock." He passed something across. "Here is a rubber glove. I have cut the wire but you had better put it on. Stand just for a moment at the window, move the catch so that it can blow open a little, and drop immediately. Now."

Another stone had rattled against the glass. For Hollyer to go through his part was the work merely of seconds, and with a few touches Carrados spread the dressing-gown to more effective disguise about the extended form. But an unforeseen and in the circumstances rather horrible interval followed, for Creake, in accordance with some detail of his never-revealed plan, continued to shower missile after missile against the panes until even the unimpressionable Parkinson shivered.

"The last act," whispered Carrados, a moment after the throwing had ceased. "He has gone round to the back. Keep as you are. We take cover now." He pressed behind the arras of an extemporized wardrobe, and the spirit of emptiness and desolation seemed once more to reign over the lonely house.

From half-a-dozen places of concealment ears were straining to catch the first guiding sound. He moved very stealthily, burdened, perhaps, by some strange scruple in the presence of the tragedy that he had not feared to contrive, paused for a moment at the bedroom door, then opened it very quietly, and in the fickle light read the consummation of his hopes.

"At last!" they heard the sharp whisper drawn from his relief. "At last!"

He took another step and two shadows seemed to fall upon him from behind, one on either side. With primitive instinct a cry of terror and surprise escaped him as he made a desperate movement to wrench himself free, and for a short second he almost succeeded in dragging one hand into a pocket. Then his wrists slowly came together and the handcuffs closed.

"I am Inspector Beedel," said the man on his right side. "You are charged with the attempted murder of your wife, Millicent Creake."

"You are mad," retorted the miserable creature, falling into a desperate calmness. "She has been struck by lightning."

"No, you blackguard, she hasn't," wrathfully exclaimed his brother-in-law, jumping up. "Would you like to see her?"

"I also have to warn you," continued the inspector impassively, "that anything you say may be used as evidence against you."

A startled cry from the farther end of the passage arrested their attention.

"Mr. Carrados," called Hollyer, "oh, come at once."

At the open door of the other bedroom stood the lieutenant, his eyes still turned towards something in the room beyond, a little empty bottle in his hand.

"Dead!" he exclaimed tragically, with a sob, "with this beside her. Dead just when she would have been free of the brute."

The blind man passed into the room, sniffed the air, and laid a gentle hand on the pulseless heart.

"Yes," he replied. "That, Hollyer, does not always appeal to the woman, strange to say."

The Last Exploit of Harry the Actor

The one insignificant fact upon which turned the following incident in the joint experiences of Mr. Carlyle and Max Carrados was merely this: that having called upon his friend just at the moment when the private detective was on the point of leaving his office to go to the safe deposit in Lucas Street, Piccadilly, the blind amateur accompanied him, and for ten minutes amused himself by sitting quite quietly among the palms in the centre of the circular hall while Mr. Carlyle was occupied with his deed-box in one of the little compartments provided for the purpose.

The Lucas Street depository was then (it has since been converted into a picture palace) generally accepted as being one of the strongest places in London. The front of the building was constructed to represent a gigantic safe door, and under the colloquial designation of "The Safe" the place had passed into a synonym for all that was secure and impregnable. Half of the marketable securities in the west of London were popularly reported to have seen the inside of its coffers at one time or another, together with the same generous proportion of family jewels. However exaggerated an estimate this might be, the substratum of truth was solid and auriferous enough to dazzle the imagination. When ordinary safes were being carried bodily away with impunity or ingeniously fused open by the scientifically equipped cracksman, nervous bond-holders turned with relief to the attractions of an establishment whose modest claim was summed up in its telegraphic address: "Impregnable." To it went also the jewel-case between the lady's social engagements, and when in due course "the family" journeyed north—or south, east or west—whenever, in short, the London house was closed, its capacious storerooms received the plate-chest as an established custom. Not a few traders also—jewellers, financiers, dealers in pictures, antiques and costly bijouterie, for instance—constantly used its facilities for any stock that they did not require immediately to hand.

There was only one entrance to the place, an exaggerated

keyhole, to carry out the similitude of the safe-door alluded to. The ground floor was occupied by the ordinary offices of the company; all the strong-rooms and safes lay in the steel-cased basement. This was reached both by a lift and by a flight of steps. In either case the visitor found before him a grille of massive proportions. Behind its bars stood a formidable commissionaire who never left his post, his sole duty being to open and close the grille to arriving and departing clients. Beyond this, a short passage led into the round central hall where Carrados was waiting. From this part, other passages radiated off to the vaults and strong-rooms, each one barred from the hall by a grille scarcely less ponderous than the first one. The doors of the various private rooms put at the disposal of the company's clients, and that of the manager's office, filled the wall-space between the radiating passages. Everything was very quiet, everything looked very bright, and everything seemed hopelessly impregnable.

"But I wonder?" ran Carrados's dubious reflection as he reached this point.

"Sorry to have kept you so long, my dear Max," broke in Mr. Carlyle's crisp voice. He had emerged from his compartment and was crossing the hall, deed-box in hand. "Another minute and I will be with you."

Carrados smiled and nodded and resumed his former expression, which was merely that of an uninterested gentleman waiting patiently for another. It is something of an attainment to watch closely without betraying undue curiosity, but others of the senses—hearing and smelling, for instance—can be keenly engaged while the observer possibly has the appearance of falling asleep.

"Now," announced Mr. Carlyle, returning briskly to his friend's chair, and drawing on his grey suède gloves.

"You are in no particular hurry?"

"No," admitted the professional man, with the slowness of mild surprise. "Not at all. What do you propose?"

"It is very pleasant here," replied Carrados tranquilly. "Very cool and restful with this armoured steel between us and the dust and scurry of the hot July afternoon above. I propose remaining here for a few minutes longer."

"Certainly," agreed Mr. Carlyle, taking the nearest chair and eyeing Carrados as though he had a shrewd suspicion of something more than met the ear. "I believe some very interesting people rent safes here. We may encounter a bishop, or a winning jockey, or even a musical comedy actress. Unfortunately it seems to be rather a slack time."

"Two men came down while you were in your cubicle," remarked Carrados casually. "The first took the lift. I imagine that he was a middle-aged, rather portly man. He carried a stick, wore a silk hat, and used spectacles for close sight. The other came by the stairway. I infer that he arrived at the top immediately after the lift had gone. He ran down the steps, so that the two were admitted at the same time, but the second man, though the more active of the pair, hung back for a moment in the passage and the portly one was the first to go to his safe."

Mr. Carlyle's knowing look expressed: "Go on, my friend; you are coming to something." But he merely contributed an encouraging "Yes?"

"When you emerged just now our second man quietly opened the door of his pen a fraction. Doubtless he looked out. Then he closed it as quietly again. You were not his man, Louis."

"I am grateful," said Mr. Carlyle expressively. "What next, Max?"

"That is all; they are still closeted."

Both were silent for a moment. Mr. Carlyle's feeling was one of unconfessed perplexity. So far the incident was utterly trivial in his eyes; but he knew that the trifles which appeared significant to Max had a way of standing out like signposts when the time came to look back over an episode. Carrados's sightless faculties seemed indeed to keep him just a move ahead as the game progressed.

"Is there really anything in it, Max?" he asked at length.

"Who can say?" replied Carrados. "At least we may wait to see them go. Those tin deed-boxes now. There is one to each safe, I think?"

"Yes, so I imagine. The practice is to carry the box to your private lair and there unlock it and do your business. Then you lock it up again and take it back to your safe."

"Steady! our first man," whispered Carrados hurriedly. "Here, look at this with me." He opened a paper—a prospectus—which he pulled from his pocket, and they affected to study its contents together.

"You were about right, my friend," muttered Mr. Carlyle, pointing to a paragraph of assumed interest. "Hat, stick and spectacles.

He is a clean-shaven, pink-faced old boy. I believe—yes, I know the man by sight. He is a bookmaker in a large way, I am told."

"Here comes the other," whispered Carrados.

The bookmaker passed across the hall, joined on his way by the manager whose duty it was to counterlock the safe, and disappeared along one of the passages. The second man sauntered up and down, waiting his turn. Mr. Carlyle reported his movements in an undertone and described him. He was a younger man than the other, of medium height, and passably well dressed in a quiet lounge suit, green Alpine hat and brown shoes. By the time the detective had reached his wavy chestnut hair, large and rather ragged moustache, and sandy, freckled complexion, the first man had completed his business and was leaving the place.

"It isn't an exchange lay, at all events," said Mr. Carlyle. "His inner case is only half the size of the other and couldn't possibly be substituted."

"Come up now," said Carrados, rising. "There is nothing more to be learned down here."

They requisitioned the lift, and on the steps outside the gigantic keyhole stood for a few minutes discussing an investment as a couple of trustees or a lawyer and a client who were parting there might do. Fifty yards away, a very large silk hat with a very curly brim marked the progress of the bookmaker towards Piccadilly.

The lift in the hall behind them swirled up again and the gate clashed. The second man walked leisurely out and sauntered away without a backward glance.

"He has gone in the opposite direction," exclaimed Mr. Carlyle, rather blankly. "It isn't the 'lame goat' nor the 'follow-me-on,' nor even the homely but efficacious sand-bag."

"What colour were his eyes?" asked Carrados.

"Upon my word, I never noticed," admitted the other.

"Parkinson would have noticed," was the severe comment.

"I am not Parkinson," retorted Mr. Carlyle, with asperity, "and, strictly as one dear friend to another, Max, permit me to add, that while cherishing an unbounded admiration for your remarkable gifts, I have the strongest suspicion that the whole incident is a ridiculous mare's nest, bred in the fantastic imagination of an enthusiastic criminologist."

Mr. Carrados received this outburst with the utmost benignity.

"Come and have a coffee, Louis," he suggested. "Mehmed's is only a street away."

Mehmed proved to be a cosmopolitan gentleman from Mocha whose shop resembled a house from the outside and an Oriental divan when one was within. A turbaned Arab placed cigarettes and cups of coffee spiced with saffron before the customers, gave salaam and withdrew.

"You know, my dear chap," continued Mr. Carlyle, sipping his black coffee and wondering privately whether it was really very good or very bad, "speaking quite seriously, the one fishy detail—our ginger friend's watching for the other to leave—may be open to a dozen very innocent explanations."

"So innocent that to-morrow I intend taking a safe myself."

"You think that everything is all right?"

"On the contrary, I am convinced that something is very wrong."

"Then why——?"

"I shall keep nothing there, but it will give me the *entrée*. I should ad-advise you, Louis, in the first place to empty your safe with all possible speed, and in the second to leave your business card on the manager."

Mr. Carlyle pushed his cup away, convinced now that the coffee was really very bad.

"But, my dear Max, the place—'The Safe'—is impregnable!"

"When I was in the States, three years ago, the head porter at one hotel took pains to impress on me that the building was absolutely fireproof. I at once had my things taken off to another hotel. Two weeks later the first place was burnt out. It *was* fireproof, I believe, but of course the furniture and the fittings were not and the walls gave way."

"Very ingenious," admitted Mr. Carlyle, "but why did you really go? You know you can't humbug me with your superhuman sixth sense, my friend."

Carrados smiled pleasantly, thereby encouraging the watchful attendant to draw near and replenish their tiny cups.

"Perhaps," replied the blind man, "because so many careless people were satisfied that it was fireproof."

"Ah-ha, there you are—the greater the confidence the greater the risk. But only if your self-confidence results in carelessness. Now do you know how this place is secured, Max?"

"I am told that they lock the door at night," replied Carrados, with bland malice.

"And hide the key under the mat to be ready for the first arrival in the morning," crowed Mr. Carlyle, in the same playful spirit. "Dear old chap! Well, let me tell you——"

"That force is out of the question. Quite so," admitted his friend.

"That simplifies the argument. Let us consider fraud. There again the precautions are so rigid that many people pronounce the forms a nuisance. I confess that I do not. I regard them as a means of protecting my own property and I cheerfully sign my name and give my password, which the manager compares with his record-book before he releases the first lock of my safe. The signature is burned before my eyes in a sort of crucible there, the password is of my own choosing and is written only in a book that no one but the manager ever sees, and my key is the sole one in existence."

"No duplicate or master-key?"

"Neither. If a key is lost it takes a skilful mechanic half-a-day to cut his way in. Then you must remember that clients of a safe-deposit are not multitudinous. All are known more or less by sight to the officials there, and a stranger would receive close attention. Now, Max, by what combination of circumstances is a rogue to know my password, to be able to forge my signature, to possess himself of my key, and to resemble me personally? And, finally, how is he possibly to determine beforehand whether there is anything in my safe to repay so elaborate a plant?" Mr. Carlyle concluded in triumph and was so carried away by the strength of his position that he drank off the contents of his second cup before he realized what he was doing.

"At the hotel I just spoke of," replied Carrados, "there was an attendant whose one duty in case of alarm was to secure three iron doors. On the night of the fire he had a bad attack of toothache and slipped away for just a quarter of an hour to have the thing out. There was a most up-to-date system of automatic fire alarm; it had been tested only the day before and the electrician, finding some part not absolutely to his satisfaction, had taken it away and not had time to replace it. The night watchman, it turned out, had received leave to present himself a couple of hours later on that particular night, and the hotel fireman, whose duties he took over, had missed being notified. Lastly, there was a big riverside blaze at the same time and all the engines were down at the other end of the city."

Mr. Carlyle committed himself to a dubious monosyllable. Carrados leaned forward a little.

"All these circumstances formed a coincidence of pure chance. Is it not conceivable, Louis, that an even more remarkable series might be brought about by design?."

"Our tawny friend?"

"Possibly. Only he was not really tawny." Mr. Carlyle's easy attitude suddenly stiffened into rigid attention. "He wore a false moustache."

"He wore a false moustache!" repeated the amazed gentleman. "And you cannot see! No, really, Max, this is beyond the limit!"

"If only you would not trust your dear, blundering old eyes so implicitly you would get nearer that limit yourself," retorted Carrados. "The man carried a five-yard aura of spirit gum, emphasized by a warm, perspiring skin. That inevitably suggested one thing. I looked for further evidence of making-up and found it—these preparations all smell. The hair you described was characteristically that of a wig—worn long to hide the joining and made wavy to minimize the length. All these things are trifles. As yet we have not gone beyond the initial stage of suspicion. I will tell you another trifle. When this man retired to a compartment with his deed-box, he never even opened it. Possibly it contains a brick and a newspaper. He is only watching."

"Watching the bookmaker."

"True, but it may go far wider than that. Everything points to a plot of careful elaboration. Still, if you are satisfied——"

"I am quite satisfied," replied Mr. Carlyle gallantly. "I regard 'The Safe' almost as a national institution, and as such I have an implicit faith in its precautions against every kind of force or fraud." So far Mr. Carlyle's attitude had been suggestive of a rock, but at this point he took out his watch, hummed a little to pass the time, consulted his watch again, and continued: "I am afraid that there were one or two papers which I overlooked. It would perhaps save me coming again to-morrow if I went back now——"

"Quite so," acquiesced Carrados, with perfect gravity. "I will wait for you."

For twenty minutes he sat there, drinking an occasional tiny cup of boiled coffee and to all appearance placidly enjoying the quaint atmosphere which Mr. Mehmed had contrived to transplant from the shores of the Persian Gulf.

At the end of that period Carlyle returned, politely effusive about the time he had kept his friend waiting but otherwise bland and unassailable. Anyone with eyes might have noticed that he carried a parcel of about the same size and dimensions as the deed-box that fitted his safe.

The next day Carrados presented himself at the safe-deposit as an intending renter. The manager showed him over the vaults and strong-rooms, explaining the various precautions taken to render the guile or force of man impotent: the strength of the chilled-steel walls, the casing of electricity-resisting concrete, the stupendous isolation of the whole inner fabric on metal pillars so that the watchman, while inside the building, could walk above, below, and all round the outer walls of what was really—although it bore no actual relationship to the advertising device of the front—a monstrous safe; and, finally, the arrangement which would enable the basement to be flooded with steam within three minutes of an alarm. These details were public property. "The Safe" was a showplace and its directors held that no harm could come of displaying a strong hand.

Accompanied by the observant eyes of Parkinson, Carrados gave an adventurous but not a hopeful attention to these particulars. Submitting the problem of the tawny man to his own ingenuity, he was constantly putting before himself the question: How shall I set about robbing this place? and he had already dismissed force as impracticable. Nor, when it came to the consideration of fraud, did the simple but effective safeguards which Mr. Carlyle had specified seem to offer any loophole.

"As I am blind I may as well sign in the book," he suggested, when the manager passed him a gummed slip for the purpose. The precaution against one acquiring particulars of another client might well be deemed superfluous in his case.

But the manager did not fall into the trap.

"It is our invariable rule in all cases, sir," he replied courteously. "What word will you take?" Parkinson, it may be said, had been left in the hall.

"Suppose I happen to forget it? How do we proceed?"

"In that case I am afraid that I might have to trouble you to establish your identity," the manager explained. "It rarely happens."

"Then we will say 'Conspiracy.' "

The word was written down and the book closed.

"Here is your key, sir. If you will allow me—your key-ring——"

A week went by and Carrados was no nearer the absolute solution of the problem he had set himself. He had, indeed, evolved several ways by which the contents of the safes might be reached, some simple and desperate, hanging on the razor-edge of chance to fall this way or that; others more elaborate, safer on the whole, but more liable to break down at some point of their ingenious intricacy. And setting aside complicity on the part of the manager—a condition that Carrados had satisfied himself did not exist—they all depended on a relaxation of the forms by which security was assured. Carrados continued to have several occasions to visit the safe during the week, and he "watched" with a quiet persistence that was deadly in its scope. But from beginning to end there was no indication of slackness in the business-like methods of the place; nor during any of his visits did the "tawny man" appear in that or any other disguise. Another week passed; Mr. Carlyle was becoming inexpressibly waggish, and Carrados himself, although he did not abate a jot of his conviction, was compelled to bend to the realities of the situation. The manager, with the obstinacy of a conscientious man who had become obsessed with the pervading note of security, excused himself from discussing abstract methods of fraud. Carrados was not in a position to formulate a detailed charge; he withdrew from active investigation, content to await his time.

It came, to be precise, on a certain Friday morning, seventeen days after his first visit to "The Safe." Returning late on the Thursday night, he was informed that a man giving the name of Draycott had called to see him. Apparently the matter had been of some importance to the visitor for he had returned three hours later on the chance of finding Mr. Carrados in. Disappointed in this, he had left a note. Carrados cut open the envelope and ran a finger along the following words:—

"*Dear Sir,*—I have to-day consulted Mr. Louis Carlyle, who thinks that you would like to see me. I will call again in the morning, say at nine o'clock. If this is too soon or otherwise inconvenient I entreat you to leave a message fixing as early an hour as possible.

"Yours faithfully,

Herbert Draycott.

"*P.S.*—I should add that I am the renter of a safe at the Lucas Street depository.   *H.D.*"

A description of Mr. Draycott made it clear that he was not the

West-End bookmaker. The caller, the servant explained, was a thin, wiry, keen-faced man. Carrados felt agreeably interested in this development, which seemed to justify his suspicion of a plot.

At five minutes to nine the next morning Mr. Draycott again presented himself.

"Very good of you to see me so soon, sir," he apologized, on Carrados at once receiving him. "I don't know much of English ways—I'm an Australian—and I was afraid it might be too early."

"You could have made it a couple of hours earlier as far as I am concerned," replied Carrados. "Or you either for that matter, I imagine," he added, "for I don't think that you slept much last night."

"I didn't sleep at all last night," corrected Mr. Draycott. "But it's strange that you should have seen that. I understood from Mr. Carlyle that you—excuse me if I am mistaken, sir—but I understood that you were blind."

Carrados laughed his admission lightly.

"Oh yes," he said. "But never mind that. What is the trouble?"

"I'm afraid it means more than just trouble for me, Mr. Carrados." The man had steady, half-closed eyes, with the suggestion of depth which one notices in the eyes of those whose business it is to look out over great expanses of land or water; they were turned towards Carrados's face with quiet resignation in their frankness now. "I'm afraid it spells disaster. I am a working engineer from the Mount Magdalena district of Coolgardie. I don't want to take up your time with outside details, so I will only say that about two years ago I had an opportunity of acquiring a share in a very promising claim— gold, you understand, both reef and alluvial. As the work went on I put more and more into the undertaking—you couldn't call it a venture by that time. The results were good, better than we had dared to expect, but from one cause and another the expenses were terrible. We saw that it was a bigger thing than we had bargained for and we admitted that we must get outside help."

So far Mr. Draycott's narrative had proceeded smoothly enough under the influence of the quiet despair that had come over the man. But at this point a sudden recollection of his position swept him into a frenzy of bitterness.

"Oh, what the blazes is the good of going over all this again!" he broke out. "What can you or anyone else do anyhow? I've been robbed, rooked, cleared out of everything I possess," and tormented by recollections and by the impotence of his rage the unfortunate engineer beat the oak table with the back of his hand until his knuckles bled.

Carrados waited until the fury had passed.

"Continue, if you please, Mr. Draycott," he said. "Just what you thought it best to tell me is just what I want to know."

"I'm sorry, sir," apologized the man, colouring under his tanned skin. "I ought to be able to control myself better. But this business has shaken me. Three times last night I looked down the barrel of my revolver, and three times I threw it away. . . . Well, we arranged that I should come to London to interest some financiers in the property. We might have done it locally or in Perth, to be sure, but then, don't you see, they would have wanted to get control. Six weeks ago I landed here. I brought with me specimens of the quartz and good samples of extracted gold, dust and nuggets, the clearing up of several weeks' working, about two hundred and forty ounces in all. That includes the Magdalena Lodestar, our lucky nugget, a lump weighing just under seven pounds of pure gold.

"I had seen an advertisement of this Lucas Street safe-deposit and it seemed just the thing I wanted. Besides the gold, I had all the papers to do with the claims—plans, reports, receipts, licences and so on. Then when I cashed my letter of credit I had about one hundred and fifty pounds in notes. Of course I could have left everything at a bank, but it was more convenient to have it, as it were, in my own safe, to get at any time, and to have a private room that I could take any gentlemen to. I hadn't a suspicion that anything could be wrong. Negotiations hung on in several quarters—it's a bad time to do business here, I find. Then, yesterday, I wanted something. I went to Lucas Street, as I had done half-a-dozen times before, opened my safe, and had the inner case carried to a room. . . . Mr. Carrados, it was empty!"

"Quite empty?"

"No." He laughed bitterly. "At the bottom was a sheet of wrapper paper. I recognized it as a piece I had left there in case I wanted to make up a parcel. But for that I should have been convinced that I had somehow opened the wrong safe. That was my first idea."

"It cannot be done."

"So I understand, sir. And, then, there was the paper with my name written on it in the empty tin. I was dazed; it seemed impossible. I think I stood there without moving for minutes—it was more like hours. Then I closed the tin box again, took it back, locked up the safe and came out."

"Without notifying anything wrong?"

"Yes, Mr. Carrados." The steady blue eyes regarded him with pained thoughtfulness. "You see, I reckoned it out in that time that it must be someone about the place who had done it."

"You were wrong," said Carrados.

"So Mr. Carlyle seemed to think. I only knew that the key had never been out of my possession and I had told no one of the password. Well, it did come over me rather like cold water down the neck, that there was I alone in the strongest dungeon in London and not a living soul knew where I was."

"Possibly a sort of up-to-date Sweeney Todd's?"

"I'd heard of such things in London," admitted Draycott. "Anyway, I got out. It was a mistake; I see it now. Who is to believe me as it is—it sounds a sort of unlikely tale. And how do they come to pick on me? to know what I had? I don't drink, or open my mouth, or hell round. It beats me."

"They didn't pick on you—you picked on them," replied Carrados. "Never mind how; you'll be believed all right. But as for getting anything back——" The unfinished sentence confirmed Mr. Draycott in his gloomiest anticipations.

"I have the numbers of the notes," he suggested, with an attempt at hopefulness. "They can be stopped, I take it?"

"Stopped? Yes," admitted Carrados. "And what does that amount to? The banks and the police stations will be notified and every little public-house between here and Land's End will change one for the scribbling of 'John Jones' across the back. No, Mr. Draycott, it's awkward, I dare say, but you must make up your mind to wait until you can get fresh supplies from home. Where are you staying?"

Draycott hesitated.

"I have been at the Abbotsford, in Bloomsbury, up to now," he said, with some embarrassment. "The fact is, Mr. Carrados, I think I ought to have told you how I was placed before consulting you, because I—I see no prospect of being able to pay my way. Knowing that I had plenty in the safe, I had run it rather close. I went chiefly yesterday to get some notes. I have a week's hotel bill in my pocket, and"—he glanced down at his trousers—"I've ordered one or two other things unfortunately."

"That will be a matter of time, doubtless," suggested the other encouragingly.

Instead of replying Draycott suddenly dropped his arms on to the table and buried his face between them. A minute passed in silence.

"It's no good, Mr. Carrados," he said, when he was able to speak. "I can't meet it. Say what you like, I simply can't tell those chaps that I've lost everything we had and ask them to send me more. They couldn't do it if I did. Understand sir. The mine is a valuable one; we have the greatest faith in it, but it has gone beyond our depth. The three of us have put everything we own into it. While I am here they are doing labourers' work for a wage, just to keep going . . . waiting, oh, my God! waiting for good news from me!"

Carrados walked round the table to his desk and wrote. Then, without a word, he held out a paper to his visitor.

"What's this?" demanded Draycott, in bewilderment. "It's—it's a cheque for a hundred pounds."

"It will carry you on," explained Carrados imperturbably. "A man like you isn't going to throw up the sponge for this set-back. Cable to your partners that you require copies of all the papers at once. They'll manage it, never fear. The gold . . . must go. Write fully by the next mail. Tell them everything and add that in spite of all you feel that you are nearer success than ever."

Mr. Draycott folded the cheque with thoughtful deliberation and put it carefully away in his pocket-book.

"I don't know whether you've guessed as much, sir," he said in a queer voice, "but I think that you've saved a man's life to-day. It's not the money, it's the encouragement . . . and faith. If you could see you'd know better than I can say how I feel about it."

Carrados laughed quietly. It always amused him to have people explain how much more he would learn if he had eyes.

"Then we'll go on to Lucas Street and give the manager the shock of his life," was all he said. "Come, Mr. Draycott, I have already rung up the car."

But, as it happened, another instrument had been destined to apply that stimulating experience to the manager. As they stepped out of the car opposite "The Safe" a taxicab drew up and Mr. Carlyle's alert and cheery voice hailed them.

"A moment, Max," he called, turning to settle with his driver, a transaction that he invested with an air of dignified urbanity which almost made up for any small pecuniary disappointment that may have accompanied it. "This is indeed fortunate. Let us compare notes for a moment. I have just received an almost imploring message from the manager to come at once. I assumed that it was the affair of our colonial friend here, but he went on to mention Professor Holmfast Bulge. Can it really be possible that he also has made a similar discovery?"

"What did the manager say?" asked Carrados.

"He was practically incoherent, but I really think it must be so. What have you done?"

"Nothing," replied Carrados. He turned his back on "The Safe" and appeared to be regarding the other side of the street. "There is a tobacconist's shop directly opposite?"

"There is."

"What do they sell on the first floor?"

"Possibly they sell 'Rubbo.' I hazard the suggestion from the legend 'Rub in Rubbo for Everything' which embellishes each window."

"The windows are frosted?"

"They are, to half-way up, mysterious man."

Carrados walked back to his motor-car.

"While we are away, Parkinson, go across and buy a tin, bottle, box or packet of 'Rubbo.' "

"What is 'Rubbo,' Max?" chirped Mr. Carlyle with insatiable curiosity.

"So far we do not know. When Parkinson gets some, Louis, you shall be the one to try it."

They descended into the basement and were passed in by the grille-keeper, whose manner betrayed a discreet consciousness of something in the air. It was unnecessary to speculate why. In the distance, muffled by the armoured passages, an authoritative voice boomed like a sonorous bell heard under water.

"What, however, are the facts?" it was demanding, with the causticity of baffled helplessness. "I am assured that there is no other key in existence; yet my safe has been unlocked. I am given to understand that without the password it would be impossible for an unauthorized person to tamper with my property. My password, deliberately chosen, is 'anthropophaginian,' sir. Is it one that is familiarly on the lips of the criminal classes? But my safe is empty!"

What is the explanation? Who are the guilty persons? What is being done? Where are the police?"

"If you consider that the proper course to adopt is to stand on the doorstep and beckon in the first constable who happens to pass, permit me to say, sir, that I differ from you," retorted the distracted manager. "You may rely on everything possible being done to clear up the mystery. As I told you, I have already telephoned for a capable private detective and for one of my directors."

"But that is not enough," insisted the professor angrily. "Will one mere private detective restore my £6000 Japanese 4½ per cent. bearer bonds? Is the return of my irreplaceable notes on 'Polyphyletic Bridal Customs among the mid-Pleistocene Cave Men' to depend on a solitary director? I demand that the police shall be called in—as many as are available. Let Scotland Yard be set in motion. A searching inquiry must be made. I have only been a user of your precious establishment for six months, and this is the result."

"There you hold the key of the mystery, Professor Bulge," interposed Carrados quietly.

"Who is this, sir?" demanded the exasperated professor at large.

"Permit me," explained Mr. Carlyle, with bland assurance. "I am Louis Carlyle, of Bampton Street. This gentleman is Mr. Max Carrados, the eminent amateur specialist in crime."

"I shall be thankful for any assistance towards elucidating this appalling business," condescended the professor sonorously. "Let me put you in possession of the facts——"

"Perhaps if we went into your room," suggested Carrados to the manager, "we should be less liable to interruption."

"Quite so; quite so," boomed the professor, accepting the proposal on everyone else's behalf. "The facts, sir, are these: I am the unfortunate possessor of a safe here, in which, a few months ago, I deposited—among less important matter—sixty bearer bonds of the Japanese Imperial Loan—the bulk of my small fortune—and the manuscript of an important projected work on 'Polyphyletic Bridal Customs among the mid-Pleistocene Cave Men.' Today I came to detach the coupons which fall due on the fifteenth, to pay them into my bank a week in advance, in accordance with my custom. What do I find? I find the safe locked and apparently intact, as when I last saw it a month ago. But it is far from being intact, sir. It has been opened, ransacked, cleared out. Not a single bond, not a scrap of paper remains."

It was obvious that the manager's temperature had been rising during the latter part of this speech and now he boiled over.

"Pardon my flatly contradicting you, Professor Bulge. You have again referred to your visit here a month ago as your last. You will bear witness of that, gentlemen. When I inform you that the professor had access to his safe as recently as on Monday last you will recognize the importance that the statement may assume."

The professor glared across the room like an infuriated animal, a comparison heightened by his notoriously hircine appearance.

"How dare you contradict me, sir!" he cried, slapping the table sharply with his open hand. "I was not here on Monday."

The manager shrugged his shoulders coldly.

"You forget that the attendants also saw you," he remarked. "Cannot we trust our own eyes?"

"A common assumption, yet not always a strictly reliable one," insinuated Carrados softly.

"I cannot be mistaken."

"Then can you tell me, without looking, what colour Professor Bulge's eyes are?"

There was a curious and expectant silence for a minute. The professor turned his back on the manager and the manager passed from thoughtfulness to embarrassment.

"I really do not know, Mr. Carrados," he declared loftily at last. "I do not refer to mere trifles like that."

"Then you can be mistaken," replied Carrados mildly yet with decision.

"But the ample hair, the venerable flowing beard, the prominent nose and heavy eyebrows——"

"These are just the striking points that are most easily counterfeited. They 'take the eye.' If you would ensure yourself against deception, learn rather to observe the eye itself, and particularly the spots on it, the shape of the finger-nails, the set of the ears. These things cannot be simulated."

"You seriously suggest that the man was not Professor Bulge—that he was an impostor?"

"The conclusion is inevitable. Where were you on Monday, Professor?"

"I was on a short lecturing tour in the Midlands. On Saturday I was in Nottingham. On Monday in Birmingham. I did not return to London until yesterday."

Carrados turned to the manager again and indicated Draycott, who so far had remained in the background.

"And this gentleman? Did he by any chance come here on Monday?"

"He did not, Mr. Carrados. But I gave him access to his safe on Tuesday afternoon and again yesterday."

Draycott shook his head sadly.

"Yesterday I found it empty," he said. "And all Tuesday afternoon I was at Brighton, trying to see a gentleman on business."

The manager sat down very suddenly.

"Good God, another!" he exclaimed faintly.

"I am afraid the list is only beginning," said Carrados. "We must go through your renters' book."

The manager roused himself to protest.

"That cannot be done. No one but myself or my deputy ever sees the book. It would be—unprecedented."

"The circumstances are unprecedented," replied Carrados.

"If any difficulties are placed in the way of these gentlemen's investigations, I shall make it my duty to bring the facts before the Home Secretary," announced the professor, speaking up to the ceiling with the voice of a brazen trumpet.

Carrados raised a deprecating hand.

"May I make a suggestion?" he remarked. "Now, I am blind. If, therefore——?"

"Very well," acquiesced the manager. "But I must request the others to withdraw."

For five minutes Carrados followed the list of safe-renters as the manager read them to him. Sometimes he stopped the catalogue to reflect a moment; now and then he brushed a finger-tip over a written signature and compared it with another. Occasionally a password interested him. But when the list came to an end he continued to look into space without any sign of enlightenment.

"So much is perfectly clear and yet so much is incredible," he mused. "You insist that you alone have been in charge for the last six months?"

"I have not been away a day this year."

"Meals?"

"I have my lunch sent in."

"And this room could not be entered without your knowledge while you were about the place?"

"It is impossible. The door is fitted with a powerful spring and a feather-touch self-acting lock. It cannot be left unlocked unless you deliberately prop it open."

"And, with your knowledge, no one has had an opportunity of having access to this book?"

"No," was the reply.

Carrados stood up and began to put on his gloves.

"Then I must decline to pursue my investigation any further," he said icily.

"Why?" stammered the manager.

"Because I have positive reason for believing that you are deceiving me."

"Pray sit down, Mr. Carrados. It is quite true that when you put the last question to me a circumstance rushed into my mind which —so far as the strict letter was concerned—might seem to demand 'Yes' instead of 'No.' But not in the spirit of your inquiry. It would be absurd to attach any importance to the incident I refer to."

"That would be for me to judge."

"You shall do so, Mr. Carrados. I live at Windermere Mansions with my sister. A few months ago she got to know a married couple who had recently come to the opposite flat. The husband was a middle-aged, scholarly man who spent most of his time in the British Museum. His wife's tastes were different; she was much younger, brighter, gayer; a mere girl in fact, one of the most charming and unaffected I have ever met. My sister Amelia does not readily——"

"Stop!" exclaimed Carrados. "A studious middle-aged man and a charming young wife! Be as brief as possible. If there is any chance it may turn on a matter of minutes at the ports. She came here, of course?"

"Accompanied by her husband," replied the manager stiffly. "Mrs. Scott had travelled and she had a hobby of taking photographs wherever she went. When my position accidentally came out one evening she was carried away by the novel idea of adding views of a safe deposit to her collection—as enthusiastic as a child. There was no reason why she should not; the place has often been taken for advertising purposes."

"She came, and brought her camera—under your very nose!"

"I do not know what you mean by 'under my very nose.' She came with her husband one evening just about closing time. She brought her camera, of course—quite a small affair."

"And contrived to be in here alone?"

"I take exception to the word 'contrived.' It—it happened. I sent out for some tea, and in the course——"

"How long was she alone in here?"

"Two or three minutes at the most. When I returned she was seated at my desk. That was what I referred to. The little rogue had put on my glasses and had got hold of a big book. We were great chums, and she delighted to mock me. I confess that I was startled —merely instinctively—to see that she had taken up this book, but the next moment I saw that she had it upside down."

"Clever! She couldn't get it away in time. And the camera, with half-a-dozen of its specially sensitized films already snapped over the last few pages, by her side!"

"That child!"

"Yes. She is twenty-seven and has kicked hats off tall men's heads in every capital from Petersburg to Buenos Ayres! Get through to Scotland Yard and ask if Inspector Beedel can come up."

The manager breathed heavily through his nose.

"To call in the police and publish everything would ruin this establishment—confidence would be gone. I cannot do it without further authority."

"Then the professor certainly will."

"Before you came I rang up the only director who is at present in town and gave him the facts as they then stood. Possibly he has arrived by this. If you will accompany me to the boardroom we will see."

They went up to the floor above, Mr. Carlyle joining them on the way.

"Excuse me a moment," said the manager.

Parkinson, who had been having an improving conversation with the hall porter on the subject of land values, approached.

"I am sorry, sir," he reported, "but I was unable to procure any 'Rubbo.' The place appears to be shut up."

"That is a pity; Mr. Carlyle had set his heart on it."

"Will you come this way, please?" said the manager, reappearing.

In the boardroom they found a white-haired old gentleman who had obeyed the manager's behest from a sense of duty, and then remained in a distant corner of the empty room in the hope that he might be over-looked. He was amiably helpless and appeared to be deeply aware of it.

"This is a very sad business, gentlemen," he said, in a whispering, confiding voice. "I am informed that you recommend calling in the Scotland Yard authorities. That would be a disastrous course for an institution that depends on the implicit confidence of the public."

"It is the only course," replied Carrados.

"The name of Mr. Carrados is well known to us in connection with a delicate case. Could you not carry this one through?"

"It is impossible. A wide inquiry must be made. Every port will have to be watched. The police alone can do that." He threw a little significance into the next sentence. "I alone can put the police in the right way of doing it."

"And you will do that, Mr. Carrados?"

Carrados smiled engagingly. He knew exactly what constituted the great attraction of his services.

"My position is this," he explained. "So far my work has been entirely amateur. In that capacity I have averted one or two crimes, remedied an occasional injustice, and now and then been of service to my professional friend, Louis Carlyle. But there is no reason at all why I should serve a commercial firm in an ordinary affair of business for nothing. For any information I should require a fee, a quite nominal fee of, say, one hundred pounds."

The director looked as though his faith in human nature had received a rude blow.

"A hundred pounds would be a very large initial fee for a small firm like this, Mr. Carrados," he remarked in a pained voice.

"And that, of course, would be independent of Mr. Carlyle's professional charges," added Carrados.

"Is that sum contingent on any specific performance?" inquired the manager.

"I do not mind making it conditional on my procuring for you, for the police to act on, a photograph and a description of the thief."

The two officials conferred apart for a moment. Then the manager returned.

"We will agree, Mr. Carrados, on the understanding that these things are to be in our hands within two days. Failing that——"

"No, no!" cried Mr. Carlyle indignantly, but Carrados good-humouredly put him aside.

"I will accept the condition in the same sporting spirit that inspires it. Within forty-eight hours or no pay. The cheque, of course, to be given immediately the goods are delivered?"

"You may rely on that."

Carrados took out his pocket-book, produced an envelope bearing an American stamp, and from it extracted an unmounted print.

"Here is the photograph," he announced. "The man is called Ulysses K. Groom, but he is better known as 'Harry the Actor.' You will find the description written on the back."

Five minutes later, when they were alone, Mr. Carlyle expressed his opinion of the transaction.

"You are an unmitigated humbug, Max," he said, "though an amiable one, I admit. But purely for your own private amusement you spring these things on people."

"On the contrary," replied Carrados, "people spring these things on me."

"Now this photograph. Why have I heard nothing of it before?"

Carrados took out his watch and touched the fingers.

"It is now three minutes to eleven. I received the photograph at twenty past eight."

"Even then, an hour ago you assured me that you had done nothing."

"Nor had I—so far as result went. Until the keystone of the edifice was wrung from the manager in his room, I was as far away from demonstrable certainty as ever."

"So am I—as yet," hinted Mr. Carlyle.

"I am coming to that, Louis. I turn over the whole thing to you. The man has got two clear days' start and the chances are nine to one against catching him. We know everything, and the case has no further interest for me. But it is your business. Here is your material.

"On that one occasion when the 'tawny' man crossed our path, I took from the first a rather more serious view of his scope and intention than you did. The same day I sent a cipher cable to Pierson of the New York service. I asked for news of any man of such and such a description—merely negative—who was known to have left the States; an educated man, expert in the use of disguises, audacious in his operations, and a specialist in 'dry' work among banks and strong-rooms."

"Why the States, Max?"

"That was a sighting shot on my part. I argued that he must be an English-speaking man. The smart and inventive turn of the modern

Yank has made him a specialist in ingenious devices, straight or crooked. Unpickable locks and invincible lock-pickers, burglar-proof safes and safe-specializing burglars, come equally from the States. So I tried a very simple test. As we talked that day and the man walked past us, I dropped the words 'New York'—or, rather, 'Noo Y'rk'—in his hearing."

"I know you did. He neither turned nor stopped."

"He was that much on his guard; but into his step there came—though your poor old eyes could not see it, Louis—the 'psychological pause,' an absolute arrest of perhaps a fifth of a second; just as it would have done with you if the word 'London' had fallen on your ear in a distant land. However, the whys and the wherefores don't matter. Here is the essential story.

"Eighteen months ago 'Harry the Actor' successfully looted the office safe of M'Kenkie, J. F. Higgs & Co., of Cleveland, Ohio. He had just married a smart but very facile third-rate vaudeville actress —English by origin—and wanted money for the honeymoon. He got about five hundred pounds, and with that they came to Europe and stayed in London for some months. That period is marked by the Congreave Square post office burglary, you may remember. While studying such of the British institutions as most appealed to him, the 'Actor's' attention became fixed on this safe-deposit. Possibly the implied challenge contained in its telegraphic address grew on him until it became a point of professional honour with him to despoil it; at all events he was presumedly attracted by an undertaking that promised not only glory but very solid profit. The first part of the plot was, to the most skilful criminal 'impersonator' in the States, mere skittles. Spreading over those months he appeared at 'The Safe' in twelve different characters and rented twelve safes of different sizes. At the same time he made a thorough study of the methods of the place. As soon as possible he got the keys back again into legitimate use, having made duplicates for his own private ends, of course. Five he seems to have returned during his first stay; one was received later, with profuse apologies, by registered post; one was returned through a leading Berlin bank. Six months ago he made a flying visit here, purely to work off two more. One he kept from first to last, and the remaining couple he got in at the beginning of his second long residence here, three or four months ago.

"This brings us to the serious part of the cool enterprise. He had funds from the Atlantic and South-Central Mail-car coup when he

arrived here last April. He appears to have set up three establish-
ments; a home, in the guise of an elderly scholar with a young wife,
which, of course, was next door to our friend the manager; an
observation point, over which he plastered the inscription 'Rub in
Rubbo for Everything' as a reason for being; and, somewhere else,
a dressing-room with essential conditions of two doors into different
streets.

"About six weeks ago he entered the last stage. Mrs. Harry, with
quite ridiculous ease, got photographs of the necessary page or two
of the record-book. I don't doubt that for weeks before then everyone who entered the place had been observed, but the photographs
linked them up with the actual men into whose hands the 'Actor's'
old keys had passed—gave their names and addresses, the numbers
of their safes, their passwords and signatures. The rest was easy."

"Yes, by Jupiter; mere play for a man like that," agreed Mr.
Carlyle, with professional admiration. "He could contrive a dozen
different occasions for studying the voice and manner and appearance
of his victims. How much has he cleared?"

"We can only speculate as yet. I have put my hand on seven
doubtful callers on Monday and Tuesday last. Two others he had
ignored for some reason; the remaining two safes had not been
allotted. There is one point that raises an interesting speculation."

"What is that, Max?"

"The 'Actor' has one associate, a man known as 'Billy the Fon-
dant,' but beyond that—with the exception of his wife, of course—
he does not usually trust anyone. It is plain, however, that at least
seven men must latterly have been kept under close observation. It
has occurred to me——"

"Yes, Max?"

"I have wondered whether Harry has enlisted the innocent
services of one or other of our private inquiry offices."

"Scarcely," smiled the professional. "It would hardly pass muster."

"Oh, I don't know. Mrs. Harry, in the character of a jealous wife
or a suspicious sweetheart, might reasonably——"

Mr. Carlyle's smile suddenly faded.

"By Jupiter!" he exclaimed. "I remember——"

"Yes, Louis?" prompted Carrados, with laughter in his voice.

"I remember that I must telephone to a client before Beedel
comes," concluded Mr. Carlyle, rising in some haste.

At the door he almost ran into the subdued director, who was wringing his hands in helpless protest at a new stroke of calamity.

"Mr. Carrados," wailed the poor old gentleman in a tremulous bleat, "Mr. Carrados, there is another now—Sir Benjamin Gump. He insists on seeing me. You will not—you will not desert us?"

"I should have to stay a week," replied Carrados briskly, "and I'm just off now. There will be a procession. Mr. Carlyle will support you, I am sure."

He nodded "Good-morning" straight into the eyes of each and found his way out with the astonishing certainty of movement that made so many forget his infirmity. Possibly he was not desirous of encountering Draycott's embarrassed gratitude again, for in less than a minute they heard the swirl of his departing car.

"Never mind, my dear sir," Mr. Carlyle assured his client, with impenetrable complacency. "Never mind. *I* will remain instead. Perhaps I had better make myself known to Sir Benjamin at once."

The director turned on him the pleading, trustful look of a cornered dormouse.

"He is in the basement," he whispered. "I shall be in the board-room—if necessary."

Mr. Carlyle had no difficulty in discovering the centre of interest in the basement. Sir Benjamin was expansive and reserved, bewilder-ed and decisive, long-winded and short-tempered, each in turn and more or less all at once. He had already demanded the attention of the manager, Professor Bulge, Draycott and two underlings to his case and they were now involved in a babel of inutile reiteration. The inquiry agent was at once drawn into a circle of interrogation that he did his best to satisfy impressively while himself learning the new facts.

The latest development was sufficiently astonishing. Less than an hour before Sir Benjamin had received a parcel by district messenger. It contained a jewel-case which ought at that moment to have been securely reposing in one of the deposit safes. Hastily snatching it open, the recipient's incredible forebodings were realized. It was empty—empty of jewels, that is to say, for, as if to add a sting to the blow, a neatly inscribed card had been placed inside, and on it the agitated baronet read the appropriate but at the moment rather gratuitous maxim: "Lay not up for yourselves treasures upon earth ——"

The card was passed round and all eyes demanded the expert's pronouncement.

" '—where moth and rust doth corrupt and where thieves break through and steal.' H'm," read Mr. Carlyle with weight. "This is a most important clue, Sir Benjamin——"

"Hey, what? What's that?" exclaimed a voice from the other side of the hall. "Why, damme if I don't believe you've got another! Look at that, gentlemen; look at that. What's on, I say? Here now, come; give me my safe. I want to know where I am."

It was the bookmaker who strode tempestuously in among them, flourishing before their faces a replica of the card that was in Mr. Carlyle's hand.

"Well, upon my soul this is most extraordinary," exclaimed that gentleman, comparing the two. "You have just received this, Mr.— Mr. Berge, isn't it?"

"That's right, Berge—'Iceberg' on the course. Thank the Lord Harry, I can take my losses coolly enough, but this—this is a facer. Put into my hand half-an-hour ago inside an envelope that ought to be here and as safe as in the Bank of England. What's the game, I say? Here, Johnny, hurry and let me into my safe."

Discipline and method had for the moment gone by the board. There was no suggestion of the boasted safeguards of the establishment. The manager added his voice to that of the client, and when the attendant did not at once appear he called again.

"John, come and give Mr. Berge access to his safe at once."

"All right, sir," pleaded the harassed key-attendant, hurrying up with the burden of his own distraction. "There's a silly fathead got in what thinks this is a left-luggage office, so far as I can make out —a foreigner."

"Never mind that now," replied the manager severely, "Mr. Berge's safe: No. 01724."

The attendant and Mr. Berge went off together down one of the brilliant colonnaded vistas. One or two of the others who had caught the words glanced across and became aware of a strange figure that was drifting indecisively towards them. He was obviously an elderly German tourist of pronounced type—long-haired, spectacled, outrageously garbed and involved in the mental abstraction of his philosophical race. One hand was occupied with the manipulation of a pipe, as markedly Teutonic as its owner; the other grasped a carpet-bag that would have ensured an opening laugh to any low comedian.

Quite impervious to the preoccupation of the group, the German made his way up to them and picked out the manager. "This was a safety deposit, *nicht wahr?*"

"Quite so," acquiesced the manager loftily, "but just now——"

"Your fellow was dense of gomprehension." The eyes behind the clumsy glasses wrinkled to a ponderous humour. "He forgot his own business. Now this goot bag——"

Brought into fuller prominence, the carpet-bag revealed further details of its overburdened proportions. At one end a flannel shirt cuff protruded in limp dejection; at the other an ancient collar, with the grotesque attachment known as a "dickey," asserted its presence. No wonder the manager frowned his annoyance. "The Safe" was in low enough repute among its patrons at that moment without any burlesque interlude to its tragic hour.

"Yes, yes," he whispered, attempting to lead the would-be depositor away, "but you are under a mistake. This is not——"

"It was a safety deposit? Goot. Mine bag—I would deposit him in safety till the time of mine train. *Ja?*"

"*Nein, nein!*" almost hissed the agonized official. "Go away, sir, go away! It isn't a cloakroom. John, let this gentleman out."

The attendant and Mr. Berge were returning from their quest. The inner box had been opened and there was no need to ask the result. The bookmaker was shaking his head like a baffled bull.

"Gone, no effects," he shouted across the hall. "Lifted from 'The Safe,' by crumb!"

To those who knew nothing of the method and operation of the fraud it seemed as if the financial security of the Capital was tottering. An amazed silence fell, and in it they heard the great grille door of the basement clang on the inopportune foreigner's departure. But, as if it was impossible to stand still on that morning of dire happenings, he was immediately succeeded by a dapper, keen-faced man in severe clerical attire who had been let in as the intruder passed out.

"Canon Petersham!" exclaimed the professor, going forward to greet him.

"By dear Professor Bulge!" reciprocated the canon. "You here! A most disquieting thing has happened to me. I must have my safe at once." He divided his attention between the manager and the professor as he monopolized them both. "A most disquieting and— and outrageous circumstance. My safe, please—yes, yes, Rev. Henry Noakes Petersham. I have just received by hand a box, a small box of no value but one that I *thought*, yes, I am convinced that it was the one, a box that was used to contain certain valuables of family interest which should at this moment be in my safe here. No. 7436? Very likely, very likely. Yes, here is my key. But not content with the disconcerting effect of that, professor, the box contained—and I protest that it's a most unseemly thing to quote *any* text from the Bible in this way to a clergyman of my position—well, here it is. 'Lay not up for yourselves treasures upon earth——' Why, I have a dozen sermons of my own in my desk now on that very verse. I'm particularly partial to the very needful lesson that it teaches. And to apply it to *me!* It's monstrous!"

"No. 7436, John," ordered the manager, with weary resignation.

The attendant again led the way towards another armour-plated aisle. Smartly turning a corner, he stumbled over something, bit a profane exclamation in two, and looked back.

"It's that bloomin' foreigner's old bag again," he explained across the place in aggrieved apology. "He left it here after all."

"Take it upstairs and throw it out when you've finished," said the manager shortly.

"Here, wait a minute," pondered John, in absent-minded familiarity. "Wait a minute. This is a funny go. There's a label on that wasn't here before. *'Why not look inside?'* "

" 'Why not look inside?' " repeated someone.

"That's what it says."

There was another puzzled silence. All were arrested by some intangible suggestion of a deeper mystery than they had yet touched. One by one they began to cross the hall with the conscious air of men who were not curious but thought that they might as well see.

"Why, curse my crumpet," suddenly exploded Mr. Berge, "if that ain't the same writing as these texts!"

"By gad, but I believe you are right," assented Mr. Carlyle. "Well, why not look inside?"

The attendant, from his stooping posture, took the verdict of the ring of faces and in a trice tugged open the two buckles. The central fastening was not locked, and yielded to a touch. The flannel shirt, the weird collar and a few other garments in the nature of a "top-dressing" were flung out and John's hand plunged deeper. . . .

Harry the Actor had lived up to his dramatic instinct. Nothing was wrapped up; nay, the rich booty had been deliberately opened out and displayed, as it were, so that the overturning of the bag, when John the keybearer in an access of riotous extravagance lifted it up and strewed its contents broadcast on the floor, was like the looting of a smuggler's den, or the realization of a speculator's dream, or the bursting of an Aladdin's cave, or something incredibly lavish and bizarre. Bank-notes fluttered down and lay about in all directions, relays of sovereigns rolled away like so much dross, bonds and scrip for thousands and tens of thousands clogged the down-pouring stream of jewellery and unset gems. A yellow stone the size of a four-pound weight and twice as heavy dropped plump upon the canon's toes and sent him hopping and grimacing to the wall. A ruby-hilted kris cut across the manager's wrist as he strove to arrest the splendid rout. Still the miraculous cornucopia deluged the ground, with its pattering, ringing, bumping, crinkling, rolling, fluttering produce until, like the final tableau of some spectacular ballet, it ended with a golden rain that masked the details of the heap beneath a glittering veil of yellow sand.

"My dust!" gasped Draycott.

"My fivers, by golly!" ejaculated the bookmaker, initiating a plunge among the spoil.

"My Japanese bonds, coupons and all, and—yes, even the manu-script of my work on 'Polyphyletic Bridal Customs among the mid-Pleistocene Cave Men.' Hah!" Something approaching a cachinna-tion of delight closed the professor's contribution to the pande-monium, and eyewitnesses afterwards declared that for a moment the dignified scientist stood on one foot in the opening movement of a can-can.

"My wife's diamonds, thank heaven!" cried Sir Benjamin, with the air of a schoolboy who was very well out of a swishing.

"But what does it mean?" demanded the bewildered canon. "Here are my family heirlooms—a few decent pearls, my grandfather's collection of camei and other trifles—but who——?"

"Perhaps this offers some explanation," suggested Mr. Carlyle, unpinning an envelope that had been secured to the lining of the bag. "It is addressed 'To Seven Rich Sinners.' Shall I read it for you?"

For some reason the response was not unanimous, but it was sufficient. Mr. Carlyle cut open the envelope.

"My dear Friends,—Aren't you glad? Aren't you happy at this moment? Ah yes; but not with the true joy of regeneration that alone can bring lightness to the afflicted soul. Pause while there is

yet time. Cast off the burden of your sinful lusts, for what shall it profit a man if he shall gain the whole world and lose his own soul? (Mark, chap. viii, *v.* 36.)

"Oh, my friends, you have had an all-fired narrow squeak. Up till the Friday in last week I held your wealth in the hollow of my ungodly hand and rejoiced in my nefarious cunning, but on that day as I with my guilty female accomplice stood listening with worldly amusement to the testimony of a converted brother at a meeting of the Salvation Army on Clapham Common, the gospel light suddenly shone into our rebellious souls and then and there we found salvation. Hallelujah!

"What we have done to complete the unrighteous scheme upon which we had laboured for months has only been for your own good, dear friends that you are, though as yet divided from us by your carnal lusts. Let this be a lesson to you. Sell all you have and give it to the poor—through the organization of the Salvation Army by preference—and thereby lay up for yourselves treasures where neither moth nor rust doth corrupt and where thieves do not break through and steal. (Matthew, chap. vi, *v.* 20.)

"Yours in good works,
                    "*Private Henry, the Salvationist.*

"*P.S.* (in haste).—I may as well inform you that no crib is really uncrackable, though the Cyrus J. Coy Co.'s Safe Deposit on West 24th Street, N.Y., comes nearest the kernel. And even that I could work to the bare rock if I took hold of the job with both hands— that is to say I could have done in my sinful days. As for you, I should recommend you to change your T.A. to 'Peanut.'
                    "*U. K. G.*"

"There sounds a streak of the old Adam in that postscript, Mr. Carlyle," whispered Inspector Beedel, who had just arrived in time to hear the letter read.

The Ingenious Mr. Spinola

"You seem troubled, Parkinson. Have you been reading the Money Article again?"

Parkinson, who had been lingering a little aimlessly about the room, exhibited symptoms of embarrassed guilt. Since an unfortunate day, when it had been convincingly shown to the excellent fellow that to leave his accumulated savings on deposit at the bank was merely an uninviting mode of throwing money away, it is not too much to say that his few hundreds had led Parkinson a sorry life. Inspired by a natural patriotism and an appreciation of the advantage of $4\frac{1}{2}$ over $1\frac{1}{4}$ per cent., he had at once invested in consols. A very short time later a terrible line in a financial daily —"Consols weak"—caught his agitated eye. Consols were precipitately abandoned and a "sound industrial" took their place. Then came the rumours of an impending strike and the Conservative press voiced gloomy forebodings for the future of industrial capital. An urgent selling order, bearing Mr. Parkinson's signature, was the immediate outcome.

In the next twelve months Parkinson's few hundreds wandered through many lands and in a modest way went to support monarchies and republics, to carry on municipal enterprise and to spread the benefits of commerce. And, through all, they contrived to exist. They even assisted in establishing a rubber plantation in Madagascar and exploiting an oil discovery in Peru and yet survived. If everything could have been lost by one dire reverse Parkinson would have been content—even relieved; but with her proverbial inconsequence Fortune began by smiling and continued to smile—faintly, it is true, but appreciably—on her timorous votary. In spite of his profound ignorance of finance each of Parkinson's qualms and tremors resulted in a slight pecuniary margin to his credit. At the end of twelve months he had drawn a respectable interest, was somewhat to the good in capital, and as a waste product had acquired an abiding reputation among a small but choice coterie as a very "knowing one."

"Thank you, sir, but I am sorry if I seemed engrossed in my own affairs," he apologised in answer to Mr. Carrados's inquiry. "As a matter of fact," he added, "I hoped that I had finished with Stock Exchange transactions for the future."

"Ah, to be sure," assented Carrados. "A block of cottages Acton way, wasn't it to be?"

"I did at one time consider the investment, but on reflection I decided against property of that description. The association with houses occupied by the artisan class would not have been congenial, sir."

"Still, it might have been profitable."

"Possibly, sir. I have, however, taken up a mortgage on a detached house standing in its own grounds at Highgate. It was strongly recommended by your own estate agents—by Mr. Lethbridge himself, sir."

"I hope it will prove satisfactory, Parkinson."

"I hope so, sir, but I do not feel altogether reassured now, after seeing it."

"After seeing it? But you saw it before you took it up, surely?"

"As a matter of fact, no, sir. It was pointed out to me that the security was ample, and as I had no practical knowledge of house-valuing there was nothing to be gained by inspecting it. At the same time I was given the opportunity, I must admit; but as we were rather busy then—it was just before we went to Rome, sir—I never went there."

"Well, after all," admitted Carrados, "I hold a fair number of mortgage securities on railways and other property that I have never been within a thousand miles of. I am not in a position to criticise you, Parkinson. And this house—I suppose that it does really exist?"

"Oh yes, sir. I spent yesterday afternoon in the neighbourhood. Now that the trees are out there is not a great deal that can be actually seen from the road, but I satisfied myself that in the winter the house must be distinctly visible from several points."

"That is very satisfactory," said Carrados with equal seriousness. "But, after all, the title is the chief thing."

"So I am given to understand. Doubtless it would not be sound business, sir, but I think that if the title had been a little worse, and the appearance of the grounds a little better, I should have felt more secure. But what really concerned me is that the house is being talked about."

"Talked about?"

"Yes. It is in a secluded position, but there are some old-fashioned cottages near and these people notice things, sir. It is not difficult to induce them to talk. Refreshments are procurable at one of the cottages and I had tea there. I have since thought, from a remark made to me on leaving, that the idea may have got about that I was connected with the Scotland Yard authorities. I had no apprehension at the time of creating such an impression, sir, but I wished to make a few casual inquiries."

Carrados nodded. "Quite so," he murmured encouragingly.

"It was then that I discovered what I have alluded to. These people, having become suspicious, watch all that is to be seen at Strathblane Lodge—as it is called—and talk. They do not know what goes on there."

"That must be very disheartening for them."

"Well, sir, they find it trying. Up to less than a year ago the house was occupied by a commercial gentleman and everything was quite regular. But with the new people they don't know which are the family and who are the servants. Two or three men having the appearance of mechanics seem to be there continually, and sometimes, generally in the evening, there are visitors of a class whom one would not associate with the unpretentious nature of the establishment. Gentlemen for the most part, but occasionally ladies, I was told, coming in taxis or private motor cars and generally in evening dress."

"That ought to reassure these neighbours—the private cars and evening dress."

"I cannot say that it does, sir. And what I heard made me a little nervous also."

Something was evidently on the ingenuous creature's mind. The blind man's face wore a faintly amused smile, but he gauged the real measure of his servant's apprehension.

"Nervous of what, Parkinson?" he inquired kindly.

"Some thought that it might be a gambling-house, but others said it looked as if a worse business was carried on there. I should not like there to be any scandal or exposure, sir, and perhaps the mortgage forfeited in consequence."

"But, good heavens, man! you don't imagine that a mortgage is like a public-house licence, to be revoked in consequence of a rowdy tenant, surely?"

Parkinson's dubious silence made it increasingly plain that he had, indeed, associated his security with some such contingency, a conviction based, it appeared, when he admitted his fears, on a settled belief in the predatory intentions of a Government with whom he was not in sympathy.

"Don't give the thing another thought," counselled his employer. "If Lethbridge recommended the investment you may be sure that it is all right. As for what goes on there—that doesn't matter two straws to you, and in any case it is probably idle chatter."

"Thank you, sir. It is a relief to have your assurance. I see now that I ought to have paid no attention to such conversation, but being anxious—and seeing Sir Fergus Copling go there——"

"Sir Fergus Copling? You saw him there?"

"Yes, sir. I thought that I remembered a car that was waiting for the gate to be opened. Then I recognised Sir Fergus: it was the small dark blue car that he has come here in. And just after what I had been hearing——"

"But Sir Fergus Copling! He's a testimonial of propriety. Do you know what you are talking about, Parkinson?"

The excellent man looked even more deeply troubled than he had been about his money.

"Not in that sense, sir," he protested. "I only understood that he was a gentleman of position and a very large income, and after just listening to what was being said——"

Carrados's scepticism was intelligible. Copling was the last man to be associated with a scandal of fast life. He had come into his baronetcy quite unexpectedly a few years previously while engaged in the drab but apparently congenial business of teaching arithmetic at a public school. The chief advantage of the change of fortune, as it appeared to the recipient, was that it enabled him to transfer his attention from the lower to the higher mathematics. Without going out of his way to flout the conventions, he set himself a comparatively simple standard of living. He was too old and fixed, he said, to change much—forty and a bachelor—and the most optimistic spinster in town had reluctantly come to acquiesce.

Carrados had not forgotten this conversation when next he encountered Sir Fergus a week or so later. He knew the man well enough to be able to lead up to the subject and when an identifiable footstep fell on his ear in the hall of the Metaphysical (the dullest club in Europe, it was generally admitted) he called across to the baronet, who, as a matter of fact, had been too abstracted to notice him or anyone else.

"You aren't a member, are you?" asked Copling when they had shaken hands. "I didn't know that you went in for this sort of thing." The motion of his head indicated the monumental library which he had just quitted, but it might possibly be taken as indicating the general atmosphere of profound somnolence that enveloped the Metaphysical.

"I am not a member," admitted Carrados. "I only came to gather some material."

"Statistics?" queried Copling with interest. "We have a very useful range of works." He suddenly remembered his acquaintance's affliction. "By the way, can I be of any use to you?"

"Yes, if you will," said Carrados. "Let me go to lunch with you. There is an appalling bore hanging about and he'll nab me if I don't get past under protection."

Copling assented readily enough and took the blind man's arm.

"Where, though?" he asked at the door. "I generally"—he hesitated, with a shy laugh—"I generally go to an A.B.C. tea-shop myself. It doesn't waste so much time. But, of course——"

"Of course, a tea-shop by all means," assented Carrados.

"You are sure that you don't mind?" persisted the baronet anxiously.

"Mind? Why, I'm a shareholder!" chuckled Carrados.

"This suits me very well," remarked the ex-schoolmaster when they were seated in a remote corner of a seething general room. "Fellows used to do their best to get me into the way of going to swell places, but I always seem to drift back here. I don't mind the prices, Carrados, but hang me if I like to pay the prices simply to be inconvenienced. Yes, *hot* milk, please."

Carrados endorsed this reasonable philosophy. Carlton or Coffee-house, the Ritz or the tea-shop, it was all the same to him—life, and very enjoyable life at that. He sat and, like the spider, drew from within himself the fabric of the universe by which he was surrounded. In that inexhaustible faculty he found perfect content: he never required "to be amused."

"No, not statistics," he said presently, returning to the unfinished conversation of the club hall. "Scarcely that. More in the nature of topography, perhaps. Have you considered, Copling, how every-thing is specialised nowadays? Does anyone read the old-fashioned unpretentious *Guide-book to London* still? One would hardly think so to see how the subject is cut up. We have 'Famous London Blind-alleys,' 'Historical West-Central Door-Knockers,' 'Footsteps of Dr. Johnson between Gough Square and John Street, Adelphi,' 'The Thames from Hungerford Bridge to Charing Cross Pier,' 'Oxford Street Paving Stones on which De Quincey sat,' and so on."

"They are not familiar to me," said Sir Fergus simply.

"Nor to me; yet they sound familiar. Well, I touched journalism myself once, years ago. What do you say to 'Mysterious Double-fronted Houses of the outer Northern Suburbs'? Too comprehensive?"

"I don't know. The subject must be limited. But do you seriously contemplate such a work?"

"If I did," replied Carrados, "what could you tell me about Strathblane Lodge, Highgate?"

"Oh!" A slow smile broke on Copling's face. "That is rather extraordinary, isn't it? Do you know old Spinola? Have you been there?"

"So far I don't know the venerable Mr. Spinola and I have not been there. What is the peculiarity?"

"But you know of the automatic card-player?"

The words brought a certain amount of enlightenment. Carrados had heard more than once casual allusions to a wonderful mechanical contrivance that played cards with discrimination. He had not thought anything more of it, classing it with Kempelen's famous imposture which had for a time mystified and duped the chess world more than a century ago. So far, also, some reticence appeared to be observed about the modern contrivance, as though its inventor had no desire to have it turned into a popular show: at all events not a word about it had appeared in the Press.

"I have heard something, but not much, and I certainly have not seen it. What is it—a fraud, surely?"

Copling replied with measured consideration between the process of investigating his lightly boiled egg. It was plain that the automaton had impressed him.

"I naturally approached the subject with scepticism," he admitted, "but at the end of several demonstrations I am converted to a position of passive acquiescence. Spinola, at all events, is no charlatan. His knowledge of mathematics is profound. As you know, Carrados, the subject is my own and I am not likely to be imposed on in that particular. It was purely the scientific aspect of the invention that attracted me, for I am not a gambler in the ordinary sense. Spinola's explanation of the principles of the contrivance, when he found that I was capable of following them, was lucid and convincing. Of course he does not disclose all the details of the mechanism, but he shows enough."

"It is a gamble, then, not a mere demonstration?"

"He has spent many years on the automaton, and it must have cost thousands of pounds in experiment and construction. He makes no secret of hoping to reimburse his outlay."

"What do you play?"

"Piquet—rubicon piquet. The figure could, he claims, be set to play any game by changing or elaborating the mechanism. He had to construct it for one definite set of chances and he selected piquet as a suitable medium."

"It wins?"

"Against me invariably in the end."

"Why should it win, Copling? In a game that is nine-tenths chance, why should it win?"

"I am an indifferent player. If the tactics of the game have been reduced to machinery and the combinations are controlled by a dispassionate automaton, the one-tenth would constitute a winning factor."

"And against expert players?"

Sir Fergus admitted that to the best of his knowledge the figure still had the advantage. In answer to Carrados's further inquiry he estimated his losses at two or three hundred pounds. The stakes were whatever the visitor suggested—Spinola was something of a grandee, one inferred—and at half-crown points Sir Fergus had found the game quite expensive enough.

"Why do people go if they invariably lose?" asked the blind man.

"My dear fellow, why do they go to Monte Carlo?" was the retort, accompanied by a tolerant shrug. "Besides, I don't positively say that they always lose. One hears of people winning, though I have never seen it happen. Then I fancy that the novelty has taken with a certain set. It is a thing at the moment to go up there and have the rather bizarre experience. There is an element of the creep in it, you know—sitting and playing against that serene and unimpressionable contrivance."

"What do the others do? There is quite a company, I gather."

"Oh yes, sometimes. Occasionally one may find oneself alone. Well, the others often watch the play. Sometimes sets play bridge on their own. Then there is coffee and wine. Nothing formal, I assure you."

"Rowdy ever?"

"Oh no. The old man has a presence; I doubt if anyone would feel encouraged to go too far under Spinola's eye. Yet practically nothing seems to be known of him, not even his nationality. I have heard half-a-dozen different tales from as many cocksure men—he is a South American Spaniard ruined by a revolution; a Jesuit expelled from France through politics; an Irishman of good family settled in Warsaw, where he stole the plans from a broken-down Polish inventor; a Virginia military man, who suddenly found that he was dying from cancer and is doing this to provide a fortune for an only and beautiful daughter, and so on."

"Is there a beautiful daughter?"

"Not that I have ever seen. No, the man just cropped up, as odd people do in great capitals. Nobody really knows anything about him, but his queer salon has caught on to a certain extent."

Now any novel phase of life attracted Carrados. The mixed company that Spinola's enterprise was able to draw to an out-of-the-way suburb—the peculiar blend of science and society—was not much in itself. The various constituents could be met elsewhere to more advantage, but the assemblage might engender piquancy. And the man himself and his machine? In any case they should repay attention.

"How does one procure the entrée?" he inquired.

Copling raised a quizzical eyebrow.

"You also?" he replied. "Oh, I see; you think——Well, if you are going to discover any sleight-of-hand about the business I don't mind——"

"Yes?" prompted Carrados, for Sir Fergus had pulled up on an obvious afterthought.

"I did not intend going up again," said Copling slowly. "As a matter of fact, I have seen all that interests me. And—I suppose I may as well tell you, Carrados—I made someone a sort of promise to have nothing to do with gambling. She feels very strongly on the subject."

"She is very wise," commented the blind man.

Elation mingled with something faintly apologetic in the abrupt bestowal of the baronet's unexpected confidence.

"It was really quite a sudden and romantic happening," he continued, led on by the imperceptible encouragement of his companion's attitude. "She is called Mercia. She does not know who I am—not that that's anything," he added modestly. "She is an orphan and earns her own living. I was able to be of some slight service to her in the science galleries at South Kensington, where she was collecting material for her employer. Then we met there again and had lunch together, and so on."

"At tea-shops?"

"Oh yes. Her tastes are very simple. She doesn't like shows and society and all that."

"I congratulate you. When is it to be?"

"It? Oh! Well, we haven't settled anything like that yet. Of course this is all in confidence, Carrados."

"Absolutely—though the lady has done me rather an ill turn."

"How?"

"Well, weren't you going to introduce me to Mr. Spinola?"

"True," assented Sir Fergus. "And I don't see why I shouldn't," he added valiantly. "I need not play, and if there is any bunkum about the thing I should certainly like to see how it is done. What evening will suit you?"

An early date had suited both, and shortly after eight o'clock— an hour at which they were likely to find few guests before them— Carrados's car drew up at Strathbane Lodge. By arrangement he had picked up Copling, who lived—"of all places in the world," as people had said when they heard of it—in an unknown street near Euston. Parkinson, out of regard for the worthy man's feelings, had been left behind on the occasion and in ignorance of his master's destination.

The appearance of the place was certainly not calculated to reassure a nervous investor. The entirely neglected garden seemed to convey a hint that the tenant might be contemplating a short occupation and a hasty flight. Nor did the exterior of the house do much to remove the unfortunate impression. Only a philosopher or an habitual defaulter would live in such a state.

The venerable Mr. Spinola received them in the salon set apart for the display of the automaton and for cards in general. It was a room of fair proportions—doubtless the largest in the house—and quite passably furnished, though in a rather odd and incongruous style. But probably any furniture on earth would have seemed incongruous to the strange, idol-like presence which the inventor had thought fit to adapt to the uses of his mechanism. The figure was placed on a low pedestal, sufficiently raised from the carpet on four plain wooden legs for all the space underneath to be clearly visible. The body was a squat, cross-legged conception, typical of an Indian deity, the head singularly life-like through the heavy gilding with which the face was covered, and behind the merely contemplative expression that dominated the golden mask the carver had by chance or intention lined a faint suggestion of cynical contempt.

"You have come to see my little figure—Aurelius, as we call him among outselves?" said the bland old gentleman benignly. "That is right; that is right." He shook hands with them both, and received Mr. Carrados, on Sir Fergus's introduction, as though he was a very dear friend from whom he had long been parted. It was difficult indeed for Max to disengage himself from the effusive Spinola's affection without a wrench.

"Mr. Carrados happens to be blind, Mr. Spinola," interposed Copling, seeing that their host was so far in ignorance of the fact.

"Impossible! Impossible!" exclaimed Spinola, riveting his own very bright eyes on his guest's insentient ones. "Yet," he added, "one would not jest——"

"It is quite true," was the matter-of-fact corroboration. "My hands must be my eyes, Mr. Spinola. In place of seeing, will you permit me to touch your wonderful creation?"

The old man's assent was immediate and cordial. They moved across the room towards the figure, the inventor modestly protesting:

"You flatter me, my dear sir. After all, it is but a toy in large; nothing but a toy."

A weary-looking youth, the only other occupant of the room, threw down the illustrated weekly that he had picked up on the new arrivals' entrance and detained Copling.

"Yes, I had been toying a little before you arrived," he remarked flippantly. "I came early to cut Dora Lascelle off from the idle crowd and the silly little rabbit isn't coming, it appears. I didn't want to play, because, for a fact, I have no money, but the old thing bored me to hysterics. Good God! how he can talk so little on anything really entertaining, like *The Giddy Flappers* or Trixie Fluffs divorce, and so much about strange, unearthly things that no other living creature has ever seen even in a dream, baffles my imagination. What's an 'integral calculus,' Copling? No, don't tell me, after all. Let me forget the benumbing episode as soon as possible."

"Do you wish for a game, Sir Fergus?" broke in Spinola's soft voice from across the room. "Doubtless Mr. Carrados might like to follow someone else's play before he makes the experiment."

Copling hesitated. He had not come to play, as he had already told his friend, but Max gave no sign of coming to his assistance.

"Perhaps you, Crediton?" said the mathematician; but young Crediton shook his head and smiled wisely. Copling was too easygoing to stand out. He crossed the room and sat down at the automaton's table.

"And the stake?"

"Suppose we merely have a guinea on the game?" suggested the visitor.

Spinola acquiesced with the air of one to whom a three-penny bit or a kingdom would have been equally indifferent. The deal fell to Copling and the automaton therefore had the first "elder hand," with the advantage of a discard of five cards against its opponent's three.

Carrados had already been shown the theory of the contrivance. He now followed Spinola's operations as the game proceeded. The old man picked up the twelve cards dealt to the automaton and carefully arranged them in their proper places on a square shield that was connected with the front of the figure. As each fell into its slot it registered its presence on the delicate mechanism that the figure contained.

"The discard," remarked Spinola, and moved a small lever. The left hand of the automaton was raised, came over the shield which hid its cards from the opponent, touched one with an extended finger, and affixing it by suction, lifted the selected card from the slot and dropped it face downwards on the table.

"A little slow, a little cumbersome," apologised the inventor as the motions were repeated until five cards had been thrown out. "The left hand is used for the discard alone, as a different movement is necessary." He picked up the five new cards from the stock and arranged them as he had done the hand. "Now we proceed to the play."

Crediton strolled across to watch the game. He stood behind

Copling, while Carrados remained near the automaton. Spinola opened the movements.

"Aurelius has no voice, of course," he said, studying the display of cards, "so I—point of five."

"Good," conceded the opponent.

Spinola registered the detail on one of an elaborate set of dials that produced a further development in the machinery.

"Spades," he announced, declaring the suit that he had won the "points" on. "Tierce major."

"Quart to the queen—hearts," claimed Copling, and Spinola moved another dial to register the opponent's advantage.

"Three kings."

"Good," was the reply.

"Three tens," added the senior player, as his three kings, being good against the other hand, enabled him to count the lower trio also. "Five for the point and two trios—eleven." Every detail of the scoring and of the ensuing play was registered as the other things had been.

This finished the preliminaries and the play of the hands began. The automaton, in response to the release of the machinery, moved its right arm with the same deliberation that had marked its former action and laid a card face upwards on the table. For the blind man's benefit each card was named as it was played. At the end of the hand Copling had won "the cards"—a matter of ten extra points—with seven tricks to five and the score stood to his advantage at 27—17.

"Not bad for the junior hand," commented Crediton. "Do you know"—he addressed the inventor—"there is a sort of 'average,' as they call it, that you are supposed to play up to? I forget how it goes, but 27 is jolly high for the minor hand, I know."

"I have heard of it," replied Spinola politely. Crediton could not make out why the other two men smiled broadly.

The succeeding hands developed no particular points of interest. The scoring ruled low and in the end Copling won by 129 to 87. Spinola purred congratulation.

"I am always delighted to see Aurelius lose," he declared, paying out his guinea with a princely air.

"Why?" demanded Crediton.

"Because it shows that I have succeeded beyond expectation, my dear young sir: I have made him almost human. Now, Mr. Carrados——"

"With pleasure," assented the blind man. "Though I am afraid that I shall not afford you the delight of losing, Mr. Spinola."

"One never knows, one never knows," beamed the old man. "Shall we say——"

"Half-crown points—for variety?"

"Very good. Ah, our deal." He dealt the hands and proceeded to dispose the twelve that fell to the automaton on the shield. There was a moment of indecision. "Pray, Mr. Carrados, do you not arrange your cards?"

"I have done so." He had, in fact, merely spread out his hand in the usual fan formation and run an identifying finger once round the upper edges. The cards remained as they had been dealt, face downwards.

"Wonderful! And that enables you to distinguish them?"

"The ink and the impression on a plain surface—oh yes." He threw out the full discard as he spoke and took in the upper five of the stock.

"You overwhelm us; you accentuate the tiresome deliberation of poor Aurelius." Spinola was hovering about the external fittings of the figure with unusual fussiness. When at length he released the left hand it seemed for an almost perceptible moment that the action hung. Then the arm descended and carried out the discard.

"Point of five," said Carrados.

"Good."

"In spades. Quint major in spades also, tierce to the knave in clubs, fourteen aces"—*i.e.* four aces; "fourteen" in the language of piquet as they score that number. He did not wait for his opponent to assent to each count, knowing, after the point had passed, that the other calls were good against anything that could possibly be held. "Five, twenty, twenty-three, ninety-seven." Having reached thirty before his opponent scored, and without a card having so far been played, his score automatically advanced by sixty. That is the "repique."

"By Jove!" exclaimed Crediton, "that's the first time I've ever known Aurelius repiqued."

"Oh, it has happened," retorted Spinola almost testily.

The play of the hand was bound to go in Carrados's favour—he held eight certain tricks. He won "the cards" with two tricks to spare and the round closed at 119—5.

"You look like being delighted again, Mr. Spinola," remarked Crediton a little cruelly.

"Suppose you make yourself useful by dealing for me," interposed Carrados. "Of course," he reminded his host, "it does not do for me to handle any cards but my own."

"I had not thought of that," replied Spinola, looking at him shrewdly. "If you had no conscience you would be a dangerous opponent, Mr. Carrados."

"The same might be said of any man," was the reply. "That is why it is so satisfactory to play an automaton."

"Oh, Aurelius has no conscience, you know," chimed in Crediton sapiently. "Mr. Spinola couldn't find room for it among the wheels."

The second hand was not eventful. Each player had to be content to make about the "average" which Crediton had ingenuously discovered. It raised the scores to 33—130. Two hands followed in the same prudent spirit; the fifth—Carrados's "elder"—found the position 169—67.

"Only two this time," remarked Carrados, taking in.

"Jupiter!" murmured Crediton. It is unusual for the senior hand to leave even one of the five cards to which he is entitled. It indicated an unusually strong hand. The automaton evidently thought so too. It availed itself of all the six alternative cards and, as the play disclosed, completely cut up its own hand to save the repique by beating Carrados on the point. It won the point, to find that its opponent only held a low quart, a tierce and three kings. As a result Carrados won "the cards" and the score stood 199—79. The discard was, in fact, an experiment in bluff. Carrados *might* have held a quint and fourteen kings for all the opposing hand disclosed.

"What on earth did you do that for?" demanded Copling. He himself played an eminently straightforward game—and generally lost.

"I'll bet I know," put in Crediton. "You are getting rather close, Mr. Spinola—the last hand and you need twenty-one to save the rubicon." The "rubicon" means that instead of the loser's score being deducted from the winner's in arriving at the latter's total, it is *added* to it—a possible difference of nearly 200 points.

"We shall see; we shall see," muttered Spinola with a little less than his usual suavity.

Whatever concern he had, however, was groundless, for the game ended tamely enough. Carrados ought to have won the point and divided tricks, leaving his opponent a minor quart and a solitary trio—about 15 on the hand. By a careless discard he threw away both chances and the final score stood at 205—112. Copling, who had come to regard his friend's play as rather excellent, was silent. Crediton almost shrieked his disapproval and seizing the cards demonstrated to his heart's content.

"Ninety-three and the hundred for the game—twenty-four pounds and one half-crown," said the loser, counting out notes and coin to the amount. "It has been an experience for both of us—Aurelius and myself."

"And certainly for me," added Carrados.

"Look here," interposed Crediton, "Aurelius seems off his play. If you don't mind taking my paper, Mr. Spinola, I should like another go."

"As you please," assented the old man. "Your undertaking is, of course——" The gesture suggested "quite equal to that of the cashier of the Bank of England." The venerable person had, in fact, regained his lofty pecuniary indifference. "The same point?"

"Right-o," cheerfully assented the youth.

"I will go and think over my shortcomings," said Carrados.

He started to cross the room to a seat and ran into a couch. With a gasp Copling hastened to his assistance. Then he found his arm detained and heard the whisper. "Sit down with me."

Across the room the play had begun again and with a little care they could converse without the possibility of a word being overheard.

"What is it?" asked Sir Fergus.

"The golden one will win. It is only when the cards are not exposed that you play on equal terms."

"But I won?"

"Because it is well to lose sometimes and, by choice, when the stake is low. That witless youth will have to pay for both of us."

"But how—how on earth do you suggest that it is done?"

"Look round cautiously. What eyes overlook Crediton's hand as he sits there?"

"What eyes? Good gracious! is there anything in that?"

"What is it?"

"There is a trophy of Japanese arms high up on the wall. An iron mask surmounts it. It has glass eyes. I have never seen anything like that before."

"Any others round the walls?"

"There is a stuffed tiger's head on our right and a puma's or something of that sort on the left."

"In case a suspicious player asks to have the places changed or holds his cards awkwardly. Working the automaton from other positions is probably also arranged for."

"But how can a knowledge of the opponent's cards affect the automaton? The dials——"

"The dials are all bunkum. While you were playing I took the liberty of altering them and for a whole hand the dials indicated that you must inevitably be holding eight clubs and four spades. All the time you were leading out hearts and diamonds and the automaton serenely followed suit. The only effective machinery is that indicating the display of cards on the shield and controlling the hands, and that is worked by a keyboard and electric current from the room below. The watcher behind the mask telephones the opposing hand, the discard and the take-in. The automaton's hand has already been indicated below. You see the enormous advantage the hidden player has? When he is the minor hand he knows everything that is to be known before he discards. When he is the elder he knows almost everything. By concentrating on one detail he can practically always balk the pique, the repique and the kapot, if it is necessary to play for safety. You remember what Crediton said—that he had never known Aurelius repiqued before. The leisurely manipulation of the dials gives plenty of time. An even ordinary player in that position can do the rest."

Copling scarcely knew whether to believe or not. It sounded plausible, but it reflected monstrously.

"You speak of a telephone," he said. "How can you definitely say that such a thing is being used? You have never been in the room before and we've scarcely been here an hour. It—it may be awfully serious, you know."

Carrados smiled.

"Can you hear the kitchen door being opened at this moment or detect the exact aroma of our host's mocha?" he demanded.

"Not in the least," admitted Copling.

"Then of course it is hopeless to expect you to pick up the whisper of a man behind a mask a score of feet away. How fearfully in the dark you seeing folk must be!"

"Can you possibly do that?" Even as he was speaking the door opened and a servant entered, bringing coffee and an assortment of viands sufficiently exotic to maintain the rather Oriental nature of entertainment.

"Stroll across and see how the game is going," suggested Carrados. "Have a look at Crediton's discard and then come back."

Sir Fergus did not quite follow the purpose, but he nodded and proceeded to comply with his usual amiable spirit.

"It stands at 137 to 75 against Crediton and they are playing the last hand. Our young friend looks like losing thirty or forty pounds."

"And his discard?"

"Oh—seven and nine of clubs and the knave of hearts."

Carrados held out a slip of paper on which he had already pencilled a few words. The baronet took it, looked and whistled softly. He had read: "Clubs, seven, nine. Hearts, knave."

"Conjuring?" he interrogated.

"Quite as simple—listening."

"I suppose I must accept it. What staggers me is that you can pick out a whisper when the room is full of other louder sounds. Now if there had been absolute stillness——"

"Merely use. There's nothing more in it than in seeing a mouse and a mountain, or a candle and the sun, at the same time. Well, what are we going to do about it?"

Copling began to look acutely unhappy.

"I suppose we must do something," he ruminated, "but I must say that I wish we needn't. I mean, I wish we hadn't dropped on this. You know, Carrados, whatever is going on, Spinola is no charlatan. He does understand mathematics."

"That makes him all the more dangerous. But I should like to produce more definite proof before we do anything. . . . Does he ever leave us in the room?"

"I have never known it. No, he hovers round his Aurelius."

"Never mind. Ah, the game is finished."

The game was finished and it needed no inquiry to learn how it had gone. Mr. Crediton was handing the venerable Spinola a memorandum of indebtedness. His words and attitude did not convey the impression of a graceful loser.

"I wish you two men would give me the tip for beating this purgatorial image," he grumbled as they came up. "I thought that he'd struck a losing line after your experience and this is the result." He indicated the spectacle of their amiable host folding up his I.O.U. preparatory to dropping it carelessly into a letter-rack, and shrugged his shoulders with keen disgust.

"I'll tell you if you like," suggested Sir Fergus. "Hold the better cards."

"And play them better," added Carrados. "Good heavens!"

A very untoward thing had happened. They had all been standing together round the table, Spinola purring appreciatively, Crediton fuming his ill-restrained annoyance, and the other two mildly satirical at his expense. Carrados held a cup of coffee in his hand. He reached towards the table with it, seemed to imagine that he was a full foot nearer than he was, and before anyone had divined his mistake, cup, saucer and the entire contents had dropped neatly upon Mr. Spinola's startled feet, saturating his lower extremities to the skin.

"Good heavens! What on earth have I done?"

Crediton shrieked out his ill-humour in gratified amusement; Sir Fergus reddened deeply with embarrassment at his friend's mishap. Victim and culprit stood the ordeal best.

"My unfortunate defect!" murmured Carrados with feeling. "How ever can I——"

"I who have eyes ought to have looked after my guest better," replied Spinola with antique courtliness. He reduced Crediton with a glance of quiet dignity and declined Carrados's handkerchief with a reassuring touch on the blind man's arm. "No, no, my dear sir, if you will excuse me for a few minutes. It is really nothing, really nothing, I do assure you."

He withdrew from the room to change. Copling began to prepare a reassuring phrase to meet Carrados's self-reproaches when they should break forth again. But the blind man's tone had altered; he was no longer apologetic.

"Play them better," he repeated to Crediton, as if there had been no interruption, "and play under conditions that are equal. For instance, it might be worth while making sure that a Japanese mask does not conceal a pair of human eyes. If I were a loser I should be inclined to have a look."

Not until then did it occur to Sir Fergus that his friend's clumsiness had been a calculated ruse to force Spinola to withdraw for a few minutes. Later on he might be able to admire the simple ingenuity of the trick, but at that moment he almost hated Carrados for the cool effrontery with which he had duped all their feelings.

No such subtleties, however, concerned Crediton. He stared at the blind man, followed the indication of his gesture and all at once grasped the significance of the hint.

"By George, I shouldn't wonder if you aren't right!" he exclaimed. "There are one or two things——" Without further consideration he rushed a table against the wall, swung up a chair on to it, and mounting the structure began to wrench the details of the trophy from side to side and up and down in his excited efforts to displace them.

"Hurry up," urged Copling, more nervous than excited. "He won't be long."

"Hurry up?" Crediton paused, panting from his furious efforts, and found time to look down upon his accomplices. "I don't think that it's for us to concern ourselves, by George!" he retorted. "Spinola had better hurry up and bolt for it, I should say. There's light behind here—a hole through the wall. I believe the place is a regular swindling hell."

His eyes went to the group of weapons again and the sight gave him a new idea.

"Aha, what price this?" he cried, and pulling a short sword out of its sheath he drove it in between mask and wall and levered the shell away, nails and all. "By God, if the eyes aren't a pair of opera-glasses! And there's a regular paraphernalia here——"

"So," interrupted a quiet voice behind them, "you have been too clever for an old man, Mr. Carrados?"

Spinola had returned unheard and was regarding the work of detection with the utmost benignness. Copling looked and felt ridiculously guilty; the blind man betrayed no emotion at all and both were momentarily silent. It fell to Crediton to voice retort.

"My I.O.U., if you don't mind, Mr. Spinola," he demanded, tumbling down from his perch and holding out an insistent hand.

"With great pleasure," replied Spinola, picking it out from the contents of the letter-rack. "Also," he continued, referring to the contents of his pocket-book, while his guest tore up the memorandum into very small pieces and strewed them about the carpet, "also the sum of fifty-seven pounds, thirteen shillings which I feel myself compelled to return to you in spite of your invariable grace in losing. I have already rung; you will find the front door waiting open for you, Mr. Crediton."

" 'Compelled' is good," sneered Crediton. "You will probably find a train waiting for you at Charing Cross, Mr. Spinola. I advise you to catch it before the police arrive." He nodded to the other two men and departed, to spread the astounding news in the most interested quarters.

Spinola continued to beam irrepressible benevolence.

"You are equally censorious, if more polite than Mr. Crediton in expressing it, eh, my dear young friends?" he said.

"I thought that you were a genuine mathematician—I vouched for it," replied Sir Fergus with more regret than anything else. "And the extent of your achievement has been to contrive a vulgar imposture—in the guise of an ingenious inventor to swindle society by a sham automaton that doesn't even work."

"You thought that—you still think that?"

"What else is there to think? We have seen with our own eyes."

"And"—turning to his other guest—"Mr. Carrados, who does not see?"

"I am waiting to hear," replied the blind man.

"But you, Sir Fergus, you who are also—in an elementary way—a mathematician, and one with whom I have conversed freely, you regard me as a common swindler and think that this—this tawdry piece of buffoonery that is only designed to appeal to the vapid craze for novelty of your foolish friends—this is, as you say, the extent of my achievement?"

Copling gave a warning cry and sprang forward, but it was too late to avert what he saw coming. In his petulant annoyance at the comparison Spinola had laid an emphasising hand upon Aurelius and half unconsciously had given the figure a contemptuous push. It swayed, seemed to poise for a second, and then toppling irretrievably forward crashed to the floor with an impact that snapped the golden head from off its shoulders and shook the room and the very house itself.

"There, there," muttered the old man, as though he was doing no more than regretting a broken tea-cup; "let it lie, let it lie. We have finished our work together, Aurelius and I. Now let the whole world——"

It would have been too much to expect the remainder of the mysterious household, whoever its members were, to ignore the tempestuous course of events taking place within their midst. The door was opened suddenly and a young lady, with consternation charged on every feature of her attractive face, burst into the room. For the moment her eyes took in only two figures of the curious group—the aged Spinola and his fallen handiwork.

"Granda!" she cried, "whatever's happened? What is it all? Oh, are you hurt?"

"It is nothing, nothing at all; a mere contretemps of no importance," he reassured her quickly. Then, with a recurrence of his most grandiloquent manner, he recalled her to the situation. "Mercia, our guests—Sir Fergus Copling, Mr. Carrados. Sir Fergus, Mr. Carrados—Miss Dugard."

"Then it *is* Mercia!" articulated the bewildered baronet. "Mercia, you here! What does it mean? What are you doing?"

"What are you doing, Sir Fergus?" retorted the girl in cold reproach. "Is this the way you generally keep your promises? Gambling!"

"Well, really," stammered the abashed gentleman, "I—I only——"

"Sir Fergus only played a game for a mere nominal stake, to demonstrate the working to his friend," interposed Spinola with a shrewd glance—a curious blend of serpentine innocence and dovelike cunning—at the estranged young people.

"And won," added Sir Fergus *sotto voce*, as if that fact condoned his offence.

"Won indeed!" flashed out Miss Dugard. "Of course you won— I let you. Do you think that we wished to take money from you now?"

"You—*you* let me!" muttered Sir Fergus helplessly. "Good heavens!"

"I am grateful that your consideration also extends to your friend's friend," put in Carrados pleasantly.

Miss Dugard smiled darkly at the suavely-given thrust and showed her pretty little teeth almost as though she would like to use them.

"There, there, that will do, my child," said the old man indulgently. "Sir Fergus and Mr. Carrados are entitled to an explanation and they shall have it. The moment is opportune; the work of a lifetime is complete. You have seen, Sir Fergus, the sums that Aurelius— assisted, as we will now admit, by a little external manipulation— has gathered into our domestic exchequer. Where have they gone, these hundreds and thousands that you may estimate? In lavish living and a costly establishment? Observe this very ordinary apartment—the best the house possesses. Recall the grounds through which you entered. Sum up the simple hospitality of which you have partaken. In expensive personal tastes and habits? I assure you, Sir Fergus, that I am a man of the most frugal life; my granddaughter inherits the propensity. In what, then? In advancing science, in benefitting humanity, in furthering human progress. I am going to prove to you that I have perfected one of the greatest mechanical inventions of all ages, and I ask you to credit the plain statement that all my private fortune and all the winnings that you have seen upon this table—with the exception of a bare margin for the necessities of life—have been spent in perfecting it."

He paused with a senile air of triumph and seemed to challenge comment.

"But surely," ventured Copling, "surely on the strength of this you would have had no difficulty in obtaining direct financial support. Well, I myself——"

Spinola smiled a peculiar smile, shaking his head sagely.

"Take care, my generous young friend, take care. You may not quite comprehend what you are saying."

"Why?"

Still swayed by his own gentle amusement, the old man crossed the room to a desk, selected a letter from a bulky pile and handed it to his guest without a word.

Copling glanced at the heading and signature, then read the contents and frowned annoyance.

"This is from my secretary," he commented lamely.

"That is what a secretary is for, is it not—to save his employer trouble?" insinuated Spinola. "He took me for a crank or a begging-letter imposter, of course." Then came the pathetic whisper. "They *all* took me for that."

Sir Fergus folded the letter and handed it back again.

"I am very sorry," he said simply.

"It was natural, perhaps. Still, something had to be done. My work was all arrested. I could no longer pay my two skilled mechanics. Time was pressing. I am a very old man—I am more than a hundred years old——"

The girl shot a sudden, half-frightened, pleading glance at her lover, then at Mr. Carrados. It checked the exclamation that would have come from Copling; the blind man passed the monstrous claim without betraying astonishment.

"—a very old man and my work was yet incomplete. So I contrived Aurelius. I could, of course, have perfected a model that would have done all that has been claimed for this—mere child's play to me—but what would have been the good? Such a mechanical player would have lost as often as he would have won. Hence our little subterfuge, a means amply justified by so glorious an end."

He was smiling happily—the weeks of elaborate deception were, at the worst, an innocent ruse to him—and concluded with an emphasising nod to each in turn, to Mercia, who regarded him with implicit faith and veneration, to Copling, who at that moment surely had ample justification for declaring to himself that he was dashed if he knew what to think, and to Carrados, whose sightless look agreed to everything and gave nothing in reply. Then the old man stood up and produced his keys.

"Come, my friends," he continued; "the moment has arrived. I am going to show you now what no other eye has yet been privileged to see. My mechanics worked on the parts under my instruction, but in ignorance of the end. Even Mercia—a good girl, a very clever girl—has never yet passed this door." He had led them through the house and brought them to a brick-built, windowless shed, isolated in the garden at the back. "I little thought that the first demonstration——But things have fallen so, things have fallen, and one never knows. Perhaps it is for the best." An iron door had yielded to his patent key. He entered, turned on a bunch of electric lights and stood aside. "Behold!"

The room was a workshop, fitted with the highly finished devices of metal-working and littered with the scraps and débris of their use. In the middle stood a more elaborate contrivance —the finished product of brass and steel—a cube scarcely larger than a packing-case, but seemingly filled with wheels and rods, relay upon relay, and row after row, all giving the impression of exquisite precision in workmanship and astonishing intricacy of detail.

"Why, it's a calculating machine," exclaimed Sir Fergus, going forward with immense interest.

"It is an analytical engine, or, to use the more common term, a calculating machine, as you say," assented the inventor. "I need hardly remind you, of course, that one does not spend a lifetime and a fortune in contriving a machine to do single calculations, however involved, but for the more useful and practical purpose of working out involved series with absolute precision. Still, for the purpose of a trial demonstration we will begin with an ordinary proposition, if you, Sir Fergus, will kindly set one. My engine now is constructed to work to fifty places of figures and twelve orders of difference."

"If you have accomplished that," remarked Copling, accepting the pencil and the slip of paper offered him, "you have surpassed the dreams of Babbage, Mr. Spinola."

There was a sudden gasp from Mercia, but it passed unheeded in the keen excitement of the great occasion. Spinola received the paper with its row of signs and figures and turned to operate his engine. He paused to look back gleefully.

"So you never guessed, Sir Fergus?" he chuckled cunningly. "We kept the secret well, but it doesn't matter now. *I am Charles Babbage!*"

The noise of wheel and connecting-rod cut off the chance of a reply, even if anyone had been prepared to make one. But no one, in that bewildering moment, was.

"The solution," announced Spinola with a flourish, and he passed a little slip of metal stamped with a row of figures into Sir Fergus's hand. Then, with a curious indifference to their verdict, he turned away from the group and applied himself to the machine again.

"What is it? Is it not correct?" demanded Mercia in an agonised whisper. She had not looked at the solution, but at her lover's face, and her hand suddenly gripped his arm.

"It is incomprehensible," replied Sir Fergus, dropping his voice so that the old man could not overhear. "It isn't a matter of right or wrong—it is a mere farrago of nonsense."

"But harmless nonsense—quite harmless," interposed Carrados softly from behind them. "Come, we can safely leave him here; you will always be able to leave him safely here. Help Miss Dugard out Copling. It is better, believe me, to leave him now."

Spinola did not turn. He was bending over the machine to which he had given life, brain and fortune, touching its wheels and sliding rods with loving fingers. They passed silently from his presence and crept back to the deserted salon, where the deposed head of Aurelius leered cynically at them from the floor.

Note on Sources

The stories in this collection have been taken from the following sources:

"The Coin of Dionysius," "The Knight's Cross Signal Problem," "The Tragedy at Brookbend Cottage," "The Last Exploit of Harry the Actor" from *Max Carrados* (Methuen, London, 1914).

"The Disappearance of Marie Severe," "The Mystery of the Poisoned Dish of Mushrooms," "The Ghost at Massingham Mansions," "The Ingenious Mr. Spinola" from *The Eyes of Max Carrados* (Doran, New York, 1924).

"The Mystery of the Vanished Petition Crown," "The Holloway Flat Tragedy" from *Max Carrados Mysteries* (Hodder and Stoughton, London, 1927).

A CATALOGUE OF
SELECTED DOVER BOOKS
IN ALL FIELDS OF INTEREST

A CATALOGUE OF SELECTED DOVER
BOOKS IN ALL FIELDS OF INTEREST

RACKHAM'S COLOR ILLUSTRATIONS FOR WAGNER'S RING. Rackham's finest mature work—all 64 full-color watercolors in a faithful and lush interpretation of the *Ring*. Full-sized plates on coated stock of the paintings used by opera companies for authentic staging of Wagner. Captions aid in following complete Ring cycle. Introduction. 64 illustrations plus vignettes. 72pp. 8⅝ x 11¼.   23779-6 Pa. $6.00

CONTEMPORARY POLISH POSTERS IN FULL COLOR, edited by Joseph Czestochowski. 46 full-color examples of brilliant school of Polish graphic design, selected from world's first museum (near Warsaw) dedicated to poster art. Posters on circuses, films, plays, concerts all show cosmopolitan influences, free imagination. Introduction. 48pp. 9⅜ x 12¼.
23780-X Pa. $6.00

GRAPHIC WORKS OF EDVARD MUNCH, Edvard Munch. 90 haunting, evocative prints by first major Expressionist artist and one of the greatest graphic artists of his time: *The Scream, Anxiety, Death Chamber, The Kiss, Madonna*, etc. Introduction by Alfred Werner. 90pp. 9 x 12.
23765-6 Pa. $5.00

THE GOLDEN AGE OF THE POSTER, Hayward and Blanche Cirker. 70 extraordinary posters in full colors, from Maitres de l'Affiche, Mucha, Lautrec, Bradley, Cheret, Beardsley, many others. Total of 78pp. 9⅜ x 12¼.   22753-7 Pa. $6.95

THE NOTEBOOKS OF LEONARDO DA VINCI, edited by J. P. Richter. Extracts from manuscripts reveal great genius; on painting, sculpture, anatomy, sciences, geography, etc. Both Italian and English. 186 ms. pages reproduced, plus 500 additional drawings, including studies for *Last Supper*, Sforza monument, etc. 860pp. 7⅞ x 10¾. (Available in U.S. only)
22572-0, 22573-9 Pa., Two-vol. set $19.90

THE CODEX NUTTALL, as first edited by Zelia Nuttall. Only inexpensive edition, in full color, of a pre-Columbian Mexican (Mixtec) book. 88 color plates show kings, gods, heroes, temples, sacrifices. New explanatory, historical introduction by Arthur G. Miller. 96pp. 11⅜ x 8½. (Available in U.S. only)   23168-2 Pa. $7.95

UNE SEMAINE DE BONTÉ, A SURREALISTIC NOVEL IN COLLAGE, Max Ernst. Masterpiece created out of 19th-century periodical illustrations, explores worlds of terror and surprise. Some consider this Ernst's greatest work. 208pp. 8⅛ x 11.   23252-2 Pa. $6.00

DRAWINGS OF WILLIAM BLAKE, William Blake. 92 plates from Book of Job, *Divine Comedy, Paradise Lost,* visionary heads, mythological figures, Laocoon, etc. Selection, introduction, commentary by Sir Geoffrey Keynes. 178pp. 8⅛ x 11. 22303-5 Pa. $5.00

ENGRAVINGS OF HOGARTH, William Hogarth. 101 of Hogarth's greatest works: *Rake's Progress, Harlot's Progress, Illustrations for Hudibras, Before and After, Beer Street and Gin Lane,* many more. Full commentary. 256pp. 11 x 13¾. 22479-1 Pa. $12.95

DAUMIER: 120 GREAT LITHOGRAPHS, Honore Daumier. Wide-ranging collection of lithographs by the greatest caricaturist of the 19th century. Concentrates on eternally popular series on lawyers, on married life, on liberated women, etc. Selection, introduction, and notes on plates by Charles F. Ramus. Total of 158pp. 9⅜ x 12¼. 23512-2 Pa. $6.00

DRAWINGS OF MUCHA, Alphonse Maria Mucha. Work reveals drafts-man of highest caliber: studies for famous posters and paintings, render-ings for book illustrations and ads, etc. 70 works, 9 in color; including 6 items not drawings. Introduction. List of illustrations. 72pp. 9⅜ x 12¼. (Available in U.S. only) 23672-2 Pa. $4.50

GIOVANNI BATTISTA PIRANESI: DRAWINGS IN THE PIERPONT MORGAN LIBRARY, Giovanni Battista Piranesi. For first time ever all of Morgan Library's collection, world's largest. 167 illustrations of rare Piranesi drawings—archeological, architectural, decorative and visionary. Essay, detailed list of drawings, chronology, captions. Edited by Felice Stampfle. 144pp. 9⅜ x 12¼. 23714-1 Pa. $7.50

NEW YORK ETCHINGS (1905-1949), John Sloan. All of important American artist's N.Y. life etchings. 67 works include some of his best art; also lively historical record—Greenwich Village, tenement scenes. Edited by Sloan's widow. Introduction and captions. 79pp. 8⅜ x 11¼. 23651-X Pa. $5.00

CHINESE PAINTING AND CALLIGRAPHY: A PICTORIAL SURVEY, Wan-go Weng. 69 fine examples from John M. Crawford's matchless private collection: landscapes, birds, flowers, human figures, etc., plus calligraphy. Every basic form included: hanging scrolls, handscrolls, album leaves, fans, etc. 109 illustrations. Introduction. Captions. 192pp. 8⅞ x 11¾. 23707-9 Pa. $7.95

DRAWINGS OF REMBRANDT, edited by Seymour Slive. Updated Lipp-mann, Hofstede de Groot edition, with definitive scholarly apparatus. All portraits, biblical sketches, landscapes, nudes, Oriental figures, classical studies, together with selection of work by followers. 550 illustrations. Total of 630pp. 9⅛ x 12¼. 21485-0, 21486-9 Pa., Two-vol. set $17.90

THE DISASTERS OF WAR, Francisco Goya. 83 etchings record horrors of Napoleonic wars in Spain and war in general. Reprint of 1st edition, plus 3 additional plates. Introduction by Philip Hofer. 97pp. 9⅜ x 8¼. 21872-4 Pa. $4.50

THE EARLY WORK OF AUBREY BEARDSLEY, Aubrey Beardsley. 157 plates, 2 in color: *Manon Lescaut, Madame Bovary, Morte Darthur, Salome,* other. Introduction by H. Marillier. 182pp. 8⅛ x 11. 21816-3 Pa. $6.50

THE LATER WORK OF AUBREY BEARDSLEY, Aubrey Beardsley. Exotic masterpieces of full maturity: *Venus and Tannhauser, Lysistrata, Rape of the Lock, Volpone,* Savoy material, etc. 174 plates, 2 in color. 186pp. 8⅛ x 11. 21817-1 Pa. $5.95

THOMAS NAST'S CHRISTMAS DRAWINGS, Thomas Nast. Almost all Christmas drawings by creator of image of Santa Claus as we know it, and one of America's foremost illustrators and political cartoonists. 66 illustrations. 3 illustrations in color on covers. 96pp. 8⅜ x 11¼. 23660-9 Pa. $3.50

THE DORÉ ILLUSTRATIONS FOR DANTE'S DIVINE COMEDY, Gustave Doré. All 135 plates from Inferno, Purgatory, Paradise; fantastic tortures, infernal landscapes, celestial wonders. Each plate with appropriate (translated) verses. 141pp. 9 x 12. 23231-X Pa. $5.00

DORÉ'S ILLUSTRATIONS FOR RABELAIS, Gustave Doré. 252 striking illustrations of *Gargantua and Pantagruel* books by foremost 19th-century illustrator. Including 60 plates, 192 delightful smaller illustrations. 153pp. 9 x 12. 23656-0 Pa. $6.00

LONDON: A PILGRIMAGE, Gustave Doré, Blanchard Jerrold. Squalor, riches, misery, beauty of mid-Victorian metropolis; 55 wonderful plates, 125 other illustrations, full social, cultural text by Jerrold. 191pp. of text. 9⅜ x 12¼. 22306-X Pa. $7.00

THE RIME OF THE ANCIENT MARINER, Gustave Doré, S. T. Coleridge. Dore's finest work, 34 plates capture moods, subtleties of poem. Full text. Introduction by Millicent Rose. 77pp. 9¼ x 12. 22305-1 Pa. $4.50

THE DORE BIBLE ILLUSTRATIONS, Gustave Doré. All wonderful, detailed plates: Adam and Eve, Flood, Babylon, Life of Jesus, etc. Brief King James text with each plate. Introduction by Millicent Rose. 241 plates. 241pp. 9 x 12. 23004-X Pa. $6.95

THE COMPLETE ENGRAVINGS, ETCHINGS AND DRYPOINTS OF ALBRECHT DURER. "Knight, Death and Devil"; "Melencolia," and more—all Dürer's known works in all three media, including 6 works formerly attributed to him. 120 plates. 235pp. 8⅜ x 11¼. 22851-7 Pa. $7.50

MECHANICK EXERCISES ON THE WHOLE ART OF PRINTING, Joseph Moxon. First complete book (1683-4) ever written about typography, a compendium of everything known about printing at the latter part of 17th century. Reprint of 2nd (1962) Oxford Univ. Press edition. 74 illustrations. Total of 550pp. 6⅛ x 9¼. 23617-X Pa. $7.95

THE COMPLETE WOODCUTS OF ALBRECHT DURER, edited by Dr. W. Kurth. 346 in all: "Old Testament," "St. Jerome," "Passion," "Life of Virgin," Apocalypse," many others. Introduction by Campbell Dodgson. 285pp. 8½ x 12¼. 21097-9 Pa. $7.50

DRAWINGS OF ALBRECHT DURER, edited by Heinrich Wolfflin. 81 plates show development from youth to full style. Many favorites; many new. Introduction by Alfred Werner. 96pp. 8⅛ x 11. 22352-3 Pa. $6.00

THE HUMAN FIGURE, Albrecht Dürer. Experiments in various techniques—stereometric, progressive proportional, and others. Also life studies that rank among finest ever done. Complete reprinting of Dresden Sketchbook. 170 plates. 355pp. 8⅜ x 11¼. 21042-1 Pa. $7.95

OF THE JUST SHAPING OF LETTERS, Albrecht Dürer. Renaissance artist explains design of Roman majuscules by geometry, also Gothic lower and capitals. Grolier Club edition. 43pp. 7⅞ x 10¾ 21306-4 Pa. $3.00

TEN BOOKS ON ARCHITECTURE, Vitruvius. The most important book ever written on architecture. Early Roman aesthetics, technology, classical orders, site selection, all other aspects. Stands behind everything since. Morgan translation. 331pp. 5⅜ x 8½. 20645-9 Pa. $5.00

THE FOUR BOOKS OF ARCHITECTURE, Andrea Palladio. 16th-century classic responsible for Palladian movement and style. Covers classical architectural remains, Renaissance revivals, classical orders, etc. 1738 Ware English edition. Introduction by A. Placzek. 216 plates. 110pp. of text. 9½ x 12¾. 21308-0 Pa. $10.00

HORIZONS, Norman Bel Geddes. Great industrialist stage designer, "father of streamlining," on application of aesthetics to transportation, amusement, architecture, etc. 1932 prophetic account; function, theory, specific projects. 222 illustrations. 312pp. 7⅞ x 10¾. 23514-9 Pa. $6.95

FRANK LLOYD WRIGHT'S FALLINGWATER, Donald Hoffmann. Full, illustrated story of conception and building of Wright's masterwork at Bear Run, Pa. 100 photographs of site, construction, and details of completed structure. 112pp. 9¼ x 10. 23671-4 Pa. $5.95

THE ELEMENTS OF DRAWING, John Ruskin. Timeless classic by great Viltorian; starts with basic ideas, works through more difficult. Many practical exercises. 48 illustrations. Introduction by Lawrence Campbell. 228pp. 5⅜ x 8½. 22730-8 Pa. $3.75

GIST OF ART, John Sloan. Greatest modern American teacher, Art Students League, offers innumerable hints, instructions, guided comments to help you in painting. Not a formal course. 46 illustrations. Introduction by Helen Sloan. 200pp. 5⅜ x 8½. 23435-5 Pa. $4.00

THE ANATOMY OF THE HORSE, George Stubbs. Often considered the great masterpiece of animal anatomy. Full reproduction of 1766 edition, plus prospectus; original text and modernized text. 36 plates. Introduction by Eleanor Garvey. 121pp. 11 x 14¾.   23402-9 Pa. $8.95

BRIDGMAN'S LIFE DRAWING, George B. Bridgman. More than 500 illustrative drawings and text teach you to abstract the body into its major masses, use light and shade, proportion; as well as specific areas of anatomy, of which Bridgman is master. 192pp. 6½ x 9¼. (Available in U.S. only)
22710-3 Pa. $4.50

ART NOUVEAU DESIGNS IN COLOR, Alphonse Mucha, Maurice Verneuil, Georges Auriol. Full-color reproduction of *Combinaisons ornementales* (c. 1900) by Art Nouveau masters. Floral, animal, geometric, interlacings, swashes—borders, frames, spots—all incredibly beautiful. 60 plates, hundreds of designs. 9⅜ x 8-1/16.   22885-1 Pa. $4.50

FULL-COLOR FLORAL DESIGNS IN THE ART NOUVEAU STYLE, E. A. Seguy. 166 motifs, on 40 plates, from *Les fleurs et leurs applications decoratives* (1902): borders, circular designs, repeats, allovers, "spots." All in authentic Art Nouveau colors. 48pp. 9⅜ x 12¼.
23439-8 Pa. $5.00

A DIDEROT PICTORIAL ENCYCLOPEDIA OF TRADES AND IN-DUSTRY, edited by Charles C. Gillispie. 485 most interesting plates from the great French Encyclopedia of the 18th century show hundreds of working figures, artifacts, process, land and cityscapes; glassmaking, paper-making, metal extraction, construction, weaving, making furniture, clothing, wigs, dozens of other activities. Plates fully explained. 920pp. 9 x 12.
22284-5, 22285-3 Clothbd., Two-vol. set $40.00

HANDBOOK OF EARLY ADVERTISING ART, Clarence P. Hornung. Largest collection of copyright-free early and antique advertising art ever compiled. Over 6,000 illustrations, from Franklin's time to the 1890's for special effects, novelty. Valuable source, almost inexhaustible.
Pictorial Volume. Agriculture, the zodiac, animals, autos, birds, Christmas, fire engines, flowers, trees, musical instruments, ships, games and sports, much more. Arranged by subject matter and use. 237 plates. 288pp. 9 x 12.
20122-8 Clothbd. $15.00

Typographical Volume. Roman and Gothic faces ranging from 10 point to 300 point, "Barnum," German and Old English faces, script, logotypes, scrolls and flourishes, 1115 ornamental initials, 67 complete alphabets, more. 310 plates. 320pp. 9 x 12.   20123-6 Clothbd. $15.00

CALLIGRAPHY (CALLIGRAPHIA LATINA), J. G. Schwandner. High point of 18th-century ornamental calligraphy. Very ornate initials, scrolls, borders, cherubs, birds, lettered examples. 172pp. 9 x 13.
20475-8 Pa. $7.95

ART FORMS IN NATURE, Ernst Haeckel. Multitude of strangely beautiful natural forms: Radiolaria, Foraminifera, jellyfishes, fungi, turtles, bats, etc. All 100 plates of the 19th-century evolutionist's *Kunstformen der Natur* (1904). 100pp. 9⅜ x 12¼.   22987-4 Pa. $5.00

CHILDREN: A PICTORIAL ARCHIVE FROM NINETEENTH-CENTURY SOURCES, edited by Carol Belanger Grafton. 242 rare, copyright-free wood engravings for artists and designers. Widest such selection available. All illustrations in line. 119pp. 8⅜ x 11¼.
23694-3 Pa. $4.00

WOMEN: A PICTORIAL ARCHIVE FROM NINETEENTH-CENTURY SOURCES, edited by Jim Harter. 391 copyright-free wood engravings for artists and designers selected from rare periodicals. Most extensive such collection available. All illustrations in line. 128pp. 9 x 12.
23703-6 Pa. $4.95

ARABIC ART IN COLOR, Prisse d'Avennes. From the greatest ornamentalists of all time—50 plates in color, rarely seen outside the Near East, rich in suggestion and stimulus. Includes 4 plates on covers. 46pp. 9⅜ x 12¼.   23658-7 Pa. $6.00

AUTHENTIC ALGERIAN CARPET DESIGNS AND MOTIFS, edited by June Beveridge. Algerian carpets are world famous. Dozens of geometrical motifs are charted on grids, color-coded, for weavers, needleworkers, craftsmen, designers. 53 illustrations plus 4 in color. 48pp. 8¼ x 11. (Available in U.S. only)   23650-1 Pa. $1.75

DICTIONARY OF AMERICAN PORTRAITS, edited by Hayward and Blanche Cirker. 4000 important Americans, earliest times to 1905, mostly in clear line. Politicians, writers, soldiers, scientists, inventors, industrialists, Indians, Blacks, women, outlaws, etc. Identificatory information. 756pp. 9¼ x 12¾.   21823-6 Clothbd. $65.00

HOW THE OTHER HALF LIVES, Jacob A. Riis. Journalistic record of filth, degradation, upward drive in New York immigrant slums, shops, around 1900. New edition includes 100 original Riis photos, monuments of early photography. 233pp. 10 x 7⅞.   22012-5 Pa. $7.00

NEW YORK IN THE THIRTIES, Berenice Abbott. Noted photographer's fascinating study of city shows new buildings that have become famous and old sights that have disappeared forever. Insightful commentary. 97 photographs. 97pp. 11⅜ x 10.   22967-X Pa. $6.00

MEN AT WORK, Lewis W. Hine. Famous photographic studies of construction workers, railroad men, factory workers and coal miners. New supplement of 18 photos on Empire State building construction. New introduction by Jonathan L. Doherty. Total of 69 photos. 63pp. 8 x 10¾.
23475-4 Pa. $4.00

THE DEPRESSION YEARS AS PHOTOGRAPHED BY ARTHUR ROTH-STEIN, Arthur Rothstein. First collection devoted entirely to the work of outstanding 1930s photographer: famous dust storm photo, ragged children, unemployed, etc. 120 photographs. Captions. 119pp. 9¼ x 10¾.
23590-4 Pa. **$5.95**

CAMERA WORK: A PICTORIAL GUIDE, Alfred Stieglitz. All 559 illustrations and plates from the most important periodical in the history of art photography, Camera Work (1903-17). Presented four to a page, reduced in size but still clear, in strict chronological order, with complete captions. Three indexes. Glossary. Bibliography. 176pp. 8⅜ x 11¼.
23591-2 Pa. **$6.95**

ALVIN LANGDON COBURN, PHOTOGRAPHER, Alvin L. Coburn. Revealing autobiography by one of greatest photographers of 20th century gives insider's version of Photo-Secession, plus comments on his own work. 77 photographs by Coburn. Edited by Helmut and Alison Gernsheim. 160pp. 8⅛ x 11.
23685-4 Pa. **$6.00**

NEW YORK IN THE FORTIES, Andreas Feininger. 162 brilliant photographs by the well-known photographer, formerly with Life magazine, show commuters, shoppers, Times Square at night, Harlem nightclub, Lower East Side, etc. Introduction and full captions by John von Hartz. 181pp. 9¼ x 10¾.
23585-8 Pa. **$6.95**

GREAT NEWS PHOTOS AND THE STORIES BEHIND THEM, John Faber. Dramatic volume of 140 great news photos, 1855 through 1976, and revealing stories behind them, with both historical and technical information. Hindenburg disaster, shooting of Oswald, nomination of Jimmy Carter, etc. 160pp. 8¼ x 11.
23667-6 Pa. **$6.00**

THE ART OF THE CINEMATOGRAPHER, Leonard Maltin. Survey of American cinematography history and anecdotal interviews with 5 masters—Arthur Miller, Hal Mohr, Hal Rosson, Lucien Ballard, and Conrad Hall. Very large selection of behind-the-scenes production photos. 105 photographs. Filmographies. Index. Originally Behind the Camera. 144pp. 8¼ x 11.
23686-2 Pa. **$5.00**

DESIGNS FOR THE THREE-CORNERED HAT (LE TRICORNE), Pablo Picasso. 32 fabulously rare drawings—including 31 color illustrations of costumes and accessories—for 1919 production of famous ballet. Edited by Parmenia Migel, who has written new introduction. 48pp. 9⅜ x 12¼. (Available in U.S. only)
23709-5 Pa. **$5.00**

NOTES OF A FILM DIRECTOR, Sergei Eisenstein. Greatest Russian filmmaker explains montage, making of Alexander Nevsky, aesthetics; comments on self, associates, great rivals (Chaplin), similar material. 78 illustrations. 240pp. 5⅜ x 8½.
22392-2 Pa. **$7.00**

HOLLYWOOD GLAMOUR PORTRAITS, edited by John Kobal. 145 photos capture the stars from 1926-49, the high point in portrait photography. Gable, Harlow, Bogart, Bacall, Hedy Lamarr, Marlene Dietrich, Robert Montgomery, Marlon Brando, Veronica Lake; 94 stars in all. Full background on photographers, technical aspects, much more. Total of 160pp. 8⅜ x 11¼. 23352-9 Pa. $6.95

THE NEW YORK STAGE: FAMOUS PRODUCTIONS IN PHOTO-GRAPHS, edited by Stanley Appelbaum. 148 photographs from Museum of City of New York show 142 plays, 1883-1939. *Peter Pan, The Front Page, Dead End, Our Town,* O'Neill, hundreds of actors and actresses, etc. Full indexes. 154pp. 9½ x 10. 23241-7 Pa. $6.00

DIALOGUES CONCERNING TWO NEW SCIENCES, Galileo Galilei. Encompassing 30 years of experiment and thought, these dialogues deal with geometric demonstrations of fracture of solid bodies, cohesion, leverage, speed of light and sound, pendulums, falling bodies, accelerated motion, etc. 300pp. 5⅜ x 8½. 60099-8 Pa. $5.50

THE GREAT OPERA STARS IN HISTORIC PHOTOGRAPHS, edited by James Camner. 343 portraits from the 1850s to the 1940s: Tamburini, Mario, Caliapin, Jeritza, Melchior, Melba, Patti, Pinza, Schipa, Caruso, Farrar, Steber, Gobbi, and many more—270 performers in all. Index. 199pp. 8⅜ x 11¼. 23575-0 Pa. $7.50

J. S. BACH, Albert Schweitzer. Great full-length study of Bach, life, background to music, music, by foremost modern scholar. Ernest Newman translation. 650 musical examples. Total of 928pp. 5⅜ x 8½. (Available in U.S. only) 21631-4, 21632-2 Pa., Two-vol. set $12.00

COMPLETE PIANO SONATAS, Ludwig van Beethoven. All sonatas in the fine Schenker edition, with fingering, analytical material. One of best modern editions. Total of 615pp. 9 x 12. (Available in U.S. only) 23134-8, 23135-6 Pa., Two-vol. set $17.90

KEYBOARD MUSIC, J. S. Bach. Bach-Gesellschaft edition. For harpsichord, piano, other keyboard instruments. English Suites, French Suites, Six Partitas, Goldberg Variations, Two-Part Inventions, Three-Part Sinfonias. 312pp. 8⅛ x 11. (Available in U.S. only) 22360-4 Pa. $7.95

FOUR SYMPHONIES IN FULL SCORE, Franz Schubert. Schubert's four most popular symphonies: No. 4 in C Minor ("Tragic"); No. 5 in B-flat Major; No. 8 in B Minor ("Unfinished"); No. 9 in C Major ("Great"). Breitkopf & Hartel edition. Study score. 261pp. 9⅜ x 12¼. 23681-1 Pa. $8.95

THE AUTHENTIC GILBERT & SULLIVAN SONGBOOK, W. S. Gilbert, A. S. Sullivan. Largest selection available; 92 songs, uncut, original keys, in piano rendering approved by Sullivan. Favorites and lesser-known fine numbers. Edited with plot synopses by James Spero. 3 illustrations. 399pp. 9 x 12. 23482-7 Pa.$10.95

PRINCIPLES OF ORCHESTRATION, Nikolay Rimsky-Korsakov. Great classical orchestrator provides fundamentals of tonal resonance, progression of parts, voice and orchestra, tutti effects, much else in major document. 330pp. of musical excerpts. 489pp. 6½ x 9¼.   21266-1 Pa. **$7.50**

TRISTAN UND ISOLDE, Richard Wagner. Full orchestral score with complete instrumentation. Do not confuse with piano reduction. Commentary by Felix Mottl, great Wagnerian conductor and scholar. Study score. 655pp. 8⅛ x 11.   22915-7 Pa. **$13.95**

REQUIEM IN FULL SCORE, Giuseppe Verdi. Immensely popular with choral groups and music lovers. Republication of edition published by C. F. Peters, Leipzig, n. d. German frontmaker in English translation. Glossary. Text in Latin. Study score. 204pp. 9⅜ x 12¼.
23682-X Pa. **$6.50**

COMPLETE CHAMBER MUSIC FOR STRINGS, Felix Mendelssohn. All of Mendelssohn's chamber music: Octet, 2 Quintets, 6 Quartets, and Four Pieces for String Quartet. (Nothing with piano is included). Complete works edition (1874-7). Study score. 283 pp. 9⅜ x 12¼.
23679-X Pa. **$7.50**

POPULAR SONGS OF NINETEENTH-CENTURY AMERICA, edited by Richard Jackson. 64 most important songs: "Old Oaken Bucket," "Arkansas Traveler," "Yellow Rose of Texas," etc. Authentic original sheet music, full introduction and commentaries. 290pp. 9 x 12.   23270-0 Pa. **$7.95**

COLLECTED PIANO WORKS, Scott Joplin. Edited by Vera Brodsky Lawrence. Practically all of Joplin's piano works—rags, two-steps, marches, waltzes, etc., 51 works in all. Extensive introduction by Rudi Blesh. Total of 345pp. 9 x 12.   23106-2 Pa. **$15.95**

BASIC PRINCIPLES OF CLASSICAL BALLET, Agrippina Vaganova. Great Russian theoretician, teacher explains methods for teaching classical ballet; incorporates best from French, Italian, Russian schools. 118 illustrations. 175pp. 5⅜ x 8½.   22036-2 Pa. **$2.75**

CHINESE CHARACTERS, L. Wieger. Rich analysis of 2300 characters according to traditional systems into primitives. Historical-semantic analysis to phonetics (Classical Mandarin) and radicals. 820pp. 6⅛ x 9¼.
21321-8 Pa. **$12.50**

THE WARES OF THE MING DYNASTY, R. L. Hobson. Foremost scholar examines and illustrates many varieties of Ming (1368-1644). Famous blue and white, polychrome, lesser-known styles and shapes. 117 illustrations, 9 full color, of outstanding pieces. Total of 263pp. 6⅛ x 9¼. (Available in U.S. only)   23652-8 Pa. **$6.00**

AN ETYMOLOGICAL DICTIONARY OF MODERN ENGLISH, Ernest Weekley. Richest, fullest work, by foremost British lexicographer. Detailed word histories. Inexhaustible. Do not confuse this with *Concise Etymological Dictionary*, which is abridged. Total of 856pp. 6½ x 9¼.
21873-2, 21874-0 Pa., Two-vol. set **$13.00**

A MAYA GRAMMAR, Alfred M. Tozzer. Practical, useful English-language grammar by the Harvard anthropologist who was one of the three greatest American scholars in the area of Maya culture. Phonetics, grammatical processes, syntax, more. 301pp. 5⅜ x 8½.   23465-7 Pa. $4.00

THE JOURNAL OF HENRY D. THOREAU, edited by Bradford Torrey, F. H. Allen. Complete reprinting of 14 volumes, 1837-61, over two million words; the sourcebooks for *Walden,* etc. Definitive. All original sketches, plus 75 photographs. Introduction by Walter Harding. Total of 1804pp. 8½ x 12¼.   20312-3, 20313-1 Clothbd., Two-vol. set $80.00

CLASSIC GHOST STORIES, Charles Dickens and others. 18 wonderful stories you've wanted to reread: "The Monkey's Paw," "The House and the Brain," "The Upper Berth," "The Signalman," "Dracula's Guest," "The Tapestried Chamber," etc. Dickens, Scott, Mary Shelley, Stoker, etc. 330pp. 5⅜ x 8½.   20735-8 Pa. $4.50

SEVEN SCIENCE FICTION NOVELS, H. G. Wells. Full novels. *First Men in the Moon, Island of Dr. Moreau, War of the Worlds, Food of the Gods, Invisible Man, Time Machine, In the Days of the Comet.* A basic science-fiction library. 1015pp. 5⅜ x 8½. (Available in U.S. only)
       20264-X Clothbd. $15.00

ARMADALE, Wilkie Collins. Third great mystery novel by the author of *The Woman in White* and *The Moonstone.* Ingeniously plotted narrative shows an exceptional command of character, incident and mood. Original magazine version with 40 illustrations. 597pp. 5⅜ x 8½.
       23429-0 Pa. $7.95

FLATLAND, E. A. Abbott. Science-fiction classic explores life of 2-D being in 3-D world. Read also as introduction to thought about hyperspace. Introduction by Banesh Hoffmann. 16 illustrations. 103pp. 5⅜ x 8½.
       20001-9 Pa. $2.75

AYESHA: THE RETURN OF "SHE," H. Rider Haggard. Virtuoso sequel featuring the great mythic creation, Ayesha, in an adventure that is fully as good as the first book, *She.* Original magazine version, with 47 original illustrations by Maurice Greiffenhagen. 189pp. 6½ x 9¼.
       23649-8 Pa. $3.50

ORIENTAL RUGS, ANTIQUE AND MODERN, Walter A. Hawley. Persia, Turkey, Caucasus, Central Asia, China, other traditions. Best general survey of all aspects: styles and periods, manufacture, uses, symbols and their interpretation, and identification. 96 illustrations, 11 in color. 320pp. 6⅛ x 9¼.   22366-3 Pa. $6.95

CHINESE POTTERY AND PORCELAIN, R. L. Hobson. Detailed descriptions and analyses by former Keeper of the Department of Oriental Antiquities and Ethnography at the British Museum. Covers hundreds of pieces from primitive times to 1915. Still the standard text for most periods. 136 plates, 40 in full color. Total of 750pp. 5⅜ x 8½.
       23253-0 Pa. $10.00

UNCLE SILAS, J. Sheridan LeFanu. Victorian Gothic mystery novel, considered by many best of period, even better than Collins or Dickens. Wonderful psychological terror. Introduction by Frederick Shroyer. 436pp. 5⅜ x 8½.   21715-9 Pa. **$6.95**

JURGEN, James Branch Cabell. The great erotic fantasy of the 1920's that delighted thousands, shocked thousands more. Full final text, Lane edition with 13 plates by Frank Pape. 346pp. 5⅜ x 8½.
                                                                                      23507-6 Pa. $4.50

THE CLAVERINGS, Anthony Trollope. Major novel, chronicling aspects of British Victorian society, personalities. Reprint of Cornhill serialization, 16 plates by M. Edwards; first reprint of full text. Introduction by Norman Donaldson. 412pp. 5⅜ x 8½.   23464-9 Pa. $5.00

KEPT IN THE DARK, Anthony Trollope. Unusual short novel about Victorian morality and abnormal psychology by the great English author. Probably the first American publication. Frontispiece by Sir John Millais. 92pp. 6½ x 9¼.   23609-9 Pa. $2.50

RALPH THE HEIR, Anthony Trollope. Forgotten tale of illegitimacy, inheritance. Master novel of Trollope's later years. Victorian country estates, clubs, Parliament, fox hunting, world of fully realized characters. Reprint of 1871 edition. 12 illustrations by F. A. Faser. 434pp. of text. 5⅜ x 8½.   23642-0 Pa. $6.50

YEKL and THE IMPORTED BRIDEGROOM AND OTHER STORIES OF THE NEW YORK GHETTO, Abraham Cahan. Film *Hester Street* based on *Yekl* (1896). Novel, other stories among first about Jewish immigrants of N.Y.'s East Side. Highly praised by W. D. Howells—Cahan "a new star of realism." New introduction by Bernard G. Richards. 240pp. 5⅜ x 8½.   22427-9 Pa. $3.50

THE HIGH PLACE, James Branch Cabell. Great fantasy writer's enchanting comedy of disenchantment set in 18th-century France. Considered by some critics to be even better than his famous *Jurgen*. 10 illustrations and numerous vignettes by noted fantasy artist Frank C. Pape. 320pp. 5⅜ x 8½.   23670-6 Pa. $4.00

ALICE'S ADVENTURES UNDER GROUND, Lewis Carroll. Facsimile of ms. Carroll gave Alice Liddell in 1864. Different in many ways from final Alice. Handlettered, illustrated by Carroll. Introduction by Martin Gardner. 128pp. 5⅜ x 8½.   21482-6 Pa. $2.50

FAVORITE ANDREW LANG FAIRY TALE BOOKS IN MANY COLORS, Andrew Lang. The four Lang favorites in a boxed set—the complete *Red, Green, Yellow* and *Blue* Fairy Books. 164 stories; 439 illustrations by Lancelot Speed, Henry Ford and G. P. Jacomb Hood. Total of about 1500pp. 5⅜ x 8½.   23407-X Boxed set, Pa. $16.95

HOUSEHOLD STORIES BY THE BROTHERS GRIMM. All the great Grimm stories: "Rumpelstiltskin," "Snow White," "Hansel and Gretel," etc., with 114 illustrations by Walter Crane. 269pp. 5⅜ x 8½.
21080-4 Pa. $3.50

SLEEPING BEAUTY, illustrated by Arthur Rackham. Perhaps the fullest, most delightful version ever, told by C. S. Evans. Rackham's best work. 49 illustrations. 110pp. 7⅞ x 10¾. 22756-1 Pa. $2.95

AMERICAN FAIRY TALES, L. Frank Baum. Young cowboy lassoes Father Time; dummy in Mr. Floman's department store window comes to life; and 10 other fairy tales. 41 illustrations by N. P. Hall, Harry Kennedy, Ike Morgan, and Ralph Gardner. 209pp. 5⅜ x 8½. 23643-9 Pa. $3.00

THE WONDERFUL WIZARD OF OZ, L. Frank Baum. Facsimile in full color of America's finest children's classic. Introduction by Martin Gardner. 143 illustrations by W. W. Denslow. 267pp. 5⅜ x 8½.
20691-2 Pa. $4.50

THE TALE OF PETER RABBIT, Beatrix Potter. The inimitable Peter's terrifying adventure in Mr. McGregor's garden, with all 27 wonderful, full-color Potter illustrations. 55pp. 4¼ x 5½. (Available in U.S. only)
22827-4 Pa. $1.50

THE STORY OF KING ARTHUR AND HIS KNIGHTS, Howard Pyle. Finest children's version of life of King Arthur. 48 illustrations by Pyle. 131pp. 6⅛ x 9¼. 21445-1 Pa. $5.95

CARUSO'S CARICATURES, Enrico Caruso. Great tenor's remarkable caricatures of self, fellow musicians, composers, others. Toscanini, Puccini, Farrar, etc. Impish, cutting, insightful. 473 illustrations. Preface by M. Sisca. 217pp. 8⅜ x 11¼. 23528-9 Pa. $6.95

PERSONAL NARRATIVE OF A PILGRIMAGE TO ALMADINAH AND MECCAH, Richard Burton. Great travel classic by remarkably colorful personality. Burton, disguised as a Moroccan, visited sacred shrines of Islam, narrowly escaping death. Wonderful observations of Islamic life, customs, personalities. 47 illustrations. Total of 959pp. 5⅜ x 8½.
21217-3, 21218-1 Pa., Two-vol. set $14.00

INCIDENTS OF TRAVEL IN YUCATAN, John L. Stephens. Classic (1843) exploration of jungles of Yucatan, looking for evidences of Maya civilization. Travel adventures, Mexican and Indian culture, etc. Total of 669pp. 5⅜ x 8½. 20926-1, 20927-X Pa., Two-vol. set $7.90

AMERICAN LITERARY AUTOGRAPHS FROM WASHINGTON IRVING TO HENRY JAMES, Herbert Cahoon, et al. Letters, poems, manuscripts of Hawthorne, Thoreau, Twain, Alcott, Whitman, 67 other prominent American authors. Reproductions, full transcripts and commentary. Plus checklist of all American Literary Autographs in The Pierpont Morgan Library. Printed on exceptionally high-quality paper. 136 illustrations. 212pp. 9⅛ x 12¼. 23548-3 Pa. $12.50

AN AUTOBIOGRAPHY, Margaret Sanger. Exciting personal account of hard-fought battle for woman's right to birth control, against prejudice, church, law. Foremost feminist document. 504pp. 5⅜ x 8½.
20470-7 Pa. $7.50

MY BONDAGE AND MY FREEDOM, Frederick Douglass. Born as a slave, Douglass became outspoken force in antislavery movement. The best of Douglass's autobiographies. Graphic description of slave life. Introduction by P. Foner. 464pp. 5⅜ x 8½.
22457-0 Pa. $6.50

LIVING MY LIFE, Emma Goldman. Candid, no holds barred account by foremost American anarchist: her own life, anarchist movement, famous contemporaries, ideas and their impact. Struggles and confrontations in America, plus deportation to U.S.S.R. Shocking inside account of persecution of anarchists under Lenin. 13 plates. Total of 944pp. 5⅜ x 8½.
22543-7, 22544-5 Pa., Two-vol. set $12.00

LETTERS AND NOTES ON THE MANNERS, CUSTOMS AND CONDITIONS OF THE NORTH AMERICAN INDIANS, George Catlin. Classic account of life among Plains Indians: ceremonies, hunt, warfare, etc. Dover edition reproduces for first time all original paintings. 312 plates. 572pp. of text. 6⅛ x 9¼.
22118-0, 22119-9 Pa.. Two-vol. set $12.00

THE MAYA AND THEIR NEIGHBORS, edited by Clarence L. Hay, others. Synoptic view of Maya civilization in broadest sense, together with Northern, Southern neighbors. Integrates much background, valuable detail not elsewhere. Prepared by greatest scholars: Kroeber, Morley, Thompson, Spinden, Vaillant, many others. Sometimes called Tozzer Memorial Volume. 60 illustrations, linguistic map. 634pp. 5⅜ x 8½.
23510-6 Pa. $10.00

HANDBOOK OF THE INDIANS OF CALIFORNIA, A. L. Kroeber. Foremost American anthropologist offers complete ethnographic study of each group. Monumental classic. 459 illustrations, maps. 995pp. 5⅜ x 8½.
23368-5 Pa. $13.00

SHAKTI AND SHAKTA, Arthur Avalon. First book to give clear, cohesive analysis of Shakta doctrine, Shakta ritual and Kundalini Shakti (yoga). Important work by one of world's foremost students of Shaktic and Tantric thought. 732pp. 5⅜ x 8½. (Available in U.S. only)
23645-5 Pa. $7.95

AN INTRODUCTION TO THE STUDY OF THE MAYA HIEROGLYPHS, Syvanus Griswold Morley. Classic study by one of the truly great figures in hieroglyph research. Still the best introduction for the student for reading Maya hieroglyphs. New introduction by J. Eric S. Thompson. 117 illustrations. 284pp. 5⅜ x 8½.
23108-9 Pa. $4.00

A STUDY OF MAYA ART, Herbert J. Spinden. Landmark classic interprets Maya symbolism, estimates styles, covers ceramics, architecture, murals, stone carvings as artforms. Still a basic book in area. New introduction by J. Eric Thompson. Over 750 illustrations. 341pp. 8⅜ x 11¼.
21235-1 Pa. $6.95

GEOMETRY, RELATIVITY AND THE FOURTH DIMENSION, Rudolf Rucker. Exposition of fourth dimension, means of visualization, concepts of relativity as Flatland characters continue adventures. Popular, easily followed yet accurate, profound. 141 illustrations. 133pp. 5⅜ x 8½.
23400-2 Pa. $2.75

THE ORIGIN OF LIFE, A. I. Oparin. Modern classic in biochemistry, the first rigorous examination of possible evolution of life from nitrocarbon compounds. Non-technical, easily followed. Total of 295pp. 5⅜ x 8½.
60213-3 Pa. $5.95

PLANETS, STARS AND GALAXIES, A. E. Fanning. Comprehensive introductory survey: the sun, solar system, stars, galaxies, universe, cosmology; quasars, radio stars, etc. 24pp. of photographs. 189pp. 5⅜ x 8½. (Available in U.S. only)
21680-2 Pa. $3.75

THE THIRTEEN BOOKS OF EUCLID'S ELEMENTS, translated with introduction and commentary by Sir Thomas L. Heath. Definitive edition. Textual and linguistic notes, mathematical analysis, 2500 years of critical commentary. Do not confuse with abridged school editions. Total of 1414pp. 5⅜ x 8½.
60088-2, 60089-0, 60090-4 Pa., Three-vol. set $19.50

Prices subject to change without notice.

Available at your book dealer or write for free catalogue to Dept. GI, Dover Publications, Inc., 180 Varick St., N.Y., N.Y. 10014. Dover publishes more than 175 books each year on science, elementary and advanced mathematics, biology, music, art, literary history, social sciences and other areas.